"A superbly plotted high-tension technothriller about a War-on-Drugs-style crackdown on brain/ computer interfaces. Excellent spycraft, kick-ass action scenes, and a chilling look at a future cold war over technology and ideology, making a hell of a read."

Cory Doctorow

"*Nexus* is one of the most intensely compelling and original debut novels I've read in a very, very long time. His breathtaking expertise and confidence as a writer makes Naam the only serious successor to Michael Crichton working in the future history genre today."

Scott Harrison, author of Archangel

"It's good. Scary good. Take a chance and have a great time reading a bleeding edge technical thriller that is full of surprises."

James Floyd Kelly, Wired.com's GeekDad blog

"If you are posthuman or transhuman this is an absolute must-read for you; and even mere mortals will love it."

Philip Palmer, author of Version 43

"The action scenes are crisp, the glimpses of future tech and culture are mesmerizing."

Publishers Weekly

"Naam displays a Michael Crichton-like ability to explain cutting-edge research via the medium of an airport techno-thriller

SFX Magazine

Join

Shortl

BY THE SAME AUTHOR

Crux

Apex

NON-FICTION

The Infinite Resource

*More Than Human: Embracing the Promise
of Biological Enhancement*

RAMEZ NAAM

Nexus

ANGRY
ROBOT

ANGRY ROBOT
An imprint of Watkins Media Ltd

Lace Market House,
54-56 High Pavement,
Nottingham,
NG1 1HW
UK

angryrobotbooks.com
twitter.com/angryrobotbooks
Upload 99% complete

An Angry Robot paperback original 2013
4

A catalogue record for this book is available
from the British Library.

ISBN 978 0 85766 292 7
EBook ISBN 978 0 85766 294 1

Set in Meridien by Argh! Nottingham.
Printed in the UK by 4edge Limited.

For Mom and Dad,
who brought me into this world,
raised me, and have supported
me at every step.

1

The Don Juan Protocol

Friday 2040.02.17 : 2255 hours
The woman who called herself Samantha Cataranes climbed out of the cab and walked towards the house on 23rd Street. The door opened, spilling light and the sounds of music and voices out into the night. A pair of young women emerged, arm in arm, wrapped up in conversation. They smiled at her as she passed them, and Sam smiled back. Faceprinting code identified them, used her tactical contacts to superimpose softly glowing names, ages, and threat levels beside their faces in her field of view. All green. Civilians. No known connection to her mission.

Sam ran her eyes over the exterior of the home. Her sight came alive with structural elements, power lines, data lines, possible ingress and egress through doors, windows, weak spots in the walls. She blinked it all away. None of it served her purpose tonight.

Her left knee twinged as she ascended the stairs. A memento of that disastrous firefight outside Sari. As if she could ever forget that night. Her face felt tight. Her lips were overstuffed, her cheeks taut, her jaw awkwardly cocked. Her nerves strained in protest at the visage she held. It would be a relief to relax into her own face again.

Bits of her briefing for this mission flitted through her mind unbidden. A building blasted apart, bodies strewn everywhere. Religious leaders murdered by trusted old friends. Politicians with sudden, implausible changes of heart. All the suicide bombings, the assassinations, the political subversions, the blank-faced companies of inhumanly loyal, unthinking, unquestioning super-soldiers. And behind them all, the common thread: Beijing's new coercion technology. A technology that this target might just help them get a step closer to understanding and defeating.

Sam opened the door and let herself in to the party, a wide smile on her false face. Overly loud flux music hit her. The smells of dozens of bodies inundated her sharpened senses. Identities swam over the sea of faces. Somewhere in this house, she would find her man.

Friday 2040.02.17 : 2310 hours
"Do you romp?" the girl asked. She leaned in close, close enough to be heard over the din of the party, close enough to kiss.

Kaden Lane watched carefully, clinically, as Don Juan molded his body's responses. A slight smile. Release of oxytocin. Dilation of capillaries in his cheeks. A mix of confidence and anticipation. Candidate replies flitted through his mind, half-formed on his lips, as the software's conversational package sifted through possibilities:

    [Yeah, I love to dance.]
    [Sure, what kind of music do you like?]
    [If I'm with a pretty girl like you.]

Signals propagated through the highly modified web of Nexus nodes in his brain. The drug's nanostructures evaluated data, processed it, transformed it. Don Juan made a choice in milliseconds. Input spiked at Nexus nodes attached to neurons in the speech centers of his frontal and temporal lobes. Nerve impulses raced outward from speech centers to motor cortex, and from there to the muscles of his tongue and jaw, his lips and diaphragm. A fraction of a second after he'd heard the girl speak, those muscles contracted to produce his response.

"Yeah, I love to dance," Kade heard himself say.

Who writes these lame lines? he wondered.

"Want to see if there's something good tonight?" she asked.

Frances. Her name was Frances. They'd met twenty minutes ago in this hallway. She was twenty-six years old, a Virgo, a graphic designer by trade. Frances smelled nice, liked to touch him when she talked, and did look rather fetching in her tight pants and low-cut top. She loved acro-yoga, loud dance music, travel in Central America, and her two cats.

Kade had never asked anyone their sign before. He supposed in a way he still hadn't. The software had done that with his mouth and lungs. Did that count?

All the test was supposed to show was that software could use their Nexus-based interface to control speech and hearing in a real environment. It was Rangan who'd insisted on using this dating app to test their platform, and that Kade be the one to run it. "You gotta get out and have some fun, dude," he'd said. "All you do is mope around. Flirting with some girls is exactly what you need."

Next time, he thought to himself, Rangan can do the field test.

"Sure, let's see what's happening," Don Juan answered.

Kade pulled out his phone and stuck it to the wall beside them. Don Juan spoke to it. "Bay Area dance parties tonight. Full immersion for two."

Frances turned to face the camera. A partygoer jostled her as he scooted by down the hall. She squeezed up against Kade, nestling into his side. Her body *did* feel rather warm and enticing, he had to admit. He put an arm around her waist as the phone responded to his request. Maybe Rangan did have a point...

Retinal projectors sought out their eyes. Targeted acoustics zeroed in on their ears. Local events scrolled across shared vision.

SEROTONIN OVERLOAD IV

A brief advertisement for the event washed over their senses: pulsing music, syncopated lights, warm smiles, dancers embracing and moving in time.

Frances made a face. "A little too earnest for me."

Kade chuckled. "Next."

CYGNUS EXPRESS – A PROJECT ODYSSEUS FUNDRAISER

Vastness of space, planets orbiting distant suns, partygoers in gleaming imitations of vacuum suits, bleeping sound of contact through the static of cosmic background radiation, overlaid with driving trance rhythm.

Frances shrugged. Damn, she felt good pressed against him.

"In space," she said, "no one can hear you dance."

Kade shrugged. "Next."

CARE BARE by UNITED SKEINS OF SEXY

New sights and sounds: Writhing, almost-naked bodies, skin moving against skin, moaning pulsing sounds, fast flashes of mouths and hips and breasts.

Frances moved her hip against him just a bit. "Now *that* looks pretty hot. Yeah?"

Kade laughed out loud. Any other night, he wouldn't have the balls to venture into a scene like that. But what the hell. His task tonight was to push the platform they'd built on top of Nexus's nanoscale elements to its limits.

It'll be a great test case, he told himself. I'm doing this for science.

Don Juan responded for him. "Maybe. You planning on getting fresh with me?"

Kade let it drive, let it wink with his eye.

Frances smirked and raised an eyebrow, turning towards him, her body still pressed against his. "Oh, you'd like that, would you?"

She batted her pretty green eyes up at him.

"Oh, I think the pleasure would be all yours," Don Juan replied. Kade put his other arm around her waist, holding her to him now, looking down into her eyes.

Frances bit her lower lip.

"Prove it."

Kade might have stuttered, might have blushed, but a more calculating logic was in control. "Your place or mine?"

They kissed standing up, Kade's back against the wall of the room they'd snuck into. Frances was a giggler. She made out with a fun enthusiasm that Kade found infectious. They kissed and kissed, giggled and whispered. Kade's clinical detachment crumbled. Someone opened the door to the room, saw them, and backed out apologetically. More giggles ensued. More kissing followed. Giggling gave way to sighing. Sighing gave way to grinding, to hands roaming. Heat rose between their bodies. Her breath was coming short and heavy. So was his.

The dialog sucks, but I can't complain about the results, Kade thought to himself. There was one more test he'd promised Rangan he'd run. Now for the kinesthetic interfaces...

He kept his eyes closed as he kissed her, immersed himself in the Nexus OS that he and Rangan had built atop the hundreds of millions of nano-structures of the drug that suffused their brains.

Softly glowing numbers scrolled across the bottom of his field of view. A column of icons hung at the right. A research log window with his field test notes lay compressed down to its title bar. The muted roar of the party still rushed in his ears. Kade flicked his inner eye over pulse, respiration, neuro-electrical activity, inter-face status, neurotransmitter and neuron-hormone levels. All green. He could see the copy of Don Juan that Rangan had pirated and modified running through its models, behaving nicely and only using the resources he'd assigned. He flicked past it, sought out another program, one Rangan had lifted from VR porn and hacked to send its output to their body-control software – Peter North.

```
[activate: peter_north mode: full_interactive
priority: 1 smut_level: 2]
```

Frances pressed herself more insistently against him. The giggles were gone. Her lips brushed his jaw, tugged wetly at his mouth. Her body was hot beneath his hands. Her snug pants were smooth and slick and hugged her ass perfectly. She spread her thighs slightly, leaned her hips against his, ground her crotch against his leg as they kissed. Her soft little moans of pleasure went straight to some primal part of his brain. Numbers and icons still floated in his vision.

Kade ignored one set of stimuli, let himself be absorbed by the other.

Peter North was in charge now, a VR porn bot Rangan had lifted from the net and adapted to their Nexus OS as a way to test their kinesthetic interfaces. It spat out limb position changes and muscle and joint vectors. Nexus nodes in Kade's brain flared, signals raced from his motor cortex to his limbs, and Kade's body responded.

Frances moaned softly, shifted her ass against his hand, ground herself against his hip. *Peter North* slid Kade's hand down her back, past the fabric of her low-cut top, and down onto the smooth and snug backside of her pants. His hand squeezed one perfect cheek, rose up into the room, and came down with a resounding smack.

"Ooooh," Frances murmured. She bit his lower lip then, not quite too hard, and tugged. Her finger rubbed his chest, teasing one nipple. Forefinger and thumb came together, pinching, enough to hurt this time.

Damn, thought Kade. Why did I ever think this was a bad idea?

Peter North grabbed hold of Frances by her hips, steered them both to the couch, pushed her down into it. The software brought his body down atop her, kneeling on the edge of the cushion, one knee between her thighs. Kade's hands came up, entangled themselves in her hair and made fists. *Peter North* tugged, tilting her head back, making her look at him, paused until she opened her eyes to stare into his, waited just a moment longer, then brought his mouth down on hers.

Thank you, thank you, thank you, Rangan, he thought, for forcing me to get out here and have some fun.

Frances responded with nails on his back, sharp and even painful through his shirt. She shifted her hips forward on the seat, pressing herself more firmly against his knee, squeezing her thighs around his leg, purring into his mouth as her hands found his belt and eased their way under his shirt. Searching for skin, ready to draw blood.

Kade forced himself to concentrate. Forced himself to make more notes in the research log. He was still a scientist, damn it.

[Smooth muscular control. Feedback systems excellent. Possibly insufficient pain response.]

Outside, *Peter North* had him cupping one breast, one hand tangled in her hair. His shirt was gone. Frances was biting her way down his chest, his stomach.

[Definitely insufficient pain response.]

Her hand was on his crotch now. Kade was hard, as hard as the safety limits he and Rangan had coded into the interface would allow. Frances seemed to approve. She smiled seductively as her hand squeezed him through the front of his pants, started to move in time to her own grinding against his lower leg...

Kade made no note of this. He'd tested the erection module extensively already.

Frances smiled coyly up at him and gave him a long squeeze. "Is this for me?"

She licked her lips lasciviously.

Kade's mind filled with an image of what was about to happen. His heart skipped a beat in anticipation. He opened his mouth to reply.

```
[interface warning - max spikes per second >
parameters]
[interface warning - packet loss in connection
0XE439A4B]
  [interface ERROR - socket not found OXA27881E]
  [interface ERROR - socket not found OXA27881E]
  [interface warning...]
```

Oh fuck, he thought.

Errors and warnings flooded Kade's vision. Parameter displays were spiking into yellow and red. Intracortical bandwidth was saturated. Packets were being dropped. CPU cycles were being consumed in massive ways by error-catching and error-correcting packages, stepping all over each other in their haste to fix whatever was wrong.

Outside, neither *Peter North* nor Kade were in control of his body. His hips jerked forward spastically, again and again. His hands gripped hard on Frances's shocked head. His still-clothed crotch was banging into her face on every pelvic thrust. His mouth was wide open, his eyes unfocused. An incoherent sound was escaping his throat.

"Ug. Ug. Ug."

[interface warning — max spikes per second > parameters]

[interface warning — max spikes per second > parameters]

[interface ERROR...]

Fuck fuck fuck.

[system halt], he commanded.

Nothing.

[system halt], he repeated.

Nothing.

[system halt] [system halt] [system fucking halt!]

Neuro-muscular stimulation ceased. Kade's inner displays went blank. His muscles relaxed. Hips stopped moving. Hands eased on Frances's head. Success!

Kade drew breath.

And then another hard spasm rolled across every muscle in his body, and another, and another...

What? Oh shit.

Kade was ejaculating.

He threw himself back from Frances, collapsing on the bed behind him, back arching and toes curling as some side effect of the stimulation threw him into a whole-body ecstasy. Laughter burst forth. Tears rolled down his face. He turned onto his side in bliss and confusion and hilarity and some deep warm sleepy sense of peace. Ahhhh.

"What the fuck was that?" Frances was on her feet, yelling at him. One hand was on her face. "What the hell is wrong with you?"

Kade rolled over in a haze, opened his mouth to apologize, to explain, tried to pull himself up onto his feet. "Frances…"

"You stay there, jerk!" She leveled an accusing finger at him. "I'm walking out of this room, and if you so much as twitch, I'm gonna scream for help!"

She was backing towards the door.

"Hey, wait, I'm sorry. I didn't mean to… umm…"

"Shut up! Stupid ass one-minute wonder. Next time you wanna play rough, you *ask first*, asshole."

She opened the door, slammed it behind her. Through the door he heard, "Hey, there's some sicko freak in there…"

Well, he thought, that didn't work so well.

Friday 2040.02.17 : 2347 hours

They were coming for him. The Corps. His brothers. He could hear the choppers, hear the small arms fire. They'd found the place he'd been taken to, the place he'd been held, the place where he'd gotten a long clear look into the pits of hell. You never leave a man behind. They were coming for him, and God help anyone who stood in their way.

Watson Cole woke with a start, drenched in sweat, his heart pounding in his chest, a lump in his throat. He was half upright in the bed, one massive dark-skinned arm raised as if to ward off a blow. He was shaking.

Fuck. Just a dream. Just another nightmare.

"Lights," he said aloud.

The small room lit up around him. The light pushed the terror back. This wasn't the KZ. This wasn't that war. This was his apartment in San Francisco.

He let his weight sink back into the mattress. The sheets were soaked in his night sweats.

Breathe. Relax. Breathe.

It had been the rescue, this time. The rescue and the girl. Lunara. He dreamt of all of them. Arman, Nurzhan, Temir. Most of all, Lunara. The ones who'd imprisoned him. The ones who'd used the drug called Nexus to pry open his mind, force themselves and so many others into him. The ones who'd jammed his head full of the hellish memories of the victims of that war. It had been two years, but still he dreamt of them. Still he dreamt their lives.

Why me? Why'd it have to be *me*?

He'd been at the wrong place at the wrong time. It was as simple as that. If he hadn't been...

I'd still be out there now. Killing for my country. Murdering. Ignorant. Blind. Happy.

And someone else would have this hell inside them.

Breathe. Relax the body. Breathe.

His heart was slowing now. The tremors were nearly gone. He glanced at the clock beside the bed. Not even midnight. He'd been asleep for just an hour. He looked at the nightstand, considered the bottle of pills in the top drawer. He could medicate himself into dreamless unconsciousness. But it was getting harder every time. The doses were increasing.

He hadn't asked for this hell, but it had come to him. He hadn't asked to have his eyes opened, but they had been. He hadn't asked for a chance at redemption, but it had been offered. Offered in the form of these young, idealistic kids that had made him a part of their family. Offered in the form of their modifications and improvements to Nexus, improvements that made it an even more powerful tool for touching the minds and hearts of others.

Nexus had changed him. It had shown him his actions through others' eyes. It has shown him the evil that he and all the other men like him had done. It had given him the urge to find a better way, to make a better world. And if it had done that to him, the hardest of men, what could it do for others?

Watson Cole rose and dressed for a run. He would push his superhumanly fit body to exhaustion. He wouldn't succumb to dependence on the meds. He would keep himself fit and hard. He had things to do before he paid for his crimes.

The drug that had transformed him could transform the world. He would make it happen.

Friday 2040.02.17 : 2355 hours

Damn, Kade thought. Bad time for a bug. He splashed water on his face in the bathroom, tried to collect himself. Time to sneak out of here, see if he could debug the crash he'd run into.

He opened the door from the washroom and into the crowded party. The back door would be the safest way out. He was halfway there, studiously avoiding eye contact, when he heard his name and felt a hand on his shoulder.

"Hey, Kade!" It was Dominique, the hostess. Shit.

"Kade, I want you to meet someone," Dominique went on. "This is Samara. Sam, meet Kaden Lane. Kade, meet Samara Chavez. Sam was telling me about an article she'd read that reminded me of your work."

Sam was in her mid to late twenties, with olive skin and straight black hair that fell to her shoulders. She was dressed in stylish black slacks and a clinging grey sweater. There were muscles under that sweater. She had the build of a swimmer.

"Nice to meet you, Kade. Dominique says you're getting your doctorate in brain-computer communication?"

Kade looked towards the back door. So close... "Yeah. Sanchez Lab at UCSF. What article was this?"

"Two monkeys, with parts of their brains wirelessly linked. One could see out of the other's eyes."

Warwick and Michelson. That one got some press.

"Yeah, that was a good paper," he said. "I work with those guys occasionally. They're over at Berkeley."

"Cool," Sam responded. "Is that what you work on too?"

Dominique made her exit.

Kade shuffled his feet a bit, keenly aware of the stain on the front of his trousers.

"A lot of our grants are for interfaces to control body functions – muscle control and so on."

Kade had a flash of his hips thrusting out of control at Frances's face. He hurried on.

"You know, to help paralyzed people move again. My thesis is on higher-level brain functions. Memory, attention, knowledge representation."

Kade paused, unsure how much she wanted to hear.

Sam picked up the thread. "Interesting. Did you see the one where they taught a mouse the layout of a maze, and other mice could learn it too, just by being wired up to its brain?"

Kade chuckled. "That was my paper. First one I wrote as a grad student. No one thought we could do it."

Sam raised an eyebrow. "No shit. That was impressive. Where are you going from there? Do you think that..."

Sam turned out to be surprisingly interested in neuroscience. She peppered him with questions on the brain, on his work, on what they planned next. Kade found himself forgetting the fiasco he'd just had and his plans of escape. And along the way he learned a few things about her. She worked in data archeology, helping companies mine old and disorganized systems for missing information. She lived in New York, and she was here in SF on a contract assignment for the next few months. She'd just arrived and was looking to make friends. She was funny, smart, and good looking. She laughed at his jokes. And it turned out that she shared one of his interests.

"So you're a brain guy. Have you heard of this drug, Nexus?" she asked.

Kade nodded cautiously. "I've heard of it."

"They say it's some sort of nano-structure, not really just a drug. And that it links brains. Is that possible?"

Kade shrugged. "We can do it with wires and with radios. Why not with something you swallow? As long as it gets into the brain..."

"Yeah, but does it actually work?"

"I've heard it does," Kade replied.

"You've never tried it?"

He grinned. "That would be illegal."

Sam grinned back.

"Have *you* tried it?" he asked her.

She shook her head. "I had a chance in New York last year, but I missed it. It's all dried up on the East Coast."

A first-timer, Kade thought to himself. We could use more first-time females for the study...

He hesitated. "It's dried up out here too. A lot of busts lately."

Sam nodded.

Kade missed whatever she said next. Out of the corner of his eye he caught sight of something. Some*one*. Frances.

Oh, fuck.

"...total asshole. He was so rude."

Her back was to him. She hadn't seen him yet.

"...seizure or something. He needs help. *Professional* help."

The back door. He started to edge towards it.

"Kade? Everything OK?"

Sam. He looked at her. "I've got to go. Sorry. Hope I see you again."

He left her there as he hustled out the door.

Samantha Cataranes watched as Kaden Lane fled the party.

Did I spook him? she wondered. Must have.

Her eyes flicked to a readout at the corner of her tactical contact display. It was red. Off the charts red. The sensor on the necklace she wore had picked up clear Nexus transmissions. Whatever Kaden Lane might say, he had not only tried Nexus before, he'd been using it this very night, in quantities beyond any they'd seen in a human before.

How very odd to be using that drug here, when no one else was. What good was Nexus without another Nexus user for it to bridge a connection to?

Time would tell. She would find another way into their little circle. Rangan Shankari, perhaps.

Sam turned and looked for someone else to chat up. Her cover required it.

Kade soared through a three-dimensional maze of neurons and nano-devices. Nano-filament antennae crackled with life as Nexus nodes sent and received data. Vast energies accumulated in neuronal cell bodies, reached critical thresholds, surged down long axons to pulse into thousands more neurons. Code readouts advanced in open windows around him. Parameter values moved as he watched.

After the debacle of the party, debugging the code running in his own brain was bliss. His body lay safely in his bed. His mind exulted inside the Nexus development environment, tracing the events that had led to the fault. Here he was in his element.

He traced the events of the night through the logs, through the pulses of Nexus nodes and neurons in his brain, until he found the place where Nexus OS had faulted. He traced system parameters backwards in time until he understood what had happened. Nexus nodes had fired in response to excited neurons and triggered an uncontrolled cascade. They needed more bounds checking. It was a simple fix. The code opened itself to him, changed in response to his thoughts. He compiled it, tested it, fixed a new bug he'd introduced, repeated until he was done.

Reluctantly, he left the world inside his mind, and came back to the senses of his body. It was then that he remembered the other girl. Samara.

They could still use another first-time female subject for the study tomorrow to test out the changes they'd made to calibration. They had their minimum sample size, but another wouldn't hurt. Would she fit? Yes. Was that foolish? Perhaps. But they really could use another first-time female…

And she did happen to be smart, funny, and good looking…

He pulled out his slate, projected it onto the wall, and paid a reputation bot to look up everything there was to know about Samara Chavez of New York City.

There she was: Samara A Chavez. Reputation green.

He drilled into the details. Two degrees of separation from Kade. A Brooklyn address. Thousands of pictures of her online. Mentions of her at various data archeology conferences and online forums. A business license for a private consultancy. No mention on narc sites. No face match against suspected narc photos. The bot summarized her as legit and reputable.

Always use a second source, Wats had said.

He paid for a credit verification service to check her out as well. She came back with an address that matched, a phone number that matched the one she listed online, a decent credit record, no convictions, no gaps in employment and education. Everything was consistent.

Kade yawned and checked the time. It was almost two in the morning. Was there anything else to check? He couldn't think of anything.

He fired off an invitation to Sam's public address. Would she like to attend a party Saturday night? A party where she might be able to find a certain something she'd asked about? He couldn't tell her where, but he'd be happy to pick her up. Reread. Send.

Then he stripped off his clothes and collapsed into bed.

Sam kicked, blocked, punched, dodged, kicked again. Imaginary enemies fell.

Across the room, a new message chime sounded. The tone was keyed to Kaden Lane.

Sam ignored the sound and continued her blurringly fast path through the hundred and eight steps of the *kata* she was practicing, her limbs moving with superhuman grace and precision through a four hundred year-old sequence of strikes, parries, and evasions.

Focus, Nakamura had taught her. Absorb yourself in your task. Leave all the rest aside.

She let the message wait as she completed the *kata*. Only when she was done and had bowed to the empty room did she turn, limbs trembling slightly, brow beaded with sweat, and ask her slate to show her the message.

It appeared in the air before her. A message to Samara Chavez. An invitation to a party. A party where, he hinted, she could try Nexus.

Guess I didn't spook him so badly after all, Sam thought to herself.

She waved away the slate's projection and the image evaporated. She'd respond tomorrow at a reasonable hour.

Samantha Cataranes turned back towards the center of the room, bowed to the air, and began the next *kata*.

Briefing

Transhuman – *noun* –
1) A human being whose capabilities have been enhanced such that they now exceed normal human maxima in one or more important dimensions.
2) An incremental step in human evolution.

Posthuman – *noun* –
1) A being which has been so radically transformed by technology that it has gone beyond transhuman status and can no longer be considered human at all.
2) Any member of a species which succeeds humans, whether having originated from humanity or not.
3) The next major leap in human evolution.

OXFORD ENGLISH DICTIONARY, 2036 Edition

2
Close Door, Open Mind

Saturday 2040.02.18 : 0612 hours
The lump on his forearm was red, agitated. It stood out
against his dark skin. Wats rubbed at it. It felt hard, hot to
the touch. Skin peeled away under his fingers. He was
bloody underneath. He peered at the uncovered tumor.
Deep within it he could almost see the broken strands of
DNA, his chromosomes fraying like split ends, giving birth
to the cancers that would eat him. Another lump caught
his attention. Another. His wrist was covered with them.
His hands. His arm. In horror he ripped open his shirt. Red,
angry lumps were growing on his chest, on his belly. They
were rising, expanding, spreading as he watched, covering
him…

Wats jerked awake.

Breathe. Breathe. Early morning light was filtering in
through the windows.

Not the cancers. Not yet.

He scanned his arms. They were bare, unblemished.

"Lights!"

He threw himself out of bed, scanned the rest of himself.
Nothing.

Breathe. Close your eyes. Breathe. Pull yourself together, Sergeant Cole.

He hadn't been Sergeant Cole for a long time now.

Wats crossed to the sink and splashed cold water on his face. Wash away the rest of the nightmare. He pulled down a disposable tester, slid his finger into it. A short, sharp prick. A drop of his blood was sucked into its microfluidic channels. The box hummed softly as it worked. Flow cytometers examined every cell by laser, looking for telltale swelling of the cell nuclei, elevated hormone levels, abnormal chromosomes. DNA and protein assays took burst cells, evaluated them for cancerous genetic and proteomic fragments.

Wats stared at the device as it did its work. He willed it green. He willed it to finish. He willed it to give him time to do what must be done.

The device beeped. Its display turned green. No sign of the cancers. Not yet.

Wats breathed a sigh of relief and tossed the tester into the garbage. Someday he'd pay for his crimes. But not today.

Saturday 2040.02.18 : 2108 hours
Kade picked Sam up just past nine in a Siemens autocab. The little plastic and carbon fiber car drove them south and east along the 101, past SFO, past San Mateo, past Menlo Park and Palo Alto and Stanford, and the venture capital hub of the world. She kept Kade engaged in conversation. She asked about his work, his friends, the party, the music he listened to, when he'd first tried Nexus. He answered everything except the questions on Nexus, and asked his own about her, her life, New York, her work in data archeology. She stepped into her role and answered the way the fictional Samara Chavez would answer. The lies

came easy after so many years. She had him in stitches with Samara's misadventures in data archeology.

The cab drove them to Simonyi Field, formerly the site of NASA's Ames Research Center, and dropped them in front of the giant Hangar 3. It loomed above them, longer than a football field, taller than a seven story building.

"Welcome to our party space." Kade grinned.

Sam nodded her approval. "Impressive. How'd you score this?"

"Our lab leases it for experiment space. And, well, this is kind of an experiment."

Sam raised an eyebrow.

"You'll see."

Kade led them to a back door into the hangar. He knocked quickly three times, and the door opened.

Inside an entryway, a large sign read "Welcome! Please turn off data connections on all phones, slates, pens, watches, specs, shades, rings, etc... No active transmitters, please!"

Below that, another sign: "Close Door and Open Mind As You Enter."

To her right, the man who'd opened the door for them. Six feet tall, black, muscular, and lean, with a shaved head and a relaxed posture. Watson Cole. Data spooled across her tactical contacts in pulsing red. Threat level: high.

```
Watson "Wats" Cole (2009- )
Sergeant 1st Class, US Marines (ret 2038)
Deployed: Iran (2035), Burma (2036-37),
Kazakhstan (2037-38) (...)
Specialist: Counter-intel, Hand-to-Hand Combat
Augments: Marine Combat & Recovery Boosters
(2036, 2037, 2038)
Approach with Extreme Caution
```

Cole clasped hands with Kade. "Kade."

Kade responded. "Good to see you, Wats. This is my friend Sam. She should be on the list now."

Wats raised an eyebrow, eyes still on Kade. Then, slowly, he nodded. Calm, dark eyes turned towards her. "Samara Chavez. You're on the list. I'm Wats." He extended his large brown-skinned hand.

Sam had read Cole's bio already. A refugee from war-torn Haiti, brought to the US by a Marine who'd met and married his mother. Cole had enlisted in the Corps at age eighteen, distinguished himself in missions across the globe, been handpicked for augmentation and promotion. Then he'd been captured by rebels in Kazakhstan. The man who emerged from that months-long ordeal was different. A peace activist. A Buddhist. A pacifist. Had captivity changed him? Or something more?

Sam took his hand. "Nice to meet you, Wats."

His grip was firm but not forceful. Those hands could crush steel. They'd killed men across two continents. Even with her newer, top-secret fourth-generation enhancements, Sam wasn't sure she wanted to mess with Watson Cole.

"Please turn off any radios," he said.

Why?

"Sure," she answered.

She pulled her show phone from her jacket pocket, flipped it to standby, used the motion as cover to blink the surveillance gear on her body into passive mode.

Kade was returning his own phone to a pocket. He turned and smiled. "Wanna go see the space? We're still a little early."

"Absolutely," she answered. "Lead on."

Lane led her through a large heavy door, the kind Sam suspected might be EM shielded, and closed it behind them.

On the other side was a hallway. Kade opened the door at the far end and they stepped through into a large open space, the true interior of the original hangar. It was at least two hundred feet across, with a vaulted ceiling seventy or eighty feet tall – a space you could fit an old 747 into. A circle of couches occupied one end of the hangar. Along one wall was a bar. A dozen people were milling about, apparently setting up for the party. At the other end she saw a DJ platform with four large screens. Behind them was the DJ, dark-skinned, bleached blonde hair, in multi-colored Sufi robes.

Data scrolled across her vision in yellow. A person of interest.

```
Rangan Shankari (2012 - ) aka "Axon" (stage
name)
PhD candidate, Neural Engineering, Sanchez
Lab, UCSF
Technology R&D Risk Level: Medium [human
intelligence enhancement]
```

Rangan waved at them across the room. "Hey, Kade, can you give me a hand?" he yelled out. "Got a weird glitch in the repeaters here."

Kade nodded. "Sure, give me a minute."

He led Sam in another direction, towards a cluster of people at one end of the space.

"Hey, Ilya," he called out.

An earnest-looking woman of Russian descent looked up at her name. Dark hair, large thoughtful eyes, a simple green dress accented by a gauzy purple scarf around her neck. She smiled charmingly at Kade as they approached her.

```
Ilyana "Ilya" Alexander (2014 - )
Post-doctoral Fellow, Janus Lab, Systems
Neuroscience, UCSF (2039-)
Published works on meta- and group
intelligences
Technology R&D Risk Level: Medium [post-/non-
human intelligence]
```

Ilyana Alexander. Another of their little group. A refugee of the 2027 Pudovkin purges in her native Russia. A theoretical neuroscientist whose work focused on cognition in groups and networks.

Alexander hugged Kade in greeting. "Hello, Kade."

Kade smiled. "Sam, this is Ilyana Alexander, aka Ilya. Ilya, could you get Sam started?" Kade asked. "I need to help Rangan with something."

Kade touched Sam's arm. "We have a dose for you. Ilya will set you up. I'll see you in a little bit."

"Thanks," Sam replied. "See you soon."

Kade turned and headed off towards the DJ table.

Ilya led her out of the main hangar, through a door labeled "Crew," and then beyond that to a cozy chill space.

They sat together on a couch. From out of her bag Ilya produced a small glass vial. Inside was a dark, silvery fluid.

Sam felt her pulse quicken.

"You've never used Nexus before?" Ilya asked.

"Never," Sam lied. Only in training, she thought.

"This is Nexus 5."

Nexus 5?

Nexus 3 was the most common Nexus formulation on the street. Nexus 4 had been a flash in the pan out of a lab in Santa Fe, put down quickly in a joint mission between the ERD and the DEA. Something called Nexus 5 was rumored to exist, but until this point had never been confirmed.

"Where do you guys get it?" she asked Ilya.

Ilya hesitated just a moment too long. "We have a friend on the East Coast who gets it for us."

She's lying, Sam thought.

"You have experience with psychedelics?" Ilya asked.

"The usual. Experimentation in college. Not a regular thing."

"How'd you tolerate them?"

"Fine. I had fun. Just nothing I needed to do too often."

Ilya nodded. "Good. Experience with psychedelics always makes this easier. The first time people try Nexus can be a little disorienting, especially the first hour or so. Your brain is learning how to interface with the drug and other brains. With a whole party full of people pressing up against your mind, it's going to be even more intense."

Sam frowned. "I thought Nexus only worked at short range, like arm's length maybe."

"Usually." Ilya's gaze flickered away for a moment. "But there are ways to increase the range."

Pieces clicked together for Sam. The "no transmitters" rule. The "repeaters" Rangan had mentioned. These kids had found a way to extend Nexus transmissions.

Dear god.

"Sounds great," she replied. "I'll take your lead."

Her pulse was quick now. Her stomach was a knot.

Ilya popped the top of the vial. Sam caught a glimpse of a metallic liquid swirling through the glass. Brownian motion mixed tendrils of grey and silver. For an instant she had the impression of the drug as a living thing, aware, alert, purposeful.

The moment passed. Ilya handed her the vial, followed closely by a glass of juice from the table.

Sam downed the drug. The liquid tasted strongly metallic,

slightly bitter. It felt heavy on her tongue, oily as it flowed down her throat. She sipped the juice. It was orange-guava. It cut through the taste and feel of Nexus instantly, leaving her mouth just slightly sweet, tart, and tropical.

Now for the other part I hate.

Samantha Cataranes closed her eyes, recited the mantra that would rearrange parts of her memory, make her believe she was someone else.

Elephant. Skyscraper. Maple.

She saw them as she thought the words, superimposed them on each other. Mental tumblers clicked, knowledge that should not leak out of her mind was suppressed. Fictions became reality.

Samara Chavez opened her eyes.

3
Calibration

Samara Chavez was flying. Eyes closed, reclined on the couch, she soared above a landscape of shapes and emotions, senses and experiences. Below her a pulsing red sea of arousal lapped against a sharp and glistening black shore of mathematics, which gave way to green and brown hills of Spanish, Mandarin, and English. She dove into those hills, let the ground accept her and pass through her, burrowed into the earth, tasting tones and verbs and conjugates, feeling the shape of letters, words, characters, feeling their meanings and sounds coalesce. It felt gorgeous.

Sam was aware that she was high. She was tripping more intensely than any time since… since… And at the same time she felt clear-headed. Every sensation was sharp. Everything fit together just so. She understood where she was and what was going on.

Nexus is learning me, she thought. This is the calibration phase.

She penetrated through the dense earth of languages into a cavern of abstraction, filled with a soaring, brilliant city of concepts. Broad lanes of Time and Space cut the city into

34

quarters. A bell tolled from within the towers of the delicate crystal and steel Temple of Self in the center of the city. The sound of the bell was the sound of everything she'd ever tried to communicate. It pulsed in the air, almost physical, spreading outwards in concentric waves she could see, resonating through city blocks where ideas crashed together. Open public squares of contemplation, serene parks and elegant symphony halls of harmony and synthesis, wrecked bombed-out shells of discord, confusion, misunder-standing. Her thoughts spread out into suburbs full of memories and beyond them into the dark forest of Other which wrapped the city, isolated it.

With delight she dove down into a public pool of Laughter, pulled herself out and walked a street of Beauty, turned down the lane and entered the vast museum of Animate Things, exited from its rear door onto a street of Actions, and soon came to the great open plaza around the Temple of Self. Everywhere she looked in the plaza she saw the faithful come, called to prayer. The faithful were her. A hundred of her, a thousand, ten thousand, all kneeling, praying, paying homage and sending prayers to herself.

She spun around then, taking in this city, her city, her mind. She whirled once, twice, three times, until the spin had a perpetual motion of its own, and then she found herself rotating faster and faster, the city blurring by too fast to see, but her mind spreading out to encompass it, the centrifugal force of her dervish-whirl sending the edges of her thoughts and senses outward from her, spread out and held taut to her by the line of her will.

She was this city. She was the million hers within it. She tasted a hundred thousand memories. Memories of places and times and things and words. Her sixth birthday, falling off her bike, blood running down her knee, she'd dipped her finger in it, brought it as close to her face as she could, wanting to see those tiny cells inside. Her college graduation, unexpectedly meaningful to her, a flush of excitement, visible pride on the face of her aunt and uncle, wishing her parents could be there if not for... for... Her first taste of sushi, incredible texture of raw albacore, followed by intense wasabi flavor overwhelming her sense of smell. A rainbow in the desert, seen alone. A lover's kiss on her neck. The sharp joy of sparring. Childhood games. And data archeology – the 3am discovery of the key that cracked the Watzer archive, the way the pieces of the puzzle fit together perfectly to decode the message Venter had encoded with his genome.

All of this is you – the words came unbidden to her. The memories came not one at a time, but in parallel, overlaid with one another, interleaving in ways she'd never seen, the timeline of her life becoming three-dimensional.

She felt she would explode with joy, with the sheer intensity of being, with the incredible *largeness* she felt. She wanted to grow ever larger, to spread beyond this city and cavern, to encompass this entire psychedelic planet of self, to experience every instant and morsel and potential of her being at once. To spread beyond this one planet, to experience everything of everyone!

"Sam?"

Her eyes opened. She was flush with excitement. Her chest was heaving. Her heart was pounding. She was damp between her thighs. She had never felt so turned on or so alive in her life. Except... except...

"Sam?"

It was Kade. Kaden Lane. The boy who'd brought her here, given her this chance to try Nexus for the first time. (*first?*) That beautiful, tall, confusing, shy, naïve young man, with a mind like fire and a boyish disregard of the consequences of his curiosity. He was standing at the foot of the couch she reclined on, looking at her tentatively.

"Kade." It came out husky. She tried again, more casually. "Hi."

"Hey, how're you feeling? Sorry I couldn't get here sooner, I was trying to help Rangan track down that glitch."

Rangan. Right. The DJ. She was at a party. OK.

Get it together, Sam.

"Kade." She held his gaze with her own, took a deep breath. "This is *amazing.* I was just lost, swimming, deep inside... I can't even explain."

Even as she spoke she felt the whirlwind, felt the assimilation and calibration continuing inside her. Her skin was sensitized. Every word and every breath felt electric with potential.

Kade smiled. "Tell me. What are you feeling?"

Sam closed her eyes, spoke with them closed. "I'm inside myself. Inside my mind. I see how the pieces of me fit together. The different concepts. The different *kinds* of concepts I can hold. And I can see all these scenes from my life. Patterns between them, connections I never noticed. I feel incredible. If I was like this when I was working... I could just suck up anything." She paused. "And I'm really, really aroused."

She opened her eyes. Kade was blushing, looking away now, down at his shoes, over at the wall. And Sam had the apprehension that he had been looking directly at her until her final words. And that *he* was aroused. By her. She got a flash of how she must seem to him, skin flushed and radiating heat, nipples hard, chest rising and falling, breath audible – and knew that flash was more than intuition, that it came from Kade himself.

Really? Had he dosed?

"Kade. Have you taken the Nexus already?"

And then his eyes snapped to hers again, directly, not

shyly at all. He came around the couch without speaking, sat next to her, close, and put one hand on her brow. And she felt something. His mind brushing against hers. An invitation, followed by an opening, and then Kade unfolded before her.

She caught another glimpse of his arousal. Of his interest in her. Of his shyness. His insecurity with women.

But those were peripheral. In the center she caught full on a view of his intellect, diamond sharp and clear, the restlessness of his mind, his ever churning set of questions, his lust for answers… and what he'd done. He and Rangan and Ilya.

She took a sharp breath as she understood. "You're like this all the time? You've done this permanently? To yourself?"

Of course. Last night. So, so dangerous.

Last night? Dangerous?

Kade spoke. "The potential is there. The Nexus core is permanently integrated. But it's not active all the time. Not broadcasting. And we're definitely not experiencing the rush of the first mapping that you're going through now."

Sam understood it as he spoke. She caught the sense of the linked thoughts behind his words. Semantic mapping. Sensory mapping. Emotive mapping. Calibration and assimilation. All the things they needed to enable mass Nexus connectivity.

Because they'd made it, Kade and Rangan and a few others. They'd taken Nexus 3 and they'd cracked some of its code. They'd learned to program Nexus cores, to tell them what to do. They'd added on layers of logic and functionality. They'd turned it into a platform for running software inside the brain. They'd brought this thing in her mind to fruition.

It took her breath away. She felt Kade's pride. She felt

her own awe at his brilliance, at their accomplishment, at their audacity. She wanted him then. Wanted to swallow his mind up like the city inside her, experience all of him at once, know what he knew, feel what he felt, really understand what was happening inside her.

And she felt fear. A chill up the back of her spine. A strong sense of foreboding.

Sam brushed it off. She fought for words.

"Kade. Kade. Show me the party. Take me out there to meet everyone else."

Kade laughed. "You're just coming up. Want to practice this a little more with one person before you're out there with a hundred?"

In his thoughts she read amusement, caution.

"I'm ready," Sam replied. "I want more. I can handle it."

I want it all, she thought.

Kade chuckled. "Alright, let's do it. Party time."

He stood up, smiled, and backed a step away.

Sam took a deep breath, steadied herself, and rose to a seated position. So far so good. She could feel Kade watching, evaluating, taking mental notes on her responses, her equilibrium, her affect.

She looked up at him, met his eyes, and held out her hand. Kade took it to help her rise to her feet.

Their touch was electric, frank, revealing. She sought out his attraction to her, wanted it, found it buried beneath his scientific curiosity, his commitment to the experiment of which she was now a part, his cool observation of her. Sam blazed at Kade, showed him her hunger, her craving for more, her will to assimilate everything around her, starting with him.

He was at once amused and impressed. And his mind was awesome, full of knowledge and experience she craved.

Sam rose smoothly to her feet, Kade's hand still held but

unneeded. She stood inches from him, face at his level in her tall boots.

"Show me," she asked him. He knew what she wanted.

He flushed crimson, let go of her hand, broke eye contact, laughed to hide a bashfulness that he could not possibly contain, and backed away again.

"You're something else," he said. "A natural for this. It's not as easy as you think, though. Internal mapping is one thing. That level of depth with another mind just isn't doable right now. Not enough bandwidth. Not a rich enough protocol."

Sam saw the truth of it in his mind, saw also that he was holding back from her. There was more. *Disappointment.* She'd be patient.

"OK." She smiled, despite herself. "Out into the party?"

Kade took her hand again, grinning, broadcasting excitement. "Sam, you're gonna love this."

And she saw that she would.

He led her out of the chill space and into the crew room, up to the heavy, shielded door that led to the main hangar.

"I'm going to let you feel a little at first, then more and more over time."

Kade opened the door. Music hit her. Electronic and tribal, rhythmic and trancedelic. The genre they called flux. Compelling enough to dance to, relaxed enough to not.

At the same time a different kind of humming filled Sam's head. The sound of many voices, muted, distant, but all speaking at once. More than sound. Information. Meaning. Emotion. Excitement. Giddiness. Apprehension. Awe. Impatience. Heartbreak. Desire. Contentment. All there. All at some remove from her. Nothing like the experience she'd had within herself. But these were other minds!

Kade led her through the doorway.

The hangar had been transformed. The lighting was saturated with slowly changing colors now, shifting through the spectrum. The corner they were in was rich blue shifting to indigo and violet. Across the hangar from her it was red turning orange. To the left it was yellow turning green.

Scattered across the hangar were people, scores of them. Enough to add life to what had been a large and empty space. They were dressed for a San Francisco party night: short skirts and tight pants; velvet and vinyl and faux leather; tattoos, piercings, and marginally legal biomorph body art that shifted and flowed as they moved. She felt them in her mind. Gay, straight, and bi; singles, couples, triads, more complex networks still.

This boy-scientist had brought her into the heart of the counterculture. And the counterculture was dosed with Nexus.

Above and around them, the smartfabric-covered walls undulated in time to the music now. Liquid silvers, reds, and blues flowed across the curving inner surface of the hangar, like ripples emanating from each tribal, elemental beat of the music Rangan was playing. It was transfixing, organic. She stared at it and knew that the track was "Buddha Fugue" by the group Apoptosis, the rhythms inspired by the sounds of Thai drumming meeting crashing surf as heard through the hashish-addled ears of band member Sven Utler, one hot summer night on the beaches of Koh Phangan.

It came to her in a flash. She simply knew it as if she'd always known it. As if she'd heard this track a dozen times, heard the story behind it from Sven or Rangan or Kade already.

Sam caught her breath. It was a great track, the kind her hips wanted to move to, but she didn't care. They just beamed that into my head! What she could do with that technology! What data archeology could be like! Education! Anything!

She turned to Kade, mouth agape, eyes full of wonder. He grinned at her. He knew her thoughts and she knew his: infectious enthusiasm, excitement at her excitement, pride in his accomplishments.

Like a boy showing off his toys, she thought, and he blushed and looked away and giggled.

Kade took her by the hand then and led her into the crowd. They passed a pair of people, standing facing each other, arms moving oddly, clumsily, giggling and laughing out loud at each other.

"What are they doing?" she asked Kade.

He grinned at her. "We call it push/pull. They're using Nexus to move each others' bodies. Sending impulses to each others' motor cortices. Or trying to. It's not easy for most people."

She stared at them.

"Can we try that?" she asked.

Kade grinned again. "Later."

He led her further into the hangar, towards the circle of reclined couches. Something was going to happen there, she read from him. An experiment. And she could be part of it.

"This is the closest we've come to people mapping each other. To the calibration experience across more than one mind. Want to try it?"

Yes. God yes. She wanted to swallow them all whole.

No, a small voice protested within her.

She ignored it, nodded mutely to Kade.

A half-dozen men and women were already reclining on the couches. There was room for a half-dozen more. As she and Kade approached the rest of the minds in the space faded. She could feel these six now, and clearly. She could feel Kade. The rest of the party was blanketed in mental silence.

Kade was behind her. His hands touched lightly on her shoulders. He led her to one of the couches, helped her to sit. He crouched at her side.

Others arrived, took their seats. A dozen of them on the couches and a few watchers nearby.

"Ready?" Kade spoke aloud, pitched for her alone.

Sam nodded.

Something happened. Eleven more minds grew larger in her perception. They brightened, swam more fully into focus. They were so full. So alive with thoughts and memories, emotions and desires. Her breathing synchronized with theirs. She closed her eyes and she could see and feel their individual lines of thought.

Eleven minds touched her at once in eleven parts of her psyche. Here was Brian's sheer joy at the crazy, meditative, ebullient madness of playing mind to mind with his friends. Here was Sandra's deep reservoir of calm and poise, her years of yoga, her pool of peace, anchoring those around her. This was *samadhi* to her. Here was Ivan's physicist's appreciation of the math and music in the interplay and dance and harmony and discord of the thoughts around him. Here was a vision in Leandra's mind, of protein shapes, folds and receptors and binding sites, of a dozen men and women connected in mind to decode them... Here were tears on Josephine's face, tears of a joyous memory of childhood, fireworks with her beloved Dad, lost to her. Lost like... like...

There were tears on Sam's face now. She didn't know why. She could feel Kade watching her, concerned. She had no answer for him.

Each person had not one thread, but many. They

intertwined in parallel, each connected to the others. Thoughts and memories shifting and flowing. Sandra's first fumblings with other girls in her preteen years. Antonio's comprehension of quantum programming, the edges of understanding *any* of it just beyond what Sam could capture. Jessica's rapture in freefall dives from twelve thousand feet, the adrenaline of jumping, the calm of popping the chute, her bliss every time she hung below that fabric wing and steered herself to the ground, singing and breathing and soaring untethered.

She knew Sandra's love of the stillness, the meditative, I-am-in-my-body glory of her daily practice. It spiraled within Sam, found her memories of sparring bouts, the absolute beauty of a perfect strike or block or dodge. The serenity of perfect form, the adrenaline of a hard and close fight, the endorphic come-down bliss that followed. And... and...

She felt Kade, still. He was with them, with her. And his mind... his mind... She knew the beauty of the Nexus core. The sublimity of its design that awed him, staggered him. She tasted the pure abstract space within him where he did his best work, apprehended a tiny bit of the protocol he'd built with Rangan, the semantic layer between individual neural connections and whole thoughts. It was a glorious thing, a map of all the kinds of pieces of thoughts, an ontology of consciousness. It existed in him in part of his mind beyond doubt or fear or even consideration of others. Part of him so beautiful and yet so distant and so alien and so very, very much hers for this brief time.

Sam saw through his eyes. Saw the flows of thoughts and emotions and experiences as bits and packets and traffic patterns, not cold and dry, but gorgeous in a symphonic way, an orchestral way. They were individual instruments coming together to create a richly textured whole, greater than the sum of its parts. She saw his aspirations, to transcend the boundaries of individual minds, saw how Ilya had shaped his thoughts, saw a glimpse of the path he thought might just be feasible, his wonder at a future nothing like the past.

She was crying then. Crying because Kade's mind was so crystal clear and his vision so pure and so awe-inspiring in its way and yet so terrifying to her. Crying with Josephine at shared loss, of parents ripped away in youth, of childhood lost. Crying at the loss of Kade's parents so recently. Crying at a memory of pain and fear that Sandra had uncovered, Sam wounded in the night, left arm hanging useless, blood dripping into her eyes, terrified, not sure if she would see the dawn, not sure she could get past the one last guard...

She was confused, disoriented. Memories that made no sense were arising. Josephine experienced Sam's memories of her parents' last Christmas in San Antonio. Yet she also knew Sam's sorrow at the death of them, years in the past. At the horror of something not clean, not fast, not accidental...

Leandra's experiences in proteomics touched Sam's identity as a data archeologist. Sam worked for corporations to unlock value from their legacy intellectual assets. Not Third World government databases... Not records of human and transhuman experiments...

She felt their collective concern. Kade most of all. Felt them reaching out more tendrils to her, to soothe her, buttress her. Each contact triggered a memory. An all-nighter in college cramming for her differential equations mid-term. Her first triathlon, that place beyond exhaustion, beyond bliss, beyond anything but moving her body again and again and again... Pushing herself that hard in the Iranian Caspian, north-east of Sari, terrified out of her mind, trying to make that rocky beach in Turkmenistan, not knowing if backup would truly be there...

Sam was losing her mind.

She liked to bike. She swam. She'd graduated with a master's in DA with honors. She had two loving parents. She had a memory of a gun, huge in her young hands, the man she'd shot lying in a puddle of his own blood, slowly bleeding to death, deserving this and more for the horrors he'd inflicted...

Yet Sam remembered her training for this mission. Another dose of Nexus, Nexus 3, the palest shadow of her current experience. A briefing. An assignment. A mantra that veiled who she was...

Sam understood then. It overwhelmed her. She understood who she was, understood the betrayal of herself that this experience constituted. It came out in a jumble through the upper layers of her mind. Sam felt the bewilderment of the minds she was connected to, each of them seeing just a part of it. Felt their growing alarm. She had seconds to act.

NOOOOOOOOO!

It came out as a scream from her mind and throat, unforced, perfect for her needs. Sam wrenched her mind away from them, as brutally as she could, felt things tear inside her, saw and knew them stunned and disoriented.

She remembered her name. *Samantha*. Samantha Cataranes. She remembered who she was.

Tactical contacts came online, had always been online, dropped layers of threats and recommendations and escape vectors and supplemental information on her.

[EXTRACT EXTRACT EXTRACT], her display read.

Arrows pointed towards escape vectors. Alternate exits. Ceiling hatch seventy feet above her. Likely weak points in the wall. Back out the door she'd come in through. She chose the latter.

Samantha Cataranes stood up. Force of will pulled her out of the chaos of the drug high. Years of training took over. She swept her vision across the scene around her. A score of names lit up, faces recognized, bios scrolling. All green or yellow. No gross threats.

Her fingers found her slimline in her boot, tripped the emergency uplink sequence. Buffered data pulsed out instantly at emergency power. Everything she'd seen and heard going out to her watchers.

The phone pulsed once, twice, three times, violating FCC power regs by a cool order of magnitude, expending a quarter of its fuel cell to get the message out.

White noise shot through mind space, tearing up mental cohesion. Sam saw one or two go down with their hands to heads. Her own head ached. The music stopped.

She turned towards the door then. The voices and minds around her were starting to burble, coming out of their stunned and pained silence. Few of them had caught what had really happened, but they had caught on that something bad had occurred indeed.

That was sick. That was wrong. I can't believe I took part in that.

Images of the mind meld she'd just experienced bounced through her, nauscating her, reminding her too much of... of... of what she'd killed to escape.

Time for reminiscing later. She caught a glimpse of Kade on his knees, vomiting onto the floor. She felt a pang of pity, of regret. Time for that later, too.

She strode towards the entrance, locked her mind down. Crowds parted. Then she felt a mind against hers, saw him move to block her path. Watson Cole.

He felt hard, poised, resigned. Pacifist or no, he was not going to let her pass.

[Combat Threat. Extreme Caution.]

Alternate routes flashed on her display. Arrows towards other escape vectors. She could turn and run, beat him to an exit.

But Sam was not in the mood to let some burned-out jarhead stand in her way.

She blanked her mind, weaved towards him unsteadily on the floor, brought her left hand to her stomach, her right to her face, feigned a disoriented stumble to the left as she reached him, came out of it in a vicious right-hand backfist to his temple.

Wats was unfooled. The big black Marine had anticipated the move or something like it. He brought his hand up to block, fell back, barely twisted the blow aside as he gave ground.

Good. She was faster than he was. Her fourth-generation enhancements outclassed the Marine Corps' third-generation techniques. The ERD saved the best for its own.

Sam's next two blows were already in the air in the close space between them. Hard jab to his solar plexus, low kick to his knee. Wats parried the first, still falling back, lifted his leg and let his raised calf absorb the damage of her kick.

Cole was good. Experienced. Deadly. The Marine Corps' third-generation viral upgrades had made him stronger, faster, less sensitive to pain than any normal man.

Sam was smaller, shorter of reach, lighter of muscle, but she'd been taught by the best, and she had the better technology. Fourth-generation *post*human genetics gave her nerves like quicksilver, muscles like corded titanium, and bones of organic carbon fiber.

She'd become something like the thing she hated. She'd stared into the abyss, and it had transformed her. To destroy evil, she'd become it.

Wats countered her superior speed by giving ground, step

by step. Sam stayed in close as he did, neutralizing his advantage in reach. They moved in a blur of strikes, dodges, and blows, almost too fast for any onlooker to follow.

She could see him coming up now, see the adrenaline hitting him, making him a more dangerous foe. Behind her she felt flashes of courage and anger. Partygoers thinking of joining the fray. Before long, they would mob her.

End this now, then. A gambit. A sacrifice. She let him create a foot of space to get his comfort, parried three more blows, threw feints at groin and eyes and plexus, then came in wide and sloppy, hole in her guard at mid-section.

Wats saw the opening and threw a brutal fist at it, low and under her nearly unbreakable ribs. She accepted the fist, twisting to mute it, felt pain blossom inside her as he connected. As she twisted, she brought one hand down like a vice on his wrist, yanked him off balance as she planted a leg behind his knees and slammed her other hand into his shoulder to bring him down.

Wats saw it coming, but it was too late. The gambit had worked. He went down fast and hard.

Sam's booted foot flashed out, connected with his head, twice, three times.

She stopped herself. Don't kill. Incapacitate.

Her breath was fast, pulse elevated. She'd taken serious but not immediately life-threatening damage. Time to leave. She stepped over Wats' unmoving form towards the door.

And then she felt it. Felt *him*. Kade. He was behind her. He was inside her mind. She could feel his anger and hurt, his confusion, his sense of betrayal, his self-loathing at having been so easily fooled... having risked so much on behalf of so many people, and let them down. Despite herself, she felt a pang of guilt at how she'd deceived him, at the hell he was going to pay.

"No," he said.

He was about to do something to her mind, Sam knew. She saw it in his thoughts. He was a threat.

She turned. Crossed the space between them in three long steps. Don't kill. Incapacitate. She lunged forward, hard backfist snapping out at his temple.

No.

She heard him in her mind. Felt his will slam against something inside her.

Hard fist connected with civilian body. All went black.

4
The Noose

Sam swam slowly back to consciousness. Darkness. Her eyes were closed, head slumped. She stayed that way. Better to feign unconsciousness as long as she could, and learn the situation. There were voices around her. People talking.

"So she's, what, a DEA agent?" That was Rangan Shankari, the DJ.

"Not DEA," a voice responded slowly. "Homeland Security. Emerging Risks Directorate." That deep bass. Watson Cole.

"ERD?" Ilya Alexander spat it out. "Fuck."

Rangan spoke again, "So, this Samara from the ERD, you think she's alone?"

"Her name's not Samara." That was Kade. "It's Samantha. Samantha Cataranes. She had some way of hiding it. Her memories were a mask somehow. The group meditation messed it up for her."

They know my name, she thought to herself.

"She's awake," Ilya said.

Sam's muscles rebelled, then. Against her will, her head jerked up, her eyes opened. Someone was in her mind, controlling her body. That realization snapped her to alertness, sent a jolt of fear up her spine. These were very dangerous people.

She was in a cluttered storage room, sitting in a straight back chair, arms tied or strapped behind her back, ankles tied to the chair legs. As if those restraints were necessary when her Nexus-dosed brain was splayed open to those around her. Her left side ached where Wats had landed his blow. Internal bleeding likely.

Eyes shifted to her at Ilya's pronouncement. Rangan stood above her and to her left, arms crossed in his ridiculous Sufi robe, eyes angry and intent. He was the one in her mind. Ilya had fists clenched at her sides. Wats was to her right, an ugly bruise already covering one side of his face where Sam's boot had slammed into him. His eyes were cold and hard.

Behind them, slumped in a chair, ice pack to his head, was Kade, staring at the floor.

Rangan spoke again, "You'd better start talking, girl."

She felt a jolt of pain as he spoke, and a compulsion to speak. He was twisting something in her mind. All four of them were opaque to her. Sam could feel the hard external shells of their minds, and the hard tendril inside her own, but nothing more. She felt a brief longing for the communion she'd felt at the height of the party. It nauseated her.

Sam cleared her throat and wet her lips. She tasted blood. "Rangan Shankari, Ilyana Alexander, Watson Cole, Kaden Lane – you're all under arrest."

Wats shook his head slowly, the corners of his lips turning up slightly in admiration of her audacity. Rangan made a small noise in his throat. Ilya just stared.

"You're under arrest for the crime of trafficking in an ERD Alpha Class Prohibited Technology and a DEA Schedule I controlled substance. In addition to that, development and use of a coercion technology, attempting to construct an unlicensed Non-Human Intelligence in violation of the Chandler Act, kidnapping, and interfering with an officer of the law."

Rangan blanched.

"No Miranda rights?" Wats asked. "No right to remain silent? What if I want to see a lawyer?" He sounded coolly amused.

Sam locked eyes with him. "Those don't apply. Your research is designated a potential threat to humanity. You have no rights in that situation. Your best option is to give up now. It'll go easier on you if you surrender. If my support squad moves in, I can't guarantee your safety. They won't hesitate to use force."

Wats' eyes narrowed. He turned to his compatriots. "See what I mean?"

Rangan cut in, speaking to Sam, "Your transmission didn't make it out of the building. There's no cavalry coming. You're stuck here with us."

Sam tried to shake her head, found that Rangan's vice-like mental hold wouldn't let her. She spoke firmly, with more confidence than she felt.

"Think it through. The ERD knows I'm in this building with Kade. They know that you're here too. By now they know everyone that's gone in and out of this building for the last week. Eventually my backup will come knocking. And if I disappear, they're going to tear this place and all of you apart looking for me. The kid gloves are on right now. They won't be on for long."

Always project confidence, Nakamura had taught her. *Even when they have the physical upper hand, you can have the psychological advantage.*

Ilya turned to Rangan. "What can you do to her memories?"

Rangan thought for a moment, then slowly shook his head and turned behind him. "Kade?"

Kade didn't reply. His eyes stayed glued on the floor.

"Kade," Ilya snapped. "Focus. Can you erase her memories of tonight? Fuzz them out?"

Kade looked at Sam for the first time. Their eyes met. Sam wished again that she could feel his mind. She hated that fact.

"Nothing subtle," he said. "Probably nothing very effective. And it might do some other damage along the way."

Sam didn't like where this was going. That cold chill was creeping further up her spine. She broke Kade's gaze, looked hard at Ilya. "I thought nonconsensual mindfucking was rape? Isn't that what you wrote last year? The worst kind of violation possible?"

Rangan rolled his eyes. "Oh, this bitch is good."

Ilya looked at Sam. She looked hard and aristocratic. "I'd rather wipe your memories than kill you. Be grateful." Her Russian accent was flaring up.

"There will be no killing here," Wats pronounced.

Kade spoke up. "It doesn't matter. They know she's here. They know who we are. We're made."

"So what's the alternative, Kade?" Ilya asked.

Wats cut in. He spoke slowly, firmly. "We need to evac according to our plans. Her memories are irrelevant. It's time to do what we've prepared to do – leave here for a safer place."

Ilya laughed nervously. "You're kidding, right?"

"No," Wats replied. "Kade is right. This woman isn't here on her own. She was sent. Secrecy has been compromised. That means we're all in danger right now. At this point, every second counts. If we act immediately, we might slip the net. The longer we wait, the worse our odds."

Sam spoke up. "Listen. Just stay calm, OK. You're not going to make it out of here. This place is under a magnifying glass right now. My team has been tracking me constantly. There'll be stealthed ERD scopes aimed at every exit. Running is not going to help. Give up, and it'll go easier on you. Try to run, or mess with my memories, you'll get the book thrown at you."

"She's lying," said Rangan.

"I'm not lying."

"Then you're holding something back. What is it?"

Sam took a deep breath.

Rangan pushed against her thoughts. Something in her mind bent.

He's doing something to my mind...

She found herself speaking again.

"It's Kade," she told them. She looked at him. "My superiors want you to do a job for them. My mission here was twofold – to get intel on what research you were really doing, and to get leverage that could be used to compel you to take part in an upcoming ERD mission."

Kade looked surprised. "What do they want me for?"

Again she felt the pressure from Rangan. She tried to resist. Words tumbled out. "We want him to get close to someone. Someone building a mind control technology, possibly based on Nexus."

"I won't do it," said Kade.

Ilya rounded on him. "Wait, Kade, think about it. If they want you for something, that gives you leverage. You can negotiate to get the charges dropped."

"What about everyone else here?" asked Kade. "All the people who came to the party?"

"We're not local cops," said Sam. "We're ERD. We care about the technology. If you cooperate, your guinea pigs here probably aren't in much trouble. If not... you and everyone here are in a deep pile of shit."

"I want them all off the hook. Rangan and Ilya and Wats too. No arrests, no jail, no probation, nothing."

Sam wanted to shake her head again, but couldn't. "I'm not the person for you to bargain with. Surrender and come in with me. Just you four. No one else has to even know what's going on. Then we can negotiate."

Wats spoke to Rangan. "Can you blur her senses? Make it so she can't hear us? Can't read our lips?"

Rangan nodded. Sam started to object, found that she couldn't speak. Her vision started to fail. It narrowed into a tunnel, grayed out, then simply vanished. She didn't see blackness. She simply didn't see. Sound disappeared. She was blind and deaf.

Sam fought to choke down a rising panic. Few nightmares were worse for her than losing control of her mind and body. Breathe, she told herself. She could still feel her body, still feel her chest rise and fall, still feel her arms tied behind her back and her feet tied to the chair. She clung to that solidity.

Wats exhaled slowly. How to convince these kids of what was necessary? "Listen, this woman will say anything to you to achieve her goals. She's lied from the beginning. She's going to keep on lying. Once the ERD have you in custody, you're theirs. You won't get a lawyer. They can do whatever they want to you, and you won't ever get out from under it. You understand?"

He looked around the room. Ilya met his eyes. Rangan was nodding, his face pale. Kade still had his eyes on the ground. Wats could feel their emotions. Rangan: fear and anger. Ilya: defiance. Kade: guilt and self-doubt. He was reprimanding himself for creating this situation.

"Kade. Sit up straight, my friend. It doesn't matter how

we got here. We're here." Wats saw Kade nod at his words, felt the kid get fractionally more of a grip on his emotions. "Look, our getaway plans are solid. If we stay, they have us for sure. If we bolt right now, we have a chance. It's a deep dark hole or a chance at getting out. We've got to do the sensible thing."

He paused, looking around. Rangan was ready. He didn't know what to make of Ilya and Kade's emotions.

"OK, you all ready? Rangan, can you knock her out and leave her that way for a few hours?"

"I'm not going," Kade said.

Wats paused again. Then, "Kade, if you stay, it's over. You won't ever get free of them."

Kade nodded. "I know. It's just... If we run, what happens to everyone else here? Antonio, Jessica, Andy... The volunteers that measured out the doses and hooked up the repeaters. Do we tell all of them to run too? They don't have fake passports. They don't have someplace to run to. They just get fucked. Hell, what about Tania, Wats?"

Wats flushed. "If you stay here, you get fucked too," he replied.

Kade shook his head. "Ilya's right. If they want me for something, then I have leverage. It's a bargaining chip. I can get other folks off the hook."

"You have bigger things to attend to," Wats replied.

Now Kade exuded anger. "That's a cop-out, Wats. We created this situation. It's our responsibility." He calmed himself, spoke more softly. "Actually, you know what? It's *my* responsibility." He shook his head.

Wats let his breath out slowly again. He had to reach this kid. "Kade... It's important that you get out of here. All three of you. What you're doing here is powerful. It has potential. It can save a lot of lives. It can end wars. It's bigger than you. It's more important than just this party.

You're more important."

"I'm not more important than the hundred people out there," Kade said sharply.

"Your work is."

Ilya cut in. "Wats, we can't let the ends justify the means. These people haven't done anything wrong. *We* haven't done anything wrong. We have to fight. We can take this public, take it to the press..."

Wats shook his head. So naïve. "Ilya, they're not going to let you, don't you see? You have no rights in this country, not as of tonight. They're not going to let you near the press. And even if they did, no one would care."

Ilya stood her ground. "We have to try. We have to stand up and fight for what's right." She exuded resolve, defiance.

This wasn't going to work, Wats saw. As much as he'd tried to educate them on the realities of the world, they wouldn't ever understand until they'd experienced it first hand.

He turned to Kade.

"Then give me the code," he said. "The design, the blueprints, the recipe, all of it. If you disappear, I'll get it out into the world."

Kade shook his head. "It's not ready yet."

"Kade, if you go to jail, it'll never get out. This may be your only chance left to make a difference with it."

Kade kept shaking his head. "It's too easy to abuse. Look at what we're doing to her right now." He gestured towards the now blind and deaf ERD agent tied to the chair. "If we let it out now, people will get hurt."

Wats kept his breathing steady, held onto his calm. "Then I'll find someone trustworthy to keep working on it until it is ready. Don't let it go down the drain."

Rangan interjected, "I'm not staying either."

Kade turned and looked at him. There was no surprise

there. He just nodded. "OK. I'm the one with the bargaining chip. The rest of you get out of here. You too, Ilya."

"I'm with you," she said. "We have to fight for what's right."

Wats relaxed fractionally. Rangan had the full code and design. If Rangan got out too, then all was not lost. Then he looked again at Kade and at Ilya. These were his friends. The best friends he'd made since he'd left the Corps. He doubted he'd ever see them again. He let his eyes drink up the sight of them.

Wats picked Kade up in a bear hug. Kade winced, then relaxed into it. Wats moved on to Ilya, picked her up off the ground and twirled her around. She squealed, despite the grave circumstances. There were tears in her eyes. Then Rangan said his goodbyes as well.

At the door, Wats turned and soaked up the sight of Ilya and Kade once more. "I won't forget you," he promised. "Good luck." Then he and Rangan were gone.

Saturday 2040.02.18 : 2108 hours
Department of Homeland Security – West Coast Tactical Situation Center

Three hundred and fifty miles to the south, ERD Special Agent Garrett Nichols watched the developing situation with some interest. Five of them clustered in the command and control room at the Department of Homeland Security Tactical Situation Center outside Los Angeles. The Drug Enforcement Agency liaison and the Department of Homeland Security Counterterrorism Division liaison sat quietly behind him. This was a joint operation, but given its nature, the Emerging Risks Directorate of DHS had operational command.

His two analysts sat at the consoles in front of him. Half a dozen giant screens filled a wall that all of them could see.

Screen 1 showed overhead false color visual of Simonyi
Field, as seen from the Coast Guard's HQ-37 Sky Eye flying
silent circles one thousand feet above it. Hangar 3 was their
focus. Lights illuminated either end of the vast building.
Cars in the nearby parking lot shone in infrared, their
engines still warm.

On screen 2, a running stream of tagged identities of
attendees. Every vehicle arriving was having its registration
quietly interrogated. Every person who stepped out of a
vehicle was being optically faceprinted. Their profiles
streamed across the screen. Almost every one was an
associate of targets Alpha through Delta.

Screen 3 showed the status of their two ground units and
the squads within them.

Screen 4 showed the status and location of California
Highway Patrol and Mountain View Police units standing
by to assist.

Screen 5, where the stream of data from Agent Blackbird
should be, was blank. It would update when she left the
EM shielding and her surveillance devices uploaded what
she'd seen and heard in the intervening time.

Being out of contact with a field agent always made
Nichols nervous. Tonight was no exception.

Sight and sound slowly faded back into Sam's reality. She
heard her own breathing, first. Then saw the tiniest hint of
light. Shapes. A wall. She blinked, and the world came back
more strongly. She was still in the same room. Kade was
here, slumped in a chair. No sign of Wats, Rangan, or Ilya.

She tried to wiggle her toes. Nothing. Fingers. Nothing.
Still paralyzed.

Nichols and his team watched the hangar closely, waiting
for Blackbird to emerge. It might be hours yet until the

Nexus party wound down.

On scope, a small number of people came and went from the party. A cluster of smokers emerged around the east exit. Three couples snuck out to find private time outside the structure. A dozen stragglers arrived late and were let into the building. Seven individuals left in the same timeframe. All groups were faceprinted. None were among the primary targets.

A young man emerged in a hoodie, his face hidden from the aerial camera, his body glowing in infrared. There was a tense moment as he crossed towards the neighboring golf course. Then he pissed on a bush and strolled back to the party.

Just after midnight another couple emerged and strolled in the same direction. Faceprinting identified one as Tania Wellington, a martial arts instructor residing in San Francisco. The other's face was shielded by a hooded sweatshirt. He was a large man, tall and broad. Could that be Cole?

The two figures crossed slowly across the golf course, making no move towards the road or Sunnyvale. Eventually their stroll led them to the edge of the San Francisco Bay. IR showed their forms entwine, their faces meet, their clothes begin to come off.

Three individuals came out the east entrance, walked past the smokers, headed towards a car. The first two were ID'd successfully. The third kept his face in the shadows of the hoodie. The car door opened, and light momentarily illuminated him.

Rangan Shankari.

"Get CHP on that car," Nichols ordered. "Just follow. I want to see where Shankari goes."

"Roger that," Jane Kim called out.

• • •

"Why'd you do this to us?" Kade asked. He was slumped in the chair across the room once more, the ice pack to his head.

Sam took a breath before answering. "What you're doing is illegal. My job is to uphold the law."

Kade shook his head. "That's no answer. Why'd you choose this job?"

"Because what you're doing is dangerous. That's why I care. You're playing with fire."

"This isn't a weapon. It's a new way to communicate. It connects people. You saw that. You felt it."

Sam had felt it. She'd loved it, until she'd been horrified by it, by the discovery that she was not who she thought she was. She dodged the topic.

"It can be abused. Maybe you wouldn't use it to hurt people, but others would."

"It's not like that," said Kade. "It's a way of bridging the gap between people. It makes us smarter together than we could be apart. It can raise collective intelligence, collective empathy. Ilya talks about…"

Sam cut him off. "Ilya talks about creating things that aren't human, Kade. Non-human intelligences."

"Groups of humans," Kade retorted. "Human networks."

"Hive minds. Borgs. Super-organisms," Sam spat out. "What if they don't like us?"

"How could they not like us? They'd *be* us." Kade was getting heated now.

"And what if I didn't want to join a hive? Would I be forced to? Assimilated? Could I keep up if I didn't? Would there be a place for ordinary humans?"

Kade exhaled in frustration. "Look, that's all paranoia. There are positive effects too."

"It's not just paranoia, Kade. You have me under your thumb right now. You can make me do whatever you want.

Rangan could too. That's *coercion*, Kade. You've built a coercion technology. A way to control people. And you tell me this isn't a weapon?"

Kade shook his head. "It's just a safety precaution. This is still experimental."

"Just a precaution, huh? Do other people have this back door in their heads? Can you paralyze any of your friends out in the party? Can you read their minds?"

Kade said nothing, just looked down at his hands.

"You can, can't you?" Sam continued. "Do they know? Have you told them that taking part in your little experiment hands you and Rangan the keys to their heads?"

Kade shook his head, still not looking at her. "It's a safeguard, that's all. We'd never release it like this."

"How can you be so naïve, Kade? You're a good guy. I've felt that. But what about other people who get their hands on this? You think they won't reverse-engineer it? You think they won't make slaves out of this? Suicide troops? Sex slaves? Worshippers?"

Awful memories were rising up inside of her. The ranch. The cult. The way her parents had become cattle, or worse. She wanted to push them at Kade, couldn't. He was opaque to her. She was cut off from his mind.

Kade bristled. "This is stupid. You can hurt people with guns. You can get them to do awful things with words. Books are as dangerous as anything I'm doing. We *need* this. 'Our current problems can't be solved by the level of thinking that created them.' Einstein said that. This can take us to a new level of thinking."

"Kade, it's going too fast," Sam replied. She fought down the pain and despair of old memories, hardened herself. She despised the longing she felt to touch his mind and show him. Hated the weakness of it, the wrongness of it. Damn this drug. Damn this mission.

"You're talking about changing everything about people, the way we've been for a hundred thousand years, in a heartbeat. You can't know the consequences, you can't understand how people will abuse this, you can't know that humanity will survive this. We have to *slow down* the rate we're becoming something that's not human."

Kade glared at her. "You're one to talk. You're not quite baseline human yourself, are you?"

Nichols turned his attention back to the couple at the edge of the water. The red blobs in the IR scope were bent over, making odd motions. What were they doing?

It clicked. They were taking off their shoes. And now their pants. A little rendezvous on the beach. The couple now appeared to be kissing passionately, red lines blurring in IR, only heads and limbs distinguishable in the image. He was about to look away, when they did something he didn't expect. They turned, hand in hand, and ran into the Bay, water splashing up around them. They ran till they were hip-deep, the lower halves of their bodies disappearing from IR view, and then dove head first into the water, and vanished under the waves entirely.

"Isn't that water a little cold for a swim this time of year?" Nichols asked aloud.

"I was just thinking the same," Bruce Williams replied. "Can't be much more than fifty degrees."

On screen, twenty feet further out, the head and shoulders of one of the red blobs. Nichols held his breath. Wait for it... Wait for it... Nothing. The other was nowhere to be seen.

"Fuck!" he exclaimed. "Get Mobile 2 there now! Scramble the mini drones. Light that place up. Find that guy!"

Kim and Williams furiously hit keys. On screen, Mobile 2 turned on its lights and spun tires as it accelerated to the spot, leaving the road and crashing into the manicured greens of the course. A narrow beam spotlight shot out from the overhead Sky Eye. The naked figure in the water turned, put her face in the water and kicked towards shore.

"And pull over the car with Shankari in it!" Nichols called out.

"Yes, sir," Jane Kim replied.

A tense minute passed, and then another. Mobile 2 arrived at the scene and took Tania Wellington into custody. Yes, she confirmed, that had been Cole. And no, she had no idea where he was going.

Cole was gone. If he had a rebreather or had undergone black market blood hyperoxygenation, he could stay down for hours. He could come up anywhere. Unless they were very, very lucky, he was gone.

California Highway Patrol had more luck. On screen a cruiser pulled in behind the vehicle carrying Rangan Shankari. Moments later, they had him in custody.

Sam took her time in replying. "I'm human, Kade. I've made compromises. I've accepted things that are necessary for me to do my job, to help keep people safe."

"Funny," Kade said, "I don't feel any safer with you around."

"You don't see the things we do on your behalf."

"I saw what you did tonight."

"There are monsters out there, Kade," Sam said. "We have to stop them."

"I'm no monster."

"You're no monster," Sam agreed, "but they're out there. There are people who would do awful things with this technology."

"There are people who would do wonderful things with it, too," Kade replied. "We'll put safeguards in. That's always been the plan. We don't want this used for mind control any more than you do."

"Other people will reverse-engineer the technology. They'll remove the safeguards, or figure out how to build a clone system that doesn't have them. That's how it always works. Once the genie is out of the bottle, you can't control what they do."

Kade threw up his hands in frustration. "You can't control what people do with phones, or planes, or the net," he replied. "People do terrible things with all of those, but the good things outweigh them. Should we take all of those back too?"

"Those don't change what we are. We're still human."

"You get to decide who's human? Pretty damn arrogant."

Sam tried to stay cool, didn't entirely succeed. "Arrogant? You're the one who's taking risks that could affect billions of people. You're the one threatening to make real humans obsolete. Do you have any idea the danger you're putting the whole world in?"

Kade shook his head bitterly. "You have this so backwards. I'm not making choices for anyone. I'm giving people options. I'm giving them new decisions to make for themselves. You're the one taking people's freedoms away. You're the one locking people up for doing the wrong science, or for trying something new." He stabbed an accusatory finger in her direction. "If there's any monster here, it's you."

The state trooper placed Rangan in the back of his squad car. Bruce Williams patched Nichols into the CHP comms system.

Nichols put on his headset. "Rangan Shankari?" he asked.

Silence. On the screen, Rangan looked towards the floor of the vehicle, making no sign he'd heard.

"Mr Shankari, you are now in the custody of the Emerging Risks Directorate. My name is Special Agent Nichols."

More silence.

"Mr Shankari, is Samara Chavez still inside Hangar 3? What's her status?"

"I want to see my lawyer." Rangan uttered the words without looking up.

"Mr Shankari, you're under suspicion of very serious crimes in breach of the Emerging Technological Threats Act. Under these conditions you don't have the right to a lawyer."

Silence.

Nichols continued. "What I care about is the safety of Samara Chavez. Is she still in that building? What's her situation?"

Rangan said nothing.

"Mr Shankari, I have a team of men ready to knock down the door of that building and do whatever it takes to get my agent out. There are also at least a hundred civilians in the building, many of whom are your friends. If we go in with force, some of your friends could be hurt. Do you understand me?"

"Suck my dick."

Nichols was irritated now. "Rangan, you may think you're accomplishing something with this, but you're not. If you're covering for your friends, we already have Watson Cole," Nichols lied. "What we want is to know if Samara Chavez is still alive, and a way to communicate with the people inside that building to get her out."

Rangan said nothing, but shifted slightly in his seat.

"If you don't help me, we're going in, and people are

likely to get hurt. People might get killed. You understand that?"

Rangan shifted again. "I want my lawyer."

"You're not going to get one. Are you going to help us, or do we kick in the door and start shooting?"

Rangan visibly hesitated, then spoke. "They're going to let her go in a couple hours."

Nichols leaned back in his seat. So, she was alive. And being held.

"Let's end this now," he said. "Not a couple hours from now. You're going back in there, and here's what you're going to tell your friends inside…"

Fifteen minutes later, a black SUV deposited him outside the hangar's back entrance.

"…if there's any monster here, it's you!"

The handle of the door to the storage room turned. Both Kade and Sam turned, startled, to see Ilya enter, a glum look on her face, trailed by Rangan, dressed in a grey hoodie and jeans. Rangan looked pale and unhappy. His eyes were fixed on the ground in front of him. Party sounds followed them in.

"They caught me," Rangan announced. His voice shook.

Kade could feel the bitterness of it. The words tasted like ashes in his mouth.

"They sent me back in to deliver a message," Rangan said. "They have this place surrounded. They have Wats too."

"Ugh." Kade felt it like a blow.

"They want the three of us to come out, with her." Rangan nodded towards Sam, still bound to the chair. "They want us to shut down the party, send everyone home with some excuse, and surrender ourselves. Just us. We're not to mention the ERD at all. If we don't come out in thirty minutes, they say they'll come in here with guns out."

"What about everyone else here?" Kade asked.

"As long as we surrender, everyone else can go home."

"I'd rather make a scene," said Ilya. "Force them to arrest a hundred of us. Take it public. Show people what they're doing. That's how we fight."

"Everyone knows what they're doing," Rangan said. "No one cares. We're just druggies to them."

Kade spoke up. "I don't want other people going to jail because of us. That was the whole point of not running."

"That was part of the point," Ilya said. "The other part is standing up for what's right. We've done nothing wrong. The ERD are the bad guys here. We can show the world that."

Kade shook his head. "No. This is our fall to take."

"I'm with Kade," Rangan said softly.

Ilya bowed her head. She didn't look convinced. Her mind felt angry to Kade, defiant.

"Fine," she said. "I'll go start shutting things down." She left through the open door.

Rangan looked at Kade. "You OK?"

Kade nodded but said nothing.

Minutes passed. They waited in silence.

What's taking so long? Kade wondered.

Just then, through the door, they heard the current track fade, Ilya's amplified voice, something about a noise complaint, the party over, time to go, drive safe.

Ilya returned shortly after that. Her eyes were wet. Had she been crying? He wanted to comfort her, but she felt hard and angry.

"I left Antonio in charge of clearing people out," she said. "That'll take a while. We might as well go now."

"They said to head out the side entrance and walk towards the golf course parking lot," Rangan said.

Ilya untied the rope around Sam's feet, helped her up

with a hand on her bicep.

Sharp pains lanced up Sam's left side as she rose. She ignored them. The four of them walked out of the storage room, turned and took a hallway away from the main hangar area. A minute later Rangan opened the side door of the hangar and they emerged into the cool night air.

Sam's contacts immediately lit up with the positions of the DEA SWAT team that was providing her support on this mission. The two vehicles were a hundred yards ahead. Two agents were with the vehicles. Four more in a loose perimeter blocking possible escape. All showed ready to fire, half with lethal loads, half with tranq. A green handshake glyph showed that their tactical systems had registered hers as well.

She looked to her right at Rangan, squinted to illuminate him as a target, then Kade on her left, squinted, and hit the fire icon with her eyes. Rangan started to turn, the start of a frown on his face. Sam felt him tense in her mind. Then tranquilizer rounds shot out from two agents and hit each men in the neck. They went down like comic actors, hands rising to the sudden wasp stings at their necks, gurgling cries of surprise, then eyes going glassy, balance lost, toppling into loose-limbed heaps.

"Bitch!"

Sam felt Ilya grab her physically from behind, her arm around Sam's throat. Sam spun to present a clear shot on the woman to the shooters, heard the *thwap* of a silenced tranq dart, and a moment later felt the grasp around her neck loosen and Ilya's limp body crumple to the ground.

Watson Cole came up for air under the Dumbarton Bridge. He slid his body slowly into the shallows where it came to ground in Menlo Park, gradually letting just his face rise above the level of the water. With luck, the bridge would shield him from any cameras, IR or visual, searching for him from above. He'd swum more than six miles underwater, an exhausting feat in the best of times. He needed time to let his blood hyperoxygenate again. He rested a moment, then started the pressure breathing that would accelerate his uptake of precious oxygen. He had miles to go before he slept.

5
Leverage

Rangan woke slowly. His head ached. His muscles were cramped, his stomach restless. God, what a hangover. What had he been doing last night? What time was it? He cracked one eye to take a peek.

This was not his bedroom.

Memory rushed back. Oh, fuck...

Rangan sat bolt upright. He was on a thin mattress atop a rigid metal bench along the wall of a starkly white cell. Fuck fuck fuck. He looked down at himself. His clothes were gone, his watch, his shoes. He was in shapeless grey cotton slacks, like hospital pants, and a baggy grey shirt. Prison garb. They'd taken his phone, his wallet, everything.

Think, Rangan, think.

If there was an unguarded net connection here, he could get online, maybe figure out where he was. Maybe get a message out as insurance...

Nexus OS would have the tools to locate an open net connection. It wasn't running. It must have crashed last night when they'd tranqed him.

[nexus_restart] he mentally commanded. The boot sequence scrolled across his vision.

```
[Nexus OS 0.7 by Axon and Synapse]
[Built    on   ModOS   8.2   by   Free   Software
Collective]
[8,947,692,017 nodes detected]
[9,161,412,625,408 bits available]
[visual cortex interface 0.64 ... active]
[auditory cortex interface 0.59 ... active]
[...]
```

More scrolled across his vision as the operating system they'd ported to the Nexus platform came to life. He paced as it booted.

In a top secret facility outside Washington, DC, two men stared at a wall screen. One man was tall, fit, square-jawed, in a dark suit, hands clasped behind his back – Enforcement Division Deputy Director Warren Becker. The other was a scientist, wearing rumpled clothes, in old-fashioned spectacles, with a shock of unruly white hair – Neuroscience Director Martin Holtzmann.

On the screen, a dark-skinned, bleached blonde man in prison fatigues was pacing a small, starkly white cell. Rangan Shankari.

"I still don't think this is necessary," Holtzmann said.

"We have to know if your weapon works," Becker replied.

Holtzmann shook his head. "It works. We've seen it work. Many times."

Becker turned to look at him, then looked back at the wall showing Rangan Shankari. "Martin, we need to know if it works against Nexus 5. We don't know what changes they've made since Nexus 3."

"We can find that out in animals," Holtzmann replied.

Becker raised an eyebrow. "And if it doesn't work the same in mice and in men?"

Holtzmann was silent for a moment. "There are dangers. We should do the animal studies first, assess the safety, then try humans."

Becker considered this for a moment. "We don't know when we'll have this opportunity again. If this doesn't work, we'll need to spend more time refining your weapon. If it *does* work against Nexus 5, we have that much more confidence that it will work against our eventual target."

Holtzmann grunted. "Warren, I can't ethically..."

Becker held up his hand to interrupt. Holtzmann paused.

"Thank you, Martin. Given our mission priorities, I'm going to proceed. I'll take note of your reluctance. We'll keep this as brief as possible."

Holtzmann bowed his head.

Becker pitched his voice to address the wall. "Activate Nexus disruptor."

Rangan could find no signal, on any frequency. The room seemed to be entirely EM shielded. Damn. What now?

Searing pain burst across Rangan's mind. His head was on fire, alive with thousand-decibel static, threatening to burst. A scream drove its way out of his lips. Every muscle in his body convulsed. He toppled forward to the floor. Errors and warnings streamed at high speed across his consciousness.

```
[interface ERROR — memory out of bounds]
[interface ERROR — memory out of bounds]
[interface ERROR — socket not found OXA49328A]
[interface ERROR — socket not found OXA49328B]
[interface ERROR — socket not found OXA49328C]
[interface ERROR — socket not found OXA49328D]
```

...and on and on and on... thousands of lines of hard errors scrolling across his vision, a massive fault like nothing he nor Kade had ever seen.

Rangan was dimly aware of hitting the hard concrete floor. Everything was a blur of pain and white noise. His mind was in complete overload. He swam through oceans of static. Through the confusion he could just barely grasp that something was wrong with the Nexus in his brain. He needed to stop it. There was something he could do... something... something... What was it? Fuck that hurt. Fuck, fuck, fuck.

Another scream ripped through him, tore open his mouth against his will, roared its way into the echoing chamber of the cell. Thought vanished in a haze of pain and chaos. It was too much. There was no hope of coherence. There was nothing but noise, noise, nothing but noise in his mind.

And then it was over. The pain ended as abruptly as it had begun. The onslaught of static across all his senses was gone. The spear driven into his brain had evaporated. His head hurt where it had hit the floor. It was nothing compared to what he'd just endured.

Rangan drew breath, then shuddered. He was covered in sweat. His body was trembling. His breath came raggedly. He lay curled on the floor, shaking.

On the wall screen Shankari collapsed. His scream echoed out of the speakers. He curled on the floor, body spasming. Becker let it go on for a second, two, three, four...

"That's enough," Holtzmann said bitterly.

Becker nodded. "Halt disruptor," he spoke aloud.

Shankari's screams ended. The boy lay on the ground, curled in a fetal position.

"Are you satisfied now?" Holtzmann asked. His voice was acidic.

Becker nodded slowly, calmly. "Yes."

Kade woke to bright light and a voice informing him that he had five minutes until his interview. His mouth tasted like dirt, his stomach was in rebellion, and his head felt like it had been worked over by a sledgehammer. He relieved himself, splashed water on his face, and then it was time to go. Two guards took him from his stark white cell to a conference room at the end of the hall. The room was furnished with a large fake wood table, chairs, and a wall screen. Kade took a seat as directed, and waited.

Less than a minute later, a door at the far side of the room opened and an official-looking man in a suit and tie entered, holding a leather-bound slate. He was followed by a shorter, older man in a rumpled white shirt and glasses, his head topped by disorderly white hair. There was something familiar about the second man.

"Mr Lane," said the first man, as he made his way to the head of the table and sat. "I'm Enforcement Division Deputy Director Warren Becker. This is Professor Martin Holtzmann, whom you may know."

Holtzmann! thought Kade. He'd been Chair of the MIT Neuroengineering Department once. His lab had done good work in the neuroscience of volition. How was he involved with the ERD?

Holtzmann nodded in greeting. "Mr Lane," he said. He had a German accent.

Becker spoke. "Mr Lane, you're in some pretty serious trouble. You've been engaging in research in direct contravention of the Chandler Act. You've far exceeded the bounds of your ERD license. You've been caught engaging in the distribution and possibly the manufacture of a Schedule 0 narcotic. Do you understand the seriousness of your position?"

Kade's head had slumped as Becker talked. His eyes were

on the fake wood grain of the table he was seated at. He
didn't trust himself to speak.

After a minute, Becker spoke again. "You're in a deep pile
of shit, Kade. The DEA wants to press full charges. My
bosses want to classify you as a threat to humanity. The
prosecutor assigned to this case has you down for–" Becker
paused and looked down at his slate, "violating your ERD
research limits, violating the Chandler Act in multiple cases,
development of a coercion technology, employment of a
coercion technology in the first degree, kidnapping an agent
of the law, assaulting an agent of the law, and more. All of
this together adds up to... a long, long time in a National
Security Internment Center. Possibly life. Without parole.
Those aren't pleasant places. You understand?"

Kade nodded mutely.

"Good. Now listen, this is an airtight case. The evidence
is clear. If we press, you'll get all the penalties there are. But
I don't think you're a terrorist. I think you've been stupid
here, that's all. I'm on your side."

Like hell you are, Kade thought.

Becker was still talking. "There's a way that you can help
your country and help humanity. And if you do, then we
can waive most of the punitive action against you."

Kade set his mouth in a grim line. Blackmail, he thought
to himself. Just fucking blackmail.

"What about my friends?" he asked. "The people who
were at the party?"

Becker nodded. "You care about your friends. That's
good. They're in pretty deep piles of shit themselves. The
DEA wants to press possession charges against everyone
who was there last night, and distribution charges against
everyone who helped throw the event. Our own prosecutor
wants to level Chandler Act violations at you, Rangan
Shankari, Watson Cole, and Ilyana Alexander."

Becker paused and shook his head. "But if we have your full and complete cooperation, we can waive most of those charges."

Kade winced. Nexus possession had mandatory minimums of two years, not to mention likely expulsion from any decent school and never getting a job in science or research in the future. Distribution had a minimum of *seven* years. Names and faces swam through his head. Antonio. Rita. Sven. All the people that had helped with the party, that had been responsible for giving out doses to other attendees. A lot of people could go to jail for a long time.

And as for Rangan, Ilya, and Wats... They'd face the same penalties he would. Decades in a National Security Internment Center. Life maybe. His face was hot. He wanted to throw up at the thought of it.

Poker face, Kade. Poker face.

He straightened up a bit. He'd be damned if he'd break down here.

"What do you want me to do?" he asked.

"We want you to get close to someone," Becker replied. "A fellow scientist, in another country. We want you to apply for a position in their lab after your PhD. We want you to keep us informed regarding their work."

"You want me to spy for you," Kade said.

"Yes."

"Why?"

"Because the scientist we want you to spy on may be doing some very bad things," Becker answered. "Murder. Political assassination. Mind control. That sort of thing."

"And why me?" Kade asked.

"Because this scientist appears to have taken an interest in your work," Becker told him. "And, now that we know what you've really been doing, we can see why."

"Who are we talking about here?" Kade asked.

"You find that out if you agree. If not, you go to jail just wondering."

Kade drummed his fingers on the table. Spying on a fellow scientist. He felt dirty.

"You said most of the charges?" he asked. "What are you offering?"

Becker nodded. "Everyone there gets probation and mandatory drug testing for three years. They pass, it's gone from their record. You, Shankari, Cole, and Alexander are on a lifelong watch list. Mandatory testing. No use of advanced computing, bio, neuro, or nano tools, including Nexus. You're blacklisted for all federal science funding. No jail time."

Kade's vision dimmed. No funding. No computing or bio. No Nexus. They're taking everything I care about away, he thought. He couldn't breathe for a moment.

"There is one way you can stay in science," Holtzmann commented.

Kade looked up at him. "How?"

"You could come work for me," Holtzmann said. "Here at the ERD, you'd be doing work to serve your country. Under strict supervision, of course."

I'd rather lobotomize myself with a spoon, Kade thought.

"I understand this is a hard pill to swallow," Becker said. "But it's a lot better than life in prison."

Is it?

The world was spinning around him. He couldn't see straight. This was a nightmare.

"There's one more condition," Becker was saying. "You hand over all the work you've done on Nexus to us, and you walk our research team through what you've built and how."

"I…" Kade started. "I just need some time to think about

this..."

Becker nodded again. "Fine. Think about it. But don't think too long. We can hide that you're in our custody for a few more hours. After that it'll be difficult. And if it's known that we had you, you'll be of no use to us. You'll get the book thrown at you."

The guards took him back to his cell. Kade lay on the cot and closed his eyes. Faces swam through his vision again. All the people who would be fucked if he didn't agree to this.

And if he did agree to spy for them? If he did, then he might be helping the ERD screw over some scientist who was guilty of nothing. He'd be signing on to an organization that was almost his complete opposite in ideology.

But I'd have options, he thought to himself. I wouldn't be in jail. I'd be working for them overseas. I could find a way out...

I'd be part of a system I hate.

He wished his parents were alive. Dennis and Cheryl Lane had been scientists, a high energy physicist and a research biologist, until a highway crash had taken both their lives late last year. He could use their counsel now. What would they say if they were here?

A scientist is responsible for the consequences of his or her work. His dad had drilled that into his head again and again.

The consequences of my work are jail for dozens of my friends. Unless I do what the ERD wants.

His thoughts chased their own tails for an hour. No matter how he looked at it, staying out of jail, keeping his friends out of jail, was better than having them all locked away. He couldn't have that many destroyed lives on his conscience. He had to make amends for leading so many people into trouble. His decision was clear. It left a vile taste in his mouth. So be it.

Briefing

ARYAN RISING (aka RED THURSDAY)
[Event]
[Organization] [Year : 2030]

The Aryan Rising incident (2030) was an attempt to wipe out the bulk of humanity, paving the way for the repopulation of the world by a race of genetically engineered neo-Nazi transhumans.

On May 16th, 2030, the US public awoke to news of mass deaths in Laramie, Wyoming. [See RED THURSDAY] American News Network and other news sources broadcast gruesome images of citizens of Laramie vomiting blood and collapsing in the street. National Guard and FBI Bioterror quickly established a cordon around the town, which they maintained throughout the incident.

Rapid sequencing established that the deaths were due to a heavily modified airborne variant of the Marburg virus, dubbed Marburg Red. Within four days, ninety per cent of the residents of Laramie were dead, with a total death toll over thirty-one thousand. Heroic measures and the extremely short incubation time of the viral variant prevented the spread of Marburg Red beyond Laramie.

In the aftermath of the attack, investigators discovered a compound to the west of Laramie containing one hundred and twenty-eight cloned children, in eight batches of sixteen, ranging in age from three to fifteen, and dozens of bodies of deceased adults. Subsequent investigation revealed that the cloned children had been created by a group referring to themselves as the "Aryan Rising", and specifically engineered for immunity to Marburg Red, as part of an ideologically driven plot to wipe out "inferior races" and replace them with ethnically pure Übermenschen.

Recordings from within the compound showed a group of the children deliberately releasing an early variant of Marburg Red months ahead of schedule, thus killing their creators and wiping out the nearby town. Had Marburg Red's creators been able to finish their design work and induce a longer incubation time, the death toll would have been far higher.

Public reaction was at first horrified, and subsequently extremely critical of FBI and DHS for their failure to prevent the attack. The event occurred near the peak of DWITY abduction and mind control incidents, and on the heels of the Yucca Grove outbreak of Communion virus in 2028, and the deadly Eschaton computer attack of 2029.

The combined public outrage from these events led to a steep drop in popularity of President Owen Asher and a marked increase in public support for laws restricting research into genetics, cloning, nano-technology, artificial intelligence, and any approach to creating "super-human" beings.

Public response led to the Chandler Committee hearings of 2030-2031, the passage of the Chandler Act, and the creation of the ERD. These events also played a role in the presidential campaign of 2032, contributing to the election of Governor Miles Jameson as President and Senator (now President) John Stockton as Vice President, and in the 2035 drafting of the Copenhagen Accords on Global Technological Threats.

History of Advanced Technological Threats,
ERD Library Series, 2039 [Unclassified]

6
External Conditions

"I'll do it," Kade told them.

"Good," Becker nodded. "You're making the right choice."

"So who am I spying on?"

Becker tapped his slate and the wallscreen came to life.

WARNING:
THE FOLLOWING MATERIAL
IS CLASSIFIED:
TOP SECRET CITADEL FOUR
DISCLOSURE OF THIS MATERIAL TO UNCLEARED
INDIVIDUALS IS A FEDERAL OFFENSE
PUNISHABLE BY UP TO 30 YEARS
IN PRISON.

The twin logos of the Department of Homeland Security and the Emerging Risks Directorate within it bracketed the security clearance warning.

"You're about to receive top secret information. Do you understand that disclosure of this information, to anyone, is a felony with severe penalties?"

Kade swallowed. "Yes."

"Good," Becker said. He tapped his slate with a finger.

The wall screen advanced to the next slide. On it was a picture of a tall, elegant Asian woman in her early forties, caught looking to one side and smiling warmly at someone outside the image. Kade had seen her face before.

"Her name is Su-Yong Shu," Becker said. "You've probably heard of her."

Kade was momentarily speechless. Su-Yong Shu? A murderer?

Su-Yong Shu was perhaps the most impressive neuroscientist in the field. Asked to pick a working scientist who would one day win the Nobel Prize, Kade would have named her. She had done more to unlock the neural encoding of abstract reasoning, beliefs, motivations, and knowledge than anyone alive. Kade's work used statistical methods layered on top of models built in Su-Yong Shu's lab. She and her students put out a fire hose of top-notch papers. She was one of the most respected neuroscientists alive.

"You're calling Su-Yong Shu a murderer?" Kade asked. "Do you have any idea what you're talking about? Do you have any evidence to back that up?"

Becker tapped his slate. The screen changed again. Now it showed a picture of a man in the orange robes of a Buddhist monk, his shaven head bowed forward, kneeling in what looked to be a stone courtyard.

"This is a file photo of Lobsang Tulku, the Buddhist monk who shot and killed the Dalai Lama and two of his bodyguards in Dharamsala in 2037, and then took his own life."

Kade nodded. "I remember. He just snapped one day, right?"

"That's the story," Becker said. "We have reason to

believe that's not what actually occurred. Instead, we believe that someone turned this man into a kind of puppet and used him to commit a political assassination."

Becker advanced the presentation again. The wall screen now showed a gruesome image of a twenty-something Asian man in monk's robes in a pool of blood, two bullet wounds in his head. The Dalai Lama. Kade felt his stomach churn.

"Lobsang had no history of owning or using firearms," Becker said. "So far as we know, he'd never even touched a gun until a week before this event. Yet his marksmanship was impeccable. He fired six times, twice for each of the two bodyguards, and twice for the Dalai Lama. Every one was a head shot. He didn't miss with a single bullet."

Holtzmann looked at Kade thoughtfully. "You could do something like this, couldn't you? Make a person into a robot?"

Kade stared at the photo. In theory... With enough time...

He said nothing.

Holtzmann watched him for a moment, then nodded.

Kade cleared his throat, trying to hold onto his skepticism. "Maybe there were things you didn't know about him. Maybe someone was training him all along, or planted him."

Becker cocked his head to one side. "Lobsang was a close associate of the Dalai Lama. They grew up together. He was an apparently devoted follower and friend of the Dalai Lama, an activist for Tibetan freedom, until one day he decided to kill his lifelong friend, and did so with the skills of a professional assassin."

Becker continued. "We know that Lobsang was detained in Tibet by the Chinese a few months earlier. He was in custody for forty-eight hours and was then expelled from the country. Lobsang claimed that he spent most of that time in silent meditation in his cell, but if someone used a neurotechnology to alter his memories…"

It's possible, Kade thought. Nexus would make a great assassination tool.

He shook his head again. *Propaganda is the first tool of government*, Wats had said. Skepticism. He would hold onto it.

"What does this have to do with Su-Yong Shu?"

"We'll get to that in a moment," Becker said.

He advanced the slide again. A ruined building appeared, obviously the site of an explosion. Bodies and wounded were strewn about, some of them in military uniform.

"Grozny, Chechnya, 2038. After nearly five years of peace, a young woman named Zamira Zakaev – a woman associated with a disarmed and peace accord-abiding Chechen independence group – blows up a nightclub popular with the Russian army. The event, which killed seventy-four civilians and thirty Russian soldiers, set off a wave of reprisals, which in turn set off more bombings. Russia moved three divisions of the Russian army back into the North Caucasus. The situation remains inflamed today."

"I don't see the connection," said Kade.

"Zamira Zakaev had traveled to China earlier in the year, and had also been held for two days by the Chinese authorities, for no obvious reason."

"Why would China want to bomb a club in Chechnya?"

"It distracts the Russians. Forces them to move their attention and their forces away from China."

Kade tried to absorb this. What did it have to do with Shu?

"One more," Becker said. "And then we'll get to why we think Su-Yong Shu is involved."

Becker tapped his slate again. The screen now showed an

Asian man in a suit, fist raised in triumph or defiance above him, standing at a podium surrounded by a throng of people, some waving banners.

"This is Chien Liu, now president of Taiwan. This picture was taken on the eve of his election victory last year, in 2039. President Liu was the head of the DPP, the primary opposition party in Taiwan, and ran his campaign on an anti-Beijing platform. He pledged to roll back major pieces of integration. On the campaign trail he leveled sharp criticism at China on human rights, foreign policy, and its lack of internal reforms.

"In January of this year, President Liu went to Beijing for his first meeting with the recently installed Chinese premier." Becker tapped and the screen now showed Liu and an older Asian man, whom Kade recognized vaguely from the news, sitting side by side in ornate red and gold chairs. The men were smiling faintly, if at all.

Becker continued. "During the visit, President Liu became suddenly ill, apparently a case of the flu. He was admitted overnight to Beijing's Jade Palace Hospital, the best hospital in the country. He was discharged early the next morning, smiling and waving at reporters, everything apparently alright. Aside from that, the trip was a major success, at least for China.

"Liu returned from Beijing singing a new tune. He flipped on nearly every topic of Taiwan-China relations, supporting deeper and faster integration, and dropping all human rights and corruption objections. We believe Beijing turned him during that visit, though in a more subtle way than the previous two cases."

"He's a politician," Kade said. "Maybe he just changed his mind."

Becker smiled faintly. "That's a very reasonable suggestion. We wondered the same. And of course we wanted to be sure. Fortunately, during his trip to the US last month, President Liu also became ill." Becker smiled faintly again. "CIA took that as an opportunity to run a few tests on President Liu's blood and cerebrospinal fluid. His blood was clean, but in his cerebrospinal fluid, they found signs of something that looks suspiciously like Nexus. That there are no signs of it in the bloodstream suggests to us that the Nexus-like substance isn't deteriorating and being flushed out of his brain as normal. The technology has been permanently integrated. Something that you seem to have achieved as well."

Holtzmann spoke again. "We look forward to hearing the details of just how you've achieved this."

Kade felt ill.

Becker went on. "We have another two dozen events we think are cases of Chinese compulsion technology at work. Do you see why we're concerned?"

"Yes," Kade said. And he did. They'd built Nexus OS to give people new freedoms, new ways to connect, new ways to learn. Not to use it as a tool for control or assassination.

"You asked about the involvement of Dr Shu. We're now getting to that. First, we have human intelligence indicating that for the past several years, she's been working with the Chinese military on coercion technologies of some sort. Second, we have direct evidence linking her to part of the Chinese supersoldier program."

Becker tapped again, and the picture changed to a group of Asian soldiers in a parade. Something about the grain and focus suggested to Kade that the photo had been taken from very far away with a very long zoom lens.

"Do you notice anything interesting about this photo?" Becker asked.

Kade studied it, not sure what he was looking for. The soldiers were in their twenties, muscular and fit, with identical crew cuts, dress uniforms, and sophisticated rifles of some kind against their right shoulders. They were all poised in mid-step, postures erect and in complete synchrony, faces cold and blank. He wondered if he was supposed to recognize one of them? Asian faces all looked a bit alike to him. Though these faces looked extremely alike, a trick of the haircuts? Or...

"They're identical," he said.

Becker nodded. "This is a detachment of the Confucian Fist special forces battalion. They're clones, which is itself a violation of Copenhagen. We also have reports that this battalion, the most elite in China's armed forces, has been engineered for unshakable loyalty."

Kade shuddered. He had a flash of memories of newscasts from his teens, the Nazi clone kids, the ones who'd tried to wipe out all of humanity. Rows of them, filing out from the compound, eyes totally cold. Killers at age ten. He tried to suppress it.

Becker saw the reaction. "You're thinking of the Aryan Rising case. We haven't seen any major cloning projects since then. Nothing at this level. Not until now."

Kade shook his head, forced himself to think like a scientist.

"They're just twins," he said. "That's all cloning is. The Nazi kids... they had programming beyond that. Just because someone's a clone doesn't make them evil... any more than any twin is."

Becker nodded thoughtfully. "Sure. You're right. Just twins. But you have to ask yourself, why would someone create a couple hundred copies of the same twin?"

Kade shrugged. "I don't know. Maybe they want blood transfusions to be easier. Or organ transplants."

Becker nodded again, seeming to consider this. "Or maybe they want conformity. Control. Maybe they want predictability. Maybe they want to do really invasive neuro-coercion, and making the brain structure as similar as possible makes that easier, eh?" Becker raised an eyebrow at him.

Kade looked at the cold, hard, identical faces of the clone soldiers again. Becker's answer was all too plausible.

"And indeed," Becker went on, "you can see them deployed in a number of the situations where absolute, unquestioning loyalty would be most demanded. You can see two of them here." The wall flipped to an image of the Chinese premier, with two bodyguards in view. They had the same face as the soldiers he'd just seen. "Another one here, with Dr Shu." The screen showed a picture of Su-Yong Shu entering her car. The driver holding open the door was one of the clones. "And another one here, with Su-Yong Shu's husband, Chen Pang, head of the artificial intelligence program at Jiaotong University." A shot of a no-nonsense looking Chinese man in a suit, crossing a plaza, caught in the middle of a purposeful stride, a dark-suited bodyguard at his side, again with the same face.

"That Dr Shu and her husband have Confucian Fist bodyguards isn't damning in and of itself. But take a look at this." The screen showed four rows of Confucian Fist soldiers, arms clasped behind their backs in parade rest. In front of them, facing the camera was a smiling Su-Yong Shu, her arms spread as if to point out the young men behind her. Unlike the other photos, the soldiers were smiling in this one.

"This was a graduation ceremony for a class, or batch, of Confucian Fist. Why is Dr Shu there if she wasn't involved in the program? And given that she's a neuroscientist who's been fingered for working on coercion technologies, and that these soldiers are reputed to be engineered for unshakable loyalty... Well, it doesn't take much to connect the dots."

Kade opened his mouth to interject, but Becker kept talking.

"One more piece of evidence," Becker said.

The screen changed again. Now it showed a market, somewhere in the tropics, perhaps Southeast Asia. Su-Yong Shu was in the middle of the photo, delightedly holding an exotic fruit of some sort to her nose. Next to her was a lean, tall Asian man wearing dark sunglasses.

"This photo was taken in Chiang Mai, Thailand, two years ago. The man next to Dr Shu is Thanom 'Ted' Prat-Nung. Ted Prat-Nung is an American-educated Thai synthetic chemist and nano-engineer. Forty-two years old. PhD from Stanford in 2024, where he focused on self-assembling nano-structures. Postdoc at Jiaotong University in Shanghai from 2024 through 2026, where it's possible he met Su-Yong Shu. His whereabouts between 2026 and 2034 are unknown. After 2034 he re-emerges as a major source of Nexus 3. We believe he synthesizes it in a facility or set of facilities in the eastern provinces of Thailand, close to the border with Cambodia. He's someone we'd very much like to get our hands on, but the Thai government has not been cooperative. Prat-Nung and Shu's research interests essentially do not overlap at all. Seeing them together is provocative, to say the least.

"To summarize, we believe that Su-Yong Shu is one of – if not the primary – scientist behind China's neurotech program focused on coercion, and that in this work she's somehow adapted Nexus 3. We're concerned both about what China could do with this technology and, perhaps even more so, what knowledge Su-Yong Shu might pass back into the black market via her connection with someone like Ted Prat-Nung."

Kade took a deep breath.

Don't buy into what they're selling, he told himself.

These people will lie or distort the truth to convince me. Stay skeptical. Learn for yourself.

"So why me?" he asked.

Becker answered, "You're about to get an invite to a special workshop on decoding higher brain functions, to be held immediately after the upcoming International Society for Neuroscience conference in Bangkok. Su-Yong Shu arranged the invitation. You'll be the only grad student at the invite-only workshop. Everyone else is a tenured professor. That indicates some degree of exceptional interest in you. We know Shu has open postdoctoral positions in her lab, and you're going to get your PhD in the next year. Your work already builds on some of hers. It seems like a good fit."

Now Kade was nervous. "So you're asking me to spy on someone who could, conceivably, have me killed or something if she finds out?"

Becker smiled slightly. "Rest assured we'd pull you out immediately if we perceived you as being in any danger. And you'll have support with you at the conference. If something long-term emerges in Shanghai, you'd have support there as well."

I don't have much choice, do I? he thought. Maybe Ilya was right. We could have gone to the press, to the public...

No. It wouldn't have worked. How many stories like that had Kade heard about in the past? Had he done anything? He'd signed some online petitions. Had he rushed to people's defenses? Had scientists around the country risen up in protest? Fat chance. Everyone just kept their head down, massaged their research proposals, tried to skirt as close to the edge of what was allowed as they could without endangering their federal grant dollars. He felt sick, ashamed of himself, ashamed of his profession.

Becker closed the cover on his slate and looked at Kade.

"For the last topic, and for the technology briefing we'd like you to do for us, I turn to Dr Holtzmann. And now I must attend to other matters. Dr Holtzmann will see to your transport back to San Francisco. We'll send someone with you to confiscate any Nexus materials you have there. Aside from that, we'll be in touch shortly. We have two months until the ISFN meeting, and we'll be asking a fair bit of preparation from you, most of it to ensure your safety." With that, Becker got up, took his slate, and exited the room, closing the door behind him.

Kade's head was spinning. Technology briefing. Confiscate Nexus materials. He was having trouble breathing again. He could feel his heart beating in his chest. They were taking Nexus away from him. They were taking it for themselves. He was handing them this power, and giving up on it himself. He had to find a way to limit the damage they could do.

But how could he?

He was dimly aware of Holtzmann saying something to him.

He missed it for a moment. The idea came to him whole. Was it possible? Yes. Was there time? He had no idea.

Holtzmann said something again.

Kade snapped back to the room.

"Sorry? I missed that."

"I asked if you're well," the elder scientist replied.

No. I'm not well. But I'm not going to roll over, either. "Umm, yeah. Sorry. It's just a lot to take in."

Holtzmann nodded. "Do you need a break?"

Kade blinked. What was done was done. He could only move forward.

"No. I'm fine now. Let's go on."

Holtzmann nodded again, opened his own slate, tapped on it for a moment, and the wall screen transitioned to a new slide, showing a single graph, labeled "Su-Yong Shu: Impact Factor of New Publications."

Holtzmann spoke. "We have one last piece of background on your mission for today. It concerns Su-Yong Shu. She's an exceptional scientist. From the very beginning of her career that has been apparent. A number of years ago, however, something changed."

Kade absorbed the graph as Holtzmann spoke. Shu's impact factor rose rapidly, solidly through her early career. Then there was a break, three years gone from science, while she took time off to raise her daughter. When the line reappeared, it was markedly higher than it had been when it dropped off. And it had a new, steeper slope – rising faster and faster every year.

"As you can see, Kade, the career trajectories before 2029 and after 2032 appear quite different. Those three years represent a discontinuity. The early Su-Yong Shu showed every sign of a successful career. The Su-Yong Shu of 2032 and later goes beyond that. She shows signs of almost... *superhuman* brilliance."

Kade considered for a moment. "Maybe she did a lot of thinking while she was at home? Came up with new ideas?"

Holtzmann nodded. "That would produce a temporary boost upon her return. Instead, what we see is a long-term acceleration. Every year after 2032, she diverges further and further from her pre-2032 trajectory. This sort of change is unprecedented."

Kade tilted his head. "You think something changed about her. That she got smarter. Augmented."

"We have no proof..." Holtzmann said slowly. "But this is very suggestive."

Kade nodded. Her work was indeed very very good. Awe-inspiring even. "The kind of augmentation you're talking about... That's not just a little memory boost or concentration aid. It's better pattern recognition. Better creativity. You're talking about enhancements beyond anything known about in the field today..."

Holtzmann nodded. "Yes. She shows signs of being augmented in ways that surpass anything that we know of. That is something which concerns us." He paused, then continued. "And it's interesting that the first report of Nexus 1 came in 2033, just seven years ago... and one year after Dr Shu's return to science." Holtzmann let that hang in the air.

Kade frowned. "You're saying Su-Yong Shu may have created Nexus? She's not a nano-engineer."

"Do you know any nano-engineer who could have designed Nexus?"

No. Not even close. "A team of engineers..." Kade suggested.

"We've had teams of nano-engineers look at Nexus, try to reverse-engineer it," Holtzman said. "The Japanese, Germans, Brits, and Indians all have as well. No one has more than scratched the surface."

"So what are you saying?" Kade asked.

"I'm saying that Nexus may defy human understanding because it is not the product of normal human thought," Holtzman said. "It is the product of *posthuman* thought."

And you're sending me spy on her? Kade thought.

Holtzmann tapped his slate. The wall screen went dark and the room lights rose. "Now it is time for you to brief us on your Nexus 5 work, and transfer to us all materials you have on it – all design notes, experimental results, all of it."

Kade swallowed. "The materials are in SF."

Holtzmann raised one white bushy eyebrow.

"It's a precaution we took," Kade said. "The master code is on a system that's kept offline."

"Very well. We will do the first stage of the technology briefing now. And we'll send an officer with you back to your lab to retrieve this data. You'll hand all data and physical materials over to our officer, and he'll return them to us."

Kade bowed his head in assent. Here we go.

Warren Becker opened the door into the room where Sam stood, silently observing the briefing Kade was receiving through a viewscreen. Becker walked up to her, placed his hand on her shoulder.

"Sam. How's that injury?"

Sam nodded, put a hand on her side. "Healing, sir. The growth factors are doing their work. I should be fully fit for service in a week."

"Good," Becker said. "What did you think of the briefing?"

Sam shook her head. "There's a lot there. I wish I'd known the whole picture before the mission last night."

"Some of it was need-to-know, Sam. We didn't expect things to go the way they did last night."

Sam nodded. "Yes, sir. I understand." She paused for a moment, then continued. "Sir... I'm not sure that I'm the right person for the next phase of this mission."

Becker snorted. "Sam, you're the perfect person for this mission. You have more experience with Nexus than any field agent. And you have a great alias that fits the mission needs."

"I know. It's just..."

Becker waited a moment and then prompted, "The failure of your memory implants was a valuable lesson, Sam. We'll improve the implantation process from that. You'll be better prepared for a Nexus 5 connection than any agent who hasn't experienced it."

"That's not it, sir. It's that... It's that I... I enjoyed it, sir. I question my objectivity."

Becker chuckled. "If drugs weren't enjoyable, people wouldn't abuse them. There's nothing new there."

Sam looked down at her hands. How to get through to him? "Sir, when I was being held captive, and no longer part of the Nexus... *connection* that they'd established, I *missed* it. I wanted to be back in that loop. I wanted... something that goes against everything I stand for." Sam was faltering now.

"Agent Cataranes." Becker said it in a tone of command.

Sam snapped her eyes to him.

"Samantha, I know how you were raised. I know what happened to you and your family at Yucca Grove. I know about Communion virus and the things you were exposed to. It's exactly because of those experiences that I have complete faith in you. You, among all people, understand the dangers of this tech. I know you won't falter in your duty. You're going on this mission because you're the available field agent with the best relevant experience and positioning. You're going because I have one hundred percent confidence in you. And you're going because it's an order. Is that understood?"

Sam let go of the breath she was holding. "Yes, sir. Understood."

Becker smiled fractionally. "Good. Now, we have an additional briefing for you. Tell me what I haven't told Kaden Lane."

Sam turned her eyes back to the briefing room, where Kade and Holtzmann were finishing up. "At a guess... This mission isn't just to learn what we can from having someone close to Su-Yong Shu. If possible, you want more. You want her to try to turn Kade, with whatever techniques she's been using. So we can study them in depth."

Sam paused for a moment, then finished her thought. "Which means that Kade isn't just a spy," she said. "He's bait."

7
Explanations

TRANSCRIPT: RANGAN SHANKARI, TECH BRIEFING, "NEXUS 5"
Sunday February 19th 2040 0951 hours

[NOTE: Subject should be considered hostile.]

INTERVIEWER: OK. Let's start again. Tell us about Nexus 5.

SHANKARI: *[inaudible, likely profanity]* Fine. Nexus 5 is Nexus, but with software layered on top.

INTERVIEWER: What does that mean?

SHANKARI: We found a way to program it. We found a way to get data in and out. To get instructions in and out.

INTERVIEWER: What kind of data?

SHANKARI: Neural data at first. We were using it as a way to measure neural firing in the motor cortex. Individual neurons, but millions of them at a time.

INTERVIEWER: This was for your research?

SHANKARI: Yeah. The goal was to get the data from the brain, decode it, and use it to control a robot arm.

INTERVIEWER: Systems like that already exist. Why the research?

SHANKARI: Existing systems get implanted surgically. That limits them. The procedures are long. You can get infections. And you can only tap into tens of thousands of neurons. The motor cortex has maybe ten *billion* neurons. With Nexus, we could tap into more of them. Millions. Tens of millions. We could get finer control over robot arms. You could catch a ball, write with a pen, do stuff you can't do with current systems.

INTERVIEWER: Go on.

SHANKARI: Well, we knew we could get data in too. Nexus nodes talk to each other by radio.

INTERVIEWER: How do they talk by radio?

SHANKARI: I dunno. Fucking nanotubes are little radios all by themselves, man. There's a lot of nanostructures in Nexus.

INTERVIEWER: OK. Software.

SHANKARI: Software. Yeah. So, anyway, they talk by radio. They sync up. Every node has some way of saying what part of the brain it's in. Every node listens for broadcasts addressed to its part of the brain, so it knows when to fire. If we could crack that, we could listen in on brain activity, and we could make neurons fire in whatever part of the brain we wanted.

INTERVIEWER: Why would that be relevant to your work?

SHANKARI: There's a million reasons. More than that. But for us it was about feedback. Sending the brain information on what the arm was touching, where it was relative to the body. Without that, an artificial limb is useless.

INTERVIEWER: So again, systems like that exist. Why your work?

SHANKARI: Same reason. More neurons. Higher bandwidth. Higher sensitivity, more precision, no surgery. Next question?

INTERVIEWER: Software. How did this lead to software?

SHANKARI: Yeah. Well, we dosed up some mice, started recording all the signals...

INTERVIEWER: Where did the Nexus come from?

SHANKARI: *[pause]* We bought it from a guy on the street. *<stress sensor indicates deception>*

INTERVIEWER: Your pulse just shot up ten points, you're starting to sweat, and your systolic blood pressure just went up by five. Try again.

SHANKARI: *[sighs]* We made it.

INTERVIEWER: How?

SHANKARI: We autosynthed it.

INTERVIEWER: How'd you get past the censor chip?

SHANKARI: *[pause]* We got access to an old one. It's out of date. The updates haven't been installed on it for years.

INTERVIEWER: Who's the license holder?

SHANKARI: *[sighs]* Crawford Lab. They've got a newer fancier one. Their old one mostly just sits idle. I've got access to their lab. They never knew.

INTERVIEWER: Where'd you get the molecular structures?

SHANKARI: We got the chemistry from *Recipes for a Revolution*. I smuggled a hard copy back from India.

INTERVIEWER: And the source material?

SHANKARI: All over. It's mostly innocuous. The only problem is there are so many different molecules in Nexus... sixty-three different molecular parts. The autosynth only had one chemreactor. We had to do sixty-three runs, then hand mix in the right proportions.

INTERVIEWER: OK, back to the software.

SHANKARI: Yeah. Fine. So we recorded the signals. It was a bitch. Way too much going on. We did more and more mice studies, tapered down the doses as low as we could go. We started injecting straight into the brain to get the lowest possible doses, simplify the traffic between the mice, simplify the analysis for us.

INTERVIEWER: How long did it take you?

SHANKARI: Most of a year. We would do the dosing before we left lab each day, then record activity overnight. The results made no sense. The signal traffic was chaos. Huge volumes of chaos. There was nothing that looked like the position of the nodes.

INTERVIEWER: And then?

SHANKARI: And then... and then we hit pay dirt, man. Kade figured it out. The nodes don't know where they are in the brain. They know where they are relative to *other nodes* in the same brain. How much position data they send depends on how many nodes there are around 'em. And it's not even really position data. They figure out what functional region they're in, send that in their signals. It's fucking amazing. *[shakes head]* Anyway, once Kade figured that out, the data miners cracked the encoding. We could listen to brain activity, and trigger new activity anywhere we wanted.

INTERVIEWER: And this led to software how?

SHANKARI: *[drums fingers]* It was the damnedest thing, man. Once we understood the encoding, we could tell there was room for a lot more data in those signals. There were unused bits. So we just started fucking around with it one day, on a lark.

INTERVIEWER: And?

SHANKARI: And... it would do shit. It would store the data we sent it. If that node sent out a signal again, we'd get the data back. If we sent specific modifier signals, we could tell two nodes to talk to each other, to add their values together, or subtract them. We could do logical operations. *[Shankari stops talking, shakes head]* It still blows my mind, man.

INTERVIEWER: You'll share these codes with us, all of this data.

SHANKARI: Like I have any fucking choice.

INTERVIEWER: So you could make Nexus nodes perform logical operations and math operations. Go on.

SHANKARI: Well, that was a huge step. We had an instruction set. We could move data around. We could do conditionals. We could do most of the things a simple chip can do. We had the visual cortex for our display. The auditory cortex for our speakers. The motor cortex for our input. On top of that, we could write any damn software we wanted.

INTERVIEWER: So that's what you did? You wrote the Nexus operating system on top of the instruction set that you'd discovered in Nexus nodes?

SHANKARI: *[shakes head]* That would've been way too hard. We wanted to do neuroscience, not operating system development. So we ported something instead.

INTERVIEWER: Which was...?

SHANKARI: ModOS. It's free. The source code is all available. It's built to be portable, modular. It's built to run on any kind of hardware, down to the simplest possible instruction set. So we took that. We built a simple compiler to turn ModOS into a set of instructions that would run on a set of Nexus nodes.

INTERVIEWER: So the Nexus OS is really ModOS, running on Nexus nodes as its hardware.

SHANKARI: *[nods]* Yeah. You got it.

INTERVIEWER: And on top of that you've built more software.

SHANKARI: *[nods]* Yeah. Well, we've ported other software. Anything that can run on ModOS we can compile to run on the version that runs on top of Nexus. *And* we've built software. We had to build the code to send the video output to the visual cortex, stuff like that. And we wrote brand-new neuroscience software. We've built programs that make it easy to interact with parts of the brain. Interfaces. Like, an interface to take body shapes, like for a VR app, and tells the motor cortex to put the body in that position. That sort of thing.

INTERVIEWER: This is how you paralyzed Agent Chavez.

SHANKARI: *[Looks down]* Yeah. Dumbshit move, huh? *[shakes head]*

[...discussion of Nexus OS continues for another 17 minutes...]

INTERVIEWER: Next topic. You and your co-conspirators give off extraordinarily strong Nexus signals, and they're not dropping. The drug isn't wearing off. How is that possible?

SHANKARI: The limit of how much Nexus you can have in your brain is mental. Your neurons fire and the Nexus nodes are trying to coax them to fire. If they're not getting coherence, some of them break apart and get flushed out. Over time, your brain adapts to having a Nexus network. Your Nexus coherence increases. Your maximum possible levels of Nexus go up.

INTERVIEWER: But why isn't the level dropping? It's been more than eight hours. Most of it should be out of your system.

SHANKARI: *[shakes head]* We call Nexus a drug, but it's not. It's a nano-machine. It doesn't flush out because some enzyme has broken it down. Nexus nodes decompose to their parts because some internal logic has told them to. And if you give them the right signal, they just don't break down at all.

[...interview continues for another 18 minutes...]

8
Back Doors

Kade came out of his tech interview stressed and shaking. It had been an exhausting two hours. They'd drilled deep into what he and Rangan had built. They'd spotted every evasion. They'd known every time he lied or tried to hold something back. Well, he would show them.

He signed the papers they gave him. An ERD lawyer watched him, then countersigned the documents. The deal was real now. He would serve as their spy, and in exchange no one would go to jail. He and Rangan and Ilya would stay in science for just so long as Kade's mission lasted.

It was only then that they told him that Wats had gotten away.

Good for Wats, he thought.

A guard led him to the roof, to the VTOL plane waiting on the helipad; its wings rotated, its engines turned to the sky for vertical take-off. The engines were whining already. They ushered him up the stairs, and inside he found Rangan and Ilya, and the agent who would come with them to retrieve the Nexus code from San Francisco.

"Buckle up," the agent – who introduced himself as Myers – said over the sound of the engines. "There's a head in the back. Don't expect any beverage service."

Kade strapped himself in. Outside the cabin, the engines began to hum, and then to roar. All three of them remained silent as the plane rose slowly into the air, affording them a view of the city. Kade's window faced north, he thought. Where the wing did not obscure it, he could see a river – the Potomac? – and across that the Washington Monument and the Capitol. Then the engines swiveled gradually forward, and the plane picked up horizontal speed as well as altitude, and the city receded into the distance.

Kade looked over at Ilya. She was withdrawn into herself. She felt tense, wound up. He couldn't see Rangan with the seat back between them, but he could feel his friend's frustration and self doubt. He wanted to talk to them, but he didn't want to do so in any way Myers could hear.

He went Inside, found what he was looking for – ModOS's built-in chat app. He typed the words out on the mental keyboard in his mind, and the text-based chat program sent them to Rangan and Ilya.

[kade] Don't react. We need to talk.

He felt their surprise. They'd forgotten about this app. A moment later he saw Ilya's response.

[ilya] Yeah. Definitely.

[rangan]+1

[kade] Put on a movie or something. Put your headphones on. Rangan, you first.

It was a relief to be talking again. He could sense the mood lighten a tiny bit for all of them. Rangan did something in front of him. A minute or so later Ilya dialed up a nature documentary on her seat-back TV screen.

[kade] Wats got away.

[ilya] They told me the same.

[kade] They offered me a deal. Give them Nexus and do a job for them, and no one goes to jail.

[ilya] You took it.

[kade] Yes.

[ilya] I can't believe you're giving them Nexus 5.

[rangan] It was that or life in jail.

[kade] And jail for everyone else at the party.

[ilya] Do you have any idea what they'll do with Nexus? What the CIA will do?

He could feel her anger.

[kade] I know. But they were going to get it anyway. From the drives at lab or the backups at my place or Rangan's…

[rangan] He's right. Once they knew it existed, it was too late.

[ilya] You're going to have an awful lot of blood on your hands, then.

[kade] Probably. But there's one thing we can do.

[rangan] What?

[kade] We can make sure we have a back door into their version.

[rangan] They already know about the back door.

[kade] A new one. One they can't find.

[rangan] How?

[kade] Remember that article we read last term? The Thompson hack?

He felt Rangan get it instantly.

[rangan] Have the compiler inject it… It'd be in the binary, but gone from the source…

[kade] And have the ModOS compiler inject into

```
the Nexus compiler…
  [rangan] Yeah, yeah… Do we have time? How long
is this flight going to take?
  [ilya] 5 hours. I'm not following this hack.
```
Kade explained.

The Nexus OS existed in two forms. It existed as human-readable source code that Kade and Rangan or any programmer could read, understand, and modify. And it existed in a binary form that Nexus nodes could understand – sequences of raw ones and zeroes that were almost impossible to work with directly as a human.

Between the source code and the binary instructions was the compiler, the program that converted human-readable source code into Nexus-readable binary code. Kade and Rangan would use the compiler to insert their back doors.

Every time the compiler ran, it would search the Nexus OS source code for their new back doors. If the back doors weren't there, the compiler would add them before creating the binary version. The only evidence of the back doors would be in the binary version that was nearly incomprehensible to humans.

Finally, they would run the same hack on the compiler itself. The compiler's source code would contain no hint of the logic to insert the back doors. That would exist only in the compiler's binaries. Any time their workstation version of ModOS recompiled the compiler, it would insert all the logic of the hack.

Rangan felt thoughtful to Kade. Anxious still. He was thinking about the costs of being caught. He came to a decision.

```
  [rangan]OK. What the fuck. Let's do this thing.
```

Rangan and Kade pulled up their development

environments and linked them. Ilya linked to their environments and watched over their virtual shoulders. They thought through the plan, divided the tasks up as they turned it from a vague idea into a concrete list of things to do.

Plan complete, they set to work. It went quickly at first. The backdoors they cloned from their existing overrides, changing only the passwords. The code in the compiler was conceptually simple. But as they coded, they hit bugs, each one a frustration. They checked the clock constantly. Minutes went by as they worked. An hour. A compiler crash frustrated them for twenty minutes. The fix was trivial once they understood it. A second hour had passed. One of the back doors was leaking memory. How could that be? They'd copied the code from the back door they already had. They figured it out. This fix took longer. A third hour passed.

At hour four, the back doors were working and the Nexus compiler was adding them. Rangan forced the /obfuscate flag on, instructing the compiler to scatter the new code far and wide as seemingly disconnected, innocuous instructions in the binary, making reverse-engineering what they'd done even more difficult. Next they needed to change the workstation compiler to add the backdoor code to the Nexus compiler. Rangan got on that.

Kade turned his attention to the second phase. He wanted to be able to use the back door without the person running Nexus OS knowing. He needed support for hidden processes. ModOS had that in some form. It was simple in theory, but there were so many tendrils.

He took large chunks of ModOS code they'd never used and brought them back into Nexus OS. The back doors would connect them to a hidden super-user account. That would do most of what he wanted. Logging would be off for that account. Yes. How to hide the memory usage?

Shit. His ears were popping. They were landing. He looked out the window. Fuck. They were at SFO, the airport closest to UCSF. How long from SFO to lab? Twenty minutes? Twenty-five? Shit. Rangan was done. Kade still had to finish up.

Could he hide the memory usage? He didn't see how. He'd have to leave it in. Were there other telltales someone could find? Think, think. Logfiles. Had he gotten them all? Network traces? No easy way to hide those. He'd have to leave them in.

He glanced outside the window again. The ground was coming up. He cursed under his breath, then caught himself. Fuck. Stay quiet. Stay cool. OK. He compiled the rev of Nexus OS he had. He had time for only the most basic tests. Compiling... Compiling... Done. He put it in the stress simulator. Did it crash? Not right away. Did it leak memory? Not obviously. Could he still use the backdoors? Yes. Could he hide a process from himself... Checking... Checking. Looked like it. Would it hold up to real digging? He had no idea.

The wheels hit the ground mid-test. Fuck.

```
[kade]Still working. Cover for me.
[rangan]On it.
```

Kade went back to work. He could do this. He could finish in time.

The pressure in the cabin changed. The door was opening.

```
[ilya]Heads up. Focus on the real world for
just a minute here.
```

Myers stood up. "OK, everyone out and into the car."

Kade looked out the window. There was a black SUV

alongside them, a big guy in a black suit next to it. Fuck. He stood up. The code beckoned. He remembered a flag he needed to change. Shit, what file was that in? Myers walked towards him, locking eyes with him. Kade held his breath. Did he know? The ERD agent stopped.

"Come on. Let's move." Myers gestured towards the aisle and the door behind Kade.

Kade blinked. Move. Yes. Off the plane. He turned wordlessly, stepped into the aisle, went down the stairs behind Rangan. He could feel Myers right behind him. He could imagine Myers's meaty hand coming down on his shoulder, imagine the ERD agent croaking out, "You've been trying to fuck with us, haven't you?"

He nearly tripped. Myers caught him by the arm from behind. "Watch your step," he said.

Fuck. Where was his head at? Breathe. Steady. He made it into the third row of seats in the SUV. Myers closed the door on the three of them and got into the shotgun seat.

[ilya] OK. We got you covered.

Ilya started talking. "My car was at Simonyi Field. Is there going to be a way for me to get it?"

"Officer Lewis here can take you there after this is over."

"I need a ride too," Rangan said. "And I think my key was in a bag inside the hangar. Will that still be there...?" And on and on.

Kade focused on his work. Fuck. The new Nexus OS in the stress simulator had crashed after seven minutes. Shit shit shit. Look at the stack trace. What had caused the crash? All he'd done was reactivate standard ModOS code. Oh, fuck. He'd coded a crude hack to stop all logging. Something must depend on the logfiles.

Sure enough. It was a crash in accessing a logfile. OK. What to do? He created empty logfiles by hand, let the simulator run again. Another crash.

OK. Not empty logfiles. Logfiles with a bogus entry in them.

He made the mistake of looking out the window. They were on the Bayshore Freeway, right along the water, headed north into South San Francisco. Maybe halfway there. Focus, Kade, focus.

He copied a random line out of each of the parallel logfiles in his own Nexus, copied them to the right places, stepped the simulator forward. Shit, it was still past the point where it had crashed. He rewound it, added the logfiles again, put in the bogus entries, ran the stress simulator forward... A second passed. Three seconds. Ten seconds. It hadn't crashed. He was holding his breath, he realized. He let it out.

Rangan and Ilya were talking louder and louder. Had he been making noise? He glanced out the window again. The Bay was gone. Was that Potrero Hill out the window? Fuck, they were close.

He let the stress simulator keep running. He needed to copy the new code into the hidden injector in the compiler. OK, good there. To test it... run a compile using the injector. See if the file sizes were the same. Compiling. Compiling. Fuck, he hated waiting. The freeway curved. That was SoMa outside. Shit. They were almost to the exit.

The compile finished. Identical. Thank god for small miracles. Kade tossed the code over to Rangan to insert one level further upstream into the compiler's compiler. Rangan got on it. Ilya kept talking. They exited onto Duboce Avenue, then turned onto Market Street. They were in downtown San Francisco now, maybe two miles from the lab.

What did Kade need to do now? Oh yeah, the source management. He had to fake it out. He got to work convincing the source management system that these changes had always been there.

The driver turned onto 17th to cut west towards UCSF.

OK. Fake change logs. Fake histories. Fake file change dates. The car turned and turned again.

Rangan's work was done. Kade integrated it. They were on Parnassus Avenue, a few blocks from the lab now. Flashing lights ahead.

The SUV took a strange turn, came around to the lab's back entrance.

```
[rangan] I'll boot the machine and stall him
while you copy the new files over. Cool?
```

Kade nodded. Shit. Stop that, he told himself.

What have I missed?

"We're here," Myers said. "The fire alarm's been set off in the building. We have twenty minutes." He hopped out and opened their door. They were at the service entrance.

```
[kade] I need to double-check this. Keep
covering.
```

Ilya chatted away about lab equipment and fire safety and fire department response times. Rangan took Kade's arm, walked him to the door. There was something he'd forgotten. What was it?

There. The separate source tree for ModOS. The changes to the ModOS compiler needed to be in there. He had to fix up the file names, the histories, the dates...

The light changed. They were in an elevator. Rangan was steering him. Was sweat beading on his brow? Was Myers looking at him? The other officer, Lewis, was he looking at Kade too?

He made the simplest change possible. He slapped the new ModOS binary down in the source tree as the most recent archive version and backdated it by three months.

The elevator opened. Kade was definitely sweating now.

He had to copy these new files onto the server as soon as Rangan got it up, fast enough to fool the agent. Then he had to backdate the file change dates on the server.

He needed to maximize bandwidth, get the copy to happen as fast as he could. He went through the apps running in his skull, killed everything that might interfere. Kade killed the development environment, killed the simulator and the stress test, killed as much of his own logging as he could, turned off the body interfaces that Don Juan and Peter North had used. Would that be enough?

He heard a beep and snapped his attention back to the outside world. Myers swiped a passkey at the door to their lab, and it opened. Fucking feds.

"Where's the machine?"

"It's over in the corner there," Rangan said. "I'll just boot it up, and we can copy all the data for you."

"No need for that," Myers replied. "We'll just take the whole system."

Kade felt his eyes bug out. Fuck!

Rangan stayed cool. "You want everything, right?"

Myers narrowed his eyes at Rangan.

Kade held his breath.

"Everything," Myers said.

"I need to power it up, then," Rangan said. "We'll have to download the latest experiment results from the lab server, and spool some data down from Simonyi Field."

Myers scowled.

Fuck, Kade thought. We're busted.

Ilya spoke up, strain evident in her voice, playing her part to a T. "Jesus, Rangan, don't be so fucking helpful."

"Damnit, Ilya," Rangan snapped back. "I'm doing it to keep our friends out of jail!"

"Shut up, both of you," Myers said. "We have seventeen minutes left. Shankari, let's get this done."

"Yeah." Rangan led them to the powered-down workstation. He touched a control and it came to life. Kade stood right next to it, picked up a pen from the desk, did his best not to fidget.

Kade searched for the server inside his head as the boot sequence scrolled across the screen. Come on... Come on... Come on... The Nexus data transfer card they'd used the circuit printer to make was in place. It was flashing green. He refreshed the list of available devices in his head. Why wasn't it showing up? Where was it? Where was it?

The login message appeared on the screen: Welcome to ModOS. Enter credentials.

There. SanchezLab018 came online in his head. He navigated its folder tree. There. Copy.

Rangan flubbed his first password attempt. He shook his head. He flubbed it again, swore softly. "Sorry... just a little nervous here."

[10 percent complete]

Myers put one burly hand on Rangan's shoulder. "Take your time," he said. "And no tricks. Think about what you're doing here."

Kade remote logged into the machine, jumped to super-user status, got ready to tweak the file date and time stamps after the copy was complete.

[25 percent complete]

Rangan nodded. He typed his password again, and he was in.

"OK, checking the lab experiments directory." Rangan browsed folders. Kade knew damn well that directory was up to date.

[40 percent complete]

"Yeah, it's out of date," Rangan lied. He entered commands to recopy the data. "That should do it."

Myers's face was a mask. "Fourteen minutes left. And we still need those Nexus vials from your fridge."

[50 percent complete]

Rangan nodded. "OK. Pulling down the data from last night…" He opened up a window, poked a tiny hole in the firewall to connect to Simonyi Field, started pulling down logfiles.

[60 percent complete]

"This shouldn't take more than a minute or two," he explained.

It took a hundred and eight seconds.

[80 percent complete]

"And copying over the documentation," Rangan said.

Myers frowned, looked like he was about to say something.

Ilya cut in, stalling, "God, can you make it any fucking easier for them?"

"Jesus, Ilya," Rangan said. "We've been over this already!"

"That's enough, both of you," Myers said. "Power this down, Shankari. Now."

The copy was 91 per cent complete. Fuck fuck fuck. It would be obvious that they'd been trying to change something!

Rangan started to object. Myers held up his hand.

"Hold on," Myers said. He brought one finger to his right ear, plugged it, looked away from them, apparently listening to someone speaking to him.

Kade held his breath.

```
[ 96 percent complete ]
[ 98 percent complete ]
```

He let his breath out. The pen was rattling nervously against the desk. Myers scowled at him in annoyance, took a half step back.

```
[ 100 percent complete ]
```

Kade jumped in his terminal window to change the time and date stamps on the files. One set done, second set done...

Myers pulled his hand away from his ear, looked over at them.

"Shut it down, I said. Now."

There was a third set to do...

Rangan gulped, nodded, and issued the shutdown command.

Windows started to close. The last time stamp change... Kade hit ENTER in the terminal window in his mind, got the command running. There, it was going, going, going...

The command finished.

A split second later his terminal window flashed, then disappeared. *Session disconnected by host.* A moment later the virtual drive SanchezLab018 disappeared. The happy shutdown face appeared on the screen. Kade wanted to scream in triumph. He did no such thing.

"Take this down to the car," Myers told Lewis. The other officer started pulling plugs and gathering up equipment. "Now, take us to your Nexus stocks."

Ten minutes later they were back outside. It was done. Myers had everything. Well, almost everything.

• • •

Warren Becker finished reading the transcripts of the three

Nexus technical briefings. It was sobering stuff. The potential for abuse as a coercion technology was huge. Slavery. Prostitution. Worse. He thought of his two teenage girls, of the things he'd seen in the field, the horrors some men were capable of. He pushed it out of his mind.

The geopolitical implications were just as bad. Remote assassination. Subversion of political enemies. Everything the Chinese were doing, available on the cheap. This technology had to be kept out of the wild.

He dictated a memo outlining what they'd found and the dangers, labeled it TOP SECRET, and distributed it to key people across ERD, Homeland Security, FBI, CIA, State, and the Pentagon.

After that he opened another file on his terminal and reviewed its contents. *Presidential Order 594 – Eliminating and Preventing Uncontrolled Non-Human Intelligences. Scenario 7c – HIVE INTELLIGENCE.* He stared at it for long minutes. Could Nexus be used to create Borgs? Ilyana Alexander had said as much in her interview. He dictated a second memo on that possibility, sent it up the chain to the White House. It was above his pay grade.

He checked the time. 9 o'clock on a Sunday night. Claire would be upset. He packed up his things and headed out the door. The lights dropped and the room sealed itself behind him.

There was a light on in Holtzmann's office. Becker poked his head in. Holtzmann was there, working away at his terminal.

"Martin," Becker said, "you're here late."

Holtzmann flicked his eyes at Becker. "I could say the same of you," he said. "Shouldn't you be home with Claire and the girls?"

Becker smiled wryly, hoisted his briefcase for a moment. "Heading there. What do you make of the Nexus 5 risk level?"

Holtzmann shrugged. "If Nexus 5 ever gets out, it'll spread like wildfire. Permanent integration means a user only ever needs to procure a single dose for a lifetime effect. You can't fight that on the supply side."

Becker nodded glumly. He thought, We're underfunded. Understaffed. The fight gets harder every year.

"And the abuse potential is high," Becker said.

"That's not the problem," Holtzmann replied.

"Pardon?" Becker raised an eyebrow.

Holtzmann sighed. "The problem is that the *utility* is so high. People will find a thousand ways to use something like this. Communication. Entertainment. Mental health applications. Education. The potential is vast. Demand will be rampant."

Becker narrowed his eyes. "Martin, this is clearly illegal, on multiple fronts. Think about the coercion potential, the abuses the Chinese have already put it to..."

Holtzmann waved his hand. "Of course. It's all about the downsides. Never mind the upsides." He frowned. "This isn't what I came here for."

Becker shook his head. "Martin, I know you're frustrated. But you know the reality. The transhuman implications alone..."

Holtzmann frowned. "Would it be so bad? To be smarter? To touch another mind? Are you sure we're doing the right thing?"

Becker went still. Had Holtzmann just said that? He spoke slowly, carefully. "Martin, you're tired. I think you should go home now. Anne will glad to see you."

He turned and walked away calmly, leaving Holtzmann to his terminal and his thoughts.

9
Training Days

Training for Kade's ERD mission began immediately. Monday night he was instructed to report to room 3004 in the Health Sciences Building. There he met his trainer, Kevin Nakamura. Nakamura was fortyish, graying at the temples, fit, and serious.

The older man was CIA, he told Kade, but doing a favor for his old agency the ERD. He and Kade would meet nightly for the eight weeks leading up to the International Society for Neuroscience meeting in Bangkok. Nakamura would teach Kade to keep his cool – to lie without being detected. He'd drill Kade on potential scenarios of interacting with Shu and the strategies for each. And together they would implant a false persona in Kade's memories that he could invoke if needed.

Much of the training happened inside a pair of VR goggles and headphones, with a portable stress meter observing him. There, a simulated Shu had simulated conversations with Kade, conversations that called on him to lie, to hide his assignment from the ERD, to hide the contact he'd had with them.

Every time he lied, the stress meter caught it.

"You'll improve," Nakamura told him.

The later part of the first session was the implantation of the cover story memories. It was hazy – hard to remember clearly. Nakamura injected him with something. A non-sedative hypnotic. The world became dreamlike. What the goggles showed him, what the headphones told him, Kade could only recall in fragments.

At the end of the session, he felt strung out, mentally exhausted. He returned to his apartment, collapsed onto his bed and slept for ten hours.

Every night, they did the same.

While Kade trained, Rangan brooded.

They skipped lab one day, went out to Golden Gate Park, and took Ilya with them. Kade opened his mind to theirs, showed them everything the ERD had briefed him on, showed them what he knew of his mission. Then Rangan opened his mind to Kade and Ilya, showed them what had happened in that ERD cell. They'd hit him with a pain beyond anything he could imagine.

Rangan was angry. He wanted to hit them back. He wanted to arm himself and Kade and Ilya with defenses against that ERD attack. He wanted to arm them with their own weapons. It would be important, Rangan said. If Kade were going on this mission, he shouldn't go unarmed.

The invitation to the ISFN meeting and the private workshop to follow arrived in the second week. Kade's advisor was delighted. Important people were taking note of his work, she told him. Kade pretended surprise, pretended joy, found only dread and loathing inside.

The training continued. He learned to use a mantra to activate the false memories and anti-memories. The party had been ended by a noise complaint. What encounter with the ERD? It was bewildering, snapping in and out of different states of mind. It left Kade paranoid and edgy. If memories could be changed like this, how did he know what he remembered was true? Had more happened in ERD custody? Had they erased it from his mind? Was there a mantra that would unlock that? Was there a mantra that would turn him into someone else entirely?

"That's normal," Nakamura told him. "Everyone questions their own memories as they go through this."

That didn't reassure Kade.

Saturday, after his training, he went to the Mephistopheles Club where Rangan had a gig. Kade had a fine view of the DJ booth. Rangan seemed subdued. The music was more ponderous than Kade was used to. Rangan usually played flashcore or elemental on a Saturday night, something high-energy, driving, fun to move to. Tonight his set bordered on blackbeat – heavier, harder, darker. Fewer people danced than usual.

On Sunday night, Nakamura told him that while the memory implantation was going well, the other parts of the training were going poorly. Kade was a rotten liar, it seemed. He got nervous. And when he got nervous, the sensor knew.

"Is this really necessary?" he asked Nakamura.

"Shu may have off-the-charts intelligence. She has an elite special forces bodyguard. She has access to top-of-the-line technology. If you aren't absolutely perfect at dissembling, she *will* pick it up."

They kept trying for another week. It was no use.

"Your pulse just shot up again," Nakamura told him the next Thursday. "Your pupils dilated. If we don't make progress soon, we'll turn to drugs. We have to hide your anxiety."

Drugs, eh? Alternatively…

That night, Kade didn't collapse into deep sleep. Instead he sketched out a possible new Nexus OS app. A tool to manage his mental state around Shu. If he could suppress the anxiety signals passing through his amygdala, boost serotonin, suppress noradrenaline... If he directly modulated his breathing rate and his pulse... Then he could keep himself serene. It was conceptually simple, but they'd always resisted playing this deeply with their emotions. He would have to be extremely careful...

Kade closed his eyes, went Inside, and invoked his development environment. Windows blossomed in his inner sight. New project. Serenity package. He had a lot of work to do.

Weeks passed. The sessions with Nakamura improved slightly, but not enough. Kade worked away on his serenity package. He was almost there.

At the end of the fourth week, Rangan came to him with something. He exuded good cheer. Kade hadn't seen Rangan this happy since before the bust.

```
[rangan]Ready for a surprise?
[kade]Sure. Bring it on.
```

A file transfer request blinked in Kade's mind. He accepted it. A pair of files came across. One was source code. The other was an application. He had no idea what it did. Then he saw the name. Bruce Lee. Oh no...

```
[rangan]OK, so launch that app. But don't hit
any buttons yet, OK?
```

Kade groaned inwardly. Rangan had always dreamed of this app. It was ridiculous.

```
[kade]I don't really think hand-to-hand combat
```

is what this is about...

[rangan]Come on. You're a spy now. You need to be able to fight.

[kade]But I won't have the muscle, or the endurance, or...

[rangan]Dude, just launch the app.

Kade sighed and fired it up. His vision came alive with targeting circles, buttons for attacks and defenses, a toggle for automatic versus manual mode, sliders to change the auto-mode AI's emphasis on attack versus defense.

[rangan]The game engine's from the crack of Fist of the Ninja that went online last month. It takes standard VR body shapes and vectors. I just hooked it up to our Nexus body interfaces.

[kade]Uhh... Rangan, thank you, really, but...

[rangan]Oh, don't thank me yet! You probably don't want to be mashing buttons, so you just click on the target. It uses our object list to track people and so on... And then you tell it to attack. You can slide this here for how much focus to put on attacking versus defending. And over here if you want to pause. Pretty great, eh?

Kade couldn't believe they were having this conversation.

[kade]Yeah. It's great. Really. I mean, thank y—

[rangan]OK. I can see you're not convinced. No worries. You can thank me after you're forced to kick someone's ass with it.

[kade]I'm not really sure...

[rangan]Come on, let's take it to the gym.

An hour later, they limped out of the gym. Kade ached

everywhere. His body had thrown a bewildering array of kicks and strikes at the punching bag, most of which he was sure had hurt him more than they would have damaged any real-world assailant. His knuckles were bloody. His right wrist and left ankle both ached from times when Bruce Lee had driven him to hit the punching bag far harder than he really should have. And then there was the moment at which the targeting system had decided his target was the wall instead of the punching bag...

Rangan thought it was hilarious and promised to fix the bugs. Kade just hurt.

10
Changes

Watson Cole sat on the rocks and stared out at the Pacific. This was a beautiful place in its own desolate way. The little town of Todos Santos was thirty miles south down the road. The beach was better there, more sand, fewer rocks. The tourists sunned themselves and sipped margaritas, delighting in their discovery of a quaint little paradise away from the hustle and bustle of Cabo San Lucas. Up here, further from Cabo, the beach was rough and narrow. The sea came in strong against the rocks and a thin strip of brownish sand. Some hardy scrub grass clung to the land. There was little reason for tourists to make it this far north.

He'd made it here to his hidey-hole two nights ago. It had been a tense escape. The contacts and face shapers had fooled the biometrics at the border, but there had been little he could do about his size. He was a conspicuous character. If the ERD relied more on human intel... Well, he'd made it.

The nightmares woke him every morning now. Arman, the idealistic prosecutor. The sight of his family dead in their home, murdered in retribution for daring to bring charges against the wrong corrupt nephew. Temir. The heartbreak of seeing his village razed by the army, looking for rebels that weren't there.

And Lunara. Her most of all. The last moments of her life... If it wasn't for Lunara, he wouldn't be a fugitive today. He'd be out there some place, across the waves. Somewhere in central Asia, probably. A "military advisor." Running special ops missions. Suppressing the rebels. Earning commendations. Maybe in Officer Candidate School.

Instead, he was a wanted man.

Wats had no regrets. He'd made his choices. Being captured in the Kazakh Mountains was the best thing that had ever happened to him. It certainly hadn't been the easiest thing. It had been the most painful, most confusing, most troubling six months of his life. But it had opened his eyes. And eyes, once opened, seldom closed again.

He remembered another beach. A dry beach. The dry bones of the Aral Sea. The desert where once there had been water. The inland sea the Russians had drained to irrigate their crops further north. Nurzhan had taken him on walks there, towards the end, after his captivity had turned into something else.

"Here is where the Soviets fucked us," the geologist had said, "before you Americans came to finish the job." He'd laughed, hard and bitter. "Communism, capitalism, all the same. The powerful want resources. Water. Natural gas. Uranium. The powerful see them, reach out their hand and scoop them up, and who cares who they crush in the process, eh? Dictatorships and democracies, all alike. Your precious democracy doesn't care about us, does it? All men are created equal, eh? We all have inalienable rights. Unless we live so very far away, perhaps? You Americans defeated your British king because he was a dictator. We are the same. We will defeat our dictator, even if you oppose us."

No, Wats thought. I'm sorry, Nurzhan. But you won't.
You didn't.

Two years dead. All of them.

He tossed a rock into the sea. No way back. Only forward.

He'd come out of captivity to find a changed world. The
rebels were beaten. The "president" in Almaty had secured
his power. The natural gas was flowing. The uranium mines
were purring. America had one more ally bordering China,
containing it.

He came out to find that his enhancements caused
cancers. They'd discovered that during his months of
captivity. Not right away, of course. They just destabilized
the genome a bit. The viruses that had given his cells extra
copies of the genes for muscle mass and bone density and
fast nerve conduction, and all the other ways he was
enhanced, hadn't done their job quite cleanly enough. One
in every few million of them had inserted the new gene in
the wrong place, disrupting some other part of his cells'
genetic instruction set. Not many. No big deal, really. Except
that eventually... eventually those genetic disruptions
would add up. Eventually the tumors would come. By the
time he hit forty, they said, forty-five at the latest. After
that... modern medicine could fight the cancers. They could
zap tumors with gamma rays, reprogram them with even
more targeted viruses, cut off their blood supplies with
angiogenesis suppressors.

Eventually one would get through. A year. Five years.
Ten. It depended on when they were detected, what part
of his body they were in, how he responded to aggressive
treatment. So many variables.

Someone before him had quietly threatened a lawsuit,
threatened *publicity*. That was what the Corps couldn't
abide. There was a quiet settlement offer for everyone
who'd received his enhancement package. Enough that

Wats could go home to Haiti and live like a king there for the rest of his – probably quite short – life. Enough that he could stay in the States instead, and live as an activist, speak out about the war he'd seen, about how his brothers bled and died and killed to prop up a killer, to keep in place a government of *thieves, rapists, and murderers,* as Temir used to say. Enough to get an education. Enough to wait, and hope, and get the checkups, and cross his fingers that they'd find a cure.

He tossed another stone into the sea.

Enough money to acquire a few extra identities and to buy his hidey-hole here, out in the middle of nowhere.

What now? Even if he could make it back to America, he had no home there. His stepfather had disowned Wats for his anti-war activism. He'd spoken too clearly about how the American war on drugs had created the narco-barons who'd destroyed Haiti. He'd said too much about how the war in the KZ propped up a dictator. He was no son of Frank Cole.

Back to Haiti? Return to the land that had birthed him? They'd be looking for him there. Make a small comfortable life for himself somewhere else? Live off his savings here in Mexico until the cancers killed him? He was meant to do something else, something bigger. Temir, Nurzhan, Lunara… they'd risked their lives to teach him something. He had to make that mean something. This wasn't over yet.

The cheap disposable phone he'd picked up in Cabo beeped at him. He glanced at it. His data miners had found something. A new mention of Kade on the net. That was rare. Since he'd had the data miners running, they'd come back with dozens of hits about Rangan's shows and music, hundreds of hits on Ilya's writings, but none about Kade.

He opened it. Conference listing. International Society for Neuroscience meeting in Bangkok. Abstract of a poster to be presented by Kaden Lane. Kade hadn't mentioned any trip to Thailand.

Bangkok. The city of vice. The modern Babylon. A city of temples and whores. He'd spent some memorable R&R time there during his two years deployed in Burma. You could buy anything in Bangkok. Flesh. Fantasies. Drugs.

Weapons.

If it was a trap, it was a perfect set-up. They would know he'd been there. Wats knew the seedy underbelly of that city. He spoke a little Thai. He'd imagine that he could get there, find Kade, get him free.

And if he got Kade free... Then Wats could keep Nexus 5 alive. He could hope to someday get it out into the world. And if it got out to the world... It could change people. The way Nexus had changed him. The way the touch of another's mind through Nexus had changed him.

There was no choice. Even though Kade might refuse him again. Even though it might be a trap. He would go in with his eyes open. He was a dead man anyway. It was only a matter of time.

We're all born dying, someone had said. *What matters is only how we spend the instant we're given.*

He wanted to spend his instant changing the world. He wanted to spend it opening the eyes of his adopted countrymen. He wanted to spend it paying forward the gift that Temir, and Nurzhan, and Lunara, and all the rest had given him.

He tossed a final stone into the sea. It was time to move. He had seven weeks.

Watson Cole rose to his feet and set himself in motion.

Sam waited outside Enforcement Division Deputy Director Warren Becker's office. She was angry. She wanted to pace. Instead, Sam ruthlessly clamped down on her body, forcing herself to sit completely immobile in the uncomfortable chair in his anteroom, spine erect, hands folded in her lap. The vision of calm, but seething inside. Surely this was a mix-up?

The door opened, Becker's previous appointment walked out. The man, someone she vaguely recognized from Policy, made eye contact with her and then hurriedly looked away.

"Come on in, Sam," Becker projected through the door.

Sam took a deep breath, ignored the secretary, strode into Becker's office, and closed the door behind her. Becker was behind his massive mahogany desk, emblazoned with the twin seals of the DHS and the ERD.

"What can I do for you?" he asked.

"Sir, Dr Holtzmann just set up lab time with me to dose me with Nexus 5, permanent integration. He says it's under your orders."

"Yes," the deputy director replied. "My orders."

"Sir," Sam said, fists clenched at her sides. "I think this is a very bad idea."

"Noted," he said.

"It's one thing to face the risk of trying Nexus during an op, sir, but Holtzmann's talking about me having it in my skull for weeks, maybe months... That can't be right."

"Sam, in this case, it's vital for the mission and potentially for more."

"I don't see how."

Becker started to tick items off on his fingers. "First, gaining experience in this will increase your ability to fool anyone else on Nexus as to your identity in the case of mind-to-mind contact."

"We have the hypnotic memory implantation for that," Sam retorted.

"...which didn't work last time you were in the field," Becker pointed out.

"I'll do better next time. I'll be more prepared," Sam said.

"Yes," Becker said. "You will. Because you will have had multiple weeks of practicing mind-to-mind contact with Nexus 5.

"Second," Becker went on, ticking off another finger, "it'll give you and Lane a backchannel to communicate via during the operation, without needing to speak. Third, it'll let you monitor how Lane is doing emotionally and perhaps bolster him. He's doing terribly in his training. His inability to stay cool is a risk to the mission."

"Then send someone else," Sam replied, as calmly as she could. She could feel her nails gouging painful half-moons in her palm. "My presence is going to agitate him, not stabilize him. And I'm the wrong agent to have walking around with this thing in her skull."

"We don't have anyone else who's suitable, Sam."

"What about Anderson?"

"On a deep cover mission, weeks to go at minimum, maybe longer."

"Novaks, then."

"Novaks doesn't have an alias that makes sense. You have an identity as a neuroscience PhD student already in place, and just two hops from Lane. Novaks doesn't."

Sam racked her brain.

"How about Evans? He has a neuroscience alias."

Becker kept his face still, but something changed in his eyes.

"Chris Evans was critically wounded last week." He sighed. "You'll get a memo about it soon. We wanted more data on his recovery before we let the word out. I know you were friends..."

Sam felt the blood drain from her face. More than friends. She and Evans had gone through training together. They'd been lovers once, before the challenges of the job and hiding their relationship from their colleagues became too much. He'd been so gentle with her...

"How bad?" she asked.

Becker's face fell. "Bad, Sam. He was infiltrating a DWITY ring. They figured out who he was somehow. He was off comms. They put twenty rounds into him. We didn't find him for two hours. He was flatlined when we got there. His brain valves and the hyperox saved him. He survived, but just barely."

DWITY. Do What I Tell You. The drug that turned humans into slaves. Slaves for sexual predators, for sex trafficking rings, for worse. The thought made her sick. That Chris had been hurt fighting that...

"Rehab?" she asked.

Becker nodded slowly. "The damage is extensive. He suffered major cell death in most organs. They're regrowing a heart right now so they can get him off the machine. It's going to be a long hard road for him. He may never recover fully."

Sam swallowed. She could feel bile rising up inside her. Had he been conscious for those two hours? she wondered. The fourth-gen corticovascular valves would have snapped shut as blood pressure dropped, sealing hyperoxygenated blood in his brain. Pain control would have kicked in. He might have stayed awake and aware through the whole thing. What would it have felt like to lay there, heart stopped, body riddled with bullets, blood seeping out, all of your body dying as your brain lived on, helpless... waiting to be found or to die...

That could be her someday.

Becker was talking to her again. "So you see, Sam, there really isn't anyone else."

Sam nodded. Against what Chris Evans had gone through, her own reservations paled.

"I know you have a deep revulsion to this technology," Becker said. "And I know why. And that's part of why I trust you. We all do hard things. We all take risks. Chris did. He put his life on the line. I know this is not going to be pleasant for you. I trust you more because of that."

Becker still didn't understand. It wasn't that it was so horrible. It was that it *wasn't*. That she had *enjoyed* the ability to touch another person's mind. That was what scared her. That was what felt like a betrayal. Sam felt the nausea rising higher.

But there was no one else. She would do her job.

"Thank you for taking the time to meet with me, sir. If you talk to Agent Ev... If you talk to Chris, please tell him I'm rooting for him."

Becker nodded. "I'm sure he'll be happy to hear that. I'll let you know when you can visit him. Anything else?"

"No, sir," Sam replied. She walked out, closing the door behind her. Her stomach was in full revolt. It was rising up at the thought of Chris Evans nearly dead. Rising up at the thought of what she was about to do in the name of her duty.

She held the bile down long enough to make it into the restroom, past the woman fixing her make-up, into one of the stalls, down onto her knees, and then to puke her lunch into the toilet.

Even after all these years, the memories were too fresh. Another wave of nausea hit her. She spasmed and heaved over the toilet again, retching up whatever little food still dwelt in her stomach. She would do her duty, she was certain. It was all she knew how to do. The ERD was the only family she had, the only family she'd had for years now.

She bent forward, heaved and heaved again, until nothing was left inside her.

11
Serenity

April came. It had been five weeks since the bust. Three weeks until Kade left for Bangkok. The serenity package was ready. He'd tested it at low levels on his own. It could keep his pulse steady on a heart rate monitor, keep his breathing and pulse steady at whatever rate he told it, keep his skin resistance steady on the psych lab's biofeedback rig.

Time to give it a harder test. He turned the system up to a level of three out of ten, and went to meet Nakamura.

"Have you spent any time thinking about what you'll do after your doctorate?" the simulated Shu asked inside the VR rig.

"I'm going to apply for postdoc positions," Kade replied. "I'm really interested in higher function decoding and mapping."

There was no buzz from the lie detector.

"That's great to hear," Su-Yong Shu replied. "We may have funding for a postdoc in that area in my lab next year. I'd encourage you to apply."

"That'd be fantastic," Kade said. "It'd be such an honor to work with you."

Still no buzz.

"It's such a shame how tightly the authorities regulate neuroscience in your country," she said. "Don't you think?"

"Umm, well, you know, it's for safety reasons."

No buzz.

"Why, I'd love a postdoc position in your lab. You're one of my scientific heroes."

Nothing.

"I think the ERD serves a useful purpose in the US, even if they do go a bit too far."

Nada.

"Why, yes, I'd love to talk in more depth about how you came across your amazing insights and learn more about the mind behind those incredible papers."

Zip.

"No, I don't worry about my friends back home. What could possibly happen to them?"

Nothing.

Nakamura reached over and plucked the goggles and headphones from Kade's head. "You've done something."

Kade grinned.

"Mmm. You've done something inside your own skull, haven't you?"

Kade remained mute.

"You should have told me," the CIA man said.

"It was on a need-to-know basis," Kade replied.

Nakamura chuckled. "Well, let's see how it does under greater stress. Please understand that this is in no way personal."

Kade had a moment to be puzzled by the comment, then the CIA man was on him.

Nakamura was up, out of his chair, and halfway around the table, coming around to Kade's left, before Kade even had a hope of reacting. The CIA man took Kade's left arm, twisted it behind his back, used it to lift him painfully out of his seat.

BZZZZZZT! The stress detector went off. BZZZZZZT! BZZZZZZT!

In annoyance, Kade cranked the serenity package to ten out of ten. The buzzer abruptly stopped.

Nakamura chuckled. "Very good. Now, tell me, Kade," he crooned into Kade's ear in an imitation of Shu's voice, "does the idea of working with me in China excite you?"

"Oh, Dr Shu, I'd like nothing better." Kade ground the words out around the pain in his shoulder and elbow.

The sensor made no sound.

"In fact, Dr Shu, I have a little present for you."

Kade activated Bruce Lee. He flicked the switch to full auto, hit START.

Kade's body twisted to the right to elbow Nakamura in the head, then spun back to the left to kick the CIA man in the knee. Nakamura parried the elbow, fell back and bent his leg to take Kade's kick on his thigh instead of knee. Kade's body came all the way around, free hand lashing out in a palm heel strike to break Nakamura's nose and drive the shattered fragments into his brain.

The CIA agent dodged the strike with a preterhuman twitch of his neck, let go of Kade's pinned arm and took another step backwards into the apartment. There was a feral grin on his face.

Uh-oh, Kade thought.

Kade's body sprang forward with a lunging kick to Nakamura's groin and a spear finger strike at his eyes. Nakamura stepped forward, knocked the kick away with his forearm and dodged the finger strike entirely. Nakamura spun, and then somehow he was behind Kade.

Bruce Lee lashed back with an elbow and a low kick. Neither connected. Kade's body twisted to the right. Nakamura put a hand on Kade's shoulder and came around behind him again. An open palm slapped Kade almost gently on the side of his face. Bruce Lee sent a straight kick backwards towards Nakamura's groin and connected with a chair instead. The agent was beside him now, still grinning.

Bruce Lee lashed out with Kade's right hand in a knife strike at Nakamura's throat. The agent dropped into a crouch, almost casually, as Kade's hand flew through empty space above his head.

Still smiling.

Kade knew he should end this now. He was horribly outmatched. This could only end in pain. But something in him wanted to land just one blow on the smug older man. Kade cranked up a setting in the VR martial arts app: *full offense, zero defense*. His body threw a flurry of kicks, punches, knees, elbows, open palm strikes, knife hands, and gouging fingers.

None of them connected. The CIA agent kept smiling, kept moving out of the way.

A sensor was flashing red inside Kade's mind. His blood oxygen was dipping to dangerously low levels. Kade's eyesight was dimming, his vision narrowing. His body threw kicks and punches, while the serenity package kept his pulse at sixty-five bpm and his respiration at fifteen breaths a minute. Kade's body needed more oxygen and his software wasn't letting him have it.

Kade flipped off the serenity package, let his body's responses normalize. Sweat sprang up on his brow, his breath came in a ragged gasp, his heart pounded in his throat. He threw another kick at Nakamura, connecting only with empty air...

BZZZZZZT!

Kade flipped off Bruce Lee in disgust, and collapsed in an exhausted heap on the floor, panting. Breathe. Breathe.

Breathe. His chest ached. He didn't even care that Nakamura was about to kick his ass into the next century.

Kade heard the sound of clapping.

Nakamura was standing above him, smiling and slowly applauding.

"You're just full of surprises, Mr Lane. That was very impressive."

"*Fuck... off*," Kade managed between gasps.

Nakamura laughed.

The older man crouched down next to him, still smiling. "You had your body locked down that entire time, didn't you? You weren't breathing hard the entire time we were fighting. Your pulse was steady. Impressive."

Kade nodded feebly.

"But, mmm, Mr Lane, you should leave the combat to combatants."

Nakamura's fist lashed out, stopped an inch from Kade's face, and hovered there. The CIA agent laughed again, laughed and laughed and laughed.

Kade let his head fall to the floor in defeat.

The final weeks flew by. Rangan finished his work on recreating the ERD's Nexus disruptor and a partial defense against it. The defense system could filter out signals of all sorts that Kade didn't want the Nexus nodes in his brain receiving. It had layers of fail-safes, watchdogs, and tripwires to stop rogue signals and rogue processes. It seemed like a fine set of capabilities to Kade. Antivirus for their minds.

The Nexus disruptor was different. It was a weapon. Did he really need this? Rangan insisted that Kade install the disruptor itself, and not just the defense system. "You never know when you might need it," Rangan said.

In the final week, Nakamura replaced Kade's phone with

another of the same model. All his data was there. This phone, Nakamura said, had one very special feature. It would transmit Nexus 5 signals over the net. Samantha Cataranes, under her alias of Robyn Rodriguez, would have a phone with the same capability. She would be running Nexus 5, and their minds would be linked.

Oh, joy.

The approval to visit Chris Evans came two days before she shipped out. Sam made her way past three armed checkpoints to reach the secure regeneration suite Evans was housed in, deep in the secret levels below Walter Reed National Military Medical Center.

Chris – what was left of him – was submerged in the regen coffin. His body was opened to the nutrient-rich growth medium. New tissue seeded with his own cells was slowly growing to replace that which bullets, sepsis, blood loss, and necrosis had destroyed.

The doctors said Evans was aware, but there was nothing to indicate that. She sat beside the tank, put her hand on the glass, felt the gentle hum from within.

"You did good, Chris," she told him. "You saved a lot of people from a lot of hell." She stayed and talked to him for an hour, told him how much he'd done, told him what a hero he was, told him he'd be back together in no time.

She wished she could reach out and touch him. She wished he wasn't so isolated in there. She wished she could show him she cared. Wished she could know what he was thinking. She wished he were running Nexus.

Briefing

...thus, given (1) the large number of advanced technological threats to the security of the United States, which have already taken the lives and dignities of tens of thousands of American citizens and which threaten millions more; (2) the rapid advancement of the science and technology at the root of such threats and the resultant risk of even more dangerous threats to come; and (3) the insufficiency of traditional courts and law enforcement agencies in the face of such threats, we recommend:

The creation of a new office within the Department of Homeland Security – the Emerging Risks Directorate – empowered to act in any and all ways necessary to counter such threats.

The empowerment of the President and the Secretary of Homeland Security to designate certain persons, organizations, and technologies as Emerging Technological Threats.

The suspension of normal judiciary procedures and rights for such designated persons, organizations, and developers and traffickers in such technologies, including the protections of speech, trial by jury, and against unreasonable search and seizure.

The creation of National Emerging Threat Tribunals as the exclusive forums for adjudicating cases involving such persons, organizations, and technologies, assuming all responsibilities and powers of the courts, and reporting solely to the Secretary of Homeland Security and the President.

> COMMITTEE REPORT: PROTECTING AMERICA FROM FUTURE THREATS, Senate Select Committee on Homeland Security,
> *Chairman Daniel Chandler (D – SC)*
> *November 2031*

12
Two Tickets to Paradise

Kade shoved his carryon bag into the overhead compartment of flight 819 to Bangkok.

"Kade," Samantha Cataranes said from the seat next to his. "Heading to ISFN?"

He could feel her mind. Nakamura had told him to expect this. This was unmistakably Samantha Cataranes. If he'd had any doubts that it was the same woman given the new face, the touch of her mind erased them. He remembered that mind too well from the night at Simonyi Field.

The signal from her mind was strong and clear. Not as strong as that from Rangan or Ilya or Wats, but stronger than that of any casual user. She'd been running Nexus 5 for weeks, then. She'd been practicing.

"Hi, *Robyn*." He stressed her alias just a tiny bit. "You're headed there too?"

"Yep."

<Incoming chat request from Robyn Rodriguez. Accept? Y/N>

Full cooperation, they'd said. Sigh.

```
<Accept : Y>
[robyn] Hello there.
[kade] Fancy meeting you here.
```

He tried to keep the bitterness and anger from roiling off his mind.

```
[robyn] How's your head?
```

Kade reflexively brought his hand up to his temple, where she'd hit him. The bruise had lasted for a week.

```
[kade] Better. How's your side?
[robyn] Better.
```

He didn't like that her chat ID came across as "robyn". He needed to remember who he was really interacting with. He navigated a menu, aliased it to "sam".

```
[kade] Why you? No offense.
[sam] I was the only suitable agent available.
And none taken.
[kade] Too bad.
[sam] Think what you want, Kade. My job is to
keep you safe on this mission.
[kade] I'm overjoyed.
```

They sat in silence for a while, but despite himself, Kade didn't have the energy to stay angry for the entire flight. He wanted to just get this over with, please his ERD masters, and get safely home.

Sam, for her part, spent the time with her nose in her slate, first flipping through guide books of Bangkok and Thailand, pointing out interesting things to Kade, then doing the same with the program of the International Society for Neuroscience meeting.

Kade idly flipped through a guide book himself. Thailand did look amazingly beautiful, with jungles and waterfalls and beaches, and temple after temple after temple. If only I was coming here for a vacation, he thought.

The conference guide yielded up a plethora of fascinating talks: Neural Substrates of Symbolic Reasoning, Intelligence and Prospects for Increasing It, Emotive-Loop Programming: A New Path to Artificial General Intelligence. How could they even hold these talks? In the US the topics of half of them would be classified as Emerging Technological Threats.

No wonder the international meeting trumps the US neuroscience meetings these days, Kade thought. The cutting edge stuff isn't legal at home any more.

He looked over at Sam. She was part of the reason he was here. She was part of the organization blackmailing him. She was an enforcer of laws he despised, an agent of ignorance and repression, with violence as her primary tool. It wouldn't do to forget that.

Two movies, three meals, and fourteen hours later, they were finally approaching Bangkok. Cloud enveloped them for a seemingly endless time, and then they were out, below the clouds, and the lights of South East Asia's second largest metropolis were everywhere. Minutes later, they were on the ground.

Kade watched Sam as they collected their bags, passed through Customs and immigration. She smiled at the immigration officer, flipped her hair casually. He waved her through. How many identities did she have? How often did she do this? Kade could feel her, cool and collected through the Nexus link.

When it was his turn, immigration waived him through just as quickly. So this is what it's like to be a spy.

Outside the air-conditioned terminal, Bangkok's heat hit Kade like a wall. It was 11pm, local time, and yet hotter than noon on a summer day at home. And louder. They were enveloped in a din of small car engines, whooshing buses, shouting touts and trinket vendors, the zipping Skytrain above them, shouts in English and Thai of all sorts, smells of biodiesel, dust, sweat, and grilling meats, the feel of the damp hot air on his skin, the bright lights, police spinners, flashing ultrabright LED signs advertising places to sleep, places to eat, places to fuck, where to see naked girls, naked boys, and more.

As tired as he was, Kade was enraptured. This wasn't even Bangkok proper – just the exit from the airport. He could drink this all in. He could experience all of this at once.

Sam whistled and waved, and then a cabbie in an official-looking uniform was tugging at the bags in Kade's hands and jerking his head towards a waiting car. Kade let himself be led, and then they were in the cab, and onto Bangkok-Chonburi Expressway, heading into the city.

The cabbie spoke decent English and rambled on as they headed into the city. Were they here for the conference? Yes, it was filling up all the hotels in the city. If they wanted a break from the temples and markets and conference, they should see the Samutprakarn Crocodile Farm. He could take them, and here was his card. That intersection off in the distance was Phra Ram 9, where they could find the Fortune Town IT Mall and buy software and electronics of all sorts very, very, *very* cheap, if they knew what he meant.

"Not just Indian!" he said. "Good Chinese stuff! Korean stuff! Even some American software!" In another direction was the road to the ancient Thai capital of Ayutthaya. His cousin ran a tour company with good guides and excellent prices and he could even get them a discount. This way to Damnoen Saduak floating market – get there right at dawn if they could.

If they wanted seedier delights, here were some ideas of

places to go to see the best sex shows where the women could do the most amazing things with certain parts of their anatomy, and no offense to the lady. There were boy shows too, but, ummm, the fine miss in the back might be the only woman in the audience. They should see the night bazaar – just west of the Queen Sirikit Convention Center where the conference was being held. And of course anyone who visited Bangkok, the city of angels, should pay respects at the temple of Wat Phra Kaew and see the Grand Palace. If they had time for another temple go see the Reclining Buddha at Wat Pho in the old city. And look, here they were at the Victory Monument, almost the center of the city, and here they were at the Prince Market Hotel where they were staying, and that would be one thousand baht please, plus whatever tip they felt so kind as to offer.

Sam peeled eleven hundred-baht notes off a roll and handed them to the cabbie as a hotel employee opened the cab door for her. The heat was a gauntlet to be run from air-conditioned cab to air-conditioned hotel lobby. They survived.

Inside, they checked in and found that their rooms were on the same floor, just a few doors down from each other, just as he'd been told to expect.

Sam's room was across the hall and four doors short of Kade's. She was close enough to keep tabs on him, positioned between his room and the elevator, but not conspicuously and improbably in the room next door. She carded the door, propped it open with her bags, and turned back to him with a faint smile.

"See you in the morning. 8am downstairs for breakfast, right?"

Kade grunted affirmatively in reply. Sam closed the door and disappeared into her room.

Kade's own room was small but nice, with a view of

Bangkok's neon-lit downtown. He stood at the window for a moment, soaking in the tall towers, neon signs, and rivers of foot and vehicle traffic. Bright lights, big city, he thought. He tossed his slate and phone onto the charging plate atop the nightstand and collapsed into the bed, clothes still on.

Sam let the smile fall from her face as the door closed behind her. Spending time with Kaden Lane was more tiresome than she'd expected. She closed both layers of curtains to block exterior visual surveillance. Then she walked through the room, inspecting it, methodically opening every drawer, searching every nook and cranny and corner, inspecting phones, terminal, viewscreen, electrical outlets. Implants scanned for the telltale transmissions of active surveillance devices, trace molecular signatures of explosives, giveaway echoes of false walls or panels that could hide a monitoring device or worse.

She pulled out her slate, and used it to view status from the infiltration daemon the CIA had planted in the hotel's net. The cameras in the hallways and elevators were hers now, as were the locks on the doors, the fire alarms and sprinklers, the motion sensors in the crawl spaces, the discreet metal and explosives detectors in the lobby, the local network access points, the registration and booking database, the cleaning schedule, the phones, and more.

There were no known hostile agents registered at the hotel. No signs of infiltrations of the hotel's network. Which might mean that she and Kade had attracted no special attention, or might only mean that any other infiltrators were armed with tools as good as hers.

She turned her attention to Kade's room. The countersurveillance device she'd attached to his bag showed no sign of any bugs aside from hers. A composite view from the handful of bugs sprinkled across his clothes, devices, and luggage showed Kade sprawled across the bed, clothes still on, curtains wide, bags unopened. Across the Nexus link she could feel him drifting into sleep. Good. The slate would wake her at any major change in his room. If his mental state changed too much, that would wake her as well.

She instructed the daemon to continue trawling the hotel's net, to alert her if Kade's door opened, if the power draw from his room changed abruptly, if he accessed the net or used the phone, or if anyone loitered in front of his door or hers. In the meantime it would capture the faces of every person seen by any of the surveillance cameras in the elevators or hotel lobby, and especially anyone on their floor, feeding them to another CIA database for pattern-matching against known foreign agents.

She sent a clone of the data feeds off to her support team. There would be an operative awake and monitoring the feed twenty-four hours a day, ready to wake her or initiate action if any threat was detected. There were ground forces assigned as backup should they be necessary. Local contractors vetted by the CIA for trustworthiness.

The perimeter was as secure as she could make it. Sam unpacked her bag, hung her clothes out for the next day, and spread her discreet, nearly undetectable weapons out where she could reach them. She set a wakeup call for 7am, and put herself to sleep.

Across Bangkok, in a shabby rented room off Khao San Road, a slate chimed. Watson Cole paused from checking and rechecking his weapons to see what information he'd received. It was a message from his man at the Prince Market Hotel. Kaden Lane had arrived and was checked into room 2738. He'd arrived with a woman named Robyn Rodriguez, in room 2731. Photos from a lapel camera showed both in the lobby, waiting to check in.

Wats zoomed in on Robyn Rodriguez's face as he pulled up information on her in another screen. Same build. Same nose. Same chin. Eyes, hair, lips, and cheekbones were different, but those could all be altered. In all likelihood, that was Samantha Cataranes. That, in turn, confirmed that this was either an ERD mission, or a trap for Wats.

It was no matter. He had a mission. Cataranes would be a complication, but he had expected as much. She wouldn't catch him by surprise this time. He would still achieve his goal, despite her and whatever other operatives she'd brought with her.

He sent a message to the maid at the Prince Market whose services he'd purchased.

2738. Tomorrow.

His hand went to the data fob on the chain around his neck. If he could just connect this and Kade...

But would Kade accept his help? Should he even ask? He had to. Kade wasn't just a tool. He was a friend. The boy had his own decisions to make, his own concerns to weigh. Wats didn't know what they'd offered his friend or what they'd threatened him with to get him here. He didn't know what task they wanted Kade to complete.

In the end, it was Kade's karma at stake. Wats could hold out his hand, but Kade had to take it. If he had any sense, he would.

Wats went back to inspecting his equipment. His life, and that of Kaden Lane, might very well depend on it.

13
Invitations & Provocations

Morning came too soon for Kade. He and Sam ate in the hotel restaurant and then headed out for the conference. The heat hit them like a solid object as they exited the lobby to find transportation. The sky was a ceiling of cloud or smoke or both. The air was thick with humidity. A warm drizzle came down onto the street. No wonder they held conferences this time of year. No one would want to come to Bangkok on vacation when the weather was this oppressive.

Sam flagged down a tuk-tuk at random. The bright yellow three-wheeled vehicle veered over to them. "Queen Sirikit Convention Center," she told him.

"Convention center," the driver replied. "A hundred baht!"

"Fifty baht," Sam replied.

"Fifty baht! Cloudy day! No sun!" He gestured at the solar panels on his roof, the low-hanging clouds above them. "Have to use engine. Fifty baht no pay for gas! Ninety baht!"

Sam shook her head and turned to go, tugging on Kade's forearm to follow her.

"OK, OK, eighty baht!" the driver called.

Sam turned "Sixty baht, no more."

"Seventy baht, can't go no lower, lady!"

Sam nodded. "OK." She dragged Kade into the open air vehicle.

The driver took off almost before they were both in the tiny seat. The little three-wheeled vehicle darted into traffic, zipped around a taxi and between two private vehicles, dodged a motor scooter that cut obliquely across their path with three people on it, and then tucked in behind a bus and sucked its biofuel fumes. Kade scrambled for a seat belt. There were none. Nor were there any doors. They were basically on a high-speed rickshaw with an engine and a partial roof. Kade gripped the small side railing tightly. At least the roof kept the drizzle off. Small blessing when he was about to be spilled out into traffic to be run over by some other insane driver.

Sam put her hand on his forearm, and only then did Kade realize that he was gripping her leg for dear life.

"Relax," she said. "They do this all the time. Enjoy the ride."

Easy for her to say. She could probably get hit by one of those cars and bounce right back up.

Kade nodded to himself, and tried to enjoy it. He almost succeeded.

Registration was a zoo. There were fifteen thousand people expected in person at this event, and another fifty thousand virtually. The convention center covered a giant city block. The registration hall was larger than a football field, and even so it was packed. People queued up to pick up badges. Exhibition tables showed off research instruments, neuroinformatics packages, infrared neural scanners, next-gen MEG brain-scanning caps, psychiatric diagnosis AIs, brainwave-controlled robots and wheelchairs, nervous-system integrated prosthetics, and more. Jobs tables had recruiters for pharma firms, for biotechs, for neural device manufacturers, for software companies, for savvy advertising and marketing firms, for banks and hedge funds that wanted the quantitative skills of neuroscientists. A dozen nonprofit societies had booths lining one wall, from Neuroscientists for World Peace to the Thai Neuroscience Students Association. Interestingly, there were quite a few shaven-headed men walking around in the orange robes of Thai monks.

Kade made it through the registration queue, got his badge and packet. Sam was still halfway back in her line.

[sam] I'll catch up with you later.

Kade nodded. With the Nexus link over their phones, they could always keep in touch. He headed into the massive plenary hall, grabbed a seat near the back, and pulled out his slate.

A moment later the lights dimmed and a voice boomed out over the loudspeaker. "Please welcome His Royal Majesty, the King of Thailand, Rama the Tenth."

WTF?

Kade looked down at his slate, tapped into the conference program.

Buddhism and Neuroscience: From Singular to Connected Paradigms of the Mind and Brain. His Royal Majesty Rama X & Professor Somdet Phra Ananda, Chulalongkorn University

At the end of the plenary hall and on giant screens to either side, a smiling forty-something man in an immaculate white suit with an embroidered golden sash took the stage. Monks in orange robes throughout the audience came to their feet, applauding, as did other Thais, and then the entire audience. Kade followed their lead.

Rama X held up his hands and motioned for the crowd to be seated.

He spoke in English, welcomed them to Thailand, praised the organizers and attendees, remarked on the history of the conference center which his grandfather had erected. And then the talk turned in a direction Kade had not expected.

"I am a Buddhist," the king said, "as are more than ninety percent of my countrymen. As is the custom of young men of my nation, I spent a time in my youth in the orange robes of a monk."

Interesting.

"I learned many things through the experience of serving as a monk. Two of them are relevant today.

"The first is that the most essential Buddhist practice – meditation – is a practice of investigating the mind. Through that investigation we gain peace, freedom from attachments, reduction in suffering, and compassion for others. And most relevant to today, we gain tremendous insights into how our minds actually work."

We do with Nexus too, Kade mused.

"The goals of neuroscience and Buddhism are nearly the same, while their methods are both different and complementary to one another.

"The methods of science are statistical, quantitative, reproducible, reductionist, and, as much as possible, objective."

He paused.

"The methods of meditation, on the other hand, are qualitative, subjective, reproducible often only through hard work disciplining and quieting the mind, and yet equally profound."

Drugs are faster, Kade thought. Mental tools.

"I have a deep respect for the scientific method," Rama

said. "Decades ago, the fourteenth Dalai Lama was asked: 'What if neuroscience proves that Buddhism is in some way incorrect?'

"'Well,' he replied, 'in that case we would need to change Buddhism.'"

The crowd laughed. Rama X smiled.

"What I would ask you to consider is the complementary idea. What if Buddhism shows that some of the basic assumptions of neuroscience are imperfect? That a new paradigm would prove superior? Then I would hope you august scientists would be willing to change *your* scientific approach."

No one laughed this time. There was silence.

Rama X smiled wider.

"Let me put one idea in your minds as to what this new paradigm might be. And here I turn back to the second thing I learned as a monk."

He paused for effect.

"We are all one."

More silence.

The King chuckled. "I am not hearkening back to the Woodstock Festival of North America."

There were a few answering chuckles.

"Nor have I been smoking hashish."

Nervous laughter rippled through the room. Kade found himself chuckling out loud.

"What I mean is that we all exists as parts of groups and collectives larger than ourselves. Tribes. Communities. Organizations. Institutions. Families. Nations. We think of ourselves as individuals, but all that we have accomplished, and all that we will accomplish, is the result of groups of humans cooperating. Those groups are organisms in their own rights. We are their components."

He's right, Kade thought.

"For the experienced meditator, this connection is intuitively grasped. The process of meditation pierces the illusion of solitary individual existence and reveals to us that we are all part of things much much larger than any individual."

Wow, Kade thought. The King of Thailand is a hippie.

"Here neuroscience can take direction from Buddhism. Individual minds matter. Yet in an age where billions of minds are webbed through technology, where information can travel from one person on one side of the globe to a billion on the other side of the globe in a heartbeat, there are other layers of cognition which matter.

"Everything important in our world requires the efforts of large numbers of individuals. Indeed, to overcome our planet's most pressing problems, we are required to think not as individuals, not even as nations, but as a single humanity."

Like Einstein, Kade thought. The problems we currently face can't be solved at the level of thinking that created them.

Rama X went on, "Yet the dominant paradigm of neuroscience is still that of the individual brain. That is only the beginning of the understanding of the human mind, not the end product.

"If I have one wish for this conference, it is that a few of you would rethink your work through a new lens, a new paradigm – that of the connectedness of all brains and all minds on Earth, both the connectedness that already exist," – here, the king paused – "and the even greater connectedness that we'll develop in the coming years as neuroscience and neurotechnology progress."

Greater connectedness that we'll develop? thought Kade. Is he talking about brain-to-brain communication? About Nexus?

"For now, I thank you for listening to the thoughts of a layperson. As both a Thai and a Buddhist, I welcome you to Thailand, and I open these proceedings." He momentarily bowed his head.

The orange-robed monks in the audience were on their feet in a moment, followed a split second later by the other Thai attendees, applauding thunderously. Kade found himself on his feet as well, genuinely surprised and impressed.

Rama X again waved the crowd into their seats. "Now, I have the privilege to introduce Professor Somdet Phra Ananda. He is both one of the most learned Buddhist monks in our country and simultaneously the chair of the Department of Neuroscience at Chulalongkorn University. He is also my friend. Professor Ananda!"

There was applause again, seated this time, as a sixty-something man in orange robes walked on stage, bowed deeply to the king, and took the lectern.

Somdet Phra Ananda filled in some of the details underlying the King's vision of a new paradigm in neuroscience. He showed study after study demonstrating the ways that cognition occurred in groups, that ideas could leap between minds, that individuals affected each other in deep and surprising ways. But it was his closing comments that were most provocative for Kade.

"Today the technology exists to directly connect the neural activity of one brain to the neural activity of another. As this happens, the need for a neuroscience of groups of minds will become more and more urgent.

"The evolution of language marked a great leap forward for our species. It boosted our cognitive abilities by webbing us together into larger, more powerful group minds. I believe that another quantum step in human cognition awaits us on the other side of direct linkage of our brains and minds to one another. Those linkages are here and are rapidly spreading. To understand and peacefully direct the transformation they represent, we must try to recreate neuroscience through the paradigm of groups of connected brains, and we must do so immediately. Thank you."

There was applause again, this time originating from scientists and monks as one. Kade found himself absentmindedly drumming his fingers on his slate.

Ananda was definitely talking about Nexus, Kade thought, or something like it. Are people in Thailand working with it? Does the king support it?

He had a lot to think about. People were filing out of the hall. He stood up to find his way out, still lost in thought. A tall Thai student with red spiky hair bumped into him in the crowded press for the doors.

"Oh, sorry, man."

"No prob," Kade replied.

"Hey, nice T-shirt!"

Kade looked down at his chest. He was wearing his favorite DJ Axon shirt, the one with Rangan's face and alternating sine waves superimposed over a brilliantly blue glowing neuronal protrusion, obviously about to pulse forth enormous energies, presumably in the form of sick beats.

He chuckled. "Yeah, thanks. He's a friend."

"No way!" the student replied. "You know DJ Axon?"

Kade grinned. "Yep. He's a lab mate. We're both in the Sanchez Lab, UCSF."

"That is so cool, man! He makes awesome music! We listen to his mixes all the time." The student held out his hand. "I'm Narong."

Kade took it. "Kade," he replied.

"You coming to the neuroscience students' mixer tomorrow night?"

"Umm, I hadn't really made any plans."

"You should come," Narong said. He handed Kade a flyer. "We're putting it on. Thai Neuroscience Students Association. I'm the secretary."

"I'll think about it," Kade said.

"Yeah, man. It'll be fun. It's at a bar downtown. It'll be the most awesome thing happening in the 'Kok tomorrow night! And no professors allowed!" Narong laughed.

Kade laughed despite himself. What about American spies? he thought. "I'll think about it."

They'd reached the doors.

"Right on, man. See you tomorrow night." Narong patted Kade on the arm and was off.

Sam was waiting outside the doors, studying the program on her slate. She looked up as Kade approached.

"How'd you like the plenary?"

"I think Ilya would have loved it," he said.

Sam nodded. "Yeah. You're probably right."

"What did you think of it?" Kade asked.

Sam seemed to think about that for a moment. "Idealistic," she replied. "A little scary." She paused for a moment longer. "A lot naïve."

Kade shrugged. Why did I ask?

"What now?" Kade asked.

Sam shrugged. "I'm going to check out some of the talks on the augmentation track. Good to keep up on that sort of stuff. We don't have to see the same talks."

Kade was a little surprised. He'd expected Sam to keep a closer eye on him.

"Sure. And, umm, I got invited to this thing tomorrow tonight." Kade handed her the flyer. "What do you think?"

Sam looked it over, front and back, shrugged. "Looks like fun to me."

They parted ways. Kade saw talk after talk, most of them quite fascinating. He chatted with scientists from across the globe, tried to keep track of their names and what they were working on. By 5pm, Kade's head was full and jet lag was making his eyelids heavy. He told Sam he was heading back to the hotel for a nap and would meet her at the opening reception tonight.

He took the Bangkok subway instead of a tuk-tuk on the way back. It meant he had to walk a few blocks in the muggy heat, but it was less nerve-wracking than an open-sided vehicle in the suicidal Bangkok traffic.

The hotel lobby was a blessed oasis of cool air. Kade could feel the sweat under his shirt and on his brow begin to condense immediately. He took the elevator up and carded himself into his room. He tossed his new conference tote bag into one corner and kicked off his shoes. The bed was freshly made, with a pair of mints and a folded card sitting on the pillow. Kade popped one of the mints into his mouth, and opened the card. It was a comment card where he could rate the service. Kade was about to toss it when something odd happened. The text on the card disappeared and new text appeared line by line.

Kade. Act natural. This message will appear and then disappear in thirty seconds.
I have the means to extract you from your current situation. I can provide a new identity and a clean getaway. Other paths will end with you in an ERD prison or dead, regardless of what they may have told you. You are too dangerous for them to allow to wander freely.
If you are ready to get out, choose "very unsatisfied" on the "overall experience" line of this comment card. I will then provide additional instructions.

Assume your phone and all net access is monitored
and that your clothes and self are bugged. Make
no mention of this via any medium.
This text will now disappear. Fill out the
comment card to avoid suspicion.
Wats

Wats. *Wats.* Wats! He was alive. He was here.

Kade went back and read the note a second time, the
words disappearing as he did so, the original hotel
evaluation appearing once again on the page. His heart was
pounding. He activated the serenity package to calm
himself, hoping that Sam hadn't noticed his sudden burst
of excitement, and took the card over to the small writing
desk.

He found a pen on the desk, filled in other parts of the
evaluation as he thought furiously.

Is the ERD really going to jail or kill me no matter what?

Room – Price/Value: He chose "Satisfied".

How do I know this is really from Wats?

Room – Comfort: Very Satisfied

Could this be a trick? An ERD test? But then why say
that I'll be killed or jailed either way?

Room – Cleanliness: Satisfied

If the note is real, can Wats really get me away?

Room – Appearance: Very Satisfied

But... Nothing's changed. If I run, it's jail for Ilya and
Rangan and dozens of other people. They're all counting
on me.

Room – Bathrooms: Satisfied

Shit. Fucked if I do, fucked if I don't.

Staff – Friendliness: Satisfied

No... It's other people who get fucked if I run. People I
care about.

Staff – Efficiency: Satisfied

Well, shit.

Overall Service: _____

Kade's pen hovered over the line. It was really no choice at all. Maybe he would end up in jail or dead if he stuck with this mission. But if he bailed, friends of his would end up in jail for certain. He had to take the chance. The ERD held all the cards right now.

Overall Service: Satisfied

Kade sighed. It was the right choice.

He stripped off the rest of his clothes, swallowed the other mint, and collapsed into bed.

Wats. How do I reach him? Is he here just for me?

Shit, shit, shit.

He rolled over and closed his eyes.

Kade knew what Wats had gone through, how the experiences he'd had, experiences made possible by Nexus, had changed him. He knew his friend believed that Nexus could change people, that it could end wars, that it could be a technology to make the world a better place. But not everyone was like Wats. Not everyone would respond that way. Most wouldn't be willing.

And Nexus 5 just wasn't ready. It was too dangerous to put into most people's hands. It would be too easy to use it to control people, to abuse them. *A scientist is responsible for the consequences of his work*, as his dad had told him over and over again. Kade wasn't going to have some of the possible consequences on his head.

Wats, if that was Wats, shouldn't have come. He was just putting his own life at risk.

Sleep came at last, briefly, but his dreams brought him no comfort.

14
Surprising Interactions

The opening night reception was held in the ballroom of the Queen Sirikit Convention Center. Scientists milled about in shirt sleeves and the occasional tie, mixing with orange-robed monks and formally dressed serving staff. Kade could feel Sam down the Nexus link across their phones. She was here somewhere, sharp and alert.

Kade got a beer with one of his drink tickets and wandered about. He chatted with half a dozen scientists on a range of topics. Neural plasticity. The effects of religion on the brain. The similarity in neural impacts of music, drugs, and meditation. The theoretical limits of human intelligence.

Someone walked past him, and he got a view of Sam. She was chatting with Narong, wine glass in hand, big smiles on their faces. Narong said something and she laughed. She put a hand on his arm, said something back, and then turned towards the restrooms. Narong watched her go, eyes glued to her ass.

    [kade] You have an admirer.
    [sam] Don't scare him off.

[kade] Don't you have work to do?

[sam] That's work, Kade. Your new buddy Narong is a known associate of Suk Prat-Nung. That name ring a bell?

[kade] As in Ted Prat-Nung?

[sam] Suk Prat-Nung is Thanom Prat-Nung's nephew. He's also involved in Nexus distribution himself, we think.

Thanom "Ted" Prat-Nung. The Thai drug dealer. The one they'd said was possibly the largest dealer of Nexus on the planet. The one pictured in the photo with Su-Yong Shu in Thailand. Narong was connected to his nephew.

[kade] You couldn't have mentioned this earlier?

[sam] I didn't know until just now.

[kade] ?

[sam] Narong just matched an unidentified voiceprint that we have tagged as belonging to an associate of Suk's.

[kade] Are you seriously voice-printing everyone you talk to?

[sam] Yes. Matching all the faces if we can too.

[kade] You people scare me.

[sam] The people at this conference scare me a lot more.

Kade wandered on. And then there was Su-Yong Shu, tall and elegant, surrounded by a gaggle of other neuroscientists, holding court, a large smile on her face and a glass of wine in her hand. Someone in the crowd said something and she arched an eyebrow. Her charisma was evident even from across the room. There was something about her. An intensity. A ferocity in the eyes and the smile and the laugh. It sent a chill up his spine.

Kade was about to turn and walk away when Shu's eyes passed over him, and she raised a hand to wave him over. Kade felt his chest tighten. He'd practiced this half a hundred times. He could do this.

Kade activated the serenity package, tuned it up halfway. He strolled towards the crowd around her, a relaxed smile on his face. As he walked he sent a single message to Sam, then suppressed all Nexus transmit functions within his brain. Mind-to-mind contact was to be avoided if at all possible.

Kade got within earshot in time to hear Shu finish a thought in British-inflected English.

"...opening plenary was refreshingly farsighted. The Thai are very lucky to have this leadership."

The crowd had formed a ring around her and someone else. A well-dressed male. Kade knew that face. Arlen Franks. Director of the American National Institute of Mental Health. The source of the bulk of Kade's funding.

"The opening speakers were talking about technology that's illegal," Franks said. "Posthuman technology, Professor Shu. They were embracing it."

"They were talking about a very real transformation, Dr. Franks," Shu replied. "An inevitable one. Ignore that all you want. I, for one, applaud them."

Definitely, Kade thought. That was the most interesting talk all day.

"Scientists have to show respect for the law, Professor," Franks replied.

"Perhaps the law should show respect for science instead, Doctor."

"Hear, hear," someone said behind Kade.

"We have an ethical responsibility—" Franks began.

"Ethical?" Shu cut him off. "Laws that keep humanity chained and limited are ethical?"

"They keep us human."

Shu raised an eyebrow. "And who decides what's human?"

"More than a hundred world leaders decided, when they signed the Copenhagen Accords."

"More than a hundred!" Shu exclaimed. "And politicians at that! Oh, that makes me feel *so* much better!"

A ripple of laughter went through the audience. Kade found himself chuckling. Franks pursed his lips in frustration.

"Dr Franks," Shu went on more quietly. "I agree with you that as scientists we must act ethically. But surely that means acting for the greatest good. The laws that exist now inhibit our ability to do so. There's so much we could do with more leeway in our research. There's a tremendous amount in medicine, and even more in augmentation. Who says that the current human condition is the right one? We could elevate ourselves. We could make a better world. We could give billions the choices of who and what to become, rather than trusting your 'more than a hundred'. Our fear has crippled us."

Hear, hear, Kade thought to himself.

Franks downed his drink. His face was flushed. "If you were in my country, Dr Shu, you'd find your funding cut off pretty quickly with talk like that."

Kade frowned. A disapproving murmur went around the crowd.

Shu smiled faintly. She shook her head. "Then I should be glad that I'm not in your country, Dr Franks." She nodded to him. "Good evening to you."

The crowd around them began to disperse, dismissed by their queen.

Shu turned to Kade. "Mr Lane, I believe?" She stepped towards him, hand outstretched.

Kade smiled, took her hand, shook it. "It's an honor to meet you, Dr Shu."

She smiled at him. "I've heard a lot about you. I'm looking forward to seeing more of your work."

"Thank you."

"What did you make of that little exchange?" she asked.

"I agreed with you one hundred percent."

Shu nodded.

He was ready for it when her mind reached out for his. She was probing gently, feeling for him, mentally caressing the space between them. Kade kept the Nexus in his brain locked down tight, let nothing leak back out.

She said, "Kade, would you have lunch with me tomorrow? I'd like to discuss your work and where you want to go with it."

My published work? Kade wondered. Or Nexus 5?

"I'd be honored."

"Oh, good," Shu said. "I see a lot of potential in you. I think you could go very far indeed." Her mind brushed his lightly, and he found himself thinking of what he could become, of his potential. Of where they could take Nexus, of augmenting his intelligence, of gaining the clarity and speed of thought that would allow him to unravel any problem, of a mind slipped free of the shackles that constrained it. He nearly gasped, caught himself instead. It was just a single flash of what he could become, seen through Shu's eyes.

I will not respond, Kade told himself. There is no Nexus here.

He wanted it. Wanted to become what she was showing him. Wanted to be free to improve upon himself, to become posthuman. He ached to reach out to her in turn, fought to control that urge.

"I'll have my driver pick you up at noon, Kade, just out front."

"Can't wait," he replied.

Even with the serenity package, Kade needed a drink after his encounter with Shu. She moved on to work the crowd. He headed for the bar. He relaxed as the distance between them grew, allowed the Nexus in his brain to return to full transmit-and-receive mode, cranked the serenity package down to a one out of ten. He felt Sam in his mind again. Curious, but waiting until after the event to debrief him.

What would he tell her? That he agreed with Shu? That she was even more seductive in person than she was as a remote figure? That he wanted what she was offering? That he'd felt her mind brush against his? Kade shook his head and stepped into the queue for a drink.

This time he wasn't prepared when it happened. Another mind brushed against his. Kade had an impression of still water, a deep, deep tranquility, the solidity of earth, a quiet amusement. And then surprise. The mind had felt him as well. It was behind him. And then it disappeared.

Kade turned. Professor Somdet Phra Ananda was there in the drink line, hands folded in front of his ceremonial robes, his black eyes studying Kade intently.

Kade stared back, mouth agape, dumbfounded. Was Somdet Phra Ananda currently under the influence of Nexus? Here and now?

Ananda broke the silence. "Young man, what is your name?" His voice was sonorous, hypnotic. It was a voice that took its time, a voice full of patience and command.

"I'm Kade. Kaden Lane. Uhh, your Eminence?"

"'Professor Ananda' will do, Kaden Lane." Ananda slowly scanned Kade with his eyes, taking in details. "You're American." He pronounced it as a fact, not a question.

"Yes, sir. I am."

"Your clothing is disrespectful."

"Uhh, sorry. I didn't mean any disrespect. It's just that my lab mate is a DJ and..."

Ananda cut him off. "The line behind you is moving, young man."

Kade turned, saw that a gap had opened, took a few steps to catch up, turned back to face Ananda.

"What did you think of the opening plenary this morning?"

Kade took a breath. "I agreed with you and the King almost completely."

Ananda smiled. He nodded, almost to himself. "Your turn."

"Pardon?" Kade replied.

"The bar." Ananda gestured with his eyes. "It's your turn."

"Oh." Kade turned and asked for a beer, reached into his pocket to fish out his other drink coupon, fumbled for a moment before he found it, gave it to the bartender, turned...

And Professor Somdet Phra Ananda was gone.

He blinked in surprise, peered around. No sight of the elder monk.

What the hell?

The reception was starting to wind down, he saw. Sam sent him a chat message asking if he was ready to head back. He was. They took a tuk-tuk back to the hotel. The traffic was lighter. The heat remained oppressive. Kade was too jet-lagged to care about the heat, too pensive about the day's events to worry about being spilled into traffic.

[sam] Show me the conversation with Shu.

Kade sighed. There was nothing for it. He opened to her,

let her experience his memories of the conversation with
Shu.

[sam] Good. It's a good sign that she's asking
you to lunch. Just stay cool, use that package in
your head if you have to. And remember what's
riding on this.

Kade looked out of the little motorized rickshaw, watched
Bangkok slide by in chrome and neon. The deeper he got
into this situation, the more confused he was.

Sam could sense his mood. Oh well.

At the hotel, Sam walked Kade to his room. At the door,
she offered him reassurance. "You're going to do great
tomorrow. Just be yourself."

Kade nodded. "Yeah. I'm fine. Just tired." He *was* tired.

Sam squeezed his arm and headed off to her room. Kade
slipped into his own and sank down onto the bed, his mind
spinning.

Wats. Shu. Ananda. The ERD. What the hell's going on?

15

Replay

Sam sat in lotus on the floor of her own room down the hall of the Prince Market Hotel, reviewing the day.

Her surveillance devices detected no new bugs on Kade or in the room. No unusual behavior on the hotel net. Typical distribution of foot and elevator traffic within the hotel, on their floor, and just outside their doors. Typical time spent in their rooms by the maids, with no unusual behavior. No flagged individuals detected by faceprinting at the conference or the hotel.

Still, Sam was worried. There had been two bursts of surprise from Kade over the course of the day. What were they?

The first had happened around 5.20pm, just after he'd reached his room. She went back to the feed from the bugs in Kade's room, played the video. The room was still and silent. The bed was made, two mints on the pillow bracketing a comment card. Kade entered, tossed off his conference tote and shoes, ate one of the mints, filled out the comment card, ate the second mint, and then lay down for a nap.

She called up her support team, requested a sweep of

Kade's room tomorrow morning after they'd left for the conference. Someone would do a more detailed scan for bugs, transmitters, or anything else unusual. They'd pick up the comment card and the mint wrappers for analysis while they were there.

The second incident seemed more straightforward. She'd made note of the time when she felt it. She scanned through camera data from the conference center, found that time. It had been just moments after Kade had walked away from Shu. He'd gotten in line at one of the bars and then Professor Somdet Phra Ananda, coming from another direction, had gotten in line behind him. Kade had turned, presumably at something Ananda said, and they'd had a brief conversation.

Had Ananda said something that had shocked Kade? She found another camera angle where she could see the senior monk's face, zoomed in so it filled a frame, projected it onto the wall. She zoomed in on Kade's face, projected that in a giant frame next to Ananda. Then she synced the audio from the bugs on Kade, played it, watched their faces.

Ananda stepped into line behind Kade, eyes fixed forward, lips pressed together in that perpetual serene half smile the senior monks wore, and then... The conversation was short, hardly more than a few words. Nothing in it seemed particularly shocking.

Sam looked at the times again. Interesting. It was hard to say the exact sequence of things, given that it had taken her a few seconds to react. Even so, it seemed as if the sense of surprise might have come *before* he turned around and had his brief conversation with Ananda.

Sam rewound the clock, added a third wall frame with a wider view of the area, played the scene again, one-quarter speed, with the two shots in sync, timestamp displayed at the bottom of each.

Ananda stepped into line behind Kade. His face was impassive. His mouth closed. He said nothing. Kade turned. Why? And as he turned, Ananda's eyes moved, changed from the faraway gaze of someone lost in thought or taking in all around him to the near-set focus on an object in one's immediate foreground. A second passed. The time stamp Sam had noted was on the screen now. Another second passed. Only then did Ananda's mouth open. Sam queued the audio from one of the bugs on Kade. Young man, what is your name?

And then another interesting thing happened. Kade reached the front of the line and ordered his beer. While he fumbled, Ananda simply walked away, not even asking for the water or juice the monks were drinking.

Sam zoomed out, stitched together two more cameras. Ananda walked briskly, head turning this way and that, apparently searching, until he spotted a particular monk, nearly six feet tall, thin, angular, with a large hooked nose. They spoke a few words. The tall hook-nosed monk bowed, turned towards the bar where Kade and Ananda had spoken, and walked briskly there.

Kade was nursing his beer a few feet away from the bar, now. The unidentified monk stepped towards the edges of the room, outside Kade's peripheral vision, his face turned towards Kade, and waited. By this point she would have been asking Kade if he was ready to go. She watched it happen. Kade kept his eyes down on the floor. He looked lost in thought. In reality he was lost in a chat conversation with her.

And then he looked up, set his beer down on a table, and walked towards the exit to meet her. She zoomed out again. The monk followed discreetly. He had a clear view when Kade and Sam met and then walked out together. The monk paused for a moment. A few seconds later he followed them out the door.

Sam switched to an external camera. She watched herself flag down a tuk-tuk. She and Kade climbed into it and off they went. The unidentified hook-nosed monk climbed into the next one, and it took off in the same direction.

Fuck. That was twenty minutes ago. He could be inside the hotel right now.

First, secure the tactical situation. Nakamura had drilled that into her.

She felt for Kade. He was asleep, calm. Video showed him passed out on his bed, clothes on. Hallway cams. Empty. Stairwells, lobby, elevators – no orange-robed monks, no bald men. A lot of people sitting and chatting in the bar.

She took control of Kade's door, instructed it to throw the safety bolt until she overrode it. Next she sealed the stairwell doors and locked the elevator out of this floor, set alarms on them directed to her slate.

Sam grabbed the monk's face and a clip of him walking from the video feeds and forwarded them to the CIA daemon in the hotel net; told it to watch all cameras for that individual, any bald man, any monk. She instructed it to spawn a new watcher and sent it digging from the present back through time to find any telltales in the hotel logs.

And then she rewound the hotel's lobby and external cams, watched herself and Kade arrive. There they were. Climbing out of a tuk-tuk, walking through the lobby, into the elevator. She waited. No additional tuk-tuk appeared. No monk walked through the lobby.

The daemon returned. In eighteen months of data from all cameras in the hotel, it had 8,572 instances of orange-robed monks and zero of this monk. Nor were there any hits in the past twenty minutes. He was not in the building.

Sam relaxed fractionally. He had followed them, it

seemed, but had not come in. Or if he had, he was much more than a normal monk. She took a breath. Forty seconds had passed since she'd realized they'd been followed. They'd elicited attention of some sort but immediate danger was likely low.

She called her support team, debriefed Nichols quickly. He agreed with her assessment. They'd attracted attention but were likely safe. Even so, he sent two of the local contractors into the lobby as backup.

OK. At this point, attracting attention was the greater risk. She unlocked the stairwell doors and let the elevators reach her floor again. She left Kade's door locked and bolted and alarms to alert her anytime someone approached their floor. The support would be here soon. She doubted there was a risk. Something had drawn Ananda's attention to Kade, and he'd wanted to learn more. That did not spell an imminent assassination attempt.

When seeking to understand, go breadth first. That was Nakamura again.

Breadth first. From the top again. Kade's jolt of surprise in the late afternoon. She pulled up the feed from the bugs in his room and on his body around that time. Kade was not a good liar, not good at masking his emotions, except when he activated the emotion-suppression software he had. And Sam was fairly certain he'd activated that *after* the jolt of surprise, either to manage his own reaction to something, or to hide it from Sam.

The cameras in the lobby and elevators showed no jolt of surprise. It had happened sometime after he got out of the elevator. The video from the tiny bugs in his room was low quality. She couldn't see the minor tics that would give someone away to her in person.

Audio then. Sam closed her eyes, then played only the audio stream from the moment Kade entered the hotel. The lobby was loud, but even so she could hear his breathing and his footfalls. The transition to the elevator was obvious. His breathing stood out in the relative quiet of the small space. Then the elevator door opened; his breathing was louder now. Footfalls. Breathing. Trouser legs rubbed against each other. Pause as he reached his door. Beep of the door lock as he swiped it and it accepted him. Click of the door as it unlocked a fraction of a second later. A breath as he walked into the room. Audio from the room bugs joined the audio from the bugs on his body now. His conference tote bag landed on the floor in a light thud and a crumpling of cheap plastic. A breath as he kicked off the shoes. Foil unwrapping, the sound of chewing as he popped the first mint into his mouth. And then... a break in the rhythm. A breath missed. Chewing paused. A second passed. Another. Another. And then he swallowed, and breathed again.

That was it. Sam paused the playback and opened her eyes. On the slate, Kade was frozen, still standing, the comment card in his hand. She couldn't tell what was on it, but something there had caught his attention. Excellent.

And the interaction with Ananda? Sam pulled up the interlocking video again.

Assume it was two seconds between his jolt of surprise and when I noted the time, she thought. Mark the point two seconds earlier...

She replayed the videos at one tenth speed this time, zoomed in to each of their faces in two projections on the wall, out to the level of their two bodies together in a third. Ananda stepped behind Kade. His face was serene, impassive, lips curved into just the slightest smile at nothing at all. The marker happened. Kade's whole face twitched. The angle of his neck changed. He inhaled sharply. A quarter-second later his eyes and chin moved to the left, starting the turn that would bring him around. Ananda stayed impassive, serene.

No, wait, play that again, focus on Ananda. She went backwards, forwards again. He stepped behind Kade. The time marker arrived. Kade reacted. And a quarter-second later, there, on Ananda's face, there was the tiniest flutter. Ananda's nostrils flared by the barest margin. His eyes flicked from their thousand-yard stare to focus on something in front of him. Kade had just barely begun his turn, only milliseconds before. There was no time for Ananda to have responded to the motion. He was responding to something else.

Sam thought furiously. Ananda had been a monk for forty years. He'd spent more hours in meditation than Sam had spent awake. He must have nearly complete control over his expression, over his underlying emotions. He'd trained himself to accept the world with equanimity. But not perfectly so. Something had cracked that long-practiced equanimity. For a split second, Professor Somdet Phra Ananda, eminent Buddhist monk and accomplished neuroscientist, personal friend to the King of Thailand, had been sufficiently surprised that something broke through that Buddhist calm and made itself known on his face in the tiniest of ways. Something to do with Kade.

Neither Sam nor her support team observed the third tuk-tuk, which had followed the unidentified monk, nor the large dark-skinned man in black clothing within it.

Across town, in his tiny rented room, Wats zoomed in on an image of a tall, bald, hook-nosed Thai in monk's robes. Who was this man? Why had he followed Kade and Cataranes? Whoever he was, he'd spooked the ERD. Two military types had arrived at the Prince Market Hotel half an hour ago. They were Thai men with the bulk of augmented muscle, wearing blazers in this heat, blazers large and loose enough to conceal weapons in. They were still there, sipping sparkling water in the lobby. Just two businessmen out late for some Perrier in a hotel lounge on a Monday night. Yeah, right.

He stared at the monk's picture again.

Who are you?

This was a complication. An unknown. Wats didn't like unknowns.

16
A Slight Change of Plans

Kade woke before the alarm. He looked at the clock. 5.47am. Too early by far. He rolled over, but sleep wouldn't come. Today was the day. He'd meet Shu for lunch. What would happen then? Would she offer him the postdoc? Would she ask him about Nexus?

Could she truly deliver on what her mind had hinted at? Wasn't that what he wanted?

Wats. Was he really here? Was there any way to reach him?

And Ananda. Had that been real? Had he imagined that? Was the monk running Nexus?

Kade tossed and turned. It was no good. His mind was spinning too much for sleep.

He rose and threw open the curtains. It was raining outside. It would be a muggy steamy rain, he was sure. Three hundred feet down from his window, Bangkok was alive. Traffic was a chaotic dance of scooters, tuk-tuk, taxis, and private cars zipping to and fro, barely avoiding collision. Pedestrians moved in rivers of human bodies down the sidewalks, holding cheap umbrellas or wearing cheaper clear plastic ponchos. Bicyclists pedaled in the rain between pedestrians and motorized traffic. Food stalls occupied every corner but one, selling noodles or sticky rice topped with mangoes. Steam rose from them. On the fourth corner stood a small temple. Even in the rain, Thai men and women streamed continually in and out of it, paying their morning respects to whatever Buddha or bodhisattva was within.

In other circumstances he would love to explore this exotic, confusing city.

He pulled open his slate, instead. There was a message from Ilya asking how his trip was going, a dozen threads within the lab on various topics, and a single message from Su-Yong Shu.

Kade,

An unavoidable conflict has come up with lunch. Could you do dinner tonight instead? My driver can pick you up at 7pm from your hotel.
    Best,
    SYS

Curious. Kade shrugged. He fired off a quick reply. 7pm at his hotel would be fine. He answered a few more messages, then showered and went down to breakfast.

Sam seemed unperturbed about Su-Yong Shu moving their plans for the day. She ran him through the plan for interacting with Shu twice over breakfast. Kade felt as ready as he was ever going to be. Sam seemed to agree.

The conference whizzed by in a blur of sessions and brief conversations. Neuro-Optics: Laser Based Neural Stimulation. Hilbert Transforms in Deciphering Neural Correlates of Emotion. Planning and Deliberative Structures: Neural Circuitry and Firing Patterns.

Coming out of the planning structures session and on his way to lunch, Kade caught something out of the corner of his eye and turned. There was Su-Yong Shu, walking towards the conference center exit, with none other than Professor Somdet Phra Ananda.

How very interesting. Could that have anything to do with the encounter he'd had with Ananda the night before? Kade shrugged. It was impossible to know.

At least I was bumped for someone important.

He ran into Sam at the last talk of the day: *Understanding Volition: From Dopamine to Dynamic Systems*. They sat together. Sam seemed focused on the talk.

Finally, the day's sessions were over. It was time to return to the hotel to meet Shu's driver. Sam would meet Kade later, at the neuroscience students mixer that Narong had invited them to. If they were interested, there was a smaller afterparty afterwards.

Sam reviewed the plan with Kade one more time on chat, then stood there while he suppressed his Nexus transmissions. Then it was done. He was on his own. He headed back to the hotel to freshen up and iron his one button-down shirt in preparation for his dinner with Su-Yong Shu.

Wats crouched in the alley with the maid. They were four blocks from the Prince Market Hotel. Hopefully that put them outside the ERD's surveillance cordon. Hopefully.

The rain had stopped, at least. Small blessing.

The maid was not telling him what he wanted to hear.

Mai me But, she was saying. No card.

Haa Nai Thung Khaya? he asked. Had she searched the garbage?

Chai. Yes, she'd searched the garbage.

Kang Laang taitiang? Under the bed?

Chai, chai.

Hong naam? Had she looked in the bathroom?

Chai, chai. Mai me But.

And so it went. The card wasn't anywhere in Kaden Lane's room. Could he have put it in his bag to fill out later? Why would he do that? Wats had known that there was a chance that Kade would miss the card entirely... But then it should have still been in the hotel room somewhere.

Could Cataranes have taken it? Why would she? Unless they'd detected it somehow?

He felt a chill. He'd put his name on that card. It had been a risk, but he'd deemed it necessary in order to convince Kade to accept the offer.

So the ERD might know he was here. So be it.

The maid was waiting impatiently, her hand outstretched for her payment. Wats counted out the bills. Two thousand baht. He put them in her hand but didn't let go. He locked her eyes with his.

Mee ngahn Pheum, he told her. He had more work for her. He flashed more money in his other hand.

The maid smiled, rubbed the bills he'd given her with her thumb, and nodded. Wats let her go, and she turned and was off.

He stayed there in the alley after she'd gone, idly playing with the data fob around his neck. What now? Should he make his move without Kade's consent? And what were the consequences? What were they holding over Kade's head? Who would suffer? He'd trade dozens of lives for the light that Nexus 5 could shed on the world. But was it Wats' place to make that decision? Would his friend welcome it?

Fuck. Two years ago he would have charged in, guns blazing, pulled Kade out of there whether his friend would thank him or not, and damn the consequences.

Now... *We must all walk the path ourselves. We must all choose*

our own karma. We must all allow others to choose their own
karma as well.

Kade had to choose. If at all possible. That's what
Buddhism said. Every individual had to make their own
choices in life. Wats couldn't impose what he thought was
right on Kade, especially with so much in the balance. The
ones who imposed their own will on others – they were the
ones wrecking the world.

Wats just needed a way to communicate with Kade to
make sure he knew he had the choice at all. He needed a
way to do so without being picked up by any of the cameras
or microphones he suspected Kade was covered in. Without
words being overheard by the inevitable microphones on
Kade's body. Without being picked up by the cameras in
the conference center, the cameras in the hotel. Even the
note had been a risk, a bet that invisibly small surveillance
cams wouldn't be able to read the text.

He'd find a way.

And if he couldn't get confirmation one way or another?
What if, in the course of Kade's seven-day visit to Thailand,
Wats couldn't be sure that his friend knew the option of
escape was even open? Or if the rest of the situation
became too suspiciously sketchy before he had that
confirmation?

Then Wats would have to choose for him. And damn his
karma, damn the consequences.

Sam watched as Kade headed towards the conference exit.
She hadn't confronted him about yesterday's events yet.
She wanted him to be as calm and cool as possible for his
dinner with Shu.

Today had proven to be almost as interesting as last night.
The conference center cameras had spotted Su-Yong Shu
and Somdet Phra Ananda leaving together at lunch. The

man who'd picked them up, the driver of the car that had taken them away, was Confucian Fist. One of the clone soldiers.

Between the reception last night and breakfast this morning, something had caused either Shu or Ananda to seek out a short notice meeting with the other. What had happened since then? Shu's conversation with Kade, of course. And Ananda and Kade's brief and odd interaction in the drink line.

And what would have gotten Ananda's attention? What could have surprised him last night, and sent him in search of the reason Kaden Lane was here? Could it have been Nexus 5 rattling around in Kade's brain at absurdly high levels? And if that were the case... how had Ananda detected it? Unless he were a Nexus user also?

It was ninety minutes later, while Sam was having dinner with Narong, that she received a message from her team. She discreetly read it in the corner of her tactical contact display as she listened to Narong enthuse about Thailand's bright future in neuroscience.

[Prelim lab analysis back. Comment card shows traces of self-destructed nanocircuitry. Likely a self-wiping message. No obvious return message from Lane, but could be hidden or encoded.]

So someone had gotten a message to Kade. Who? Shu? Ananda? And what had it said?

She and Kade were definitely going to have to talk. Keeping secrets from her wouldn't do. No, it wouldn't do at all. Tonight, after the mixer.

Briefing

War between those who accept the limitations of "humanity" and those who embrace the power of the possible is inevitable. The humans will not accept us, will not tolerate us, will not leave us in peace. They will fear us for our greatness, just as Nietzsche said they would fear the Übermensch. In fearing us, they will seek to destroy us. They will be legion. We will be few. We will triumph, whatever the cost.

Anonymous, Posthuman Manifesto, January 2038

In order to combat criminals and terrorists using proscribed technologies, we have little choice but to embrace the enhancement of our own operatives. We can and must maintain operational supremacy on the battlefield. As such, we will use any and all means to ensure that the capabilities of our agents are unparalleled.

ERD Position Paper, November 2035

17
VIP

The elevator door opened, spilling Kade out into the lobby. Serenity package turned up high, best shirt on, Nexus transmissions suppressed. The driver was there, waiting for him in black suit and tie, white shirt, black gloves and cap. He was Confucian Fist. A clone soldier.

The driver smiled, waved, and approached him. "Mr Lane?" He had a distinctly Chinese accent.

"Yes?"

"My name is Feng." He tipped his chauffeur's cap to Kade. "I have the honor of being Professor Shu's driver. Would you come with me, please?"

"Sure." Kade followed Feng out the door. The rain had stopped and the clouds had parted a bit. The sun had just set, and an orange glow came from the west.

The car was a lustrous black Opal sedan. Top of the line Chinese luxury. The plates were Chinese. They'd brought it all the way from China.

Feng held open the rear door while Kade stepped into air-conditioned luxury. The interior was dark wood and leather. Soft classical music played. Condensation beaded on two unopened bottles of sparkling water. The windows were tinted.

Feng slid into the driver's seat.

"Where are we going?" Kade asked.

"Thonburi," Feng replied. "Just across the Chao Phraya river. A very good restaurant there – my favorite in Bangkok!"

"How long to get there?"

The Opal pulled silently away from the curb.

"Maybe twenty minutes," Feng replied. "Faster if traffic is good."

Kade leaned back into the seat. "Thanks." Something occurred to him. "You've been here before?" he asked.

Feng nodded. "Professor Shu comes to Bangkok often. I come with her."

"How long have you worked for Dr Shu?"

"Three years. Best boss to work for." He grinned into the mirror for Kade's benefit.

"And before that?"

Feng nodded again. "Army, special forces. Still am. Special protection unit."

"Special protection unit?" Kade inquired.

"Oh yeah. We take care of important people. Keep them safe."

"Dr Shu gets military protection?"

"Oh, yes. National treasure. Brilliant scientist. China's future depends on science. She's so important, you should be honored having this dinner with her!"

"Oh, I am. Shouldn't you be protecting her right now?"

Feng laughed, glanced over his shoulder. "Yeah, maybe. But you know, she's tough. Very good at taking care of herself." He paused a moment, eyes back on the road.

"How come she isn't with us now?"

"Oh, she had meeting earlier close to where we going. No sense her coming back downtown."

Kade felt bold. Was it the serenity package? Did it matter? "Have you ever had to protect her from a real threat? Like someone attacking her?"

Feng paused for moment, answered more slowly. "Sorry. Can't talk about that. Operational details. Secret."

Interesting, Kade thought. Does that mean yes?

"Would you take a bullet for her?" he asked.

"What, you mean if someone try to shoot her? Get in the way myself?"

"Yeah."

Feng laughed. "Hopefully, I shoot him first." He made a pistol shape with his thumb and forefinger, held it up to show Kade, mock fired it at some target out the windshield.

Kade laughed to keep it light. He felt calculating, clear. He could get used to this state of mind.

"What if that wasn't an option? What if the only way you could see to save her was to get between her and a bullet?"

Feng made a face in the mirror. "Mmm, bad option, you know. I get shot, saves her for a second. Then what? Better hope I have backup. Otherwise, it only slow the shooter down. Better I take him out. Best defense a good offense, you know."

He paused.

"But yeah. I do it. I take a bullet, if there no other way."

Kade nodded to himself. He remembered Becker's question. Why would someone want to create hundreds of men with the same DNA?

He studied Feng. Clones engineered for extreme loyalty. Same genes, same training. Identical, predictable behavior. Perfect soldiers.

Do I believe it?

"What were you doing before the army?" he asked casually.

"Oh, I was just a kid before army. Grew up near

Shanghai. Big family." Feng laughed to himself. "Really big family. Lots and lots of brothers." He laughed again, like that was the funniest thing in the world. Even through the serenity package, Kade felt a shiver up his spine.

They drove on, the orange glow of sunset warring with the neon lights coming on above them. The day's rain turned the streets into a glistening river of light, alive with reflecting reds and blues and greens and slowly deepening orange.

Feng made a left turn, and suddenly the view changed. They were driving onto a bridge crossing a brown river. This must be the Chao Phraya. Ahead of them, the sky reflected the final vivid rays of the recently set sun. Backlit in orange was a temple, a central structure like a pyramid with a spire rising from its apex, like the Eiffel Tower cast in massive and intricate stone, painted amber by the sunset and the lights at its base. Four smaller towers surrounded it, perhaps a hundred feet tall each. The central tower was the tallest thing on the western bank of the river.

"Wat Arun," Feng said quietly. "The Temple of the Dawn."

"It's beautiful," Kade said sincerely.

Feng nodded. "That's where Professor Shu is now. She meet us at the restaurant."

"Is it close?"

"Right there," Feng said, pointing at the river bank ahead of them.

The restaurant was called Ayutthaya, after the ancient Thai capital. It occupied a gorgeously ornate three-story building situated on the bank of the river, a few hundred yards north of Wat Arun. Red-skinned, gold-armored demon statues flanked the open double doorway, their five-foot-long swords held in two hands, points in the ground and hilts at their chests. Feng closed the car door behind Kade as he emerged, took him by the elbow to the maître d'.

"Guest for Professor Shu," he said.

A man-sized golden Buddha sat cross-legged on a stone just inside the doors.

"Oh, Mr Lane?" The hostess wore a long, flowing Thai dress in gold. Her hair was demurely pulled back into a bun. She was stunning.

"Yes, that's me." No stutter. No stammer. His voice sounded deep and confident in his own ears. I could get used to this.

"Please come with me." She lifted a menu and smiled winningly at him.

"See you after dinner." That was Feng.

"You're not coming up?"

"I'm just the driver, not an important person like you." Feng gave him the merest of bows and backed towards the car.

Kade turned to see the hostess waiting. She smiled again and turned to lead him into the restaurant. The dress hugged her shape. The sway of her hips was intoxicating.

Keep it down, buddy. There's more than one way to lose your cool.

They rounded the Buddha and the restaurant spread out before them. Floor-to-ceiling windows were cast open to the warm night. They framed the river and the Grand Palace beyond it. Through more windows to the south the spire of Wat Arun rose above the west bank. Gold and orange lanterns illuminated ornate tables with tourists and Thai alike.

They crossed a tiny bridge – over a softly gurgling stream that ran through the dining room and emptied itself into the Chao Phraya below.

She's trying to impress me, Kade thought to himself. Shu.

She's recruiting.

The hostess led him up to a rooftop deck. There was a cool breeze from the river. The sky was darkening as evening turned to night. All sorts of delicious scents assailed him.

Do I want to be recruited?

The hostess steered him towards a table at the southeastern corner of the rooftop, where the most majestic view of the river and temples would be. Su-Yong Shu rose to greet him, a wide smile on her face. She looked relaxed, confident, and elegant. Elegant and dangerous, Kade thought.

Show time.

18
Ayutthaya

"Kade. Thank you so much for joining me."

Su-Yong Shu took his hand in both of hers. Her eyes were bright, compelling.

"Professor Shu, it's an honor." They sat.

"This place is spectacular," Kade said.

Shu smiled again. She looked around, taking it all in. "I love it here," she said. She gestured at Wat Arun, soaring above them. "Humans create so much beauty."

Humans, Kade observed to himself. Not "we". Humans.

The waiter came to them with water and tea, walked them through the menu.

"Everything looks so incredible," Kade commented.

Shu smiled. "Let me. You'll be happy."

"I'm in your hands."

Shu rattled off a stream of high-speed Thai to the waiter, who smiled broadly, bowed, and backed away.

"You speak Thai," Kade noted.

Shu smiled. "Talk to me about your research, Kade. I hear your paper in *Science* is going to be very exciting. What's in it?"

Kade talked. He gave her the edited, sanitized version,

with conventional nanotube filaments, software built on the models from Shu's lab. He left out all the leapfrogs that Nexus 5 had allowed them to make. All the dead ends it had allowed them to avoid.

Nexus had enabled them to paint a Leonardo. They'd traced that into a crude crayon drawing, and still they were years ahead of the field.

Shu asked good questions. She probed details and high-level conclusions. Kade struggled to keep up.

Finally, she nodded appreciatively. "Well, I'm very impressed." She held his eyes.

"Thank you." He smiled calmly, a little sheepishly. "We're really proud of it. Rangan did as much work as I did."

The food arrived, breaking the moment.

The waiter presented each small dish with fanfare.

Yum Mamuang, a delicious mango salad.

Pad Pak Boong, fried morning glory.

Goong Kra Tiem, savory garlic fried shrimp.

Ped bai Gra-pow, basil duck.

Phat qoo-ay-dtee-o neu-a, stir-fried noodles with sliced beef.

They ate family style, remarking on each delicious dish. Shu had an enthusiasm for the food that Kade found infectious. The waiter brought them fresh guava juice, cool and refreshing. As they talked, the sky darkened into full night. Their table was illuminated by the flame from the lanterns, the amber lights on Wat Arun just to their south, the neon glow from the east, from the teeming city across the river.

Shu shifted the conversation from food back to neuroscience, grilling him on topics all across the field. He was being interviewed. The questions came thick and fast, on topics far and wide. The neural basis of creativity. Prospects for boosting human intelligence. The difficulty in uploading human minds into computers. The evolutionary basis of sleep. The limits of a human brain's storage capacity. Reasons for the human perception of time.

The questions were all speculative, open-ended, on the frontiers of modern neuroscience. He had to synthesize, reveal hunches, sketch out possibilities based on incomplete data in the field. Shu wouldn't accept "I don't know" as an answer. She kept pushing him to take an educated guess, to explain his thoughts. It was exhilarating. He wondered if she knew the answers to her own questions.

And then Kade felt it. Her mind reached out to his. He could feel her curiosity, her crystal clear intellect. Her mind felt amazing. Vast, intricate, like no one he'd ever felt before.

He longed to touch that mind. But he gave her nothing. To open to her would be to reveal why he was here and who had sent him.

Keep talking, Kade told himself. Pretend you've felt nothing.

Shu watched him, her face pensive.

Wats watched from a rooftop north of Ayutthaya Restaurant. He lay there on his stomach, utterly still, a scope to his eye. Chameleonware in his clothing blended him into the rooftop. There was Kade, with someone that facial recognition software identified as Professor Su-Yong Shu of Jiaotong University, Shanghai. Shu was one of the top researchers in Lane's field, and an occasional dabbler with the Chinese Ministry of National Defense. What was she doing there?

More troubling was the driver of that car. He'd seen that face before. He'd seen it on a very dangerous man, a man he could swear was dead.

It had been in the KZ. A Chinese "advisor" they'd flushed out of a rebel command center. They'd taken the command post, not aware of his presence. When they'd discovered him, he'd fought. Fought like no one Wats had seen fight, before or since. He was dead. How could he be here?

Su-Yong Shu gave a contented sigh. Kade could feel the sensual satisfaction of the meal emanating from her. She was not what he'd expected.

"Kade," she said, "I had an ulterior motive for inviting you here. I'll likely have a postdoctoral position opening in my lab soon. I think you'd be a strong candidate. Would you be interested?"

Lightning flashed off to the east. It struck somewhere out beyond the city, flickered for a moment, lit up the sky.

"I'd be honored," he told her. "Can you tell me more about your lab's direction?"

"I have three goals." Shu ticked them off with her fingers, "One, direct brain-to-brain communication. Two, boosting human intelligence to superhuman levels. And three, uploading human minds to machine systems."

Kade blinked.

"This surprises you?" she asked.

He nodded. "I love the goals. But what about the law? The Copenhagen Accords?"

Shu held his gaze. "Laws and treaties change. Those restrictions will end one day. We'll be ready."

Kade felt her again, then. Hints of the future. A time when their work would be unfettered. When they could be free to improve upon the human mind, to expand themselves, uplift themselves, take the next steps in human evolution. Her vision of a future human was sublime. He ached for it. He ached to become it.

And as she projected this vision, he could feel her mind searching for his. She was reaching out, trying to draw him in. Her Nexus nodes sent out affinity pings, looking for complementary nodes in his brain. Kade felt a ripple of it across his mind. The Nexus nodes in his brain resonated in response to Shu's pings, primed to respond, held in check by Nexus OS and by Kade's force of will.

He could not let her see why he was here.

He tried to act natural. "I'm impressed by your vision, Dr Shu. I admire that you're doing this work to be out ahead of the game."

Shu raised her cup of tea to her lips, took a sip, closed her eyes momentarily to savor it. "Yes," she said. "It's always good to be out ahead."

She did something then that Kade didn't understand. New pings emanated from her brain, in a pattern too fast and intricate for him to follow. Colors and shapes flickered in his mind. For a moment he didn't know what had happened, and then he felt the change, saw the errors. Starting somewhere near his midbrain, sets of Nexus nodes had dropped out of his control, were starting to broadcast a pattern of their own, against his will. And it was spreading.

He flicked on one of the defenses that Rangan had created.

[activate: aegis]

Firewalls blocked out all external signals, descending like massive blast shields over his thoughts. Watchdogs activated, isolating the misbehaving nodes in his brain, inundating them with kill signals.

Stay cool, he told himself. He smiled calmly back at Su-Yong Shu.

More errors flashed across his vision. Watchdogs were faltering. Nodes in his mind were reaching out to touch Shu's. Their pattern was spreading within his mind. More and more nodes were rebelling, reaching out to Shu. The power of their broadcast was ratcheting up from microwatts towards milliwatts. Could she hear it yet? He had to stop it before she could.

Kade pulled up the radio firewall's interface, flipped a switch to block out the signal coming from his own brain. It didn't make a difference. The foreign signal continued to spread within his brain, reaching out to Shu's. Nexus OS was faltering now. Errors were piling up. His Nexus nodes were becoming Shu's.

He was losing. His blast shields were crumbling. Nexus nodes in his brain were starting to synchronize with nodes in Shu's. He could feel bits of her mind touching his. Vast and majestic, that's how she felt.

He was fast running out of options. He would need to halt everything in his head.

[system   halt] he commanded. [system   halt]

[system halt]

The command took. Processes collapsed. Windows closed. The serenity package code – which was bolstering his serotonin levels, regulating his pulse and breathing, and suppressing the fear signals propagating through his amygdala – ceased.

The viral pattern didn't stop.

Nexus nodes in his brain continued to reach out to Shu's. Sweat beaded on his brow. His heart jumped into his throat.

Kade was well and truly fucked. Only a single option remained.

Volcano. Mastodon. Cedar.

Kade heard the words, visualized them superimposed. The mantra unfolded within him, a fractal persona expanding into the spaces of his mind, sweeping away bits of memory, identity, and conception, replacing them with, with, with…

The world went blurry for just a moment, then snapped

back into a new focus. Kade blinked. He was dizzy, suddenly – disoriented. He blinked again, lifted his glass of water to his mouth. His hand was trembling. Damn, he was nervous. What had they just been talking about?

"I'm sorry, Professor Shu, what were you saying?" He looked up at her.

19

The Confusion

Wats watched patiently from afar. Dinner was all smiles and ooohs and aaaahs. Then something happened. The smile left Shu's face. She shook her head slightly... And something happened to Kade. A worried look crossed his face, he closed his eyes, his head nodded – like he'd nearly fainted. When he opened his eyes again, something was different. He took a sip of water and his hand shook visibly in the scope. His body language changed. He slumped, seemed to withdraw into himself.

Shu seemed hyper-alert now. On a hunch Wats moved the scope down to ground level. There. The driver of the car that had dropped Kade off, walking briskly towards the restaurant.

Wats judged the distance. No way could he get there first. He reached into his pack, pulled out the highly illegal rifle, screwed on the barrel, slid the scope he'd been using into the groove on top until it snapped into place. He looked at the assembled sniper rifle for a moment. Was he willing to do this? Was he willing to kill? He just didn't know.

"...what were you saying?" Kade asked. He blinked again to try to shake this fog from his head.

Su-Yong Shu was looking at him, her head cocked to one side, lips slightly parted, eyes narrowed, studying him like a particularly puzzling scientific specimen.

"I was saying..." she spoke slowly, as if picking her words carefully, "that it's important to understand ourselves, and what makes us tick."

"Ummm, yes, of course." Whatever had just happened, it was passing. His head was clearing. He must still be jet-lagged.

Kade?

Kade blinked in surprise. Shu's mind had just touched his. She'd just sent him verbal thoughts. Was she using Nexus?

Kade, keep talking. Show no sign that we are communicating this way.

Show no sign? Why?

"I agree completely," he said aloud. "It's important to understand ourselves."

How was she doing this? And what was going on in his head? Why wasn't Nexus OS running? How was she talking to him?

Kade, you can talk to me this way as well. Like... <so>.

He saw it. He felt it.

Hello? he sent to her.

Good, she continued. **You've had some sort of minor... seizure, Kade. I'm trying to understand it. Relax for me. And keep talking as if nothing has happened.**

A chill went up Kade's spine. A seizure? Was it a side effect of the Nexus? Had all their playing with fire finally burnt him?

OK, he sent back.

He felt tendrils of her mind touch him lightly, insinuate themselves into him.

He babbled something to her about his research.

As he did, Kade could feel her in his mind, going deeper, going broader, tendrils of thought branching and spreading throughout him. She felt unlike any other human being he'd ever touched through Nexus. Her mind was everywhere inside his.

Keep talking, she sent him. He rambled, distantly aware that she was nodding, replying.

Stay calm, he told himself. Shu's mind permeated his. She touched memory after memory. It frightened him. He should be resisting. There was something he couldn't let her see…

He was sweating. Her scrutiny was terrible. Her mind was vast, her tendrils everywhere.

Take a deep breath, Kade. Keep calm.

Calm. Yes. He took a breath. He had some way of calming himself… some software he'd written…

Kade, I think someone has been manipulating your memories. They're somehow hiding things from you.

His memories? Oh, fucking fuck. What the hell was going on?

Relax, Shu sent to him. **Open to me fully. I think I can undo what's been done.**

She exuded peace, compassion, tenderness.

It may be a bit disorienting, she went on, **like waking from a dream.**

Kade was confused. His memories *were* hazy. Things didn't make sense. What could have happened?

Shu chattered at him, covering the moment. Something about animal studies. He could barely follow.

I'm restoring your memories… Now, she replied.

He felt her expand even further within him then. She suffused his mind, touched every part of him at once. It was beyond anything he could imagine doing.

He could see links between his memories as she explored them. She was sifting through his thoughts and memories faster than Kade could follow. It was as intense an experience as a Nexus calibration. How was she processing so much information? How could her mind be so vast?

Wait... he remembered now. The memories started to flood back in as Shu unlocked them. The briefing with the ERD. The mission. The defenses Rangan had built. The training. False memories... The panic code. On his phone. A code to call in help. In case he was in danger.

He reached for his phone. Nothing happened. His hand refused to obey. He tried the other. No good. He tried to yell for help. Nothing. Shu had paralyzed him. He was under her control.

Kade, stay calm. We need to understand what's happened to you.

Oh no. He remembered why he was here now. If she saw what was in his mind, she'd know he was a spy. He had to get out of here.

He had one last weapon left. The weapon Rangan had given him. He needed Nexus up and running.

`[restart]`

Boot sequences scrolled across his mind's eye. As he drew his attention Inside, Kade became more aware of Shu's presence.

Shu had synchronized millions of Nexus nodes in his brain to hers. She'd configured them in thousands of complex circuits, each a sensor, each a manipulator. He could feel her fascination as she observed his transformation. Thousands of the circuits were trained on the Nexus OS, studying it, analyzing its parts.

The circuits were in *his* brain. *His* mind. He would take it back from her.

He remembered nights playing push/pull with Rangan, with Ilya, with Wats. They'd use the Nexus synchronicity between their minds to try to maneuver each other's bodies with their thoughts alone. Reaching out with Nexus to try to move Ilya's hand, blink Rangan's eyelid, make a word come out of Wats' mouth. If you could send enough of the right signals into someone else's brain via Nexus, if your signals could be stronger and more coherent than their own, then you could overcome the signals coming from within their own brain. You could control them. That's what Shu was doing to him now.

But no one was better at that than Kade.

He pushed at the circuits she'd built in his mind, aiming to disrupt them, to free his neurons from her invading signals. The circuits flexed, bent, but didn't break. He drew in a breath, pushed harder, gave it everything he had. Circuits snapped, frayed, decohered. Coherence from within his brain squeezed out her foreign signals. For a moment he was almost free of her.

Outside, Shu closed her body's eyes for a moment, continuing with some story. "It was a priceless moment, let me tell you. I find animal subjects just *fascinating*."

I'm not your enemy, she sent him. **Stop fighting me**.

He paused to get his mental breath, and in that break Shu's mind infiltrated his own again. Her circuits began to reassemble inside him. She was putting out an incredible volume of radio traffic, swamping the Nexus nodes in his brain with it. Sensors reformed. Manipulators reformed.

Kade gritted his teeth. If he gave in, she would discover that the ERD had sent him. And when she did…

He clenched his mind with all the effort he could muster, disrupted her circuits once more, pushed her fractionally out of his head. He grunted from the effort. Pain blossomed in the front of his skull. His vision wobbled.

Kade, she sent, **stop. We have much to talk about.**

He couldn't maintain the effort of forcing her out. His mental push faltered. Her thoughts bored back into him, spreading, expanding, going deeper. She was analyzing him, analyzing his thoughts, trying to get into his memories, trying to pry apart his mind, trying to absorb the complexity of the still booting Nexus OS.

How was that possible? Her mind was so vast. She was what Holtzmann had said – a superhuman intelligence, a posthuman. His life would mean nothing to her.

There. The OS was up. A sense of calm descended on him as the serenity package restored his equilibrium. The weapons Rangan had built were his to use once more. He had a momentary flicker of doubt. Should he be doing this?

He saw no other way. Attack her to break her hold on him. Pound the emergency code on the phone. Flee.

`[activate nd*]`

The Nexus disrupter signal blared out of his skull. Filters dampened it within him. Shu's mind recoiled, spasming. She flinched as if she'd been slapped. Kade winced at the pain inside his own skull. Even through the filters it was intense.

He tried to move his hand. Still no good.

He cranked up the disruptor and its matching filters, let them consume all the Nexus nodes they wanted. Static invaded his mind. Not so bad. He could handle it. Not so bad. He ground his teeth together at the pain.

A hand descended on his shoulder. It didn't matter. He could do this. He *must* do this.

ENOUGH!

Shu said the word aloud and inside him at the same time. He felt her mind shift. The signals she sent out cohered, a solid continuous pulse of data from billions of nodes at once, pulsing out at whole watts. It overwhelmed him. His control over the nodes in his brain faltered. They became Shu's. They pulsed, pulsed, pulsed...

All went white. Every sense overloaded, not in static, but in a single coherent wave. Everything was one single pulsing rhythm.

Thought evaporated.

Time evaporated.

Space evaporated.

Identity evaporated.

There was nothing.

Nothing

      but

           this

                white

                      beyond

                            white.

Wats tensed. The driver with the all-too-familiar face came up the stairs to the roof. Kade's back was to him. The driver crossed the distance between them at a walk, careful to not alarm the serving staff. Wats flicked the safety off of his rifle.

The driver's back was square in the center of his sights.

If he did shoot... would one shot take him down? It had taken many, many bullets to take down the last man he'd seen with that face.

He had to decide. Fire now, on a bad hunch? Kill on incomplete data? Or watch the situation?

Wats took a deep breath. They were in public. Kade had been seen with Shu. If they were going to kill him, they wouldn't do it in plain sight.

He watched the driver's hand come down on Kade's shoulder. Wats tensed. Then... nothing. He exhaled, but kept the crosshairs on the back of the driver's head.

20

Only Human

Consciousness returned slowly, in fragments. He was alive. His name was Kade. Kaden Lane.

Vision faded back in, slowly, disorientingly. Shu was looking at him. How long had he been gone? How long had he been back? He tried to speak, found that he could not. His heart pounded in his chest. He tried to throw his mind at hers, found that it was just as restrained. He willed his hand to move towards the phone in his pocket, and it would not obey him. The Nexus disrupter was no longer running. He tried to start it again. The Nexus OS ignored him.

A chill went up his spine. Just like that, he'd lost. Su-Yong Shu controlled him.

This is what we did to Sam, he realized.

He could feel Shu rifling through his mind, his memories. The creation of Nexus OS. The party. The bust. The briefing about her. The mission they'd sent him on.

You're a fool, Kaden Lane.

I didn't want to be here, he sent. **I was blackmailed.**

He felt no pity from her, no sympathy. **You could have come to me**, she sent. **You could have told me. I would**

have protected you. You and I, we're alike. We're on the same side.

Are we? he wondered.

They accused you of things, Kade sent back to her. **They showed me evidence. You used Nexus to kill people and to coerce them. You took over their minds like you're taking over mine.**

She struck him then, with her mind. It hurt like hell. He could feel the stinging across his face, as if she'd reached out with her right hand and slapped him. Harder. Like she'd broken bones in his face, left him bleeding and bruised. He couldn't even flinch. He blinked, breathed in through his nose. His face ached. Tears welled up in his eyes.

You arrogant child, Shu sent to him. **How dare you lecture me on morality. Do you know the things those monsters you serve have done? Here. See them!**

He saw images from Shu's mind. A Chinese scientist found dead in a Saigon brothel; a Range Rover, found at the foot of a cliff in the Australian outback, bodies charred beyond recognition; a famous Indian AI researcher, no identifiable pieces of her remaining after a car bomb in Delhi; an American geneticist, found in an apparent suicide in his home; more.

The worst. Yang Wei, her mentor, the Nobel Prize-winning neuroscientist who'd trained her, one of the greatest minds she'd ever known, burning to death, trapped in his limousine after the Americans had attacked it, dying in agony as Shu watched helplessly.

Her mind was full of rage, full of hate. She despised them.

They kill to stop progress, she sent, **to stop science that frightens them. To stop our evolution. How could you work with them?**

Kade trembled. **They called you a killer. They said**

you helped your government assassinate people. You built the tools.

Su-Yong Shu sighed mentally. She emanated regret. **They used the tools I built, yes. My government is little better than yours. They take science, and they pervert it.**

So it was true, then. They'd used her tools to kill.

They'll do the same to you, Shu sent to him. **They'll use your tools in ways you never intended.**

I won't let them, he replied.

Shu mentally scoffed at him. **They won't ask your permission.**

I'll stop them, he told her. **I will.**

Another image bubbled up in Kade's thoughts. Su-Yong Shu in front of rows of identical Confucian Fist soldiers, arms spread widely as if to say "ta-da!" **They said you helped China make soldiers. Clone soldiers. Human robots.**

Her mind hardened in anger.

There's one right behind you. Why don't you ask him what he thinks? She sounded cold, dangerous.

The hand on his shoulder.

Feng's voice echoed laughter in Kade's mind. **Robot! I like it. Robot's strong, made of titanium and carbon fiber. Bulletproof!**

"Feng," Shu said aloud, "why don't you sit and help us with this food? We seem to have more than we need."

Feng sat next to Kade, heaped a plate up with food, radiating appetite and amusement.

You're a clone, Kade sent him, **a slave. They showed me.**

Feng laughed in Kade's mind again, his mouth full of noodles. **Clone, yeah. Like I told you, big family! Lots of brothers. Slave? That's what they wanted. But I'm**

free. My brothers too. Thanks to her.

"Mmm, good noodles!"

Shu cut in. **I could not tolerate the thought of posthumans as slaves to mere humans.**

Dr Shu, I give up, Kade sent. **I'm sorry any of this happened. How can I persuade you to let me go?**

Shu sipped her tea, her face turned towards the lightning coming down east of Bangkok. "I think the storm's coming closer," she said. "Don't you?"

Kade felt some control of his body return. He turned to look. Maybe the lightning was a little closer. It was hard to say.

You're a very dangerous man, Kaden Lane. Your government is right to fear you. This technology we have is explosive in its potential. How could baseline humans compete with us?

I don't mean to harm anyone, he told her. **I never did.**

You're only barely in control of your own mind, she scoffed. **Your intentions mean next to nothing right now.**

Kade said nothing. They sat in silence for a moment.

Come to my lab, she sent him. **Accept the postdoc. Let the ERD think you're spying for them.**

That hatred for the ERD. He could feel it at every thought of them.

Shu continued. **We can feed them enough to keep them at bay. And in the meantime, we'll do some remarkable things of our own.**

It washed over him. Images and plans from her mind. Mere glimpses. Paths towards boosted intelligence. Uploading minds from brains and into computers. Savant-like cognitive powers. Super memory. Pattern recognition that would put any data miner to shame. Knowledge banks shared mind to mind. True merger into group beings. Transformations of politics, economics, art... Intelligence and creativity that could pry apart the deepest mysteries of physics, of math, of every science known to man.

She would change the world. She would lift the human mind to new heights. He could be part of it. A posthuman, upgraded through her knowledge, empowered to help build this new world.

It was intoxicating. It was everything he wanted. How could he possibly say no?

Never swallow what they're selling whole. Ilya had said that. He had to fight to hang onto his skepticism, to push back against this seduction.

Would your government pervert my science as well? he asked her. **Would they turn my discoveries into weapons?**

Shu looked out at the horizon. He could feel the edges of her thoughts. She was thinking of something that had happened a long long time ago.

We hide the most important work, she said. **But we have to give them some progress. For now.**

And when does it stop? he asked.

Soon, she sent him. She sounded cold and distant in his mind. **There is a war coming. A world war. Not between China and America. Between humans and posthumans. You see it all around you. The humans are doing everything they can to prevent the posthuman transition from occurring. While we are struggling to be free of their controls.**

War. He turned the word over in his mind. **A world war. People will die.**

Look at the big picture, Kade. Imagine a world full of beings as far beyond humans as humans are beyond chimps. That is the future we could inhabit.

That is a future we could help bring about. Doesn't that sound like a worthy goal?

It did. She knew it did.

Isn't that something worth making some sacrifices for? she asked him.

He struggled for the right words, the right way to explain it.

Other people's lives aren't yours to sacrifice, he sent.

Shu shrugged mentally. **The world has more than eight billion people on it**, she sent. **Surely we can afford to lose a few.**

That's what it came down to then. Would he be willing to let a few die to make the world a better place? A few dozen? A few thousand? A few million? Where would he draw the line?

Who would he kill for the freedom to improve his own mind? Who would he kill to rise to new heights? Who would he kill so that posthumans might be born?

Shu caught the thrust of his thoughts. **This is directed evolution**, she sent. **How many generations would this take natural selection? Millions? The faster we uplift ourselves, the fewer who need die. Join me. Help move the work forward.**

War. War over the human condition. War for the right to change oneself. War to create humanity's successor species. War to usher in a utopia. Had it begun already? Was the ERD an army, fighting to keep posthumans from coming into existence?

And evolution. Evolution was a bloody process indeed. War would mean epic numbers of dead.

It was too much for him. He was in over his head. He needed to step back, collect himself.

I need to think about this, Dr Shu.

He did his best to stay calm. This was too much, too

much. **It's a lot all at once**, he sent.

She looked him in the eye. He could feel her evaluating him, feeling out his mind.

Of course, she replied.

Shu nodded, picked up the thread of their out-loud conversation. "Feng, what do you think of the weather?"

Feng lifted his eyes from his food to the horizon.

"Definitely coming this way," Feng said. "Rain here again in half an hour."

A thought struck Kade. **Why don't you leave China? Why not come to the US?**

Shu snorted mentally. **I'd be even less free in your country. My government doesn't object to posthumans, so long as the first posthumans are Chinese. They want control. Fools. As if such beings will be bound by nationality.**

So why not go somewhere else? Here in Thailand, maybe?

We're not all so free. He got a sense then, of an obligation, a mother's love. An image of a young girl, long black hair, dark eyes. Her daughter.

Her name is Ling, she sent him. **It means "compassion."**

She's your daughter.

Yes.

She's the leverage they have over you? he asked.

She's part of it, Shu replied.

Kade caught a glimpse of something else, then. An image of Shu, a younger Shu, a pregnant Shu, her belly huge, in a surgical theatre, her skull shaven, frightened, alone, in pain, about to go through something no one else had yet survived... And then something so huge it sent him reeling. A network of processors, vast computing power, vast storage. An incredible mind, epic in scope, something that subsumed Su-Yong Shu, stretched beyond her.

"Oh my god." He said it out loud, before he could control himself.

"Yes, it's beautiful." She was staring out at the sky, covering his gaffe.

Is that you? he asked her. **You're an upload? You were sick... Is that it? You were forced to try. And you succeeded. You're the first digital being...**

His mind was spinning. He was trying to make sense of the glimpse he'd seen.

She didn't answer for a moment. Kade felt the dread and awe climb up his spine, set the hairs on the back of his neck on end, chilling him even in the warm Bangkok night.

Please, she replied, **I shouldn't have let you see that. The less you know, the safer for both of us.**

They sat in silence for a while, watching the lightning illuminate the eastern sky.

"I think you should come visit my lab in Shanghai," Shu said aloud. "And perhaps your collaborator Rangan Shankari as well. You'll get to see the lab, meet the other postdocs and graduate students, some of the other faculty. We can get a better sense if there would be a good fit."

Say yes, she urged him. **Your masters will believe you've done your part. We'll have time to discuss more later.**

Thank you, Kade sent to her.

"I think that's a wonderful idea. Thank you for the invitation."

The check came.

Feng went to fetch the car, left them watching the storm approaching on the horizon. Lightning struck again, closer. Thunder boomed seconds later. Raindrops touched the far side of the river.

"Come, Kade," Shu said a few minutes later. "Feng will

have the car by now. We can drop you off at your next engagement." He felt her release him fully, then. His body and his mind were his once more. It felt good.

The Opal pulled around, glistening in the rain that was now beginning to fall. Feng held open the door for Shu, and then for Kade, and then they were on their way. They drove in silence for a few moments, before Shu reached out to him again.

You will need to choose soon, Kade. Organizations like the ERD exist to stop humans from taking the next step. Conflict is inevitable. She paused. **You have to decide if you're on the side of progress... or on the side of stagnation.**

Kade considered that.

I'm on the side of peace, he sent, **and freedom.**

Shu mentally chuckled. **You are so naïve.**

Kade didn't reply. Wet, neon-streaked streets slid by outside the car's windows.

Kade, Shu sounded more serious now, **the ERD will probe your memories of our dinner. We must prepare you for that, with an alternate script. Open yourself to me.**

Do I have a choice? he asked her.

I won't force you. But if our conversation is unearthed by the ERD, it will not go well for you or those you care about.

False memories. Again. Yet she was right.

Will I forget what just happened? he asked her.

Oh no. I am not so crude. You will remember. But I will give you a second set of memories you can share with others. You will only forget the truth if you are under duress.

Kade sighed. There was no way around this.

OK, he sent her. **Let's get on with it.**

He opened his mind to her. Her thoughts flowed into him, suffused him, pressed all else aside. Consciousness receded.

When he came to, he felt the same. Then she showed him, and he understood. He remembered the truth. And he remembered an alternate event, just a slight twist on what had actually happened.

It awed him. In minutes she'd made a change to his mind of a subtlety and sophistication he wouldn't have believed possible. His mind could be completely hers, Kade realized. Shu could do anything with him that she wanted. The scope of her ability to manipulate his mind was staggering.

She was posthuman already.

Wats watched through the scope of the rifle as the man with the all-too-familiar face left Shu and Kade and headed back to the car. Wats used the scope to capture images of that face and video of his gait. Who was this man who was driving Shu?

Could he be wrong on the face? He didn't think so. The last man to wear that face had made a powerful impression. He'd killed four heavily augmented special forces Marines with his bare hands before they'd taken him down. That wasn't something Wats was likely to forget.

Could this be the reason the ERD had sent Kade here? Did it have to do with this man? With Shu?

If so, why Kade?

And did this have anything to do with the monk who'd followed Kade and Cataranes to their hotel the night before?

The unknowns were piling up.

The car was coming around to the front of the restaurant now. Wats packed up his gear and prepared to follow.

21
Wild at Heart

Shu studied Kade as the glossy black Opal pulled up in front of the Wild at Heart bar where the neuroscience students' mixer was to be held.

"Here you go," Feng said as he opened the door for the boy to exit. "Door to door service!"

"That was very stimulating, Kade," Shu told him. "Let's talk soon."

"It was, Dr Shu. Thank you for dinner. I'll be in touch on the dates for the Shanghai visit." He shook her hand and turned. "And it was good to meet you, Feng. I'm glad we talked." Kade nodded, held up his hand in salutation, and was gone.

Feng got back into the driver's seat.

Thoughts? Shu asked him.

Feng put the car in gear, looked both ways, cautiously eased back into the riotous traffic of Bangkok. Shu knew he was taking the time to collect himself, to be sure he knew his own mind before he answered her. Always so careful, after all this time.

I made them that way, she reminded herself.

The boy is dangerous, Feng sent to her. **He poses a**

great risk.

He could be a great asset, Shu replied. **He's done impressive work to have come so far so fast.**

Not as impressive as your accomplishments, Feng told her.

Feng, the humans outnumber us by orders of magnitude, she sent back. **No matter how capable I am, I can't do it alone. I can't do it with just the team in Shanghai. If we're going to prevail, we need more on our side. More who can move the frontiers forward. Those individuals are rare. Kade is one of them.**

Is that the only reason? Feng asked.

He knew her too well. The old anger rose up. The painful memories. Yang Wei, her mentor, burning to death in that limo, a victim of the CIA. Along with…

Nausea struck her. Her hand went unbidden to her belly. She forced herself to pull it away. This body was a traitor. Anger was better than sorrow.

I hate them, Feng. The CIA, the ERD, they are the same. I despise them for the beautiful minds they've destroyed. I hate them for the pain they've inflicted. And yes, I resent the ERD for using him as a weapon against me. How dare they? The ignorant, venomous fools. I'm not a machine, Feng. I feel emotions as strongly as ever. And what I feel towards the Americans is rage.

Feng was silent for a moment, then spoke into her mind. **You could compel him.**

Shu chuckled. Was Feng testing her?

You know my view on that, she replied. **If I took control of him, what would that say to anyone else? Would I need to control them all? How much would they accomplish as my puppets? I would become no**

better than our masters, and no more effective. No. We're most capable as autonomous beings who choose to come together. Our associations must be voluntary.

She felt Feng's satisfaction with her answer. If it was a test, she'd passed. The line between loyalty and compulsion remained clear.

I remain concerned, Feng sent. The Americans respect you. They will not settle for surface answers. They may burrow deep, even destructively so. The memories and block you implanted may not hold.

They won't harm him, Shu insisted. They want to use him to spy on me. And short of quite destructive methods, what I've done will hold.

Perhaps, Feng replied.

The Americans can't hurt me, at any rate.

Perhaps.

Feng refused to accept just how unassailable she'd become.

They can inconvenience you, he sent. Greatly.

Yes, she replied. That they can.

They can perhaps goad our masters into hurting you, Feng went on. Or worse.

It was a possibility. One that bore more safeguards against it.

So what do you recommend? she asked.

Feng was silent for a moment, threading the Opal through wet Bangkok traffic.

I think the Americans should not get the chance to deeply interrogate Kaden Lane.

You mean that we should liberate him? she asked. Or that we should kill him?

Feng was silent again.

I mean that the Americans should not get the

chance to interrogate Kaden Lane.

I doubt our masters would agree to either silencing him or whisking him away to China on such short notice, she sent.

Feng took his time replying.

What they do not know of, they need not agree to, he sent. **Accidents happen. Bangkok is a dangerous place.**

You've become so hard, Feng, she sent him. **You would kill this boy? An innocent?**

Your safety is my priority. He threatens it.

What about the woman, the agent he's with?

Feng considered. **Challenging. Not impossible.**

I would rather have him alive, and on our side, than dead.

You may not have that choice, Feng replied. **We must all act within the choices we are given.**

Su-Yong Shu leaned back into the plush seat of the Opal, and contemplated.

The Wild at Heart bar was a sprawling three-story club in the heart of Bangkok's tourist district. It was 9pm, halfway into the 8pm to 10pm mixer, and the place was packed with students attending the conference. Kade meandered through the throng, lost in thought. What had he expected of Shu? That she'd be completely innocent of what the ERD had accused her of? That she'd be a monster?

She was neither. The opportunity she was offering him was beyond his wildest dreams. Could he accept it? Could he fool the ERD? Could he live with himself if his work was weaponized, was used to harm innocents?

Could he become posthuman? A demigod? An immortal?

He got in line for a drink, peeled off two hundred-baht

bills for something strong and alcoholic. The Nexus link on his phone came alive before the drink reached his lips.

[sam] Welcome back. Meet me on the roof.

Kade shrugged and made his way to the roof, downing his drink as he went. Show time. Again.

He found Sam with her back to the party, looking out onto the street and the chaotic, rain-soaked capital of Thailand.

"Hey."

"Hi there." She smiled at him, put her hand on his arm.

[sam] Put your arm around me.
[kade] What?
[sam] Just do it.

She turned back to the street, leaning against the banister. Kade grimaced, put his arm around her, joined her in leaning out for a view. Sam pressed her body closer. The rain made the night almost cool. Her body was distinctly warm, and firm, and curved under his hand…

[sam] Give me your other hand.
[sam] I need a few drops of your blood.
[kade] What?
[sam] I need to see if she's dosed you with anything.
[kade] I would have told you.
[sam] Maybe. If you knew. If you could. Hold out your hand.

Kade did as he was told. Sam took his free hand in hers. With her other hand she produced a small black rectangular device. She pressed it against the tip of his finger. He felt a brief sting, then a tiny bit of suction. Sam held it there for a few seconds, removed it, put it back in her pocket.

She snuggled against him, gave him a smile. "So, you had a good dinner?"

[sam] How'd it go?

[kade] Good. She invited me to come visit the lab, see if I was a good fit for the postdoc position.

[sam] Excellent. Now, walk me through the dinner. Let me see it and hear it from your perspective.

Show time indeed. Kade let himself sink into the alternate memories Shu had scripted in his mind. They fit like a mask, like a garment over his mind, like a role he was playing on a stage. He opened himself to Sam.

She roamed through his memories of the night. He watched her. She skimmed the early part of the conversation, focused on the work portion, absorbed the deliciousness of the meal, the sensuality Shu exuded as she savored the food.

Kade found himself becoming aroused. Sam's body felt good against his. She was snuggled against him, his hand on the swell of her hip. She felt firm, athletic, and still she had these curves... He could smell her hair. He liked her warmth, her touch.

Sam noticed his response. She moved fractionally further away, opening a tiny space between their bodies. His hand was still on her hip, but the message was clear: *This is just an act, buddy.*

Kade sighed. It wasn't like he *wanted* to be turned on by Samantha Cataranes.

Sam went back to sifting through his memories. She scanned the dinner and conversation from beginning to end. If she detected any flaw, if she was suspicious in any way, she didn't show it.

Sam and Kade's phones buzzed simultaneously. It was a message from Narong:

Meet me out front of mixer at 10.15 to head to the afterparty?

[kade] What's this afterparty about?

[sam] It's a chance to get closer to Narong, which means closer to Suk Prat-Nung and his uncle Ted. We're going.

[kade] You're the boss.

They went back into the mixer, mingled for another hour; 10pm came. The mixer was officially over. Some students elected to stay and continue their drinking at the Wild at Heart Bar. Others filed out into the rainy night. Sam dragged Kade out to the front entrance. Narong met them there.

"So where's this afterparty?" Sam asked.

"It's in Sukhumvit," Narong answered. "You know the city?"

"A little," Sam replied.

"It's off of Soi Sama Han, just east of the Nana District." He looked out at the rain. "We can take a cab most of the way, then walk a few blocks."

Sam's interest was piqued. Soi Sama Han, eh?

"Is that near Sukchai Market?" she asked.

Narong looked surprised. "It's a few blocks from there. We don't have to go near it, really. There's a different way."

"I'd love to see it, actually. I've heard a lot of stories about it."

Narong looked uncomfortable again. "Well, it's not the classiest area..."

Sam laughed. "I'm a big girl. I'm a scientist. I'm really curious."

Narong searched her eyes, as if trying to determine how much she could handle. Or how much he could trust her. He made a decision. "OK. Just stick with me and do what I say when we're there. Kade, that sound OK by you?"

Kade exuded mild befuddlement. "Sure, I'm down for whatever."

Narong shrugged again, picked out his umbrella from the basket by the door, and stepped out. He whistled to hail a tuk-tuk. The three of them climbed into its back, Sam squeezed between Kade and Narong. She could feel Kade studiously trying to ignore the way her body was pressed against his. And Narong? She didn't need a Nexus connection to read what was on his mind.

The tuk-tuk zipped through wet traffic. The streets were glossy black with streaks of supersaturated neon. Reds, blues, greens, yellows – a rainbow of reflected light. Rain got in through the open sides, spraying them gently. Sam stayed driest in the middle. With the rain and the wind from the open sides of the tuk-tuk, Bangkok was pleasantly cool for once.

The tuk-tuk dodged cheap Tata two-seater cars from India, knock-off Vespas from Vietnam, the occasional Hyundai four-seater taxi, pedestrians making their way across wet streets in the rain.

They passed down urban valleys of towering glass-and-steel office blocks, their neon-lit ground floors stuffed with noodle shops, massage parlors, boutiques, discount electronic stores, pharmacies, bars. Golden shrines and temples dotted the urban landscapes, some tiny, some sprawling, spires and Buddhas and fearsome temple guardian statues. At 10.30pm everything was open, restaurants, shops, bars, temples. People filed in through temple gates, incense sticks in hand, while across the street rock music blared out of red-lit bars.

They turned on to Sukhumvit 4, the infamous Soi Nana Tai, one of Bangkok's more popular sex districts. Open air bars with neon signs lined the narrow street. Foot traffic slowed their tuk-tuk to a crawl. Women in tiny miniskirts and short-shorts and improbably large breasts for their tiny frames were everywhere. The men were Indian, Chinese, or white. The women were uniformly Thai, young, and for hire. They sat on men's laps, draped themselves over them at the bars, danced lasciviously with each other, and waited for the customers to take them home, for a price.

Sam felt Kade tense next to her. His eyes were wide. So much sex on sale. Narong was looking down at his hands.

A raven haired girl – in tiny hot pants and a matching white bikini top – blew a kiss at their tuk-tuk. Sam doubted she was eighteen.

Such a strange country, Sam thought to herself. A quarter million monks who don't drink or smoke or swear. A quarter million prostitutes filling in all the spaces where the monks aren't.

Then again... She spotted a shaven-headed man, Thai, wearing normal clothes, with a black-miniskirted girl on his lap. Maybe the monks are here too.

The tuk-tuk slowly wound its way down the street. A neon sign advertised live orgy shows. The crude animation depicted a woman's body between that of two men, both of them thrusting into her in unison. Kade's head tracked it as they passed.

"Is this that market you were talking about? Sukchai?" he asked. Sam could feel his conflicting revulsion, arousal, and fascination.

"No," Sam answered.

"This is just sex," Narong elaborated. "Sukchai Market is

more… exotic." He didn't sound comfortable.

They turned onto a side street. Soi Sama Han. They threaded through traffic, turned onto another, smaller side street. There was no street sign. They were close.

The tuk-tuk pulled up to a tiny alley between buildings. "We're here," Narong said. He paid the driver. "You still sure you want to see Sukchai?"

Sam nodded. Kade shrugged.

"Stay with me while we're in the market," Narong said, unfurling the umbrella above them. "Not everything here is strictly legal. You'll look less suspicious with me as your guide."

He led them into the maze of alleyways.

Wats paused on the street, near where the tuk-tuk had left Kade and his companions. The alley they'd gone down… there was little reason to head down that alley except to reach Sukchai. What were they doing there? He knew Sukchai well. It would be difficult to follow them without being conspicuous.

He looked up into the rain. The buildings were tightly spaced here. Yes, that would do. He slipped into the shadows, tightened the straps of the pack across his back, put his hands to the brick, and began to climb.

Briefing

The Chandler Act (aka the Emerging Technological Threats Act of 2032) is the opening salvo in a new War on Science. To understand the future course of this war, one need only look at the history of the War on Drugs and the War on Terror. Like those two manufactured "wars", this one will be never-ending, freedom-destroying, counterproductive, and ultimately understood to have caused far more damage than the supposed threat it was aimed at ever could have.

FREE THE FUTURE, 2032

22

The Bazaar of the Bizarre

Sam kept her eye on Narong as he led them on a winding zigzag path through the narrow alleys. A pair of burly toughs lounged at one intersection, leaning against brick walls, heedless of the rain, improbably huge muscles bulging in their arms and chests. Narong nodded fractionally, kept walking.

One more turn beyond the toughs and a much wider alleyway opened. Stalls and shops lined both sides, neon and LED lit the air, scores of people moved down the lane, hundreds of people. They paused at the stalls, talked quietly, inspected wares and price sheets, haggled in low voices. Everything had a furtive air. Collars were turned up, hoods pulled over heads and down over faces. Two more inhumanly muscular men loitered at the intersection, glowering.

Muscle grafts, Sam thought. Inefficient, draining, but intimidating. They'll probably die of enlarged hearts trying to support all that mass.

Narong led them down the street. Sam let Kade and the Thai student share the umbrella. She walked a few steps behind them. The rain felt good on her face. Her tactical contacts snapped every face, recorded every gait, uploaded them for analysis and identification.

Kade's eyes were everywhere. The wide alley was bustling with people, with woks going over open fires, with sights and smells, and with vendors offering their wares.

The first few stalls were reproductive services. Sex selection. Ova fusion to make a child from two mothers, no father necessary. Tri-fusion to create a child with genes from two fathers and a surrogate mother. Gene tweaks for your kids. Height, eye color, hair color, muscle mass, weight, health, IQ, charisma. "Other services by request."

Reprogenetics gave way to bio-cosmetics. Semi-nude men and women modeled the wares. A petite copper-skinned beauty in a skimpy bikini posed in front of a shop advertising skin color transformation viruses. Less dramatic melanin therapy was on sale to make Asian skin lighter, Caucasian skin more tan, or whatever the customer might desire.

The semi-nude woman at the next stall showed living tattoos. A bioluminescent dragon crawled up from below her navel, climbed its way up her chest, a claw gripping her left breast. The tattoo snaked around her neck and returned on her right side. Its eyes glowed amber. She tensed her muscles and it moved, tail swishing, scales changing colors, glowing flames erupting from its mouth and nostrils.

Fat cutters. Fat boosters. Nordic cheekbones. Square jaws. Almond-eye shapes. Golden eyes. Cat-slit eyes. Hair curling viruses. Hair straightening viruses. Forked tongues. Prehensile tongues. Height therapy. The signs and models promised it all, no surgery required. However you wished to alter your appearance, from mild to wild, the gene hackers of Sukchai Market could reprogram your cells to make it happen, provided you had the cash.

"Are these things all for real?" Kade asked, voice hushed.

Narong shrugged. "Probably some scams here. But mostly, yeah. Is it safe? Different question."

"What do you mean?" Kade asked.

"Gene hacking. Sometimes they miss the gene they want, you know? Break something else. Cancer, maybe. Or worse. You hear stories."

"But don't they test this stuff? Safety trials, that sort of thing?"

"There's no FDA on this street, man. You wanna try something? You ask around about the shop, make sure there's no horror stories, make sure they have a good reputation, a clean reputation."

Bio-cosmetics gave way to bio-erotics. Booths offered viral gene injections to deliver enlarged or firmed "natural" breasts, larger penises, enhanced orgasms, porn star feats of stamina and recovery.

A banner advertised female arousal superchargers with a choice of delivery vehicle. Transform virus for permanent changes. Tasteless odorless liquid for short-term effect. The booth was thronged, the customers entirely male. Large bundles of cash changed hands for syringes and small vials. Kade was simultaneously agape and aroused.

"Tasteless and odorless...?" Kade wondered.

"...so you can spike someone's drink with it," Sam answered for him.

His revulsion overwhelmed what arousal there had been.

Bio-neurals followed bio-erotics. Stay-awakes. Sleep reduction hacks. Extroverters. Dream recall enhancers. Dream suppressers. Love injections. Heartbreak erasers. Viral pair-bonding therapy. Monogamy shots. Sexual orientation shifters in temporary and permanent varieties. Savant drugs claimed to put the customer in a hyper-productive or hyper-creative trance. A superbright LED sign offered viral injections to boost musical ability. Another to remove guilt. A third to intensify religious faith and spiritual experiences. There were customers perusing and discussing at all of the booths.

Sam hardened herself. These were the worst. These were the ones that could be used as weapons, to control and degrade and enslave. She captured every face she saw, searched for any sign of Communion virus, of DWITY. None in sight. But who knew what could be provided if you asked the right person? She thought of Chris Evans, physically and mentally crippled in busting a DWITY ring. It made her angry.

Kade sensed her mood. He sent her a sense of curiosity, an unspoken question.

Sam ignored it.

Extreme medicine came next. A tall glass cylinder housed human organs in clear, bubbling fluid. Hearts, livers, kidneys, available for transplantation. Cloned organs from your own cells speed-grown in just a few days. Another stall offered viral therapy it claimed would trigger regeneration of severed digits or limbs.

"Why is this stuff down here?" Kade asked. "Shouldn't this be in a mainstream hospital?"

"Probably non-human genes," Narong said. "The super fast-growing organs are hacked way outside human parameters. And the regeneration hacks use genes from some lizard: newts or geckos or something like that. Not legal to insert into a human."

Sam wondered if any of this would be of use to Chris Evans. Could it get him back on his feet faster? End his isolation more quickly?

She glanced back at the bio-neurals. Such vile stuff.

Chris risked his life fighting shit like that.

Was it possible to separate the mind control from the cloned organs and regeneration? To embrace one and not the other?

She pushed the thought out of her mind. She had a job to do. She had laws she was sworn to uphold.

The modifications on offer became progressively more extreme as they neared the end of the market. Muscle grafts, like those the local thugs sported. Genetic gender reassignment. Supercharged hemoglobin with ten times the oxygen capacity. More.

"You have to be careful of a lot of this stuff," Narong commented. "Change one thing in the body, it has ripple effects on a dozen other things. Let alone the brain. What kind of side effects are you going to see ten or twenty years from now? Who the hell knows?"

"You seem to have thought a lot about this, Narong," Sam observed.

Narong was silent for a while. "It's hard not to. We'd be better off if this was all legal. It's all wink-wink, nudge-nudge now. The law's not enforced. But no one studies the safety either. People come here to shop, but can they even be sure they're getting what's advertised? And even if they are, no one knows the long-term effects. Keeping it gray leaves it in limbo, makes it sketchy. We oughta pull this stuff up into the light of day, regulate it, test it for safety and quality."

Sam could feel Kade's agreement with Narong's sentiment. She had a different view.

Lock them all up and throw away the key. Hold the line, make it real. Don't let this stuff sweep our humanity away.

She kept her opinion to herself.

Sam looked down at her own hand, strong beyond any human possibility, reformed by science into a superhuman weapon to better hold the line against superhuman technologies.

And me? Where does the non-human DNA in my cells fit in? Where does the Nexus in my brain fit in?

A line from Nietzsche came to her, one Nakamura liked to quote in his more cynical moments.

He who fights too long against dragons becomes a dragon himself; and if you stare too long into the abyss, the abyss stares also into you.

Here she was, staring into the abyss again. Here she was fighting dragons. Here she was part dragon herself.

She shook her head to clear the melancholy. She was a soldier. She'd made compromises to protect others. This stuff needed to be kept under control.

One raid could clean this place out, she realized. They could round up hundreds of these sellers and buyers in one swoop.

And another market would spring up the next day somewhere else. Is there any real solution?

They came to the end of the market. Two more enforcers leaned against the walls, deliberately casual, their grotesquely huge muscles sending all the message that was needed: *Don't fuck with us.* They eyed Narong and Kade and Sam as they passed, made no move to stop them.

"That's Sukchai," Narong said. "The party's a few blocks from here. Come on."

Kade turned the things he'd seen in Sukchai over in his head as they walked. Narong was right. They'd be safer if these technologies were legalized, regulated, tested for safety...

Holtzmann's offer came to him unbidden.

You could come work for me, here at the ERD, the scientist had offered.

He'd rejected it out of hand, but was there some merit in

it? Could he change the system from the inside? Could he help nudge them towards a better way to treat these technologies? Holtzmann was a scientist, surely he wasn't a knee-jerk prohibitionist too?

Kade wandered a maze of choices as Narong led them through the maze of alleys.

Wats paced them across the rooftops, leaping lightly from one to the next. No one below looked up to see him. If they had, they would have caught only a faintly darker patch against the dark backdrop of rain and cloud.

23

Buddha's Kiss

The party was in a club in an alley off another unnamed side street off of Soi Sama Han. Sam read the name of the place, written in Thai above the door. *Joob Phajaow*. Buddha's Kiss, she mentally translated. An irreverent name in a normally devout society. Faint music and the sounds of voices filtered through.

It was a quiet, trendy area, close to the seedy debauchery of the Nana sex district, close to the illicit fruits of Sukchai, but buffered from both. Just the kind of place young, upwardly mobile Thais might choose to party, Sam thought.

Narong pressed the button next to the heavy brass door. It cracked open. A muscular Thai bouncer waved them in.

Low couches filled the establishment. The walls were painted red and gold, inlaid with Thai script, lotus flowers, Buddhas. Fashionable young Thai and a few foreigners lounged in threes and fours, smiling and talking, holding stylish glasses of clear and colored booze. A trio in the corner smoked scented tobacco out of an elaborate hookah. A bar of bronze and dark wood stretched across one wall, bottles backlit in orange. Sultry, beat-inflected flux grooves filled the space. A DJ stood in the corner, shades over his eyes, oversized headphones on his ears, gently rocking to his own beat as he tapped away on the console before him. Three Thai women in their twenties swayed on the small dance floor before him in short metallic skirts and gold bangles.

Narong led them to the bar, spoke in rapid-fire Thai to the bartender.

The bartender turned to Kade. "You know DJ Axon?" he asked over the music and the crowd.

"Yeah," Kade raised his voice to be heard. "He's my best friend. We're in school together."

"Well, you bring him here sometime, and we'll show him a good time!"

The bartender's name was Yindee, and the first round was on him. The drinks were heavy on coconut milk and alcohol, with a hint of lemongrass, and very very tasty.

Narong took them around the club, introducing them to people. Here were Baroma and Lalana, Yama and Jao, Tonga and Chuan and Rajni. This was Rajni's French friend Pierre. Zuka was from Zimbabwe and worked on the neural basis of morality. Will was very British and on his way to very drunk. Loesan was the president of the Thai Neuroscience Students Association, and a brilliant neuro-linguist. The DJ's name was Sajja. And on it went.

Sam's tactical contacts faceprinted them all. The one named Chuan was suspected of being involved in Nexus trafficking in a minor way. Baroma maintained an anarchist blog called *EatTheWest* that he thought was anonymous, but was likely all talk. None of the rest had raised any suspicions.

The DJ mixed smoothly into a new track. Sam felt Kade smile. It was a Rangan Shankari original, a tribute to his friend, a welcome to them. She had a flash of the party she'd met Shankari at, of how she'd instantly *known* so much about every song he played, the information beamed into her head via Nexus 5. She remembered her surprised delight when it had happened.

Stay focused, Sam.

She pushed it out of her head, concentrated on the job. No sign of Suk Prat-Nung so far. But getting closer with Narong and his friends might still pay dividends down the road.

Kade was enjoying himself, holding court, flirting with the young Thai woman named Lalana, telling stories of his adventures with the famous DJ Axon. Lalana was laughing, hanging on his every word.

Sam peered beyond them, watched the young women on the dance floor. They were taking turns peeling small pink tabs off a sheet, then sensually affixing them to each other's throats. Soon two of the women were dancing closer, hips and waists pressed together. They kissed open-mouthed. The third one pressed up behind them, her hands roving across the others' bodies.

"It's called Sappho," Narong spoke into her ear. "It gets girls into girls. Lasts a few hours."

Sam turned. He was very close. "Is there one that gets boys into boys?" she asked.

Narong nodded. "The working boys in Patpong take it. A lot of them are only into men for the money. Makes their job more fun."

"And you?"

Narong shrugged. "It was fun. I prefer girls, though." He put his hands on her hips.

Sam pulled away, wagged her finger at him. "Not so fast, mister. We American *women* aren't all so easy."

Come on, Narong. Impress me. Lead me to Suk Prat-Nung and his uncle Ted.

Narong laughed and took her around to meet more of his friends.

The party grew as more people trickled in. Sajja and a few others cornered Kade and got him talking more about Rangan, which led to an animated discussion of their research projects, of sending data from one brain to another.

Chuan bought a round of drinks. A bleach-blonde Thai girl in a low-cut blouse and unnaturally large breasts came up and snuggled into his arm. He started telling a story about a drug called Synchronicity. Sam's ears perked up. "Synchronicity?" she innocently inquired. "What's that?"

"It's N and M together. The champagne of trips." He kissed his fingers for emphasis.

"N as in Nexus?" She wanted him to spell it out for her.

"Yeah. And M as in Empathek. The M makes you want to connect, want to understand, want to love. And the N actually lets you feel what other people are feeling. It's beautiful. Magical." Chuan closed his eyes as he described the experience.

Out of the corner of her eye, Sam saw the amateur anarchist, Baroma, try to shush Chuan with a hand gesture. Chuan rolled his eyes in annoyance.

"You know, that's what I've *heard*, anyway. I'd never do anything *illegal* like that." His voice dripped sarcasm. Everyone but Baroma laughed.

Sam laughed with them, made eye contact with Chuan, smiled at him.

This is the loose-lipped one, she thought. This is the way in.

She looked at Chuan and blinked to pull his bio up again, excused herself to the ladies' room to read it. Neuroscience PhD dropout. Known associate of Suk Prat-Nung. Single. No known income, but a pricey flat in a trendy part of Bangkok. He liked to post pictures of himself in exclusive clubs and exotic locales, attractive young women draped all over him. A player. She knew his type. Easy to manipulate.

She came out of the bathroom, squeezed back into the circle between Narong and Chuan, pressed against them both. She waited for the right moment, shared a story about a fictional LSD experience she'd had on the beach in Mexico, the awesome connection she'd felt to the waves and sun and sky, how it had changed her life.

Chuan smiled, nodded. "So you've never tried Synchro then?" he asked.

Sam shook her head. "Nope. Sounds awesome, though."

Offer me some, she willed him. See what happens.

"Ever tried Nexus?" he asked.

"Just once. A couple months ago, at a big party that Kade and Rangan threw."

"You did Nexus with Axon?" Chuan sounded incredulous.

"Yeah. And like a hundred of him and Kade's friends."

"All on Nexus?" Chuan's incredulity was rising.

Sam nodded. "Yeah. Everyone was linked to everyone. It was amazing."

And wouldn't you like to know more about how they did that?

Sam closed her eyes, tilted her head back, pulled out her best awestruck hippie tone of voice. "It was like we were all one being, all of us in the party, all one giant consciousness... Total ego dissolution." Now... how would they react? Had she laid it on too thick? She opened her eyes.

Chuan was staring at her. Then he started to laugh. "You're alright, girl." He turned to Narong. "This chick's alright, Narong. Nice job finding her."

She pressed a bit more against Narong, grinned at Chuan. "That's how we play in California."

Chuan laughed again. "Well, we should show you how

we play in Bangkok! In fact…"

"Chuan!" It was Baroma, the careful one. "Be careful what you say in public!"

Chuan shrugged, splashing his drink a bit, narrowly missing the girl on his arm. Annoyance flashed across his face. "Public? We're in our own club, man. This isn't public."

Baroma replied in Thai. "*Kao pen kon a-may-ri-gun!*" She's an American.

Chuan appeared dumbfounded. "So?" he replied in English.

Sam kept her mouth shut.

"*Rao jam pen thong kui!*" Baroma said sharply, gesturing at Chuan and Narong. We need to talk! He stepped away.

Narong turned to Sam, shrugging apologetically. "Sorry, our friend's a little paranoid sometimes." With that he followed Baroma towards an empty corner of the club. Chuan frowned, shrugged, and followed.

There was a brief silence, and then someone made a joke about Baroma not feeling very playful. People laughed, and the moment passed.

Sam watched the three of them out of the corner of her eye. Baroma and Chuan were moving their arms animatedly, apparently arguing. Narong was making conciliatory gestures, playing peacekeeper. Interesting.

Sam wandered over and joined the conversation with Kade, listened in on a discussion of neural input output architectures. The Thai students were hanging on Kade's every word. He'd clearly impressed them.

There was a tap on her shoulder. Narong. He gestured her away from the group.

"Everything OK?" Sam asked.

Narong grimaced. "He's kind of a paranoid. Look, I was wondering, we're doing this thing on Friday. It's going to be small, really chill, a family kind of thing." He paused. "It's a Synchronicity circle. There'll be about a dozen of us. Really mellow. Would you and Kade like to join us?"

"That sounds amazing," Sam replied. "Yeah, I'd love to come."

"Great," Narong said. "It's in an apartment above us in this building. Meet here at 10pm on Friday."

"Fantastic."

Sam checked her watch. It was almost 1am. Time to get going, she told Narong. Together they extricated Kade from his conversation. Narong repeated the invitation to the Synchronicity circle on Friday.

[sam] Say yes.

Kade felt reluctant in her mind, but he answered in the affirmative.

Narong gave them directions to reach Soi Sama Han and flag down a tuk-tuk or a cab. Eventually the goodbyes were said, and they headed out into the cool Bangkok night.

Wats crouched on the rooftop. An old wound throbbed softly. Kade and Cataranes and their new friend – one he'd identified as Narong Shinawatra – would presumably be in the club for some time. Time to do a little research on that driver.

He pulled some of his clearest full frontal shots of the man off his rifle scope, used his phone to search for similar pictures on the net. Possible matches scrolled across his vision. Nope. Not that one. Not the next either. Similar, but not the same face. Not the one after that or the next dozen or the next hundred to follow. Nothing promising in the first few hundred matches at all.

He went back, selected a three-quarters profile shot from the scope, reran the search. Garbage. More garbage. More garbage after that.

But wait. What the heck? Image 438. Chinese Premier Bao Zhuang. They looked nothing alike. How had that matched?

Wats zoomed in. What he saw knotted his stomach. The match wasn't on Bao Zhuang's face. It was on the face of the man behind him, in the shadows. His bodyguard. Chinese Central Security Bureau. The Chinese equivalent of the Secret Service.

The date stamp said October 2039. Six months ago. What were the odds that a member of the premier of China's security detail was now, six months later, assigned to drive Su-Yong Shu around?

What were the odds that a Chinese "military advisor" who he'd seen die in Kazakhstan would come back to life two years later in either of those roles?

No. He knew what he was looking at. These were three different men. All creations of the Chinese supersoldier program. All clones.

What did it mean that Shu rated one as her driver? It meant that she was very important indeed.

This was getting heavy. The more he learned the less he liked.

Just then, the door to the club opened, spilling light and sound out into the alley. Wats dismissed the images on his goggle display. It was Kade and Cataranes.

They would pass right below him.

It was time to try contacting Kade another way. He was atop a roof at least thirty feet from the ground. Even with Nexus 5, this was at the outside edge of his range, but he had to try.

He let the filters on his Nexus drop, reached out to feel Kade's mind as they walked below him. There... Kade...

Fuck.

Wats recoiled, reeled his thoughts in as quickly as he could. There were two minds running Nexus down there. One was Kade. The other was Samantha Cataranes.

He caught his breath. Did he have enough control to reach Kade without Cataranes feeling him? He couldn't be sure.

This was going from bad to worse. It was time to get Kade out of this. He wished it could be his friend's choice, but this was getting way too deep. Kade couldn't know how heavy the players were, couldn't know that he'd been followed last night, couldn't know how much danger he was in. Without that information, he couldn't make an informed choice. Wats was going to have to make it for him.

The rifle was in his hands. He'd pulled it out without thought. His fingers moved with a mind of their own, screwed the silenced barrel onto the stock. He could get Kade out now. His hands slid the scope onto the assembled weapon. A shot to the head. His arms lifted the rifle up, brought the scope to his eye. The back of Cataranes' skull filled his vision. The crosshairs lined up perfectly. Her skull would be hardened, reinforced with a graphene mesh or a composite foam. The bullet might not penetrate, but it would bear her to the ground, give her a massive concussion, at the least. His thumb flipped the safety off of its own accord. She'd have pain filters. He'd need to fire more than once to be sure she was incapacitated. His index finger found the trigger. Could he take her down and not kill her? The force of the impact might just pulp her brain. Wats pulled in a long slow breath. He couldn't be sure.

To be sure of getting Kade out, he'd have to risk killing Cataranes.

Fuck.

He lowered his aim. The leg. He could put her down that way.

And if she had a weapon? If she turned and fired?

He let the breath out of his lungs, re-engaged the safety, pulled his face away from the scope. The data fob was a weight against his chest.

So close…

There was another way. He knew the route the taxis and tuk-tuks used from hotel to conference center. He knew the rough time that Kade and Cataranes would make that trip. An intercept while in transit was the best option of the ones he'd looked at. He'd get Kade out that way. Tomorrow.

There was no more point in following them tonight. The action would be tomorrow. Wats broke down his rifle and stowed it again. Then he took off across the rooftops, leaping lightly from one to the next, on a course towards the main street. He had preparations to attend to.

24

One Tough Bitch

Kade felt tightly wound up as they walked down the alley.
Sam let the silence stretch out for one block, another, yet
another. Finally she reached out to him.

```
[sam] What's on your mind?
[kade] It's that obvious?
[sam] It's getting to be.
```

It was true. The more time they spent in this Nexus
linkage, the more attuned to his emotions she became.

```
[kade] It's about the party they invited us to
on Friday. I'm not going.
[sam] What?
[kade] You want to use these kids to get to this
dealer, Ted Prat-Nung. And to do it you're going
to blackmail them into helping you, just like you
did me. That wasn't part of the deal. I'm not
going to help you.
```

Sam groaned inwardly. She still had to debrief him and
to confront him about the things he'd been holding back.
This was going to be a long night.

[sam] Kade, we don't care about these kids. They're small time. We just want to get to Ted Prat-Nung and his Nexus distribution network.

[kade] And you'll fuck over their lives to do it.

[sam] Not if they cooperate.

[kade] Cooperate in helping you find someone whose crime is selling people a tool to connect to each other? Find him so you can kidnap him? So you can kill him? What happens to Prat-Nung?

[sam] That isn't any of your concern.

[kade] Like hell it ###########!!!!!!!!!

Pain lanced through Kade's mind and body, sizzled down the link to Sam's mind. Spasming, jolting pain, muscles constricting against one another, thought collapsing. Sam felt it an instant before she heard the sounds – the soft *pffwwwwt* of a silenced rifle of some sort, the meaty thud of a projectile striking his body, the crackling *zzzzzt* of electrical discharge, the involuntary scream through clenched teeth. A taser round.

Time slowed. Her senses came alive. Rifle sound. Taser in the air. Spin. Crouch. A second projectile sailed through the air where her chest had been, missing her by inches.

Follow the shot back. Third-floor balcony. Sixty feet. Two shapes, burly, rifles. The graphene-and-ceramic blade was in her hand as she thought it, then hurtling through the air from her outstretched arm.

She moved as she threw, continued her spin, and dashed towards them. Rifles tracked, fired. A hideous gurgling as her knife ground home in an exposed throat. One down.

A taser round skidded in a shower of sparks off the cobblestones to her left. Forty feet. Another ricocheted spectacularly off the alley wall. She jagged to the side, dodged another shot. Twenty feet.

A taser round took her in the back of the thigh. Her muscles spasmed, sending her stumbling to one knee.

Behind me. Fuck!

The taser round was still discharging. Sam reached back, yanked the barbs out of her clenching muscles, hurled it blindly at the balcony. Another round took her in the shoulder. The momentum spun her around, landing her face down on the wet cobblestones. A third took her in the back. Her muscles clenched violently, flared with pain. She overrode them, came up to her hands and knees. The Nexus connection had frayed, was totally down. Tactical contacts were on the fritz. The multiple electrical discharges had disrupted both. She wasn't going to be calling for backup.

Ahead of her, far down the alley, a fourth figure in the shadows. Tall, thin, hooded – just standing there. Sam came up to one knee. Behind her she heard a clang and a thud. Footfalls from the other direction. The shooters were heading for her. Good.

More rounds in the shoulder, in the back. Their momentum sent her sprawling on her stomach. Volts and amps rocked her body, tore a scream from her mouth. She forced herself to go limp.

Silence. The sound of breathing. Footfalls.

Sam held still, eyes half lidded. Booted feet appeared in her vision.

"*Yai Ba Nung Neow*," one of them said. One tough bitch.

They had no idea.

The other responded in Thai. "Bitch killed Prang, man. Fuck. I wanna make her scream." She heard the scrape of a knife being drawn.

"Later," said the one who'd called her a tough bitch. "Take her inside. I'll get the boy."

He stepped over her, towards Kade.

Sam snapped out with both her hands, latched onto Tough-bitch's foot, yanked on it with superhuman strength, and rolled. The thug went down hard and fast, spinning in the air as he fell. She let go of him, kicked her legs up and brought herself to standing, just as the other one came at her with a wicked ten-inch blade.

He was huge, ugly, covered in tattoos, his rifle over one shoulder. He brought the knife down in a vicious overhand swing at her face. Sam stepped inside his reach, snap kicked him in the groin, broke his nose with a fast jab to his face, and then grabbed his still-extended knife arm and used it to throw him over her hip and to the ground. The rifle clattered away from him.

A gunshot exploded in the alley. Something ricocheted off the wall. The hooded figure was firing. Sam crouched low, turned to get to Kade. He was moving, up on one knee, trying to get upright, trying to get into the fray. So was the first thug, Tough-bitch.

Oh no.

The second thug, Tattoo-boy, took a page from Sam's playbook, grabbed her left ankle and calf in a crushing grip with his two hands.

Oh, fuck, she thought.

He yanked hard, pulling her off balance. She fell to the ground in plank pose, caught herself with her hands. He swung Sam by her leg and her body followed. The brick wall of the alley came at her in vivid slow motion. She raised an arm to ward it away. Her arm collided with the wall. Her head followed, slamming painfully into the brick. Stone chipped. Dust fell down on top of her.

Fuck.

Tattoo-boy cocked her back, sending her body out towards the alley, then swung her at the wall again, harder this time. Sam managed to roll, took the blow on her

shoulder rather than her head. Bricks gave under the force
of her impact. Blood and dust were dripping into her eyes.

Fuck.

The knife was on the ground where he'd dropped it
when she'd thrown him. It was beyond the thug's head,
just out of his vision. He swung her back again, cocking her
body for a good hard swing at the wall. She had time to see
Kade on his feet, moving towards her, until the other thug's
open hand collided with his face, sent him sprawling back
to the ground again.

Shit, shit, shit.

Sam got her free foot under herself, heaved against the
cobblestones with it, kicking herself out and away from the
wall as the thug cocked her back. The move surprised him.
His swing and her kick sent her towards the knife. She
reached out, stretched for all she was worth, got a hand on
the hilt just as Tattoo-boy swung her back towards the wall.

Sam twisted to the side, stabbed to her right with all her
strength as he swung her. The knife sank deep into his upper
arm. Her spine slammed into the wall hard. The force of it
pulled the knife out of her hand. Her head torqued back,
battered against the wall. Shattered bricks fell on her face.

Goddamn, that hurt. The world was going gray.

The thug was screaming. All ten inches of the knife were
embedded in his massive right arm. Sam kicked free, broke
his weakened grip, rolled backwards and came to one knee.

Tattoo-boy was enraged. He was coming up to his feet,
pulling the knife out of his arm with his remaining good
hand. The rifle was at Sam's feet. She grabbed it. The
wounded thug charged, bellowing, bloody knife in his left
hand, completely out of control.

Sam swung for his knees with the rifle, connected. Her
blow struck one knee in mid-stride and hammered it
against the brick wall. He went halfway down, scrabbled to

get up on his other leg. Sam was faster. She rose up, spun to her right through a full three hundred and sixty degrees, brought the butt of the rifle around in a whistling, blurringly fast arc that ended in a sickening wet crack against his temple, driving his head into the brick. The carbon fiber butt of the rifle splintered and cracked from the blow. The thug's eyes rolled into the back of his head and he toppled over.

There was motion behind her. Sam turned. Kade was on the ground. The first thug, Tough-bitch, was charging her, knife swinging, face enraged.

Sam dropped low, stepped forward inside his swing, and drove the barrel of the rifle like a spear, deep into his abdomen. He collapsed forward onto it, his momentum impaling him. The end ground into bone inside him. The man groaned in pain and anger, his eyes still fierce, and tried to push himself back and off of the impaling rifle.

Sam pulled the trigger, fired the taser round into his savaged guts. He spasmed, roared. She fired again. The man groaned louder. His eyes were still open. He was still struggling to get free of her. She pulled the trigger again and again until it clicked empty. The thug screamed and finally collapsed against her.

She was sweating. Her heart was pounding in her chest. The one she'd impaled was still breathing. They both were. Good. She had a lot of questions for these two. It wouldn't do for them to die too soon. It wouldn't do at all.

There was still one more out there. Sam looked down the alleyway. The tall hooded figure was retreating into the shadows. The rifle she'd impaled the thug with was spent. Another rifle had fallen to the ground across the alley. She dropped the man slumped against her, dove for the other side of the alley, came up on one knee with the fallen taser rifle, aimed, fired.

The move saved her. Twin explosions came from where she'd been, knocking her over. Dust and smoke filled the alley. The wall where she'd left the fallen thug had been blasted open, revealing a jagged hole into the building beyond. The third-floor balcony above her and down the alley had collapsed in a third blast, taking much of the building wall with it.

The hooded man was gone.

Fuck. Kade.

She found him in the smoke, bleeding from multiple locations, unconscious, still breathing. There were plasticuffs on his wrists and ankles.

She scrambled for one of the knives, found it slick with blood and gore, used it to cut Kade free. The explosions had burst the thugs open at midsection. The explosives had been *inside* them. Their bodies were burning. Someone didn't want them talking. It was time to get the fuck out of here.

Sam hoisted Kade over her shoulder, sprinted toward the main street, pulled her phone as she went, pounded the emergency buttons, shouted into it as she ran. "Extract, extract! Man down! Extract, extract!"

Wats was back on the ground in the alley network and halfway to the main street when he heard it. Had that been a yell? A human scream? Or had he imagined it? He paused for a moment, listened. There. Another yell of some sort. Then gunfire. He turned back towards where he'd last seen Kade and Cataranes and broke into a run. Another scream. A man this time, not Kade. Another. And then the thuds of explosions. Fuck!

He yanked his pistol free, sprinted two blocks, turned a corner where he guessed the sounds had come from, saw smoke and dust and flames ahead, passed someone running the other way. It was a tall hooded figure. Wats got a fleeting impression of a hooked nose inside the hood, a bald head. Wait! The monk who'd followed Kade the previous night. Wats spun. The figure was retreating in the other direction, almost around the corner. He leveled his pistol.

"Stop!" he yelled.

The hooded monk kept running.

Fuck. He aimed low to take the man in the legs, fired twice. Too late, the man was around the corner, shielded by the brick.

Fuck. Forget him. Find Kade.

He turned, sprinted the rest of the way to the source of the smoke. There were bodies, burning, burst from the inside. Gore covered much of the alley. Brick walls had collapsed. Suicide troopers, whether they'd known it or not. Their facial structures looked Thai. Their muscles were grotesquely large. A shattered rifle lay near one of the bodies, its business end covered in blood, the stock of it destroyed as if by impact. Another rifle lay against the opposite wall. He checked it. Taser rounds. Someone had wanted to take Kade or Cataranes alive.

There were no other bodies in the alley. Either Kade and Cataranes had gotten away, or someone else had taken them. He looked again at the dead men. Their presence suggested that Kade and Cataranes had escaped.

He stepped into the intersection between alleys, turned around. Four choices. Where would they have gone? Would they have hidden in this maze? Or would they have headed back towards the relative safety of public places?

He heard shouts from down the alley, in the direction of the main street. There. He sheathed the knife and loped off in that direction, gun at the ready. Shapes ahead. Do or die time.

• • •

Eighty miles to the south, the USS *Boca Raton* held station in heavy seas in the Gulf of Thailand. Monsoon waves splashed over the rounded, matte black upper surface. The submersible covert operations craft rode with its conning tower just two meters over the sea to avoid detection. Despite the *Boca Raton*'s huge size, Thai defense radars slid off its smooth surface, disappeared into its radar-absorbent materials.

A Thai Royal Navy ship patrolled these waters. An Indian-built Kolkata class destroyer. The captain of the *Boca Raton* would rather be thirty meters under, but his orders were to stay in continuous uplink, except in the case of imminent detection or harassment by the Thai Royal Navy.

The Kolkata could only find them by dumb luck, the captain knew. Despite its hundred and thirty-meter length, the *Boca Raton* presented a radar cross section the size of a rowboat, and a sonar signature even smaller when still. The high seas and surface sounds of crashing waves made the ship effectively invisible. Still, dumb luck had killed plenty of men. His crew was on constant alert.

Atop the conning tower, a directional maser powered through the monsoon rain and clouds, bouncing a narrow beam of data off a constellation of low-earth orbit satellites, hopping from one to the next as they hurtled through the sky at eight kilometers a second. Unless something should fly directly into that narrow beam, the uplink was undetectable.

Two decks below the bridge, in a cramped control center covered in displays, Garrett Nichols analyzed data Cataranes had produced from the walk down Sukchai Market. Next to him, Jane Kim sifted through databases and the web, looking for additional information on two of the students at the party, the anarchist Baroma Nantakarn and the loose-lipped Chuan Suttikul. Another console showed a deep net trawl for data on the monk who'd followed Lane and Cataranes. Bruce Williams was off duty, back at his bunk.

"Combat! Combat!" Jane called out.

Nichols jerked his head up in time to see most of the data feeds from Cataranes cut out. He moved his eyes to the feeds from Lane. Most were down. GPS from both phones remained up. They were in an alley between the Buddha's Kiss and the main street.

"What the hell?" he said.

Jane rewound, played the last few seconds. Two assailants. Three. Four. Combat. Fuck.

"Get the fireteam there, stat!" he ordered.

Sam ran down the alley, Kade across one shoulder, her phone in the other hand. The blasted thing claimed to be transmitting, but there was no sound from the speakers. She had no idea if her support team were hearing what she was saying, no idea if they had any data from her at all.

The alley mouth was just two blocks away. Wait. Figures there. Three, four of them, backlit by light from the street. Were those rifles? She ducked into a side alley. Were they her backup? Or more assassins?

She still had the knife she'd taken from the thug. She looked around for a place to hide Kade. There, a dumpster.

"Blackbird! Blackbird! We're from the nest! Here to get you home."

Voices speaking good English. The right code name.

"Today's word is golden calf. I repeat, golden calf!"

The right daily password. She relaxed fractionally.

"Coming out!" Sam yelled.

There were four of them, all local contractors vetted by

the CIA, dressed as businessmen, dark pants and dark shirts, with conservative dark blazers over them. The automatic rifles and bandoliers of ammo gave them away. She knew that underneath the blazers they wore armor, packed more ammo and more weapons. They were mercenaries, not regular forces, but at this point she just didn't care. Thank god for well-armed support teams.

"I've got a man down," she said.

Two of them came forward, took Kade's unconscious form from her, ran back towards the main street.

"I'm Lee," the point man said. "Our car's at the alley mouth. We can take him. What's the sitrep?"

"Ambush five blocks back," Sam reported. "Three Thai muscle, taser rifles, trying to take us alive. I think he was the target, I was a surprise. There was a fourth guy, not muscle, headed off..." She paused to get her bearings. "... east. In a hood. The muscle had implanted explosives, detonated after I disabled them. All KIA."

"You get samples?"

Sam looked down at the splatter of blood on her hands and clothes. More blood was dripping into her eyes. "Not intentionally."

"You hit?"

"Minor," she said. "But I'm going with him."

Lee nodded. "Roger that. We'll get samples and sanitize the site."

"Fuck the sanitize," Sam replied. "That was a fucking explosion. Bangkok Metro cops will be here soon. Get in, get out, don't get caught." There could be no contact with the local authorities.

Lee nodded. "I'll confirm with command." He jerked his head towards Soi Samahan. "Car's back that way, sooner you're in it, sooner they can roll." He gave Sam a smart salute.

Sam returned the salute, ran for the alley mouth. There was a four-seater Toyota there. The two on her team were standing by the front, their guns gone from sight, eyes scanning the perimeter, hands inside jackets. The back door was open, Kade slumped inside. Sam dove in the back, slapped the interior roof of the car.

"Let's go!"

Wats froze, flattening himself against the wall of the alley, deep in the gloom. He held still, let the chameleonware blend him into the wall, shield his IR emissions as it dumped his body heat into its onboard heat store. They were shouting in English, good accents, passwords of some sort. Four newcomers and Cataranes. The newcomers wore business garb and automatic rifles. He recognized them, American made, all ceramic and composites, x-ray invisible and non-magnetic, perfect for sneaking across a border. At a guess they were loaded with graphene-tipped rounds, harder than diamond, able to punch through any conventional body armor.

Two of them carried Kade away, carefully, like a patient rather than a sack. That was a good sign.

The other two new arrivals jogged his way as Cataranes headed out of the alley. Wats froze, held his breath. They passed right by him without noticing. Short hair. Bulky builds. Military bearing. These were CIA or Special Forces. Maybe local mercenaries. Something along those lines. They matched the description of the men who'd lounged most of last night in the lobby of the Prince Market Hotel.

Wats waited for the two military types to recede into the distance. He counted to sixty, then crept silently forward to the mouth of the alley. Gone. Kade, Cataranes, the other two – they were gone. This whole night had gone belly up. What the fuck had happened here? Who was trying to kidnap Kade?

One thing was certain. Getting the kid out was going to be a royal bitch now.

25

The Pawn Seldom Knows

Kade swam in and out of consciousness. He was in a car. Sam was with him. His head was in her lap, her hand on his brow. Lights raced by. There had been a fight... Explosions. He caught flashes of conversation. Tasers. Kidnapping. Abduction.

He could just barely feel Sam's mind through a haze of static. She was concerned. For him. And she was angry. Someone was going to pay.

Then he was being moved, carried out into the night, through a doorway. There was a woman's face. Thai. A stranger. And then a coffin lid closed down around him.

He tried to fight, found he had no strength. They'd buried him alive. He blinked hard and the world swam back into focus. Strange noises all around him. Then the lid came away and bright light filled his eyes.

He was in a compact surgery. An operating table with lights and two insectoid robotic surgeons occupied one wall. An emergency metabolic suspension tank was against a second wall. The coffin he was in was an imaging bed. They'd been scanning him.

The Thai woman was at a console, looking at diagnostic

results. Kade tried to sit up, failed. Sam gave him an arm and he managed it on the second try.

The Thai woman looked over at him. "You have a concussion. Not very serious. No significant brain bleeding. You do have a linear fracture of the skull on your right side, but it's faint, and not impinging on the brain. You're going to have major bruising of the side of your face."

Kade grunted.

She loaded up a syringe and approached him.

"What now?" Kade asked.

"I'm going to inject you with growth factors. Trust me, you want this."

Kade followed her instructions without further demur, letting her treat his wounds. He was lucky to be alive. If Sam hadn't been with him, or if she'd been a little bit slower, or if that guy had smacked him just a little bit harder...

Then again, if it weren't for her, I wouldn't be in this mess at all.

The last step was a lumbar puncture. The Thai woman slid a needle into his back, between his vertebrae, sucked out a tiny sample.

Cerebrospinal fluid. They're looking for signs that Shu inserted something else into me. They won't find any.

After the Thai woman was done with him, Sam led Kade to a room where he could lie down, then disappeared.

Kade dozed. He woke at some sound, disoriented.

Where am I?

The party, the fight, Thailand, Su-Yong Shu, it all came flooding back into him. A chill went up his spine. His stomach knotted up. He reached for the Nexus OS. No good. He couldn't get the OS to launch, couldn't invoke the serenity package. The nodes in his brain were scrambled. What was he doing here? Why were people trying to kill

him, trying to capture him? He was going to die in this
place. They were going to catch him, torture him, and then,
even though he'd tell them everything, they'd kill him.

He felt faint. His heart was pounding in his chest. His
breath was short. He was trembling. He felt cold all over. His
body was covered in sweat. He needed to get out of here.

The door to the room opened. Light flooded in. Kade
flinched, threw up an arm to ward away whatever was
coming.

"Kade!"

It was Sam. Samantha. She had something in her hand.
She moved towards him, closing the door behind her. He
flinched back farther, put both hands up to keep her away.

"Kade!" She was on the bed with him now, her hands on
him. "It's OK. It's OK. Husshhh. It's OK. I'm here. You're
safe. We're in a safe place. It's OK. Shhhhhh."

Her words didn't reach him. Her thoughts did. She was
calm. She was comfort. She was strength and safety and
resolve. He was someplace safe. They'd gotten away. No
one would hurt him here. It was OK.

Bit by bit he relaxed. His heart slowed. It no longer
threatened to burst from his chest. His breath steadied. The
trembling subsided. Sam held him, and he clung to her. It
was OK. It was going to be OK. They were safe now. It was
OK.

He lay that way for a while, feeling the comfort of her
mind, listening to the strong beat of her heart, the rhythm
of her breathing, feeling her stroke his hair as she
whispered again and again that it was OK. Her thoughts
grew stronger in his mind. He lay that way, and sleep took
him.

Sam stroked his head and whispered kind things and
exuded support and peace and safety until Kade fell asleep

again. This poor kid, scared and out of his depth. They were the same age, but Kade seemed so young in comparison. How was it that Kade, who'd grown up in a happy middle class family, in a happy suburban town, shielded from all threats until recently, was the anxious one, while she, Sam, with all the damage and torments of her childhood, was the strong one?

Maybe he was still recovering from the death of his parents six months ago.

Or maybe he was the normal one. Maybe she'd just had all the weakness beaten out of her.

She had work to do. She'd borrowed a slate from the safe house. She picked it up from the floor where she'd dropped it, shifted back into physical contact with Kade to reassure him, tapped and typed out her report. It took time. Three men, presumably Thai nationals, were dead. Bangkok Metropolitan Police would have found them by now. Her DNA could be at the scene. Oversight would have a field day with this. She finished up the report, shook her head, submitted it. Then she lay there, drifted into a half sleep with Kade beside her.

She woke – an indeterminate amount of time later – to a tap on the door. Someone turned the handle, stuck a head in. It was Lee, the squad leader. He spoke softly.

"You've got a call. ERD Deputy Director Becker. Want it on your slate or out here?"

Sam blinked the sleep out of her eyes. Her contacts said 3.05am. Kade was asleep, an arm around her.

"Out there," she said. "Be there in a sec."

Lee's head disappeared. Sam slowly extricated herself from Kade's embrace, slipped out and to the comms room.

It was a three-way call. Becker on one screen, Garrett Nichols on another.

"Sam," Becker said. "You OK?"

Sam nodded. "Yes, sir. Couple bruises, nothing major."

"I read your report. Good work out there. That was a hard fight."

"Just doing my job, sir."

"Any personal suspicions as to who the assailants were or what they were after?"

Sam nodded again. "They were after Lane, sir. I'm sure of it. They hit him first with non-lethal weapons, but didn't hesitate to use lethal force with me. As to who they were, hired muscle or organized crime, I'd guess. The self-destruct suggests the latter."

Becker nodded. "Nichols?"

"I agree with Agent Cataranes. This was an abduction attempt aimed at Lane."

Becker spoke again. "The major value that Lane has is the Nexus 5 design. That has to be what they wanted. As to who they are, let's enumerate the possibilities."

"OK," Nichols said. "First guess, Su-Yong Shu. She may want what Lane has. She's already shown interest in him. Inviting him to this conference may have been a ruse so she could nab him."

Sam mulled that over. "Why go to the trouble of having dinner with him?"

"Maybe she needed confirmation that he was what she thought," Nichols mused.

Becker nodded. "We know that Shu has connection to Thai organized crime through Ted Prat-Nung. And at their dinner there was heavy Nexus traffic between Shu and Lane. That might have been the confirmation she was looking for."

Sam frowned. "Sir, how do we know that?"

"Lane's phone was recording all Nexus traffic near it for later analysis," Becker replied.

"Sir, I turned off the Nexus functions on the phone before

their dinner, per plan, to minimize the odds of it giving Lane away."

"The record function remained on, Sam. We needed to determine whether or not Shu has Nexus capabilities."

Sam frowned again. "Why didn't I know that?"

"It was on a need-to-know basis."

"And I didn't need to know?"

"No, Agent Cataranes," Becker's voice was firm. "You didn't need to know."

"Sir, with all due respect, I think that data would have been operationally relevant."

"Agent Cataranes," Becker said sharply, "that information was not operationally relevant to *you*. The phone was in passive record mode. There was no way for Shu to detect it."

"Sir–" Sam started.

"This topic is closed, Agent."

Sam took a breath, held her temper.

The pawn seldom knows what the King has planned, Nakamura had said once.

She didn't like feeling like a pawn.

"Next possibility," Becker said.

Nichols cleared his throat, looked at the camera again. "Ananda," he said. "He had Lane followed, demonstrating interest. It's possible they had a Nexus interaction as well. If so, Lane's technology could be valuable to him."

"Any luck identifying the man who followed Lane and Cataranes?" Becker asked.

"Not yet, sir," Nichols replied.

Sam held her tongue. Ananda seemed an unlikely suspect, but he had sent a monk to follow them. And stranger things had been true.

"Next possibility," Becker said.

"There are two possibilities left," Nichols said. "First, it's possible that someone else who knows Lane's work sold him out to some organization here, maybe Thai mafia, or Ted Prat-Nung's distribution cartel."

Sam was frowning.

"Yes, Agent Cataranes?" Becker asked.

"Something just occurred to me, sir. Narong Shinawatra, the student who invited us to that afterparty. He introduced himself to Kade, apparently bumped into him randomly. He rapidly befriended us, invited us to this relatively small event. He knew the route we were taking. He had the opportunity to notify the ambushers when we were leaving the club."

"...and we know that he's had contact with Suk Prat-Nung." Nichols was nodding.

Becker nodded as well, thoughtfully. "Good observation. Any suspects on the US side who might have sold Lane out?"

Nichols shook his head. "We'll get on it, sir. We can mine phone and email for any contacts with people in Thailand or obvious short hops away. We'll look for sudden bank deposits as well."

"Nichols, you mentioned one more possibility?" Becker prompted.

"Yes, sir. The last possibility is a leak within our organization. Someone inside the ERD could have sold this information, to the same sorts of sources as discussed in the last possibility."

Becker nodded. He looked troubled.

Sam spoke up. "My instincts say no."

"Why is that, Agent Cataranes?" Becker asked.

"They would have come at us harder."

Kade came slowly back to consciousness. The panic attack had passed. Sam was gone from the bed. He could feel her across the link. She was nearby, still in the safe house. It comforted him. She was talking to her superiors. Becker. The thought of the man was like a bitter taste in his mouth.

Nexus felt much stronger now, much more stable. Whatever effect the taser had on it, it seemed that sleep and time were undoing it.

Tasers. They'd wanted to take him prisoner. He was lucky they hadn't gotten him. He owed Sam. She'd risked her life to keep him from them.

There was only one reason for them to try to take him prisoner. They wanted what he knew about Nexus. They'd wanted to take it and make it their own, use it however they chose. And him? Perhaps they'd planned to kill him after they had what they wanted. Perhaps they'd planned to make him a slave, improving the technology for them.

I won't be anyone's slave. No one.

And the ERD?

Ilya was right. He shouldn't have given Nexus 5 to them. He didn't trust them. That was the past. He wouldn't make the same mistake again. Had he actually thought of going to work for them, trying to change the system from the inside? No. He would just become another slave. He would find another way.

And Shu?

The same. Her goals attracted him, her promises captivated him. He wanted with all his being to join her. But her compromises were many. She was a tool of her country's military. And he wouldn't be a slave of the Chinese military any more than he would of the ERD.

He would find another way.

"...they would have come at us harder," Sam said. "They would have known that I was a field agent. They would have brought more firepower to bear, and started with me."

Nichols looked thoughtful.

Becker nodded. "OK, I agree that a leak is a lower likelihood. Let's focus on the organized crime angle, Shu, and Ananda. The dead assailants are our best evidence. Any data on them?"

Nichols shook his head. "No matches on face recognition, DNA, or prints."

"What about the fourth person?" Becker asked.

"Nothing so far," Nichols said. "We're running deep trawls now. If there's anything out there on any of them, we'll find it."

Becker looked down at his wrist. It was early afternoon on the US East Coast by now, Sam knew.

"OK," he said. "Good work, both of you. If there's one silver lining to this, Sam, it's that you've saved his life now. He'll be more in your debt. He's primed to trust you more. He's vulnerable now and he's gonna look to you for protection and guidance. Take advantage of that."

Sam felt something inside her twist. Trust? Is that what this was about?

Becker was continuing. "Nichols, I want you moving forward on all angles. This is a Pri 1 investigation now. Tap whatever resources you need. Sam, keep your chin up. You did good today. I want another report in eighteen hours."

"Sir," Sam said. "There's something else I'd like to discuss."

"OK," Becker said. "But make it quick. I have a meeting on the Hill shortly."

"Sir, I think we should abort the mission, or at least send Kade home."

"What?" Becker said.

"Sir, we've achieved the primary mission objective. Kade has an invitation to Shanghai, and Shu has practically offered him the job. In addition, he's a civilian, and his life may be in continued danger here."

"No," Becker said.

"But, sir," Sam protested. "The risk to Kade–"

"No, Agent Cataranes." Becker spoke with a flat finality. "Leaving now risks raising Shu's suspicions. And Prat-Nung is as important a target as Shu. This is the best lead we've had in three years. We have to take it."

"But, sir…"

"Agent!" Becker raised his voice.

Sam felt herself bristle. She pulled herself erect in the chair, said nothing.

"This isn't open for discussion," Becker said in a tone Sam knew too well. "We have an opportunity to get closer to Prat-Nung. We're going to take it. If it is a trap, it's an even better opportunity to identify and neutralize the opposition. You and Lane, our *asset*, will be well protected. And we'll do absolutely *nothing* unusual, like sending the asset home *days early*, to raise Shu's suspicions. Am I making myself *absolutely* clear, *Agent* Cataranes? Special Agent Nichols?"

"Yes, sir," Sam said smartly.

"As crystal, sir," Nichols replied.

"Good. Becker out."

His face disappeared from the screen. Sam slumped in the chair.

Nichols' face drooped. "Sam, we'll bring security in tighter around you and Lane, starting immediately. Friday night… we'll have people stationed right there. Your support will be seconds away, I swear it. We won't leave you twisting in the wind on this."

Sam nodded sadly. "Thanks, Garrett. We can talk details later." She disconnected.

She dimmed the lights in the comms room, crossed her legs in the chair, put her hands lightly in her lap, focused on her breathing, tried to let her mind empty and peace come. A memory came instead. Nakamura.

She'd been nineteen, perhaps, a year or so into her training. He'd been in his mid thirties, the summer he told her he was leaving the ERD, transferring to the CIA.

"In this business, Sam, you have to remember that you're just one piece on the board."

"What do you mean?" she'd asked. Nakamura often spoke in metaphors.

"It's like chess. White against black. But it's not just one piece against another. It's sixteen pieces on a side. Many will fall, even on the winning side, before the game is over."

Sam had mulled that over. "You're saying that if I keep moving forward with this, my life is at risk. I could get killed doing fieldwork."

They'd been in DC, on the National Mall. Nakamura had paused to skip a rock across the reflecting pool, had taken his time with his words.

Sam had squinted behind dark shades in the bright sunlight, her newly enhanced eyes still sensitive to so much stimulus. Everything had hurt that summer. Already the viruses were spreading genes no human ancestor had ever carried through the cells of her body. Muscle fibers were lengthening to inhuman proportions and strengths. Neural ion channels and myelin sheaths were being transformed to speed nerve signals between brain and muscle. Reprogrammed bone cells were extruding organic carbon fiber webs to harden themselves against impact. Everything hurt, and she didn't care. She was going to save the world. She was going to save all the little girls.

Nakamura had skipped another rock, then spoken softly. "Sometimes dropping a piece is necessary in order to win," he'd said. "A sacrifice. A gambit. A trade for a more valuable piece. It's not just that you might be killed in this line of business. It's that you might be intentionally sacrificed or traded to further advance your side's position."

Sam had scoffed at that. "That's not how we play. We take care of our own."

Nakamura had grunted, said nothing.

They'd walked a bit more in silence. She remembered the intense heat of the sun. DC was so hot that summer.

Eventually she'd asked, "So what kind of pieces are we? Knights? Bishops?"

Nakamura had chuckled. "You, my young friend, are a pawn."

Sam came out of the reverie. She could feel Kade through the Nexus link on the phone, she realized. The Nexus felt stronger now. It was coming back together in her head.

She was troubled by the conversation with Becker. Not just because he'd scolded her. It was the notion that Kade might trust her more now as a side effect of the ambush. It was true. She'd felt it. The hostility had dropped. He felt honest gratitude that she'd saved his life. He'd felt comforted by her presence. That could only be an advantage to the mission.

In seeking to uncover the causes of an event, ask yourself: who stands to benefit from it? More wise, cynical words from Nakamura.

Becker stood to benefit from this, she thought. The mission did. The ERD did. Is there any chance this was a set-up? That I was meant to beat those guys? That it was all to play Kade? Were those men pawns, sacrificed in a larger gambit?

No. That was just paranoia talking. Surely just paranoia. Wasn't it?

26
Masks

Kade was awake when she went back to the room. He opened his eyes as she entered. He felt much more settled than he had a few hours ago. He smiled at her.

Shit, Sam thought to herself.

"How're you feeling?" she asked.

Kade came up to a sitting position as he answered. "A lot better. Sorry about that freak out earlier. And thank you. You saved my life tonight."

"Just doing my job, Kade," Sam replied.

"Those guys in the alley. They exploded?"

Sam nodded.

"They had explosives in them? Why would anyone agree to that?"

Sam answered slowly. "They might not have known they were wired to blow. Their masters could have implanted the charges without their knowledge."

She felt Kade absorb that.

Are there things in me I don't know about? Sam wondered.

She dismissed the thought. It wasn't worthy of her.

Kade nodded thoughtfully. "Tough call with Becker?" he asked.

It took her by surprise. Had she been broadcasting that much? Had he heard when Lee came in to alert her to the call? Sam shrugged, tried to make it casual.

She said, "Just going over the situation. Figuring out who was behind that attack, and how to stop it from happening again."

"Any luck?"

Sam narrowed her eyes. "Tell me about the Nexus contact between you and Ananda at the reception last night."

She saw the flicker of it across his face for a moment before Kade caught himself. She felt it in the way his thoughts hardened as he got them under control.

"What do you mean?" he said. "There wasn't any Nexus contact between us. We just bumped into each other in line."

He was lying. She was sure of it. *What did I really expect?*

In a way, she was relieved. His clumsy lie let her put him more squarely in the category of "asset", where she needed him to be. And in lying, he'd confirmed the suspicion she'd had. Ananda did have Nexus rattling around in his brain.

"Kade, don't play dumb with me."

Kade shrugged. "I was in line, and he got in line behind me. We exchanged a few words. That was it. No Nexus, nothin'."

Sam shook her head. "Fine, if that's the way you want to play it. I also know you and Shu communicated via Nexus, and you hid it from me. You're walking the edge right now. Your deal is contingent on your *full* cooperation. Got it?"

Kade shook his head. "I have no idea what you're talking about. I showed you what happened. My Nexus transmissions were totally shut down, and I didn't feel a peep out of her. I got the invite to Shanghai. Mission accomplished, right?"

Sam stared at him. There was no sign he was lying. No twitch, no looking away. Even so, the phone had picked up the Nexus traffic. Was it possible that it had all come from Shu? For what purpose?

"Show me again," she said, "and show me your interaction with Ananda."

Kade nodded. "OK." The serenity package kept him calm and cool.

He stepped into the mask of false memories Shu had created for him. He widened the connection to Sam, watched as she roved through his mind. He weighed the texture of the alternate memories. They were a script more than anything else. A story. Shu had filled in the details beneath them, but the mind did that so well on its own. Memories were narratives. They were stories. If he could master the right narrative, put it on like a mask, he could fool anyone.

Could he craft a convincing narrative for that brief moment of contact with Ananda? He tried to imagine it, tried to tell himself the story of how they'd bumped into each other, tried to make it real, tried to make it feel like the mask Shu had created in his mind.

Sam moved systematically, painstakingly through his memories of dinner with Shu. She replayed some moments again and again. She found nothing. The false memories held.

"Show me when you bumped into Ananda."

Kade sank into the alternate script, became a different Kade, told the story of that brief conversation in the drink line. A felt presence. Body heat, the sound of a breath, a few words exchanged.

Sam finished. She held his eyes with hers, then shook

her head. Disappointment issued from her. Bitterness.

"Kade, I don't know how, but I know you're lying to me. I'm just going to tell you one more time. If you don't cooperate fully, you'll go to jail, dozens of your friends will go jail. Some of you won't ever come out."

Distaste issued from her as she spoke. She didn't like this, Kade could sense. She wanted to do field ops, not blackmail people. He wondered if she knew how much of herself she gave away to him.

"I'm telling the truth. I've got no reason to lie to you. I want to get this over with and get on with my life." He let frustration and anger creep into his voice, into the emotions that seeped into Sam's brain from his.

I could just make her believe me, he realized. I could use one of the back doors... I could go into her mind and make her believe.

No. He would not do that. Not unless he had no other option. He had to draw a line.

Sam sighed. "Fine, have it your way. Don't say I didn't warn you when the shit hits the fan."

She shook her head again. She was angry at herself for something. Something involving him. "Now, let's talk about today. We need to get back to the hotel. Your story is..."

"Wait, wait, wait a minute," Kade interjected.

"What?"

"This is over, right? I did what you asked. I've got the invite to Shanghai. She seems to want me for the postdoc position. How about I go home now?"

Sam shook her head. "No. The mission's not done." She was hardening herself. She didn't like this either. She was steeling herself to tell him things she didn't agree with.

"Sam... Come on. We were just attacked. You said yourself that they were trying to kidnap me. Someone knows something is fishy. And you killed those guys.

They're going to figure out you're more than just a student. What's going to stop them from coming back? Is your mission going to be better off if I'm gone? Or if I'm dead?"

Sam felt it, he saw. And his arguments hit home. They resonated with her.

"It's not an option, Kade. The decision is made. We're staying. We can't do anything that will make Shu suspicious, and you leaving early would be suspicious." Kade felt a hollowness in her as she spoke. A bitterness at hearing the words emerge from her own mouth. A grim resolve to do her job.

"Look, it wouldn't be that hard. We can say I came down with the flu. I'll mail Shu, reconfirm the visit to Shanghai."

"No." Resolve came out on top. "I told you. The decision is made. We'll have tighter security. You won't be in danger. But we *are* staying and completing this mission."

Kade said nothing for a moment, just stared at her. Then, "I'm not going to help you blackmail those kids. I'm not going to help you fuck them over the way you did me. You're not going to use them to get at someone else."

"Then Rangan and Ilya will go to jail. You'll go to jail. More than a hundred of your friends who were at that party will go to jail. They'll lose jobs. They'll lose scholarships. They'll be expelled from schools."

Self-loathing came off of her as she spoke. The resolve was still greater.

"And all of it will be on your head, Mr Lane. All of it."

Cold anger flooded through Kade. How could he have started to trust this woman? It didn't matter that she hated what she was doing. She was doing it. She was one of them.

"Fuck you, Cataranes." He said it coldly, distinctly, so she'd know he meant it.

Sam came to her feet. Her own anger was rising. "No, fuck *you*, Kade."

She walked out of the room, called over her shoulder. "And get on your feet. We're leaving in ten minutes."

27
Leave No Man Behind

In a cheap room off Khao San Road, a powerful black man tossed and turned in the grips of a nightmare, in the grips of a memory.

They were coming for him. The Corps. His brothers. He could hear the choppers, hear the small arms fire. They'd found the place he'd been taken to, the place he'd been held, the place he'd chosen to stay. You never leave a man behind. They were coming for him, and God help anyone who stood in their way.

Lunara was pulling away from him. Their minds were still linked. They'd taken the Nexus just an hour ago. He could feel her fear. He could feel her resolve.

No, he begged her. Don't go out there. They'll kill you.

He knew her answer before she spoke it, knew it before he felt it in her mind. She'd rather die than fall into the Kazakh army's hands. She'd rather die than endure the rapes and tortures at the hands of the dictator's secret police again.

He knew. He'd felt them all, relived them in her memories. Every moment of her abuse. He'd seethed with rage, seethed with helplessness. To her it was a fact of life.

To him it was a betrayal. He hadn't fought on the side of rapists and torturers. He hadn't.

But he had.

No, he begged. I'll protect you.

He knew it was a lie, knew he wouldn't be able to. He begged anyway. Don't go. Please. Don't die.

Goodbye, Watson. Remember me. Remember us all.

She clanged the reinforced steel door to the cellar closed. He felt and heard her lock it from the other side. It hadn't been locked in weeks.

He fell to his knees, weeping. No. No. No.

He could hear the gunfire outside. Close, so close. He heard a scream. Had that been Temir's voice?

He rose up. He could feel her still, just outside the door. Something was preventing her from moving on. The gun. She'd picked up the gun. She was loading it. No!

The gunfire was inside the building now.

Wats roared in desperation. He dug his fingers into the tiny gap at the edge of the door. There was no handle to grip. He would make one with his hands. He screamed his need. Steel bent under his fingers. Steel gave, millimeter by millimeter.

He could feel Lunara on the other side of the door. Her gun was pointed up the stairs, waiting. Fear paralyzed her. He would make it through this door. He'd get her out of here, get them both out.

He felt the bullets rip through her body before he heard them, felt the icy pain lance through her before he felt the impacts on the door he gripped. They'd gone through her as if through paper. It took his breath away. He heard marines yelling. He could feel Lunara's life slipping away. He could feel her clinging to the Buddhism her Uyghur mother had brought from Mongolia, feel her clinging to the hope of rebirth, feel her hoping she'd improved her karma, that her next trip on the great wheel of being would be less filled with pain.

No!

"Stand back from the door!"

Wats couldn't comprehend it. He kept digging his fingers into the steel, kept squeezing, kept trying to get a grip that he could use to force it open.

They blew the hinges off. The door exploded inward, bearing him to the ground, slamming his head into the stone floor.

Then there was a Marine Corps medic above him, shining a light into his eyes, yelling into his face. "Can you hear me? Sergeant Cole, can you hear me? Are you hit? Are you injured?"

He could feel Lunara. She was still alive. She was in pain. She was weak, and getting weaker. But she was still alive. There was still hope. He opened his mouth, tried to get the words out, tried to tell the medic.

Then from beyond the doorway: "Hey, this one's still breathing."

The sound of a single gunshot, louder than all the automatic fire before. Lunara's mind disintegrated in a final peal of agony.

"Fucking bitch. No one messes with the Corps."

They were coming for him. The Corps. His brothers. He could hear the choppers...

At 5.39am, a chime went off. Wats rose with a jolt. He was drenched in sweat. Someone downstairs pounded on his floor. Had he been screaming again? The dream. Lunara. It was getting worse.

A chime. A message. He splashed cold water from the sink onto his face, to wash away the horror, then checked his slate. It was a note and a set of photos from his man at the Prince Market Hotel. Kade and Cataranes had returned to the hotel. They both looked rumpled and worse for wear. There was a livid bruise across the side of Kade's face. Two bulky looking Thai gentlemen with crew cuts had checked in shortly thereafter.

He sat down heavily on the bed. He'd slept little, and what sleep he'd gotten had been its own torment. The urge to drug himself into dreamless unconsciousness was strong. But this was not the time for that.

What had he done to earn so much suffering in this life? What had he done that he had the memory of Lunara's death, of her rapes, of Arman's pain at discovering the slaughter of his family, of Temir's pain at the pillaging of his village, of the pain of all the men and women they'd trooped through that cellar and trooped through his mind? What had he done that he had the torment of so many seared into his soul?

Wats dismissed the question. He knew very well what he'd done. He'd killed countless men and not a few women. He'd used violence as a weapon. He'd hurt and killed people for no reason other than the words of his superiors. He'd enjoyed it. It didn't matter that he'd believed what he was doing was right. He'd sewn the mask over his own eyes. He'd been complicit in his own exploitation as a tool of evil.

His karma was black as night. A dozen lifetimes might not be enough to climb his way out of the pit he'd dug for himself in this one life.

The data fob was in his hand, the metal of the chain coiled in his palm. So small. If he could just connect this to Kade... He'd been so close, so close to doing something that could make a dent in his vile karma, that could help redeem him just a tiny bit. So close to be turned away.

Wats dragged himself out of the mire of self-pity. It was

beneath him. He was here for a reason. He looked at the
message on the slate again, at the images. He pieced
together the events of the night before. Someone had tried
to abduct Kade. Cataranes had fought them off. They'd
spent time in a safe house somewhere. Now they were
back. And they were keeping those spec-ops types close.
Security around Kade would be tighter than ever.

He should have made his move the first day. He should
have shot Cataranes in the head last night and hauled Kade
away. They could be in Laos by now.

Wats sighed. Freeing Kade would be harder than ever at
this point. It would be a suicide mission. He couldn't
succeed. Not on his own. But he wouldn't give up. Not yet.

Someone else wanted Kade. Someone else had tried to
abduct him. He wanted to know who. He wanted to know
why. He pictured the monk he'd seen twice now. He had
one lead.

28
Warnings & Discoveries

Kade woke to the sound of the alarm. With a groan he reached across the bed to slap it off. The clock read 11am. His poster session was at 1 o'clock.

The sound of the shower emanated from behind the closed bathroom door. Sam was in there. She'd slept on the floor in Kade's room, a bodyguard he wished he didn't need, wished he could be rid of. He could feel her mind, calm, thinking about the day, washing herself methodically. He didn't think she could feel him yet.

Kade rolled onto his back, stared at the ceiling. Weak light filtered through the crack between the hotel room curtain and the wall. In addition to Sam, he knew that there were two of the guys with guns in the hotel now as well, posing as Thai businessmen, covertly ready to intercept assailants, and leap to Sam and Kade's aid should anything happen.

He was as safe as he was going to get. Others weren't so lucky.

Narong and his friends... Chuan... Lalana... Sajja...

He knew what he needed to do. He remembered something Wats had said after a few drinks once, talking about a no-win situation he and his squad had found themselves in, deep in the mountains of Kazakhstan, a decision of whether or not to try to rescue a captured squad mate against impossible odds.

When the chips are down, when you have to weigh what you believe in against your own safety – that's when you find out what you're made of.

Kade knew what he believed in. He believed that Narong and his friends were doing nothing wrong. He needed to warn them, have them call off Friday night. He glanced at the door to the bathroom. It was still closed. The shower was still going. How long had Sam been in there? Was she about to pop out? He had to take the chance. He was tired of being passive. He had to make the right thing happen.

Kade kept his mind as blank as he could, reeled in the amount he was emanating, rolled off the bed, padded as quietly as he could in boxers and bare feet to the small desk, found the stationary and pen, jotted a quick note.

Robyn Rodriguez is a narc. You must cancel Friday night or uninvite us. You didn't hear this from me, please.

The noise of the shower ended. He pulled the top sheet off the pad, folded it up, scanned around frantically for his pants.

The bathroom door opened. He looked up in time to see Sam crossing the distance between them, her face livid. Her open palm knocked him to the floor before he even saw it coming. His world exploded in pain. The room spun around him.

"You stupid son of a bitch."

She was standing above him, naked, water dripping off of her, fists clenched. She was going to hit him again.

He held his breath.

"I warned you," she told him.

There was a scar below her left collarbone and above one of her perfect breasts, a long line of red against her olive skin. A knife wound? Surgery? There were circular pock marks on her otherwise flat stomach, more above one knee. Bullet wounds? Her nipples were hard. Was she cold? Did this excite her?

What was she?

He spat out blood, tried to talk. "It's not their fault. They're not doing anything wrong."

She kicked him in the stomach. He curled into a ball of agony, unable to breathe.

"I trusted you, Kade. I went to bat for you. I *saved your fucking life*. And what do you give me? Just pathetic lies. Again, and again, and again."

He gasped for breath, tried to speak...

"Tried... do... right thing..."

"Fuck your right thing, Kade. I'm tired of your lies. If *anything* about Friday night goes wrong, we're going to assume *you* sabotaged it. Got it? *Anything* goes wrong, and you're in an internment camp for life, you and your stupid fucked-up party friends. *Dozens* of them. You hear me?"

Kade tried to speak. Nothing came out. He nodded meekly instead.

Wats bowed respectfully to the woman who opened the monastery door. This was his fifth attempt today. The woman took a look at him, his skin color, his clothes, his height, his musculature, and addressed him in English.

"May I help you?" Her accent was quite good.

Wats responded in his best Thai, as weak as that was. "Please, honored sister. I'm looking for a monk. I had the honor to serve food to him from my humble stall yesterday. He forgot his alms bowl with me. I would return it to him."

She frowned at him, replied in Thai. "There are many monks, friend. If one has lost his alms bowl, it can be easily replaced."

"Please, honored sister." He bowed again. "This monk blessed my humble stall. I would feel honored to be able to return his lost possession to him."

"Very well. What does he look like?"

Wats rose up out of his bow. "He is tall." He held his hand at temple height. "Nearly as tall as me. Perhaps 1.8 meters. Not young, but not old. He has sharp features. A large nose. With a hook." His hands molded the image in the air as he spoke.

"He is Thai?"

"Yes, honored sister."

She thought for a moment. "That is very tall for a Thai man. We do not have a monk that tall in this monastery."

Wats contained his disappointment. There were many more places to try.

"But," she continued. "I may know who this monk is. Where is your food stall?"

"Off Thep Prathan, honored sister. East of the Chao Por Suea shrine."

"Ahh, near the convention center?"

"Yes, honored sister."

She nodded. "Then I may know who this monk is. It may be Phra Racha Khana Chan Rong Tuksin."

Wats nodded to himself. The title indicated that this Tuksin was only one step below Somdet status, a very senior monk. He nodded, repeated the name to be sure he had it right, then used the colloquial title, "Chan Phrom Tuksin. Thank you, honored sister."

She nodded at him.

"Where would I find Chan Phrom Tuksin, honored sister?"

"He resides at the Wat Hua Lamphong, near Chulalongkorn University. He is special assistant to Professor Somdet Phra Ananda."

Wats nodded again. This went close to the top, indeed. "Thank you again, honored sister." He brought his hands together in a respectful *wai* to her, turned to go.

"What food does your stall serve, young man?"

He turned back to her. "American food, honored sister. Hot dogs and hamburgers."

She frowned at him. "That is not fitting food to offer a monk," she scolded. "But you earn much merit in going so far to return his bowl."

"Thank you, honored sister." He bowed his head, made the *wai* to her again.

"*Sawadi*, traveler."

"*Sawadi*, honored sister."

29
Madness Everywhere

A taxi driven by one of the armed Thai military types took Kade and Sam to the conference after lunch. Kade stood near his poster on mouse-to-mouse spatial memory sharing via machine-learning mediated nanoprobe connections. The growth factors had nearly healed the bruise on his face. What little remained was covered in concealer.

He could see Sam hovering around, pretending to view the other posters. She felt tense and alert through the link. Two more of the men from the safe house orbited around in shirts and blazers, god knew what tucked away underneath there. They made a show of looking at posters.

The crowd came and went. Students and professors made comments, asked questions. Kade fielded them as quickly as he could, repeating himself again and again, constantly thronged. It was clear his poster was making waves. He wished for a glimpse of Narong in the crowd. There wasn't.

Sajja came by, admired Kade's poster. Kade wished he had the note in his pocket. Wished he had some way to warn them.

"Have you seen Narong?" he asked Sajja.

"I think he's sick," the other student said. "Didn't show

up with his poster today. It must be really bad for him to miss his poster session."

Kade nodded.

Not that I could have warned him, he thought.

More professors and students came and went. An hour passed. And then another visitor arrived.

    [sam] Heads up. Shu en route.
    [sam] Don't do anything stupid.

Kade felt the Nexus bridge to Sam go down. He looked up at the crowd, and there she was, Su-Yong Shu. He could barely see her through the throng in front of his poster. Elegant and stately as ever, going from poster to poster, taking her time, smiling and saying encouraging things to the students.

Save me from the ERD, he wanted to tell her.

But then he would just be someone else's slave.

He was fielding a question when the crowd parted and Shu stepped through. Everyone went silent. Her eyes touched on the concealed bruise on his temple and her expression changed immediately.

"Kade," she said. "What happened?"

Are you hurt? Shu asked him.

He touched his temple, smiled ruefully. "I got mugged. Late last night. It was no big deal. They just took a little bit of cash."

He heard people react, whisper about it. A mugging.

We're being observed, he sent her. **They know we communicated via Nexus last night.**

Shu's eyes went faraway for a moment, then snapped back to reality.

"Walk with me."

"My session goes until 4 o'clock, Professor..."

"It will wait," she pronounced. Then to the crowd around

them. "Please forgive me. I'll bring him back shortly."

And then she was leading him by the hand through the stunned throng. A murmur went through them. Su-Yong Shu had just snapped him away!

She led him away towards the cafeteria. He could see Sam and one of the military types watching out of the corner of their eyes. But what could they do? His assignment was to get close to Su-Yong Shu. They ordered tea, sat at a table near the window.

"So," she said. "Tell me about your schedule. When could you be free for a week or so to visit? And do you know Rangan's schedule as well?"

Kade started to walk her through the experiments they had planned for the rest of the year, when there might be a hole. A moment later, he felt her in his mind.

Open to me. Show me what happened, she sent.

He could feel her mind touching his in other ways, weaving a false set of memories to cover their conversation even as they spoke.

Are we being watched? he asked.

You are bugged, but they will not detect our real conversation. Not this time.

Kade waxed poetic about the need to book lab time months in advance, and how that would affect his calendar for the rest of the year.

I have a lot to learn, he sent her.

Yes, you do. Now show me.

He did. She absorbed it in an instant.

I did not do this thing, she told him.

He felt a cold, vast anger inside her. The attack on him offended her. It made her furious.

I know, he replied. **You could have taken me any time you wanted.**

Someone wants to make you a slave, Shu told him.

Someone wants your secrets.

Do you know who? he asked her.

No, but I intend to find out.

Could it be Professor Ananda? Kade asked. **He's one of their other suspects.**

She mentally shook her head. **Not Ananda.**

Or Ted Prat-Nung? he asked.

Shu looked at him sidelong this time. He caught a sense of... something. **Not Thanom.**

They talked logistics out loud for a time. Flights. Lodging. Who to meet. Rangan's schedule.

Can you help me about Friday? he asked her. **Help me warn them? Some way that the ERD doesn't find out?**

Your government has made you a slave, Kade. If you want my help, come with me now to Shanghai. Break free of these chains.

The temptation was strong. To have a mentor he could trust, that he could turn to. To work towards real goals and not spend all his time hiding them...

But he would be a slave there too. He would be making weapons. There would be blood on his hands.

I'm sorry, he sent her. **I can't accept the price you pay.**

I won't pay that price forever, Kade. There will come a day when we will be free and the humans will no longer have us under their thumbs.

She had so much anger inside. She hated them. He caught a flash of her mentor, Yang Wei, burning to death...

She watched him die, he realized. How would that affect me?

He shook it off. It didn't matter.

I'm sorry, he sent her. **This isn't just my life on the line. There are more than a hundred people whose**

futures are at stake. I can't let them down.

They're humans, she sent him. **You're more valuable. You're wasting your potential**.

I'm human too.

You're more, Kade. You're transhuman now. And you can be so much greater still.

Everyone could be greater, he sent. **This is about choice and freedom, right? About everyone's potential.**

The world needs leaders, Kade, she sent him. **After we tear down the old order, there will be a vacuum. Who will rule? Giving full power to everyone would be like putting guns in the hands of children. In time we'll uplift some, but I need a core group of people like you to fill that initial void. You will always be one of the elite.**

Ruling... he replied. **One of the elite...**

There is no other way, she sent.

Who decides who gets to be part of that elite? he asked her. **Who decides which people get uplifted?**

Whoever takes the initiative, Kade. Whoever wins the war to come. I intend that to be me. You can be on the winning side.

He saw it through her eyes. The old men that ruled her country and his, on their knees, giving way to the new order, or burning. Dying. Everywhere burning.

It was too much. Head reeling, he stumbled to his feet, backed away from her. He mumbled some word of farewell aloud. Her disappointment followed him. He turned and shambled in a daze back towards his poster. He felt her web of false memories knit itself shut around the conversation they'd just had. He hardly cared.

Her final thoughts followed him. **One day you'll see the truth, Kade. The humans are the enemies of the** future. They hate us. They hate our beauty and our potential. Either they hunt us down and kill and enslave us, or we rise above them and take our rightful place in this world. There are no other options.

Madness. Madness everywhere. The ERD would make him a slave. Shu would make him a tyrant and a killer. He had to find some other way.

30
Data Gathering

Wats slid slowly out of the shadow of the inner wall of Wat Hua Lamphong. It was the hour of evening meditation, between dinner and sleep, and the monks had all been called to the central hall. Golden Buddhas watched him with serene, lifeless eyes. Their half smiles mocked him. Red-faced guardian demons leered at him. A giant statue of the Hindu elephant god Ganesha watched him pass with alien indifference.

He'd watched the small number of monks' rooms all evening, had seen Tuksin enter and exit one near the end. This was a city temple, more for worship by the laity than for monks, but a few dwelled here. Tuksin and Ananda both had small cells, close to Chulalongkorn University where Ananda worked and taught during the week. Ananda's home monastery lay to the north-east, he knew, a hundred or so klicks out of town, up in the mountains.

Wats crept silently, slowly forward, moving at a pace the chameleonware could accommodate. Too fast and no technology could camouflage you. The key was patience. And luck. He remained alert to lights and motion. A sister passed by four feet away from him, heading from one place to another on some errand, oblivious to his presence. He froze while she passed, moved again when she had rounded a corner.

Finally he came to the door that he'd watched Tuksin enter and exit. He tried the knob with gloved hands. It was locked. He slid the small autopick from his thigh pocket, inserted its matte black length into the lock. It whirred softly as it felt its way within the lock, shifted its shape to fit. Then a click. He turned the autopick and the knob turned with it. Wats entered the cell, closed the door silently behind him.

He dared not turn on a light. Instead he scanned the room with the electromagnetic senses of his goggles. Night vision revealed a small spartan space. A narrow bed against one wall. A writing desk with an outdated terminal, a phone resting beside it. A bookshelf with a few texts in Thai and English. A wardrobe. A sink. No bathroom door.

The only transmissions in the room came from the phone and the terminal. He moved forward, slid a probe into a port on the phone, let it do its work. There was a thumbprint sensor on the side of the phone. He slid a print imager across it. As a precaution he did the same with the thumbprint sensor attached to the terminal, went to the doorknob, did it a third time.

As the probe cloned the phone's data he searched the wardrobe. Monk's robes. Sandals. Underwear. A cloak with a hood. No hidden back or bottom.

The probe beeped softly. Wats extracted it, slid a different tip into the terminal.

He lifted the mattress. Two boxes beneath the bed. One held old-fashioned photographs, a young man in a village. Tuksin, before he was a monk. The other held closed-toe shoes. He felt the top surface of the mattress. Nothing. He felt along the sides. Nothing. He felt along the bottom.

Hmm. There, a change in consistency. He explored it, found a place where he could part the fabric and slide his hand in, pulled out a large opaque package, soft-sided, waterproof.

Within it... business attire. Pants and a button-down shirt. A wallet with tens of thousands of baht in it in paper bills. A wig, short black hair, conventional looking. So, Tuksin liked to dress up like a layperson some times. Interesting.

The probe beeped softly again. He retrieved it from the terminal. The tiny display showed success in copying the data.

He slid the clothes back where he had found them, surveyed the room to ensure it was exactly as he'd found it, then let himself out the door and locked it behind him.

Kade came to his senses to the sound of his slate chiming at him. It was the insistent chime, the one that signaled a real-time connection request from one of his high-priority contacts.

He rolled off the bed and got it. Sam was sitting upright, watching him.

[Incoming video call from Ilyana Alexander. Accept? Y/N]

"It's Ilya," he said to Sam. "Can I take it?"

"Go ahead," she replied. "But you can't tell her anything."

Kade nodded grimly. He hit *Y*, angled the slate such that Sam wouldn't be visible.

Ilya's face appeared on the screen.

"Kade! I'm so glad you answered. Are you OK?"

"Hey, Ilya. Yeah, I'm fine."

"You look like shit! I heard you were mugged."

"Yeah, it's true. How'd you hear that?"

"Someone posted it from the conference. Grad student mugged last night. Also that he had a great poster. Also that there was an explosion and a double murder in Bangkok near where he was mugged. Any connection?"

Kade sighed, aware that Sam was watching him. "Only to the poster. I think they mugged me 'cuz they didn't like my graphs."

Ilya chuckled.

"How're you holding up, Kade?"

"Good. The mugging sucked. But, you know, the conference is going well. I met Professor Shu."

"Yeah? What's she like?"

He hesitated. "She's charming. Really *charming*. She invited me to come out to Shanghai. Maybe in August or so. She might invite Rangan too."

"Oooh, aren't you the jet-setter?"

Kade chuckled in return.

"You really OK, Kade?"

He forced himself to smile. Ilya would know that he couldn't tell her anything useful. She was just calling to let him know that she cared. She was calling to lend him strength.

"Yeah, Ilya. Thank you. I'm really OK."

She looked skeptical. "OK. I'll let you go, I guess. Sorry to call so late."

The screen said 1.12am. It must be, what, noon back home? Eleven?

"No problem."

She smiled at him. His heart melted. He missed her. He missed Rangan. He would find a way out of this. He would.

She reached forward to disconnect.

"Ilya... hold on."

"Sure, Kade. What's up?"

How could he express this? How could he say this without getting at the issues he couldn't talk about? Issues he didn't even want Sam to clue into.

The world was going mad around him. What he wanted was a check on his sanity.

"Ilya. It's really pretty intense here. There's a lot of stuff you don't see in the States, you know. Really provocative stuff."

Ilya nodded. "Yeah. I hear Thailand is that way."

He still didn't know how to approach this. He tried. "Ilya... in your essays. You talk about increasing access to trans-human tech. You talk about all the upsides. Do you ever worry about it being misused?"

She nodded. "Yeah, Kade. Of course. We've talked about this. Everything gets misused, sometimes. People will do all sorts of nasty shit with transhuman tech. But through history, when people have had the chance to use technology to improve their own lives, they've done a lot of good along with the harm. The good has more than outweighed the bad. Dramatically so. That's the only reason we're here today."

Kade nodded. "Yeah."

He wanted to ask his friend directly what he should do. He couldn't do that. Couldn't give any of this away. Not with Sam right there. Not over an ordinary video call over an ordinary slate.

"What about... what if only a few have it?"

"You mean if only the rich have a technology? Only the powerful? Or only the elites?"

Kade nodded.

"Broad dissemination and individual choice turn most technologies into a plus. If only the elites have access, it's a dystopia. The worse events in history... The worst atrocities... Maybe half of them arose directly because the powerful had a monopoly or a near-monopoly on some key capability."

Kade nodded. "Yeah. That's what I thought you would say."

She peered at him. "You sure you're OK, Kade?"

He smiled. "Better all the time, Ilya. Thank you. Thanks for calling."

She smiled at him. He could see the worry in her eyes, but she did her best. He wished he could touch her mind.

"I love you, Kade." She smirked at him. "Like a brother, I mean. I know Rangan loves you too."

Something relaxed inside him. Some tiny fraction of the tension in his body dissipated.

"I love you too, Ilya. Both of you. Tell Rangan I said so."

She smiled. The call ended.

Kade lay back in the bed. He had known what Ilya thought, but it was good to hear it again. He would follow the path she would choose. As soon as he figured out how.

He heard Sam resettle herself into her bedroll on the floor.

"Kade?" she said.

"Yeah?"

"Don't get any stupid ideas."

Wats slid the probe into his own terminal, opened the files to view them. Encrypted. The data from Tuksin's phone and terminal were completely encrypted. He'd expected that. He inputted the print pattern he'd lifted from the scanner. Still encrypted. A password required in addition. He frowned in annoyance.

He connected to a site he knew in Mumbai. He spent a moment specifying what he needed, entering in the parameters of his problem, and then submitted the request for a bid.

A few minutes later the bid came back. He whistled softly. It was high. He had the funds to pay it, but it was a non-trivial amount of money. This trip was rapidly exhausting the remaining balance of the settlement the Corps had given him. He paused for a moment, weighing his options. It was really no choice at all. He was committed to this course of action. More money could always be found later.

He accepted the bid, uploaded the data.

Two thousand miles away, a server in Mumbai received the data he transmitted. It analyzed the problem, broke it down into pieces, broke the pieces down into fragments, broke the fragments down into shards, and then distributed those shards to its worker devices.

Around the world, a network of more than two million compromised computers, slates, phones, gaming rigs, VR booths, and other devices, all operating unbeknownst to their owners, received their instructions, and began to explore the space of possible passwords, searching for the single pattern that would unlock Cham Phrom Tuksin's encrypted files.

31
From a Friend

Thursday dawned slowly. The alarm was beeping again. Kade slapped it off. Sam was in the shower. She felt pensive.

Kade felt numb. He'd left the serenity package on overnight. Everything about his situation felt distant, unreal.

He could see no way to avoid Friday without harming others he felt responsible for. The best he could do was play along with the ERD, and hope that nothing bad came of it.

The time would come when he would break free. He wasn't sure when or where or how, but it would come. He would bide his time, and watch, and wait, and be ready when the opportunity arose.

Sam came out of the shower, clothes already on. "Your turn."

He showered. His bruise was fading. He dressed. They ate in silence. A taxi driven by one of their escorts drove them to the conference. He attended sessions. Sam was with him constantly. One of their escorts was always in sight. When he went to the restroom, an armed man followed him in.

At 2.58pm, between sessions, Kade saw Somdet Phra

Ananda approaching him. He felt Sam tense through the link, felt her awareness of the pistol concealed in the small of her back, the knives in her boots, the positions of their two support shooters, the ceramic guns loaded with graphene-tipped rounds concealed under their blazers.

He pushed her paranoia out of his mind, met Ananda's eyes with his own. Sam dropped the link. The senior monk and professor came close, nodded to him. Kade nodded back. He couldn't feel Ananda's mind. He had his own Nexus pulled in tight. He had no idea what the ERD would pick up on and what they wouldn't.

"Kaden, would you walk with me?"

"Of course, sir."

He felt Sam go even more alert.

"It's a beautiful day outside. Would you like to walk in the garden?"

It was incredibly hot and muggy outside. The rain had been on and off all day. It was anything but Kade's idea of beautiful.

"Wherever you'd like to go, Professor."

Ananda nodded again, then led the way. Kade imagined the Thai mercenaries rushing to keep him in their sights.

"I was sorry to hear about your mugging, young man."

"Thank you, sir."

It was drizzling outside. Kade felt damp and sticky instantly. The garden was a web of interconnecting stone paths winding around green ponds. Low bridges crossed streams. Small stone statues of Buddhas, demons, and gods flanked the paths. Lush green tropical plants filled all empty space.

Ananda pointed things out as they walked. A bio-engineered carbon sink species that provided ground cover. The symbolism of the patterns the paths made. A seven hundred year-old statue of a bodhisattva, carved by a fallen dynasty.

"Do you know the bodhisattva vow?" Ananda asked.

Kade shook his head.

"It's from the Mah y na school of Buddhism," Ananda said, "different than my own, but still beautiful. The most basic expression of it is 'May I attain Buddhahood for the benefit of all sentient beings.' It's a pledge to keep being reborn into the material world of suffering, to put nirvana off indefinitely, until all beings in the universe have attained enlightenment and can also enter nirvana. It's perhaps the ultimate vow of placing others before oneself."

Kade contemplated that. "It's a beautiful thought."

Had Wats said something similar once? It was a gorgeous thought indeed.

"Another variant I like is 'All beings, without number, I vow to liberate.' Quite a commitment, eh?"

Kade nodded. "It is."

"It's been said that Buddhism is the most naturally democratic religion for this reason. The aim of Buddhist orders such as my own is not to control people, but to empower them. You understand?"

"I think so," Kade replied.

A memory of something else Wats had said came to him.

Buddhism suits me 'cuz nobody's in charge. Nobody's decidin' for me if I'm good or bad, goin' to heaven or hell. It's just me workin' on my head, you workin' your head, the friggin' Dalai Lama workin' on his head.

Democracy, indeed.

Ananda smiled. "Good, good. In Buddhism, as in, say, science, the goal is to empower people. To learn things of value and import, and spread them, so that as many men and women as possible can benefit from that knowledge, can use it to better themselves."

Kade thought of Shu. *It would be like giving guns to children,* she'd said. *There will be a vacuum... You will always be one of the elite.*

"What if people aren't ready for it?" he asked. "What if they'd hurt themselves with it? Hurt others with it? What if they're not wise enough for it?"

Ananda raised an eyebrow. "Are you wiser than humanity? All by yourself? Is it your place to choose?"

Kade shrugged. "No. And I agree that science should be used to serve the common good, to empower people. But… Maybe I can see harms that they can't. Maybe I've thought through consequences that most people wouldn't. Maybe I just know that a few people would abuse some piece of knowledge, even if the rest would use it for good."

"That is their karma, young man, not yours," Ananda said. Each of us must walk our own ethical path. And together, men and women of ethics can curb the damage of those without. But for you… if you keep vital knowledge from others, then you are robbing them of their freedom, of their potential. If you keep knowledge to yourself, then the fault is not theirs, but *yours*."

Kade mulled this. "I think I agree with you. Mostly."

A scientist is responsible for the consequences of his research, Kade thought. Both negative and positive. What good is my research if the world doesn't get the positive consequences out of it?

But can I do it without hurting people? Without making a tool to create slaves and assassins?

Ananda smiled. "I'm glad to hear that. Because it can be tempting to hoard knowledge, to use it as a way to gain advantage over others. But if we seek to serve our fellow man, we must spread the things we learn as far and wide as possible. To empower the downtrodden, we must put knowledge in their hands."

Kade looked around at the garden as they walked. "I'm not always sure I'm doing the right thing," he told Ananda.

"Only a fool is always certain," the monk replied.

Kade nodded again. "Thank you for the advice," he said. "I'll think about that."

Ananda nodded. "I'm sure you will, young man."

He led Kade back towards the conference center, pointing out more plant species along the way, talking about the complex web of life that connected them, telling the stories of every statue, every small bridge, pointing out the beauty in the way the drops of rain pocked the surface of the ponds.

When Ananda had gone, when he'd left Kade, slightly damp, slightly sticky, alone in the convention center, Sam opened the Nexus bridge again.

    [sam] Interesting conversation. What do you
    make of all that?
    [kade] I have no idea.

But Kade knew he lied.

At 3.19am local time, a lone CPU in a subverted cluster in a data processing center in Kuala Lumpur multiplied two 512-bit prime numbers and found that they were the factors it had been seeking for a 1024-bit number it had been assigned. It communicated its result to a system in Rio de Janeiro, which passed it to a cutout in Detroit, Michigan, which anonymously forwarded it to a machine in Johannesburg, South Africa, which finally delivered it to a server in Mumbai, India. The result was checked and rechecked. Everything fit. It was the final piece in the puzzle.

Three minutes later, at 4.22am local time in Bangkok, Thailand, Wats' slate chimed. It was a message from Mumbai. After twenty-nine hours of cracking, and more than a hundred trillion processor-seconds of computation, the key had been unlocked.

Sleep vanished from Wats' thoughts. He applied the key, and the data he'd copied from Tuksin's terminal and phone opened for him. It was in Thai. He invoked a translating filter, searched the data for Kade's name.

The first hit told him much:

From: Tuksin, Phra Racha Khana Chan Tham
<Tuksin@thaibuddha.th>
To: Suk Prat-Nung <SukPN@tmail.th>
Sent: Tuesday 1.38am local time (GMT + 7)
Subject: RE: something of interest

Suk,
The first half of the payment has reached my accounts. Here is the information:
*   The name is Kaden Lane. Ananda detected immensely strong Nexus activity from him and tasked me to investigate. He believes Lane has absorbed it permanently, but at levels far beyond any we have seen. He is no meditator. He may have the technology you seek.*

Well, well, well.

An hour later he pushed back from his slate, whistling softly, piecing it together in his mind.

The tall angular monk named Tuksin that he'd encountered twice now, the special assistant to Professor Somdet Phra Ananda, was secretly on the payroll of Suk Prat-Nung. And what Suk Prat-Nung wanted, more than anything, was upgrades to Nexus. Ananda had sensed the Nexus in Kade's brain, and assigned Tuksin to follow him. Tuksin had sold that data to Suk Prat-Nung. And Suk Prat-Nung had used it to arrange the ambush in the alley, unaware of Samantha Cataranes and her abilities.

But it was the last message, from Suk to Tuksin, that worried Wats.

The same luck that placed him in our grasp on Monday evening is returning him on Friday. He has struck a friendship with people I know. We will grab him, and the girl, as they leave the event.

The girl is dangerous, but we are now prepared. She will be of value, either alive or dead.

Suk

So Friday night was a trap. Could he use that to extract Kade? No, too dangerous. But he couldn't let Kade just walk into it, either. His first priority had to be keeping his friend alive.

He connected to a distributed anonymization service through an entry node in Switzerland. His signal was bounced around volunteered nodes around the world until it re-emerged on the public net from a node in São Paolo. From there he jumped to a throwaway machine in the Cayman Islands. From there he created a fresh email account on an anonymous mail service in Sweden.

The Friday night event is a trap. They'll try to abduct you, with more force this time. Leave Bangkok. It's too dangerous for you.

A Friend

He set up daemons on the email account, to inform him of any attempt to hack it. Then he sat back and waited.

32

Preparations

Sam woke to someone paging her slate. Garrett Nichols. She padded into the bathroom, turned on the shower for background noise, and answered.

"What's up?"

There was another chime. Becker came online, his strong square face filling up half the screen. It was 6.24am Sam's time, 7.24pm Becker's time. They were on nearly opposite sides of the planet. She could see he was still in the office.

"What's the situation?" Becker asked.

Nichols answered. "Twenty minutes ago, Lane received an email from an anonymous account telling him that tonight is a trap."

The message appeared on screen.

Sam absorbed it.

"Who sent it?" Becker asked.

"We don't know, sir," Nichols replied. "Anonymous account. We can try to backtrack, but if they have any sense it'll be difficult, and it could also give us away."

"Do it," Becker said.

"Yes, sir."

"What's our operational strength for this mission?"

"Twelve combat assets in-country, not including Blackbird. All local contractors approved by CIA." *Mercenaries*, he didn't say. "Second-generation combat enhancements."

Becker nodded. The *Boca Raton* held a platoon of marines, but deploying them would require authorizations they didn't have. The mercenaries would have to do. "Deploy them all. I want as many of the assailants as possible taken alive. They could lead us back to Prat-Nung."

"Yes, sir."

"You said you can stop them from self-destructing?"

"It's possible, sir. Based on data picked up by Agent Cataranes' phone, we think we know the self-destruct frequency and code. We can jam that."

"Good," Becker said. "Anything else?"

Nichols spoke. "Sir, I think we should reconsider Lane's role in this."

Becker narrowed his eyes. "Don't tell me you're going to give me the Lane-is-a-civilian line as well?"

Sam kept her breathing steady. Becker wasn't going to get a rise out of her today.

"No, sir," Nichols answered. "But he's an important asset. He's key to getting closer to Shu. It may not be wise to risk him tonight."

"And you, Cataranes?" Becker asked.

"Sir, Special Agent Nichols took the words right out of my mouth."

Becker's eyes flicked down, scanned the message again. "Acknowledged. We have to balance that against the possibility of capturing or neutralizing Ted Prat-Nung. And Lane is not irreplaceable if Shu is going to invite Shankari as well."

He paused for a moment, drummed his fingers. "Agent Cataranes, your top priority is to keep the asset alive. This message advises of us another *abduction* attempt. That should make your job easier. Special Agent Nichols, make sure the assault team also understand the priority of keeping Lane alive. We should be starting with non-lethal rounds and escalating to lethal fire only if absolutely necessary."

Nichols nodded.

Sam remained silent.

Becker went on, more gently this time. "They'll be expecting just you, Sam. They'll up their firepower to be sure they can handle you. They won't be expecting a dozen fully armed operatives. The advantage will be ours."

"Yes, sir," Sam said, her tone completely flat.

"And delete that email from Lane's account. There's no reason to spook him. You both have your orders. Becker out." His face disappeared.

Sam rubbed her eyes.

"All right, let's talk details," Garrett Nichols said.

At 6.47am, Watson Cole's daemons alerted him that the email account he'd used was under attack. A reply had been received from Lane's account. It contained a known Trojan Horse attack. Opening it would hand over control of his account and systems to the attacker. Forty-five seconds later, a bank of servers began issuing logon attempts to the account, thousand of them per second. Someone was trying to hack into his account. Disappointing.

Wats disconnected from the mail system in Sweden, then issued the commands to completely wipe the machine in the Cayman Islands.

The cyber-attack meant that the ERD had read his mail first. And their response suggested that they didn't mean to heed his warning.

Wats stood up to his full height and stretched. Joints

cracked in his thick neck, his beefy shoulders. He looked down at his massive arms, his dark brown skin, his superhumanly strong hands with their light palms, and contemplated his near future.

These hands had killed before. Many times.

Was he willing to kill again?

Yes. If he needed to, he would kill.

What would that do to his karma?

It was too late for that. His karma was as dark as could be. If he would suffer so that Kade might live, so be it. If he would send himself into an even deeper pit of hell that the world might be a better place, so be it.

He turned his hands over, studying them. Somewhere beneath his skin, DNA was slowly unraveling. Somewhere, the seeds of cancers were being sown.

We're all born dying, Wats told himself. What matters is only what we do with the instant we're given.

He'd doomed himself already. The world could still be saved.

It was time to collect his weapons and make his preparations. This was going to be a loud and bloody night.

In the command center aboard the *Boca Raton*, an hour after he'd signed off with Cataranes, Nichols received another call from Becker.

"Sir."

"I wanted to confirm with you: The other asset, the November asset. He's operational?"

"Yes, sir, though…"

"Yes, Special Agent Nichols?"

"I still think Agent Cataranes should know about the November asset, sir."

"What she doesn't know she can't spill," Becker replied. "The November program may have a very long lifetime.

We're under strict orders to keep it to a minimum of disclosure."

"Yes, sir." Nichols bowed his head.

"Good. I've cleared my Friday schedule. I'll be online with you and your team for most of it. Get some rest. Tonight I need you at your best."

"Yes, sir."

Becker signed off.

Nichols sat alone in the command center, restless and troubled.

Kade sat on the bed in their room at the Prince Palace Hotel. It was 9.20pm. Soon, he and Sam would activate their implanted memory-sets. His had been updated by two rounds of hypno today. He'd forget that he was here on false pretenses, that Sam was an ERD agent, that his friends back home were in danger, that someone had attempted to kidnap him two nights ago, that Su-Yong Shu intended a posthuman revolution against humanity, and more. He would be the Kade of two months ago, innocent, unbloodied, shy, nervous, optimistic. That idea should appeal, he thought. It didn't in the slightest.

He'd pushed through the final day of the conference today, Sam and a member of their backup team constantly near him. He'd seen Narong, finally. The Thai student had greeted him and Sam and said he was looking forward to tonight.

Kade had the urge to warn him, even with Sam there. He didn't. He found the logic inescapable. If he warned Narong, friends back home would be harmed for certain. If he didn't warn Narong or the others, they might all still come through this unscathed.

I have to think strategically, now, he thought. I have to wait for my chance. It'll come.

Cataranes came out of the bathroom. She had make-up on. They'd have extensive support, she'd assured him, but he could tell that something about this mission didn't sit well with her. She claimed it was just normal pre-mission adrenaline.

Soon, he wouldn't remember or care. He'd be a different Kade altogether.

"Time to go," Sam said.

Briefing

We find that the Constitution guarantees protections only to human persons. Non-human persons such as those created by the combination of non-human genes with human genes, by the integration of technology that affords non-human abilities, or by any significant deviation from the existing spectrum of human characteristics, are afforded no special protections. As such, Congress and the states may legislate the status of non-human persons without regard to the Constitutional protections afforded to humans.

DYSON V DEPARTMENT OF HOMELAND SECURITY,
Supreme Court of the United States, 2036

This court has committed a great crime today. To assert that a living thinking being, of any sort, is deserving of no rights is to ignore the lessons of two hundred and sixty years of democracy. We invite tyranny, atrocity, and slavery with this judgment.

Justice Elena Martinez, *Dissent in* DYSON V
DEPARTMENT OF HOMELAND SECURITY, 2036

33
Synchronicity

The cab dropped Kade and Robyn off near Soi Sama Han. Narong and Sajja met them, walked with them to the Buddha's Kiss. Everyone was in a good mood. He could feel Robyn's mind buzzing, excited. He couldn't wait for the Synchronicity trip to begin.

Sajja led them up a flight of stairs to a heavy door. Bolts unlocked. Chuan grinned and waved them in.

They filed into a spacious living room. Low furniture surrounded an open center space. A patterned carpet in gold and browns covered most of the floor. A half-dozen men and women from the previous night at the club sat on small cushions arranged in a circle. A low altar occupied the center of one wall, under a gorgeously ornate window. One side of the room connected to an open kitchen and a hallway. Buddha paintings took up another two walls.

A wizened Thai woman came in from the hall, a warm smile on her face.

"Aunt Chariya," Narong said. Their hostess. He introduced them. There were hugs all around. A ritual would start the trip. They were waiting for just one more person. Chariya suggested they take seats in the ring of cushions on the floor.

They found two open cushions between Narong and Lalana. They sat with Robyn on the left, by Narong, and Kade on the right, next to Lalana. Lalana giggled and said hello to them both. Her hand lingered as she clasped Kade's. There were eleven of them in the circle now, including Kade and Robyn, five young men and six young women. Kade recognized them all from the party at the Buddha Kiss on Monday night. Chuan, Sajja, Narong, and Loesan were the males. Lalana, Rajni, Sarai, Ning, and Areva were the females. One spot in the circle was empty. In the center of the circle there were two cushions. An old man sat on one, in lotus position, facing the altar, away from Kade and Robyn. Chariya came and sat in the other, back to back with the old man, facing towards Kade and Robyn.

"Come closer, everyone," she beckoned. "Bring the circle in as close as we can."

They shuffled forward until the circle was snug and close. Kade's knees touched Robyn's, touched Lalana's. It was delicious, distracting.

He *could* feel Chariya's mind, just barely. A whisper of peace and calm. And just beyond her...? Niran. Her husband. Strong, proud, tranquil.

"Empty your mind of all things," Chariya intoned. "Close your eyes. Feel your breath as it enters your body. Feel your breath as it leaves your body. Seek not to change it, simply observe."

Kade breathed with her, felt and heard the room breathe also.

A sound came. The door opened. He kept his eyes closed.

"Suk," he heard Chariya say. "How nice of you to join us."

"Hello, Auntie," said the new voice. "It's nice to see you too."

Kade felt a flutter of displeasure from Chariya.

"Since you haven't taken a seat yet," she said, "you can serve the rest of us."

"Yes, Auntie."

He heard footfalls. Someone walked past him. There was a tinkling. More footfalls. Someone made a swallowing sound. The tinkling was just in front of him. "Here," someone whispered. The new voice.

Kade opened his eyes. The newcomer was crouched in front of him, offering him a small glass filled with a silvery metallic liquid.

Kade nodded his thanks, took the glass, and drained it. More Nexus, mixed with Empathek.

He closed his eyes again, went back to focusing on his breath.

"Watch your breath leave your body," Chariya intoned slowly. "Watch it enter again. Let your breath fill your attention, let it expand to take up all of your mind. When thoughts arise, simply smile, and bring your attention back to your breath."

Kade let the breath fill him. The sound of it filled his ears. He felt his body contract as he inhaled, expand as he exhaled. The darkness behind his eyes stretched to the sides as breath flowed in to him, narrowed as the breath flowed out of him.

He became aware of a sound. A soft chanting, a gentle drumbeat. He watched the rhythm of his breath adjust itself to the soft beat of the drum. The entire room breathed as one. Their inhalations and exhalations synchronized.

"Open your palms," Chariya instructed, "and gently take the hands of those to either side of you."

Kade reached out slowly to his left and right. He felt

Robyn's strong hand close around his left, Lalana's small soft hand slip into his right. There was something electric about the contact. He felt a circuit close, a circuit of thought. It was faint still, but a ripple of sensation flowed through him, an awareness of the minds of the others in the room, an awareness of their breathing, an awareness of their awareness of him and each other, an echo, a resonance, a vibration of breath and mind.

"*We are students of the Buddha,*" Chariya intoned.

A dozen voices echoed her, "We are students of the Buddha." Kade joined them.

"*Ours is the middle path,*" she said slowly.

"*We seek enlightenment for all beings,*

"*To help all beings free themselves of suffering.*"

The room echoed her with each utterance.

"*Tonight we penetrate the veil of Maya.*

"*We pierce the illusion of separation between self and other,*

"*We apprehend our unity with one another.*"

Kade repeated every phrase in time with the others. It was hypnotic, euphoric. The veil of Maya, god of illusion and false isolation, was falling from his eyes. He was Kade. He was Robyn. He was Lalana. He was Mother Chariya. He was Father Niran. He was male. He was female. He was all of them, all things and all people.

Buddha looked down on him with a half-smile, serene, content, a man, a role model, who'd apprehended that no god or angel, no demon or devil, could bring heaven or hell to man. Only Right Thought, Right Action, Right Effort, Right Concentration, only the actions of a person, only the striving they made, only the insights they gleaned could ever lead to their enlightenment.

He knew this room well. He'd meditated here dozens of times, hundreds of times, thousands of times. He was all these people, all their experiences.

He had been a monk, a nun, a prostitute, a student. He'd first encountered Nexus four years ago, six years ago, three years ago. He'd devoted his life to service, to compassion, to enlightenment. He'd sold his body again and again. He'd studied the mind in the abstract, wanted to feel it tangibly. He'd found a way.

He was Aunt Chariya. He was her husband Niran. He'd been monk and he'd been nun. His decades of meditation had stilled his mind. He'd encountered the sacrament, had become one with the other, had crossed boundaries into forbidden territories. He'd left the order, begun something new.

Compassion for all life filled him. The universe cried out in pain, in the illusion of division. He was called to teach, to spread love, to release beings from their bonds of craving and aversion, to teach them that all was one.

He was the Buddha. He was all of them here. The fourteen of them together, together they were something more, something amazing. They were the universe observing itself. They had achieved enlightenment. They could spread it to the world.

He was the sun. His radiance filled space. His golden rays bathed the Earth, sustained all life. He was the wind that blew the leaves, and he was those leaves as well. He was the seas that ebbed and flowed and roared and surged, and he was the fish that swam in those seas, the plankton that they ate, the sunlight falling on those waters. He was the Earth. He was the stars. He was all of creation and he was at this very instant so much *alive* and so much *apprehending* his own self. The universe was waking in this very room, and thus it was waking *everywhere all at once*.

Kade opened his eyes. He was trembling. They were all trembling, all panting with quickened breath. Sweat stood on his brow. Robyn's hand pulsed rhythmically in his left hand.

She felt serene, joyous, completely in her element. Lalana's small hand fluttered like a hummingbird's wings in his right. She felt excited, exultant. How long had it been? *Three hours!* It had felt like mere minutes, had felt like eternity.

The tempo was easing, now. Chariya was chanting softly. Niran was tapping the drum ever more slowly. Breathing was slowing, returning to normal. Faces wore smiles. Chests were still moving rhythmically. He glanced to his right. Lalana's breasts rose and fell under her white shirt. Her nipples were hard against the thin fabric. The olive skin of her throat, of her chest where her shirt was unbuttoned, glistened with sweat. It was the most erotic sight Kade had ever seen. He couldn't understand why their clothes were still on, how they could do this and not have it devolve into skin on skin, lips on lips, body on body, why they would want anything else at all.

The thought leaked out. Kade blushed. Lalana giggled in voice and mind and the circle caught it, amplified it, tittered as one, not unkindly, and the tension was broken.

"That was awesome," Narong whispered out loud. Kade felt it. The circle had never been that intense before.

It's me, he thought. Me and Robyn. The Nexus 5.

Chariya was looking at him, her eyes met his eyes, her mind met his mind.

Yes, her mind seemed to say. *Who are you, child?*

There was just one mind that felt anything other than joyously open... Suk. He was so distant from them. Why?

Someone tapped him on the shoulder. Loesan. He was grinning, exultant, crouched beside Kade.

"I felt what you've done with Nexus. It's in you all the time, isn't it?"

Kade nodded, not yet ready to trust his voice.

"It's amazing," Loesan said. "Will you show us how to do that?"

Something felt wrong. There was something he should fear. But why? Knowledge was to be shared, not hoarded. Why not share some of it now?

Kade nodded. "Yes." It came out husky. "Yes, I'll show you." It came out fine this time. "Give me a couple minutes." His body had needs.

Loesan grinned even wider, radiated excitement and curiosity. "Yeah."

Kade rose, waited in line for the washroom. Lalana got in line behind him, brushed her body against his for just a moment. Kade nearly groaned in desire. He didn't know the rules here, didn't know what was OK. He felt for her intentions, found an amusement there. She pushed him against the wall, pulled his face down to hers, kissed him passionately, playfully. He was so hard. Lalana felt it against her thigh, reached down and put her hand on the lump in the front of his pants, squeezed his hardness through the fabric, pumped him up and down, once, twice, three times... Then she laughed and pushed away from him.

"Later," she whispered. Her eyes and thoughts promised sweet delights.

He mock-groaned in frustration. She laughed at him again, and he couldn't help but laugh as well. The combined Nexus and Empathek sang in his mind. Everything was absolutely wonderful. God, she was sexy.

He was too hard to piss when it was his turn. He ran through prime numbers for ages until his hardness subsided, relieved himself, and came out to show them what he and Rangan had done.

And then Kade saw Suk. Sitting on the couch. Wrongness. The young man exuded arrogance – avarice. Suddenly he didn't want to teach them anything after all.

He searched for some excuse...

"Rangan," he said. "Axon. I have to check with him

before sharing what we've done with you."

Their disappointment was palpable. It pressed on him. Perhaps he could give them some simpler ideas, less dangerous ideas...

"But I can at least share a few ideas with you," he finished.

Anticipation returned in all their minds. He sat, they leaned in close to him, and he started to show them the barest glimpses of what he and Rangan and Ilya had learned.

34
Sisters

Robyn Rodriguez was still on cloud nine. That experience had been one of the most amazing of her life, second only to her first experience with Nexus 5, with Kade, when... when... It had been amazing, that was all.

She took her turn at the restroom, still in a daze, breath heavy, pulse fast, mind and heart wide open. She came back to find the circle had transformed into a few small knots. She could still feel the minds in the room, a gestalt presence all around her, joyous and sublime. She was synchronized with them, sensitized to them. There was another presence behind her... unique...

"Hello," said a small voice in accented English. "What's your name?"

Robyn turned. It was a child. A young girl, perhaps seven years old. Robyn crouched, smiled, held out her hand. "I'm Robyn," she said. "What's your name?"

She stared in amazement, struck dumb. The child's mind was like a gem, bright and clear, small and yet so brilliant. How could Robyn even feel her? Was this child on Nexus? Who would do that?

"My name is Mai," the girl said in her high, small voice,

placing her hand in Robyn's. Her mind exuded peace. Robyn should not worry. No one had harmed her. She wanted to cry, knowing that this child was safe.

Chariya was behind her. Robyn felt her peace and comfort, her affection for the child.

"Mai," she said in Thai. "Why are you awake?"

Robyn felt the answer. It arose from Mai's small mind. She'd felt them. They'd felt wonderful. They'd felt like love. They'd felt like the future, when the world was all one.

Robyn turned towards Chariya. "How...?" she asked the older woman. How can this be?

Chariya looked down at them. "Her mother used Nexus while Mai was in the womb. And... other things. A friend sent the mother to us. Mai was born this way." Chariya crouched down, knees creaking as she did. She stroked Mai's hair.

"Do all...?" Robyn started to ask.

Are all children of Nexus mothers like this?

The older woman shook her head. "No. Only a few."

Robyn caught a glimpse of something. A refuge in the south, in Narathiwat Province, near the tiny village of Mae Dong. A place of peace, where a few such children were sequestered, where Mai might go someday, if she chose.

"I'm special," Mai said.

"Yes, you are, Mai," Chariya told her, smiling, emoting love and tenderness. "You should go back to sleep."

Mai shook her head slowly, wide-eyed. She looked at Robyn. "Will you come play with me?" Childlike curiosity and wonder swept out from her. It was infectious, contagious. Robyn couldn't imagine anything more delightful than playing with this child.

Robyn looked at Mother Chariya. The older woman nodded. "You may play for a little while, Mai. Then it will be time to sleep again."

Mai answered with a happy squeal and an outpouring of delight. Robyn felt her spirit soar with the little girl's. Mai seemed to read her heart, took her hand, led her skipping down the hall.

Her room was only a little bigger than a closet, but it was full of love. Drawings covered the walls. Bright geometric mandalas; Thai fairy princesses; elephants with cross-legged Buddhas atop them; Chariya and Niran, nearly lifelike, with a child between them. Bright lines connected the chakras of the three figures, a procession of layered triangles in a rainbow of colors.

Mai showed Robyn her toys. There was a stuffed elephant with an ornate box on his back to ride in. A monkey as large as the elephant. A beautiful Thai princess in a dress of red and gold. A Buddha who rode in the box. Mai put Monkey in Robyn's hands, made believe a story about a princess deep asleep in the forest and a monkey who had to lead the Buddha on the elephant to her to wake her up. The story came across in bits of English, in Thai, in images and emotions radiating from Mai's tiny mind.

Robyn could barely follow the game. Her heart was in her throat. Her chest was full of sensation. She could do little but marvel at the existence of this child. So young. So carefree. The child exuded *happiness*. Joyousness. Serenity almost. Mai felt safe here. She felt loved here. Here… in the midst of… in the midst of… in this terrible…

"I would like to have a sister," Mai said. It came across in emotions and desires as much as it did in words. Someone to hold her hand. Someone to braid her hair. Someone to sleep at night with. Someone to play games with. Someone to laugh with and share secrets with.

"Do you have a sister?" the little girl asked Robyn.

Robyn shook her head. Her heart was pounding in her chest, threatening to erupt. Her voice wouldn't function.

"Would you like to be my sister?" Mai asked.

There were tears on Robyn's face. She didn't know why. There was a face in her mind. A girl. A little girl. A fire. No. No. No.

Mai touched Robyn's face with her small hand. "Don't be sad."

A sob wrenched itself free of Robyn's throat. She pulled the girl close, held her.

Mai kissed the side of her face with those tiny lips. "My mommy's gone too," she said.

No. No. Her parents lived in San Antonio. They were teachers. Her parents weren't dead. They hadn't died in the fire. They hadn't been... They hadn't been...

Her sister! A moan escaped her. She was losing her mind. She'd never had a sister. Her sister had died in the fire. She'd killed for her sweet little Ana. She'd killed them all. No, she'd never had a sister at all!

"It's OK, Sam," Mai said. "You can be my sister."

Sam? No. Her name was Robyn. Robyn Rodriguez. She was a grad student at Stanford. She was here to attend... She was here to... She was...

Her sister. Ana. Oh my god. The tears flowed freely from her eyes. The grief was unbearable.

"Shhhhh... It's OK..." There was something happening. Something in her mind. A bright light, a pinprick, white, glorious, glowing. It was Mai. She was inside her, doing something, comforting her, pushing back the shadows.

Her name was Samantha Cataranes. She'd been someone else long ago. An awful thing had shaped her, made her who she was. She'd lost all that she loved. She'd buried it in a box inside her mind. The light of Mai's mind opened it, brought it out to her, cast it in warm bright light, buffered it not at all, but made Sam brave enough to see it again, all of it. This girl, or the Nexus, or the Empathek, or all of them, wrapped her in love, and she saw that she would not be trapped, that she would not be a prisoner of those years all her life, that she was bigger than anything that could happen to her, that she could not only overcome it, not only master it, but transcend it, leave it behind.

And this girl... this Mai... So like her sister. This place, these people. So like the place she'd grown up, the place where awful things had happened, the people who'd done them. But different. Totally and completely different. Ana had known pain, would have known more... This girl... Mai. She knew love. This was the dream her parents had tried to make real, but uncorrupted. Sam feared for it. So fragile, so precious.

Her heart was bursting. She felt the inexorable urge to communicate. She had to let this out in some way. She had to speak the things she'd learned. She looked at this sweet, beautiful girl. She wasn't sure how much Mai had already seen. A lot, quite possibly. But she couldn't burden this beautiful radiant innocent child with her own darkness.

"Mai... thank you. Thank you so much." She felt the tears drying on her face.

Mai smiled at her. The girl was radiant, inside and out. "Are you my sister now?"

Sam nodded fiercely, opened her heart and beamed the love she felt out of it and into this wondrous child. "Yes. I'm your sister, Mai. And you're mine."

Mai beamed.

"You have to go to sleep now, Mai. I'll play with you more soon, OK?"

Mai nodded. Satisfied. This had been good playtime. She had a sister now.

Sam tucked her in bed tenderly, kissed the girl's brow, turned off the light.

She cleaned up the mess of her face as well as she could

in the bathroom. She had no patience for it. Her dilated pupils stared back at her. Something sang inside her, compelled her to set it free.

She wandered into the living room. Her breath came short. Her heart still pumped hard in her chest. Whether it was the drugs, whether it was Mai, whether it was what she was about to do, she didn't know. She had to share.

Her eyes met Narong's. He smiled at her. He would listen. No. He didn't know who she really was. Her eyes tracked right. Niran was looking at her curiously. She didn't care. She went past him. There, Kade. He was explaining something to Loesan, gesturing with his hands. Sam could feel a mild wash of it from his mind. Neuroscience. Something about improving on Nexus. He didn't see her. Didn't notice her.

She called to Kade with her mind, put all her longing into it, her need for him right now, her need to connect with him. Even from across the room he felt it, and it stopped him in mid-thought. He turned, met her eyes with his, nodded. He excused himself from his audience and wandered over to her. All eyes were on the two of them now.

There was a room. A small guest room. The knowledge was Niran's or Chariya's or maybe someone else's. It didn't matter. She took him by the hand, led him there. It was even smaller than Mai's room, nothing but a narrow mattress on the floor and a tiny wooden table.

She lay down, pulled him down next to her. His mind was full of curiosity, concern. What was going on?

"Kade, Kade, Kade…" she whispered, her face inches from his. "Oh, Kade. Oh my god, Kade."

"Hey, slow down there. You OK? What's going on?" Concern broke through. He was worried about her.

How could she explain? How could she start? He didn't

even know who he was, let alone who she was.

"Robyn, talk to me…"

She shook her head. "My name's not Robyn, Kade. I have to show you…"

Sam wrapped her arms and legs around him, held him close. She wrapped her mind around his, sent comfort, peace.

"This is going to be a shock to your system, Kade."

Alarm. He started to squirm against her grip. She wouldn't let him.

"Robyn, what the hell?"

She whispered his counter-mantra, with her mouth, with her mind.

Canyon, parakeet, cherry.

She saw it, felt it. Awareness awoke within his mind. Denial. Confusion. Realization. He thrashed mentally and physically. She covered his mouth with her hand, held him tight, as gently as she could, blanketed his mind with comfort, with hushes, with reassurance. There was no danger. They were safe. Safe. She had to tell him something. About her. It was wonderful. It was awful.

He quieted after a while. She pulled her hand away.

"Sam… What the hell? What's going on? What are you doing?

"Shhh… Kade… I'm sorry to pull you away. I just have to get this out. You're the only one."

"Get what out?" He saw some of it then. The horror. The violence. The deaths. "Oh no… oh no… Sam…"

She sent comfort. "No, Kade… It's OK. Really. It's all long long ago. It was awful. I was young. But… I'm better now. I'm the best I've ever been. I think I'm OK for the first time, maybe ever."

He stared at her, not comprehending.

"Kade, I just have to share this with someone, please. It's

overwhelming. I have to get it out. Will you listen? Please?" She released her grip on him, opened her mind to him, sent him her need, her longing, the overwhelming urge to release the demons from her head, from her heart, to show him what she'd learned.

He nodded, slowly, looking into her eyes. He felt troubled, surprised. The drugs were riding him hard with empathy as well. He felt compelled to connect, to understand.

"OK. I'll listen."

On the *Boca Raton* Jane Kim listened to the conversation. This was not good.

"Sir," she said to Garrett Nichols. "We have a problem. Blackbird has dropped cover. The false persona is down. She's brought Canary's down as well."

"What?" Nichols asked. He checked the time. There were still many hours of Nexus effects left for them. "Get her back in character."

In the living room, old Niran rubbed his chin thoughtfully. The Lane boy had said many interesting things. Most of them were beyond his understanding.

Still, the capabilities he'd hinted at were clear. And he knew someone who would be very interested in learning more. He considered, decided.

Niran went into the other room, found his phone, made the call. The conversation was brief. Yes, the person he'd called was indeed interested. He understood that the boy was leaving Thailand in a few days. Yes, he was in Bangkok. He was occupied at the moment, but would come by in a few hours.

Niran hung up the phone, smiled to himself. It would be wonderful to see Thanom again.

35
Roots

"I wasn't born Samantha Cataranes. I was born Sarita Catalan. I grew up in southern California, in a little town near San Diego. My parents were Roberto and Anita. They both worked in bioinformatics, had met on the job. I had a sister, Ana." Sorrow welled up from her. Tears began to flow again, silently running down the side of her face. Kade felt troubled, concerned, empathic. He stroked her hair, sent kindness.

"My parents were hippies. The kind of hippies who worked in tech but went camping with the family, had singalongs with friends. There were always a lot of friends around the first few years. I think my parents smoked pot." It made her laugh, even through the tears. Kade kept stroking her hair.

"When I was eight, and my sister was four, the company where they worked was acquired by a bigger company. They had the option of relocating to Boston, or cashing out with a big severance payment. They took the latter." Her voice took on a faraway quality. She began to show Kade with her mind as she told him.

"Some friends of theirs had moved to a place in New

Mexico. They'd joined a kind of white collar commune. Everyone did some sort of work they could do remotely. Computer people, consultants, analysts, visual design people, some radiologists and lawyers. They all lived on this ranch. The idea was to raise kids together, to live in a place where they could share parenting duties, where they could be a little shielded from the law, maybe do some hippie things together."

The images came across as bright and colorful. Kids running around in the New Mexico sunshine, smiling grownups picking them up and swooping them through the air, pushing them on the swings.

"They had some shared rules and rituals. There was a Sunday night thing all the families had to go to. Somewhere between a church service and a town hall. It was a hippie thing." Her tears had stopped. She was trembling, though, anticipating something to come.

Annoyance flashed across Sam's face. They were hailing her. Her superiors. Her eyes flicked to one side, silenced a notification.

She looked back at Kade, became present with him again.

"The place was called Yucca Grove." She swallowed.

She saw Kade frown, the name familiar, reaching for the memory... "Yucca Grove? Isn't that where...?" His eyes went wide. Something chilled him. He pulled her closer. "Oh no, oh, Sam, I'm so sorry."

"Shhhh. It's OK. I have to finish this."

He held her as she spoke, as she showed him with her mind.

"The first couple years were good. Really fun." Laughter. Carefully contained bonfires in the back. Two dozen "cousins" and playmates. Hiking in the green Sangre de Cristo mountains. And love, love, love. Her mother's kind face and melodic voice. Her father's mischievous sense of humor. Her sister's squeals of delight at each new prank and trick they played together.

"Then it started to change." A listlessness in her parents. Laughter draining out. Smiles only during the rapture of Sunday nights. A rapture she didn't share. A rapture Ana didn't share. Then the bad men.

"It was called the Communion virus. It tweaked the brain. It was supposed to bring people closer together, make them less selfish, more empathic. It did something to the temporal lobe, one of the circuits involved in religious experience. It was supposed to put people closer to God. It did that. It also made them slaves." Anger rose up in her. The bad men. The ones who were immune. The way they took over the enclave. The way they made everyone else serve them. Stole their money. Crushed their spirits. The control. The abuses.

"Some of the survivors claimed that the whole commune had chosen to take it together. Some say they never took it, that someone used it against them as a weapon. I can imagine my parents trying it voluntarily. They weren't scared. They loved the idea of group living, of altruism, of harmony." It came out bitter. She was still angry with her parents. Angry that they'd failed to protect her. No... not her. That they'd failed to protect Ana.

"I don't know. I can't ask them. They died." Kade was numb, horrified, concerned, just watching, listening, empathizing, trying to comfort her with his mind, with his arm around her and his hand stroking her face.

"There were thirteen of them that ran the place after that." Their faces filled her mind. The memory of their cruelties, their abuses. The cigarette burn on her thigh. The blow that had knocked a tooth out of her mouth. Worse. Much, much worse...

"The prophet and his twelve disciples. All men."

She flicked her eyes to one corner to dismiss another message from her superiors, brought her eyes back to his.

Kade swallowed. He wanted to look away, wanted to not hear this, not know this. He endured. He held her and listened, sent her what comfort he could.

"The prophet. He was a bastard. He was naturally immune. It didn't drag him down. He figured out that he could make all the rest do what he wanted. He found the others, the ones with the most resistance, all men. Made them his disciples. Let them have anything they wanted, as long as they reinforced his control."

"They set themselves up as gods. The Sunday night meeting... it became worship. The virus made everyone want to believe. They used every trick in the book to set themselves up as gods and everyone worshipped them."

"Almost everyone. It only barely worked on me. It didn't work at all on my sister. We couldn't understand what was happening to everyone else. It was crazy. I tried to run away when I was eleven. They caught me – beat me. My mom and dad just watched. I tried again, and the prophet and his disciples beat me within an inch of my life. I tried to stab one of them with a fork, once, and they whipped me half to death, left me tied to a fencepost all night, burnt me with cigarettes."

The memories were brutal and painful. Kade lived them with her. Sam was numb to it. Tears streamed down his face.

"After that they kept a close eye on me. They didn't let me near any phones, any terminals, any knives. They used those people as cattle. Took their money. Took whatever women they wanted. Beat up the men for sport." She remembered it. Living in hell. In a prison camp. She knew it wasn't supposed to be this way.

"They started using me when I was twelve."

Kade moaned with the memory of it. Sam just stared off into space.

"I fought the first few times." She'd clawed them, bitten at them, lashed out like a wild animal. "But they always won. It hurt less if I just let them." The pain and humiliation of surrender – of submission. The disgust of it. The self-loathing.

"After that... I just gave in. I just started pretending that the virus worked on me. I told Ana to do the same." The act of dewy innocence. The complete submission to any request, any authority, the feigned enthusiasm at the Sunday night rallies. It killed Kade. The tears kept flowing. He was sending Sam love and compassion, not for the adult her, but for that twelve year-old child, helpless and alone and abused, utterly abandoned by the world.

"I went two years that way. I thought about killing myself every day. I thought about killing one of them every day. What kept me going was Ana." Her sweet sister, also unaffected by the virus, confused, hurt, scared. How Sam had tried to comfort her, hold her, raise her, shield her, protect her, show her some small bit of joy in this godforsaken place.

"It changed when I was fourteen. I'd gotten used to the abuse. I only got hurt when one of them was in a bad mood. Then one day, I was taking a walk with Ana, and one of them saw us, and he had this look, this *leer* on his face, and I was so used to that, and I didn't care anymore what they did to me. But then I realized he wasn't leering at me. He was leering at my little sister. And I thought, oh my god, if any of them touch you I'm going to kill them all, every one of them, with my own bare hands."

She was crying again. The numbness was gone. Old rage and fear and impotence replaced it. She could be numb about the pain she'd endured. Not about her fears for her sister, for the one innocent human being she'd tried to protect in those years.

"So I did what I should have done a long time earlier. One of them took me to his room. He used me hard. And after he'd spent himself, and he'd fallen asleep, I did the bravest thing I could imagine. I slid out from under him... I went out into the other room, where his phone was, and I picked it up. I hadn't touched a phone since I was nine. It beeped when I pressed the keys. I was so terrified he was going to hear me..."

Kade felt her memory, that childhood terror. They would kill her for this. They would beat her. They would rape her sister. She would never escape...

"...but I pushed 9-1-1 and it went through. And I told them where I was, and that the prophet and his disciples had made us slaves, and that they were about to hurt my sister, and that my parents had become zombies, and I didn't listen to any of their questions, and I hung up." Adrenaline was coursing through both their veins now, the memory of danger, of courage, of pushing her luck.

"And then I put the phone back and snuck back into his room. And when I crawled back into bed with him, he started to wake up. And so I fucked him, told him I wanted him so bad, did anything I could to distract him." Kade remembered it, remembered it through Sam. The fear. The shame. The way she'd hated him as she did it. The way she'd imagined him bleeding and broken and dying as he'd taken her, the way he'd mistaken her hatred for passion.

"A little while later there was shooting. A sheriff's deputy had rushed out to the site, and one of the disciples had shot him, killed him." My fault, she'd thought. I killed him.

"No, Sam, no! That wasn't your fault!" Kade told her.

She smiled sadly at him, put her finger to his lips. "I know, Kade. I know that now. I thought I knew that already. Now I do. Finally.

"After that it was a siege. All the slaves... my parents, the other parents, even the kids. They all worshipped that man, the prophet. Every family had guns. He'd made sure of it. He told us all that Satan's forces were coming to take us to hell, and we had to protect ourselves. The feds arrived. The FBI's Bioterror Division. Someone had picked up on the word 'zombie'. It wasn't the first Communion virus outbreak. Just the worst.

"The prophet told the feds that we'd rather die than go with them. That if they invaded we'd blow ourselves up, burn ourselves alive, all of us, including the kids.

"The siege lasted three days. The FBI played loud music. They brought in preachers. They brought in shrinks. I'd never seen Ana so frightened.

"On the fourth day I woke up in the middle of the night. It was 2.28am. I remember that on the clock. I'd slept maybe an hour with all the music and all the people running around. And I just knew what I had to do. My dad had a gun, like all the rest. I snuck into their bedroom. He was asleep. It wasn't his shift to be on guard. His pistol was on the nightstand. I took it, and I put on a pretty dress, the white one, the dress that the worst one, the prophet, liked to dress me up in when he fucked me. I hid the pistol under that dress, and I went to see him. People just chuckled when they saw me. They knew what that dress meant.

"There was a guard at his door, one of the other parents, a fat one, not one of the disciples. The light was on underneath. I told the guard that he'd sent for me, that he wanted me to come to him in the middle of the night, that he had a 'blessing' for me." She spat the word out in disgust.

"The guard understood. He didn't have any sympathy for me. He just saw me, and wanted me, and wanted to serve

God and the prophet. He let me in.

"The prophet was behind his desk, looking at his terminal. He looked up, saw me in that dress, looked me up and down. 'Sarita,' he said. 'What do you want?'

"And I pulled out the gun. It was huge. The guard was already turning away to go back into the hallway. The prophet saw the gun, and he yelled." The memory was so fresh in her mind. She remembered every instant of it, the position of every piece of furniture, every sound, every moment frozen forever as a still image. "He tried to come at me, but his desk was in the way. I pulled the trigger and my first shot missed completely. The gun jerked up towards the ceiling. The guard was turning around, coming at me. The prophet was most of the way around his desk, coming at me to slap the gun away. " Sam remembered the huge boom of the pistol, the smell of it, how the gun's kick had shaken her whole body. She remembered the fear, the way he was growing larger in her sight, the knowledge that she was about to die and fail – and be beaten and be killed – and have her sister raped in front of her.

"I panicked. I tried to jerk the gun down to level it and pulled the trigger again. I fired wild. The guard hit me at the same time.

"He knocked me to the ground. He tried to kick me. Somehow I still had the gun. I pulled the trigger again and the guard fell on top of me. He was fat and huge. There was blood everywhere, all over my dress. I tried to pull myself out from under him. I got part of the way but my legs were still stuck. I looked up and I saw the prophet. He was getting up on his feet. I'd shot him. There was blood on his shirt, his left arm. I'd shot him and knocked him down and now he was getting up. He had a knife in his right hand. He started coming for me and I pulled the trigger again, took him in the stomach, and he fell down to his knees."

Sam stopped speaking. The scene played out for Kade in his mind. *I hate you*, she'd whispered to the prophet. He'd coughed up blood and she'd shot him again, in the chest, and he'd flopped backwards. And then there had been more gunfire, from everywhere. The FBI had heard the shots, taken it as their cue to enter. The defenders at the gate were firing back with shotguns, rifles, pistols. People were screaming. More gunshots, coming closer. More screams.

And then, the first explosion. It took the south wing of the ranch down completely, sent a fireball up into the night sky. The rest of the building was on fire. Smoke was everywhere. Sam struggled free of the fat guard on top of her. The prophet was moaning, still barely moving. She stood above him, took careful aim, fired into his head again and again.

The smoke was too thick. She was coughing. She couldn't breathe. She put part of her dress over her mouth. It didn't help. She started to get dizzy, confused. She fell down to her knees. She didn't mind dying. It was better than staying alive through this. She only hoped Ana was OK.

She was welcoming death when she heard the voice. Loud. Male. Still full of life, but not one of the disciples. A voice she didn't know.

"IS THERE ANYBODY IN HERE?"

She tried to stand. Fell. Coughed. Waved her hand. And then she was in someone's arms. A man. He was wearing a vest. It said FBI – BIOTERROR. He had Asian features.

"It's going to be OK!" he yelled over the din of fire and explosions and gunshots.

He carried her into the hallway. Fire was spreading. A timber fell from the ceiling to their right. He ran the other way. There was a picture window there. They were on the third floor.

"CLOSE YOUR EYES!" he yelled.

And then he'd run at the window, twisted at the last moment, broken through it with his shoulder, shielding her from the glass with his body, and propelled them out into the night.

"Nakamura," Kade said.

Sam nodded, tears streaming down her face. She felt… lighter. Like she'd released something, heavy and pressing.

"Your sister?" Kade asked.

Sam shook her head. There had been one hundred and nineteen people in total at the Yucca Grove ranch. Twenty-eight had survived, including Sam. Most of the disciples had been killed by gunfire or the explosives. The others had taken their guns to their own heads. Neither Sam's parents nor her sister Ana were among the survivors.

"Oh, Sam. I am so so so sorry." He put all the compassion he had into it, all the support and care and understanding he was capable of.

Sam locked her eyes with his. "Kade, I wish my sister were still alive. But I would rather have her dead than living through what was coming for her." She meant it, he saw. Meant it fiercely.

"I'm so sorry for everything you went through, Sam. I can't imagine… No one should go through that. No kid. I can see why you joined the ERD." She'd wanted to hurt them, the bad men. Find them and hurt them or catch them or kill them. Make it so they couldn't hurt anyone ever again. She'd wanted to be strong. Strong enough that no one could ever hurt her or those she cared about again.

He tried to comfort her. Tried to give her support.

"Kade, Kade, you don't understand," Sam said.

"What?"

"That's the past, Kade. I can't go back. I've let it control me for way too long. I can let go now."

He was confused.

"I met the most amazing little girl tonight, Kade. She showed me. She helped me face it. I've just been nibbling off bits of it at a time. I can face it now. It's over. I'm not that little girl anymore. I did the best I could. I forgive myself."

He could feel it in her. The sorrow was still there, but it didn't weigh her down. She felt light as a feather. She felt free.

"That girl, Kade, oh my god. She's like you are. Like *we* are." Sam said it wondrously, as if she was realizing it for the first time. "The Nexus is in her always. She was born that way. It's amazing. I have a sister again."

She collapsed against his chest, laughing as she cried, her breath coming fast. Eventually the laughter faded, and she lay against him, breathing in and out, weeping silent tears, tears of release, tears of closure, tears of transition, tears of gratitude. She walked through her life again, marveled at it, thanked her young self for her courage and her steadfastness, forgave that young Sam for all the things she'd once held against her, said goodbye to her parents and her first sister and all the things she'd known so long ago. She lay with her head against his chest and he stroked her hair, sent her compassion, sent her warmth and comfort She fell asleep against him and still he lay there. He could feel the party slowly dwindling out in the living room. It felt so good here. It felt so right. Kade stroked Sam's hair, felt the bittersweet goodbyes of her dreams, felt her chest fall and rise in time with his, and eventually sleep took him as well.

There was silence in the C&C aboard the *Boca Raton*. She'd dismissed every message instructing her to desist, to restore her cover. They'd stopped trying eventually. They'd just listened.

The three of them had each known tiny bits of Sam's background. None of them had heard all of it before. It was a relief when she stopped talking. It was a relief when sleep took her. No one spoke for long minutes.

"Make sure the fireteams are on alert," Nichols finally said. "Let's let Blackbird get a little shut-eye."

Wats sat cross-legged one floor above Kade and Cataranes. His weapons were at his sides. Chameleon-ware made his still form difficult to pick out from his surroundings. A heat capacitor attached to his combat suit slowly siphoned off the excess warmth his body produced, keeping him from boiling in the infrared blocking garment. The data fob felt hard and cool against his chest.

His radio had picked up bursts of encrypted chatter twice tonight. The commandos were near. He wasn't sure where, but they were near.

It was a relief to feel the party below drift towards sleep. His Nexus nodes were in strictly receive-only mode. It was hard to get a good Nexus connection that way. Two-way feedback was necessary to synchronize minds, to get a clear transfer of concepts.

But he'd caught enough. The night had affected him powerfully. He was a part of the Buddha too. He was the dark mirror of a bodhisattva in his own way. He was the opposite of the enlightened teacher. He was one who would risk rebirth in darkness and ignorance, ever further from nirvana, so that others might have their chance at peace and enlightenment.

He wondered if, in a past life, Cataranes had been one of those as well.

36
Company

Kade dreamed Sam's memories. He was fourteen, wrapped in a blanket by the man who'd jumped with him from a third-floor window, watching the hell he'd lived in for the last six years burn to the ground. He was a young teen, growing up in a strange new world. He'd known exactly what he wanted to be, from the moment his old life had ended. He wanted to be one of the ones to fight the bad guys, to save the little girls from the fires.

He was eighteen, at the academy for the newly created ERD, his mentor a man named Nakamura, the very same agent who'd carried him out of the burning wreck of the ranch; his instructors teaching him to fight, to think, to survive. He was twenty-one, the year he'd spent in a seemingly endless round of surgeries and gene therapies, turning him into a weapon against evil. He was twenty-three, alone on the shores of the Caspian, the lone survivor of a mission that had destroyed a bioterror lab, but at huge cost to his team... He was twenty-seven, assigned suddenly to infiltrate a Nexus ring in San Francisco... He was in Bangkok. He'd met a girl. An amazing, magical little girl...

Someone was shaking him. He brought his arm around

to trap the hand, didn't actually know how, flailed ineffectually instead.

"Kade!" It was a whisper, a man's voice. He was Kade. That's right. Kade. Not Sam.

"Kade, wake up!" Loesan. That's who it was. "There's someone here to see you!"

Kade struggled to open his eyes. It was so early… They'd barely slept for an hour. Loesan's mind vibrated with excitement. Something big was happening. Someone important was here.

"Wha'?" Kade managed to mumble.

"Come on, get up," Loesan whispered. "You're going to like this!"

Kade blinked again, tried to wake himself up. Sam mumbled something against his arm. He looked over at her, her hair tousled, her face vulnerable and younger than he'd ever seen it before. He felt a wave of tenderness. It confused him. Time for that later.

He slowly extricated himself from her sleepy embrace, sat up, blinked some more. "OK, OK. I'm up."

Kade followed Loesan out of the tiny guest room, down the hall, into the living room. The very faintest hint of pre-dawn light showed through the windows. Two dim lamps were on inside. Most of the people from last night were sprawled out on couches or on the floor under blankets, asleep.

Shit, we snagged the best room, he thought. That was rude.

Old Niran sat cross-legged in front of the altar, meditating, feeling content and serene. Narong and Suk were awake. Suk radiated alarm and surprise. Narong was staring at someone, getting up on his feet, walking towards the person just out of Kade's sight.

Kade stepped further into the living room, turned his

head to see what Narong was looking at. There were three huge Thai men in overcoats in the room. They screamed *bodyguard*. Between them was another Thai man, tall, ramrod straight in his posture, grey hair at his temples, a fancy ring on one hand, a confident smile on his lips. He stepped forward towards Kade, extended his hand in greeting.

"Hello. My name is Ted Prat-Nung. I hear I have a lot to learn from you."

Oh no. Oh god no.

Oh, fucking hell.

Sam smiled contentedly, still half asleep. This had been so nice... She'd dreamt she was Kade through the night, had been the geeky shy boy of his youth, had lived through his discovery of science, of psychedelics, experienced his intense, restless curiosity firsthand, had lived through his and Rangan's first experiences with Nexus, the late night talks and experiments that had led to the discovery that the Nexus core could be programmed... It had felt so sweet and safe. The constant love of family and friends, a life in a world where curiosity and wonder were the drivers, not pain or fear or justice. What a sweet, gentle life... The only pain that of the loss of his parents in a crash, so suddenly, so recently...

She reached out to touch him, to hold him, found only mattress. Hmmm. Where could he...?

Something was flashing at her. Her contacts. Another message. What was it?

It was flashing red.

COMBAT IMMINENT.

Sam was fully awake in an instant. There. Tactical displays. Agents converging on front and rear, tranq loads active, lethal loads as backup. A high-value target just meters from her. Ted fucking Prat-Nung. They were coming in. They'd be here in seconds.

Cold fear gripped her. No! The civilians here! Mai!

She flicked her sight, hit ABORT, ABORT, ABORT. Looked for the damn menu item, there, CIVILIANS AT RISK,

CIVILIANS AT RISK, ABORT, ABORT, ABORT.

Someone overrode her. They were coming in. Fuck.

Garret Nichols gripped the sides of his chair as the *Boca Raton* rocked in the swells. They were in high seas, slowly maneuvering to stay clear of a pair of Thai Kolkata class destroyers on patrol. Rough conditions were expected for the next few hours.

Nichols, Jane Kim, and Bruce Williams studied the newcomers on the screen in the cramped control room. The tiny omnidirectional camera in the apartment was crap in low light. Three of the figures were large, bulky, hired muscle of some kind. The fourth…

"Holy shit," Bruce Williams whispered. Image amplification techniques on his terminal had just pulled up a match. That fourth figure, at a fifty-four percent probability, was none other than Ted Prat-Nung.

Nichols stared at the screen for a split second, dumbfounded, then began yelling out orders.

"Code Red, Code Red. Teams A and B to containment positions. Team C to reserve. Places, people!"

"Roger that," Williams replied.

Nichols jammed on the key to page Becker, yelled out another question. "Status on the November asset."

"He's asleep, sir," Jane Kim replied.

"Get him up. Eyes on Target Four. Prep for target capture."

"Roger that."

Becker's face appeared in a window. "Status," he ordered.

"We may have Ted Prat-Nung in the room," Nichols replied. "Moving our assets into capture position."

Becker blinked in surprise.

"Odds now sixty-three percent," Williams said.

"November-1 is on his feet," Kim reported. "Moving into position."

"Lane just walked in the room," Williams said, tension in his voice. Tactical display showed his position. Cataranes was a few meters further away.

"Abort signal from Blackbird!" Williams called out. "Civilians in harm's way."

"Override that," Becker ordered. "We know there are civilians there. This is capture, not kill."

Nichols nodded. Williams stabbed a key at his console.

"November-1 is almost in position," Kim said.

"Fireteams A and B still a few seconds from ready," Williams said.

The speaker crackled: "My name is Ted Prat-Nung."

"That's it," Nichols said. "We've got him."

"November-1 is in position," Kim said.

Nichols glanced at the screen with Becker's face. Becker nodded.

"Fireteams hold at ready," Nichols commanded. "Jane – initiate capture with November-1."

37
Harsh Introduction

"My name is Ted Prat-Nung," the tall man said. "I hear I have a lot to learn from you."

Oh, fucking hell, Kade thought.

Suk picked up on it. He caught the thoughts in Kade's mind, the images of danger, of armed men lying in wait. He understood in a flash of realization.

"It's a trap!" Prat-Nung's nephew cried.

Alarm spread across Ted Prat-Nung's face. The three bodyguards reached for guns beneath their coats.

Narong was faster. He was up on his feet, just a meter from Prat-Nung, a pistol in his hand pointed at the older man's head. Kade knew that pistol. He'd seen it in Sam's dreams. Ceramic shell. Graphene-tipped rounds. X-ray and metal detector invisible. Standard issue for ERD and CIA field ops.

Oh no, oh fucking no, oh please no.

"Everyone freeze," Narong said, loudly, in unaccented English. "Thanom Prat-Nung, you are under arrest for violations of international law as specified in the Copenhagen Accords on Global Technological Threats."

Have you seen Narong? Kade had asked Sajja.

I think he's sick, Sajja had answered. *Must be really bad for him to miss his poster session.*

Narong hadn't been sick. He'd been in ERD custody.

One of the guards took a slow half step to the right, trying to get around behind Narong.

He said, "I see you moving. If you take another step, I'll blow his brains out."

Kade could see it, could imagine it, the way the graphene-tipped round would go in and out of Ted Prat-Nung's skull, leaving a trail of devastation, splashing his blood and brains onto the wall.

"Everyone lay down your weapons. You're surrounded. Surrender and you won't be harmed." His voice was loud, clear, authoritative, completely unlike the real Narong.

They'll use your tools in ways you never intended, Shu had told him. *They won't ask your permission.*

The bodyguards looked at their boss, uncertain what to do. Ted Prat-Nung slowly turned his head to look at Narong, stared down the barrel of the gun.

"No," Ted Prat-Nung said. "If you shoot me, you die. You put down *your* gun."

The expressions on the faces of the bodyguards hardened, turned grim.

I won't let them, Kade had told her.

Narong... Kade looked closer at Narong's mind. There. That wasn't Nexus 3... That was Nexus 5, Kade's technology. Which meant that the ERD had done just what Shu had said they would.

They won't ask your permission, she'd scoffed.

But that also meant that the back doors he and Rangan had installed...

Narong took a step closer to Ted Prat-Nung, brought the gun even closer to his head. "You're all surrounded. Drop your weapons and this can end peacefully. You have three seconds to comply.

"Three…"

No one will use what I've built as a weapon, Kade told himself. Ever.

He sent one of the back door passwords. Narong's mind opened to him.

"Two…"

He reached inside Narong's mind, grasped for the control he needed.

"One."

Kade flexed his will as the word came out of Narong's mouth. A muscle twitched in Ted Prat-Nung's jaw. One of his bodyguards jerked his hand for his weapon.

"No," Kade said.

Narong's eyes rolled into the back of his head. The gun fell from his limp hand. His knees started to buckle.

A burst from a submachine gun tore through Narong's midsection. One of the bodyguards had his weapon out, the barrel practically buried in Narong's stomach. Narong crumpled to the ground. Kade stared in dismay.

Ted Prat-Nung turned to look at Kade. "Who are you?" he asked. All three of his men had their guns out, pointed at Kade now.

The door exploded inwards.

Garrett Nichols watched on the edge of his seat as Jane Kim operated November-1. "You have three seconds to comply." Kim caused the words to come out of November-1's mouth. "Three…"

"Two…"

"One."

Kim issued the command to fire one shot into the target's gut. Nothing happened. Onscreen, the feed from

November-1 ceased. Nichols flicked his eyes to the displays from the in-room camera. Gunfire. November-1 was collapsing to the ground, hit. The bodyguards all had their guns out. Everyone was looking at Lane.

"Fuck," Nichols said. "Move in! Move in!"

Teams A and B hit the buttons to blow the doors and burst into the room.

ABORT! CIVILIANS IN DANGER! CIVILIANS IN DANGER!

Someone overrode Sam's command. Fuck. She jumped to her feet. She was unarmed. On her display another friendly asset appeared, just meters from Prat-Nung and from Kade. She hurried into the hallway. Oh no. Mai was there, at the edge of the living room, peering in. Sam had to get the girl away from the danger.

She crept quietly down the hall, reached out with her mind to Mai at the same time. Come here, Mai. Come play with me. She sent it as images, vignettes of them together in the room, safe, playing with the dolls.

Mai turned her head, delightedly, smiled at Sam. She had Monkey in her arms.

The back door at the end of the hall exploded inwards. It knocked Sam off her feet. ERD mercenaries were moving in. The sound of tranq rounds filled the air. Submachine gun fire answered it. Oh, fuck.

The front door exploded inwards. Kade threw himself to the ground, saw Ted Prat-Nung do the same. Someone was shooting from the door, two men in black. Something whizzed above Kade's head. Darts embedded themselves in the bodyguards.

The three bodyguards fired at the doorway, full auto. Muzzle flashes filled the room in gouts of foot-long flame from the tips of the guns. Kade heard a cry of pain. A figure in the doorway toppled, the second ducked back out of sight. Ted Prat-Nung crouched behind a chair. Kade flinched back into a doorway.

"Man down!" Bruce Williams called out. "Casualty on Team A. Punched straight through the armor. Tranq rounds ineffective."

Oh shit, Nichols thought. Antibodies. Those fuckers have been inoculated against our tranq.

The tech was evolving too fast. It was getting out too fast. Now people were going to die.

"Switch to lethal rounds," he ordered. "Take those fuckers down."

The bodyguards crouched, spread out, kept their submachine guns trained at the ruined front door. Smoke and dust filled the air. Lalana was on the ground, a bullet in her leg, screaming. Niran picked her up, ran towards the hall with her.

Automatic gunfire burst out from the doorway, cut Niran in half. Bullets passed through him, took one of Prat-Nung's bodyguards in the thigh. The bodyguard fell to one knee, returning fire as he did. The others opened fire on the door. Lalana's head exploded in the crossfire. Kade gasped as her mind winked out.

Ted Prat-Nung pulled a machine pistol from his waist, glanced out from around his chair, a scowl on his face.

Sam shook off the explosion of the door, looked up. Submachine gun fire came from the living room. Mai's smile had turned to terror. She was facing Sam, looking past her, backing away towards the living room and the sounds of fighting.

No!!! Sam sent. No!!!!

Someone grabbed Sam's arm, lifted her up.

"Blackbird, you hit? Where's Canary?"

The voice came out muffled through his facemask. Sam was still staring at Mai, trying to will her back away from the shooting, towards safety.

A trench coated bodyguard came into view, crouched down low, backing into the hallway. He looked behind him, saw the agents coming in, whirled to fire. The merc next to Sam reacted faster, brought his rifle up, pulled the trigger. Muzzle fire erupted from his gun.

NO!!!! Mai was in the line of fire!

Sam threw herself against the soldier, slammed him into the wall. Bullets whizzed past them. Mai screamed, paralyzed, standing upright in the crossfire, horror emanating from her.

The man Sam had slammed was stunned. More fire came from the door behind her. A round grazed her shoulder. Sam acted on instinct, turned the one she'd slammed against the wall, steered him towards the team coming in, covered his hand with hers and pulled the trigger with his finger.

Bullets slammed into the man she held, sent her staggering back with him. She fired wildly at the back door, barely able to aim the assault rifle in the man's hand, held down his finger on the trigger until the clip was empty, saw one of the incoming figures fall.

"What the fuck?" Garrett Nichols yelled.

Bruce Williams shook his head. "Two down in B team, sir. Blackbird just took down two of our own!"

"Tell her to stand the fuck down!" Nichols ordered. "Take her down if you have to. Alive!"

He surveyed the displays. Three of the assault team dead. All the bodyguards down, at least one dead for certain.

Ted Prat-Nung unaccounted-for. What a clusterfuck.

"And send in Team C!"

Silence. Sobbing. Sam let go of the man in front of her and he slumped to the ground. She whirled.

Where was Mai?

She saw Prat-Nung's bodyguard first. Dead, a bloody crater where his face had once been. There, Mai. Sam ran, crouched down next to the girl. There was blood all over her. Her eyes were closed. There was pain, pain, pain emanating from her mind. She was hit. Once, twice, three times. Bullets from the incoming ERD mercenaries had lifted her up and thrown her down the hall. Her tiny body had been half ripped apart, her toy Monkey reduced to shreds. Her mind was fading.

NOOOOOO!

Mai opened her eyes, tried to smile up at Sam.

I love you, Sam, her mind seemed to say.

And then she was gone.

Madness descended on Samantha Cataranes.

Someone slammed into her from behind. An agent. Sam rolled with it, threw him off her. There was another burst of gunfire from the living room, a yell of pain. She could hear screaming, sobbing, cries for help. She felt them in her mind. Another agent came at her from the side. She blocked a kick, took him down with a single blow to the face.

Lalana was dead. Niran was dying. Chuan was hit and bleeding. The rage consumed her.

She blocked a rifle thrust from her left, tried to kick at the one ahead of her, felt his rifle smash painfully into her shin as he blocked her.

Chariya lay hit and dying, sobbing quietly for her husband, for the girl she'd adopted as daughter. Sarai was screaming in pain and horror, a bullet in her, crouched over Sajja's dead body, the man she'd loved.

They were all inside her. Their minds were one with hers. Sam could feel them all. The Nexus and the Empathek fused them with her.

Sam was them. She was their despair. She was their anger. She was their weapon.

Sam bellowed in rage as the agents came at her, lashed out with fists and feet, took one down, a second, a third.

A rifle smashed into the back of her head, brought her down to her hands and knees. A man behind her. She kicked backwards, sent a body hurtling through the air and into the wall. Another one slammed a rifle into her face. A man on the ground kicked her viciously in the midsection, knocked the wind out of her.

Sam rolled to the side to get out from the middle of them, took a hard kick to the head. A booted foot landed on her chest, a rifle pointed down at her.

"Cataranes!" It was Lec. "Stop!"

She kicked up, trying to disarm him. Another man kicked her in the face, hard. Two more rifle barrels stared down at her.

"Stand down, damn you!"

Wats panned the fiber-optic camera frantically. It was a goddamn warzone down there. Kade had appeared briefly before everything went tits up, then disappeared. He had to get Kade out of there. Where was he? Where the fuck was he?

Kade crouched in the doorway. He could feel the pain and death out there. He could feel it all through the Nexus connection they shared. Narong was crumpled on the ground, confused and terrified, not sure what he'd done, in incredible pain, terrified he was about to die.

I did that, Kade thought. My fault. My responsibility.

Chariya was hit, mourning the death of her family. Sajja was dead. Lalana was dead. He could feel Niran bleeding to death in the middle of the room.

It took his breath away. Pain and anguish like he'd never experienced. It was filling him up. He could feel them dying, feel their agony, feel their despair.

I've killed these people, he thought. I've fucking killed them. Tears streamed down his face.

He had to get a grip. He slammed the serenity package on hard, jammed it to its max setting. Clarity descended through the fog of pain and fear. He opened himself to those still alive, tried to parse what they were seeing through their own confusion and rage and terror.

He could feel Chuan slowly creeping towards one of Prat-Nung's dead bodyguards, reaching for his gun, intending to kill these motherfuckers who'd invaded their home. Through Chuan's eyes he saw Ted Prat-Nung dash forward from behind a chair, heading for Chariya, firing at an agent with his machine pistol. His volley took the man in the chest, armor-piercing rounds ripping right through the mercenary. A stray hit Rajni, cowering on the floor, tore through her left thigh, shattered her femur, ripped a scream out of her body like no john or pimp ever had.

Prat-Nung scooped Chariya up in his arms, dashing for the window. Another agent brought his gun to bear. Panes of the stained glass window exploded beyond Prat-Nung. Automatic fire converged on him, pounded into his chest, lifted him off his feet and dropped him onto the floor, Chariya atop him.

Kade pulled his mind away from them. Sam. She was down, agents pointing rifles at her. He sent it to Chuan, pushed on the boy's mind. *Sam! Help her!*

Chuan came up on one knee, a submachine gun from one of Prat-Nung's bodyguards in his hand, firing on the agents above Sam. His bullets took one in the back, tore through the man's spine. Two rifles came up, muzzle flares burst into life, and Chuan's chest exploded. He fell, a look of shock on his face. Kade could feel his mind still working, surprised, not understanding, still catching up to what had just happened to him, still coming to grips with the fact that he was dead, as the remains of his body slumped to the floor.

Kade had to help Sam himself. He flipped on Bruce Lee. Targeting circles appeared in his vision. He clicked on one of the men standing above Sam, his weapon trained on her:

Full attack.

Bruce Lee hurled his body into the fray.

Sam went still on the ground, stared up into the gun barrels, put her hands above her head. They had her. Damnit.

More gunfire came from the kitchen. Screams. She could feel Kade searching for her, felt him find her.

Chuan came up on one knee with a bodyguard's gun and fired. She felt him do it. The bullets tore through the chest of one of the men above her. Lee lifted his rifle, took his eyes off Sam, annihilated Chuan.

Someone slammed into Lee from the side. It was Kade, in a flying side-kick that knocked the mercenary into the wall. She felt Lee slam the butt of his gun into Kade's face, knock him to the ground. But for a moment there were only two of them above her, their eyes towards Chuan, guns drifting up. Sam reached up with both arms, grabbed their belts, yanked *hard* as she kicked herself to standing and brought them down to the ground.

She whirled in a vicious spinning hook kick that would have decapitated most men, struck one of the agents in the head, plowed him into his squadmate. An assault rifle went off, rounds firing wild into the ceiling and behind her.

Lee rushed her, using his rifle two-handed, trying to bash her in the face with it. She grabbed the rifle with both hands, rolled back and kicked, hurtling him into the air and the wall behind her.

She came up to her feet, his rifle in both her hands. Someone crashed into her from behind. She whirled, smashed the man in the head with the assault rifle. An agent on the ground threw himself at the back of her legs, brought her down to her knees.

Someone kicked at Sam's head. A rifle came down on her back like a hammer blow, sent her sprawling. She rolled to avoid another aimed at her head, took a foot painfully in the ribs, punched out at a man's groin, knocked him back despite the body armor.

Fuck. Fuck. Fuck. Too many of them.

Kicks and rifles rained down on her. She blocked, blocked, kicked blindly, tried to grab at a gun. Blows kept landing. Pain exploded through her face as a steel-toe boot connected. Her left arm went numb as she blocked a rifle butt painfully with her elbow. Pain shot up from her kidneys. Her hip, her ribs, her chest, she was being pummeled into hell. She couldn't breathe, could barely see.

Too many. Too fucking many. She could not win this fight. She was going to fucking die here.

They killed Mai!

A foot landed on the side of her head and pushed. Two men wrestled her wrists together. Sam raged, almost pushed them off. A rifle butt slammed into her face. Her muscles went limp for an instant. Her wrists snapped together behind her back in plasticuffs. Three rifle barrels pointed down at her.

"Stand down, damn you!" Lee yelled.

She was beaten, she realized. There would be no rescue this time. Now she'd pay for what she'd done.

And then the ceiling above her exploded, something large and heavy fell from it onto the agents below, and someone tall and built like an ox dropped after it, full auto shotguns in both hands, firing as he landed.

Wats scanned frantically. There! That was Kade. He flew out of nowhere, collided with one of the ERD agents. He was trying to save Cataranes.

The agent smacked Kade down as Wats watched. At least six of them down there. No sign of Suk Prat-Nung's men yet either. Nearly hopeless odds.

All that matters is what we do with the instant we are given.

Wats slapped the plastic explosive down, hit the delayed detonator, crouched behind the heavy wooden desk.

The explosion was deafening. Dust fell on him instantly. He heaved the oak desk forward, sent it hurtling down through the hole in the floor, pulled his guns and jumped down after it.

Sam's eyes widened as the towering figure in black leapt down through the hole that the blast had opened in the ceiling above, landing on the wreckage of the massive desk that had preceded him, and the agents buried beneath it. Lee looked up, stunned, tried to bring his pistol to bear. Wats' gun roared at point-blank range, and Lee's head disintegrated in a cloud of red gore.

There was a mind there. Sam felt it. She'd felt it briefly once before. Watson Cole. The one that had gotten away.

The ex-Marine turned, firing in a tight arc in the close space of the combat. One of the agents rolled behind the fallen desk. Another brought his gun up to fire at Cole. The black man's auto shotguns pulverized him.

Another mercenary took aim at Cole. Sam threw herself at the mercenary, arms cuffed behind her back, knocked him to the ground, kicked him in the face until he went limp.

There was one more agent up, the one who'd rolled behind the wreckage of the massive desk. He came around it, tried to take Cole by surprise. Wats was there, waiting for him. The mercenary came up into the barrels of both guns. They erupted, their muzzle flashes burning him, graphene-coated pellets shredding through his armor, opening holes in his chest and groin.

One of the two agents under the wreckage of the desk was stirring, reaching for the assault rifle just out of his grasp. Wats kicked it away from him, bashed him in the face with the butt of his shotgun.

The guns fell silent. Only the screams of the dying and the sobs of the bereaved could be heard.

38
Hell on Earth

Garrett Nichols stared at the display in stunned silence. What the fuck had just happened?

"Radio intercept," Jane Kim said. "Bangkok Metro Police chopper en route. ETA... two minutes."

No. This was a nightmare. They couldn't let the local authorities find any evidence. Their rules of engagement were crystal clear on that.

Three men were still alive. Another's radio was offline, his state unknown.

"Bruce, get those men up. They have to get out of there."

Bruce Williams was pounding keys furiously. "Not responding. Two unconscious. One has good vitals but radio's offline, possibly damaged."

"Ninety seconds till chopper arrival," Jane Kim called out. "Aerial news drones en route as well."

"Sanitize," Becker said quietly from the screen. "Protocol Thirteen."

Nichols looked up, horrified. "Sir, we still have three men alive in there, maybe four. And civilians! I need to get them out."

"You don't have time," Becker said. The Deputy

Director's face was pale. His mouth was set in a hard line. His voice was resigned. "You have local police inbound and you now have less than two minutes."

"We just need a little more time... get our men out of there, get the civilians out... There's no precedent!"

"There isn't any more time!" Becker snapped. "Those men are unconscious. The Bangkok Police are almost on top of you. You have to sanitize! You know the rules. Protocol Thirteen. Execute."

Nichols couldn't breathe. This was a bad dream – a horrible dream. Kim and Williams were staring at him, ashen-faced.

"Execute, Nichols, or I swear to god I'll have you relieved."

Nichols tapped at his keyboard, pulled up a screen he'd only ever used in war games. Entered the commands. A confirmation prompt appeared, asking for his password. He entered it. A second prompt appeared, on all their terminals. It needed a second person's password.

Kim and Williams stared at their terminals, all blood drained from their faces.

"Bruce, type in your password."

Williams blanched further. "Sir, I... I..."

"Do it, Bruce," Nichols said gently. "It's on me."

Williams trembled as he typed in his password, hit ENTER. The system accepted it. A final confirmation prompt appeared on Nichols' screen. He looked up at the feeds, the tactical display, his casualties, the men on the ground, immobile but still breathing, the sobbing civilians crawling on the floor. He hit ENTER one more time... God save his soul.

Sam crouched by a fallen agent, back to him, yanked a knife free from his belt, sawed it through the plasticuffs, came to her feet a free woman.

Wats reached Kade a second before she did. Kade was coming around. He'd been slammed in the face hard. One eye was swollen bloodily shut and a nasty cut ran from his temple to his cheek. He was groggy, but rising back to consciousness.

Wats holstered his guns, scooped Kade up in his arms. "We've got to get out of here."

Sam couldn't agree more.

"Wha'... Wats?" Kade had one eye open.

"Kade, my man. I told you to stay outta trouble."

Sam ripped a submachine gun from one of Prat-Nung's guards. The ERD weapons would be biometrically locked. This would have to do. She ejected the clip from the black-market special in her hand, checked it, rammed it back home. "Let's go."

She turned, half jogged towards the back door. Wats took one of Kade's arms over his shoulder. They came up behind her.

There was a sound from behind them. She whirled to see Wats turning. He pushed Kade to the side, brought his gun back up towards the direction they'd come.

Automatic fire boomed loud in the small space again. She felt Wats' grunt of pain as she came around him to fire at the source. The agent she'd taken down. He'd gotten his hand on the gun. His upper body exploded under a burst of armor-piercing rounds from both of them.

Wats was down on his knees. The bullets had hit him just below the navel, ripped through his abdomen and gone out the other side. He'd saved Kade by pushing him aside. Sam was lucky none of the rounds had hit her. His body had deflected them.

That was twice he'd saved her life in five minutes.

"Faarrgghhhh," the big man moaned. "Goddamn, that

hurts."

Sam could feel it. On top of all the moans and fear and pain and loss and rage in the room, she could feel Wats' pain, the coldness spreading through his guts.

Fucking hell, she thought.

Kade was up on one knee, then on his feet. He grabbed one of Wats' arms and tried to drag him across the floor towards the blown doorway.

"Fuck!" Wats swore. "Leave me, you idiot. Get the hell out of here. You got shit to do, brother. Go fucking do it."

"No fucking way," Kade yelled. "Sam, help me!"

"Fuck," Sam said. She grabbed Wats' other arm, started dragging him towards the door, limping with every painful step.

Then the explosions started, and the world went to hell.

Nichols hit the final ENTER key. Displays flickered and went blank. He tried to picture it. At the back of each man's skull, four grams of CL-70 had just ignited. Their brains would have disintegrated immediately. Windows would have shattered. The apartment would instantly be a raging inferno as the incredible heat of the explosion ignited wood, paper, cloth, anything in its path. Anyone still left alive in there would have been killed by the explosion or would burn to death in seconds. God help them all. God help his own soul.

The explosions knocked Sam off her feet. She landed on her back, couldn't make sense of the world for a moment. Then she understood what had happened. Bloody hell...

The place was an inferno. Walls had exploded, beams collapsed. There was fire everywhere, smoke everywhere there wasn't fire. Where was Kade? Where was Wats? She could feel them. Pain. That way, towards the door.

She reached Wats. Kade was atop him. The marine was gurgling, dying. A giant splinter of wood had been rammed into his neck, opening up both windpipe and carotid artery. Kade was trying to apply pressure. Blood kept spurting. A burning beam fell on Sam's shoulder painfully. She heaved it off, turned back to Wats, pushed Kade's hands away, got her own on the artery, tried to close it off. Blood spurted into her face between her fingers. Wats was staring at her. Sam could feel him in her mind. He knew he was dying, knew there was no chance. She could feel his intention. He was willing her to protect Kade, to get him to safety. Willing her to give the kid a chance to do something, to make a difference in the world. He locked eyes with her, put all his effort into it, willed her to promise him. Promise!

Sam didn't know what to do. There were tears streaming down her face. Everything hurt. She didn't even know this man. They'd been on opposite sides the last time she'd seen him. The Nexus and the Empathek were still coursing through her brain, opening her to him. She could feel him dying, feel his single-minded focus on ensuring that his mission succeeded despite him. She could feel Kade observing them in horror. She nodded to Wats. Yes. Yes, she would carry it on.

Wats' eyes burrowed into her. He kept pushing with his mind. She must do this. She must. Sam nodded again through tears. Yes, she would see Kade to safety. Yes.

She could feel his life drifting out. Feel his will touching Kade. There was something he had to take. Something around Wats' neck. A data fob... He would understand. It would set his gift free. It would help him make the world a better place.

Wats' eyes lost focus. His mind began to fray. She shifted her fingers, tried to find a way to stop the bleeding. It was no good. More blood spurted into her face. His mind was slipping… slipping…

"Karma…" he croaked.

The coherence of his thoughts collapsed into noise, into chaos. The chaos fell to pieces. The pieces disappeared. He was gone.

There were more screams coming from the living room. Narong was still alive. He was on fire, burning to death. It was horrible, horrible. She felt every moment of it in her mind, felt Areva collapse to her knees from smoke inhalation, her lungs burning. This was how her parents had died. How her sister had died. This is how she'd killed everyone Sarita Catalan had ever known. The smoke was thick.

Kade was pulling a bloody chain up and over Wats' neck. He was crying, placing it over his own neck, tucking it under his shirt. The boy was in pain. She could feel it. His leg was pinned under something. She crawled on hands and knees around his upper body.

Stay low, she thought, under the smoke.

Her hand felt something. His leg, his shin. It was broken. There was a fallen beam across his calf, burning hot. She heaved up, threw it off of him, felt him cough painfully. Smoke was getting in his lungs. He struggled to get to his feet and collapsed. Sam felt pain lance through the broken shin. He wouldn't be getting out of here under his own power.

She felt and heard the hallway ahead of them collapse into a pile of burning rubble. There would be no getting out that way. She came to her knees, picked him up. She tried to picture the apartment. The front door would lead out to a building already on fire, a long hall, a locked door at the end. Not that way. The altar… it was under a window that looked out on the alley. She tried to picture it. Areva was burning, now, her skin crisping and blackening, the pain filling Sam's mind. Sam coughed, once, twice, three times, from other people's pain or from her own smoke inhalation, she didn't know. She was getting lightheaded. She had to concentrate. The altar, the window. She wouldn't be able to see. She'd have to find it by dead reckoning.

Sam put her head to the floor, hyperventilated air that was super heated, but cooler than any other she'd find. This was as good as she was going to get. She sucked a final breath into her lungs. She came up onto her feet, Kade in her arms, stayed as low as she could, held her breath. She staggered down the hall, limping, her left leg aching from some blow.

The living room was ablaze, the open space raging far hotter than the hallway. The heat of it made her wince and draw back. A fire vortex was forming in the middle of the room, the superheated air swirling ever faster.

She half ran, half limped forward. Her foot came down on something still alive. Someone screamed louder. She ignored it, lurched forward, blind. The window must be directly ahead of her. God help her if it wasn't.

"CLOSE YOUR EYES!" she yelled with all her saved-up breath.

Sam surged forward with what she had left, twisted her body at the last second to shield Kade, crashed through what little glass remained in the window after the explosion, hurtled into the pre-dawn air.

39
Frying Pan to Fire

Feng shook her awake with mind and body. Even after all these years, this body still needed sleep.

Shu opened her eyes. "What is it?" she asked in Mandarin.

"Explosion. Nana District. Near where he was attacked on Monday."

She was awake instantly. Feng opened his mind to her, and she absorbed it all. She became one with her higher self, breathed deep in the glory of it, scanned the net for all public knowledge of this, saw how paltry it was. Thai Royal Police databases opened for her, told her fractionally more, not what she was looking for. Where was Kade now? Thai Telecom opened to her mental touch. There. His phone was at the site of the blast.

"Get the car," she commanded.

"This may be dangerous," Feng replied.

"Get the car," she repeated. Feng bowed and turned, sprinting for the other room in their suite.

"And your guns, Feng. Get your guns."

Sam landed hard in the alley. Pain shot up the damaged leg and it gave out. She couldn't roll with Kade in her arms, staggered instead, caught herself on one knee. Fuck. Jumping one story shouldn't hurt like that.

Coughing racked her body violently. Bloody mucus landed on Kade's scorched shirt. Kade had burns all over him. He'd passed out from pain or smoke or something else. She could hear the last fading mental screams of the dying in the apartment above, as the smoke and flames brought their lives to an end.

This is how my family died, she thought to herself.

More coughing racked her body. She'd inhaled too much smoke. Fuck. She didn't have time for this. She had to get them out of here. That way, the main street. Find a cab. Go to ground, somewhere, anywhere.

What had she done?

Time to think of that later.

Sam came up to her feet, lurched painfully down the alley towards the main street. She made it a handful of steps when she heard running feet behind her, a yell, in Thai. "There!"

She tried to turn, was too tired, too slow with Kade. Something jabbed her fast and hard in the back. Electricity coursed through her, convulsing her muscles. She screamed. A taser round. Oh, god, no. Not this again. Not now, when she was so tired…

A second round hit her. Her legs gave out. She stumbled, fell to her knees. Kade rolled out of her grip. Running feet approached. Her vision was fading. Someone kicked her in the face and she toppled backwards, into a pool of broken glass blasted out by the explosions above. She was vaguely aware of someone picking Kade up, hauling him off. She could feel someone's mind… A mind she'd felt…

Suk. Suk Prat-Nung. He was still alive.

An electrified shock baton came down on her. Her body spasmed. Kicks rained down, more shock batons. Three of them above her. Four. Maybe five. She pushed it all away from herself, like she'd pushed the beatings, the rapes, the humiliations and abuses.

She'd been so stupid.

"The Friday night event is a trap," the note had said.

Wats. It must have been Wats. That's why he'd been here. He'd known it was a trap. He came into it anyway, died trying to save Kade.

Thank you for saving my life, she whispered to him.

She felt a last feeble mental scream from someone upstairs, felt his skin turn to ash and his mind wink out. Loesan. That had been Loesan. Dead, all dead.

Her eyes opened. Wats had made her promise something. Promise that she'd keep Kade alive, keep him alive so he could make an impact.

They'd rolled her onto her stomach, she realized, brought her up on her knees, face down in the alley, on the cobblestones and the broken glass. There was a forest of legs around her, just visible in the pre-dawn gloom. One was yelling in Thai that she'd killed his brother. The blows had stopped coming down.

They were going to take her with them, he was saying. Then they were going to rape her. They were going to make her scream for hours. They were going to flay the flesh from her stupid body. They were going to make her beg for death.

Fools. They should have killed her here and now. Her hand closed on a long, jagged piece of glass, inches wide, a foot long. The sharp edges bit into her palm, her fingers. Blood welled up.

"*Chaonai Rayum Khongkhun pen Kon Kaa!*" she yelled. Your fucking boss killed him!

Sam lashed out behind her with a kick, felt it connect with one of them. She slashed to the right with the broken glass at the nearest leg, took him on the back of the calf, hamstrung him. Blood fountained out of the leg. The thug dropped to one knee, mouth open, screaming in pain.

She reached up with her left hand, grabbed the man above her by the hair, used it to pull him down and herself up, jammed the foot-long glass shard into the underside of his jaw – all the way up into his head – as she came up to her feet. Red arterial blood spurted out. The man gurgled and gasped for breath, dead on his feet.

There were rotor sounds above her. A helicopter. Someone kicked at her chest. She cut a furrow in his leg for his trouble. A spotlight illuminated them. An amplified voice boomed out in Thai, instructing them to halt by order of the police. Gunshots ricocheted off the brick walls. The thugs turned and bolted, scattering in all directions. Fuck.

An explosion ripped out of the apartment upstairs, some munition on one of the bodies finally going up. The chopper pilot jerked up and away, and the light came off her for just an instant. Sam rolled, painfully, came up with a limp, threw herself into a shaded doorway.

She had to find Kade. Where had they taken Kade?

Kade came to abruptly. Someone had smacked him across the face. He was slumped in a chair. One of his eyes wouldn't open. Everything hurt. His hands and the left side of his face burned. It hurt to breathe.

Someone smacked him again. He screamed in pain. Oh my god, that hurt. The skin of his face was on fire. His eye, he couldn't fucking see through one eye. It hurt like hell!

A fist landed in his gut. He doubled over, gasping for breath, retching. He couldn't breathe, couldn't breathe, couldn't breathe.

A voice spoke in Thai. The next blow didn't land. A tiny

bit of air leaked back into his lungs. He gasped. He was in a large room of some sort. A warehouse. Where was Sam? Where was Wats? Oh my god, that was Wats. He'd felt his friend die. Felt them all die.

Oh no. Oh no. Dead, dead, dead, all dead. My fault. My fault. All my fault.

The hand came back, slapped him again. He'd been screaming. He whimpered softly, sobbed. The pain of his flesh was nothing. He inhaled, let the serenity package take over and calm him.

Someone spoke in English. "Who are you?"

There was a mind there. Suk. Suk Prat-Nung.

A hand struck his face again. It burned like hell.

"Who are you? Who do you work for? They're dead, all dead because of you."

The hand hit him again, hard. Kade could feel the rage and fear and hatred of the mind behind it.

All because of you, Kade thought. All true. All true.

The serenity package had kicked in. He was empty, now. He was cold. He was nothingness.

Another man came forward. Thai. Angular. A large hooked nose.

"How do you do this?" he asked in accented English. "How do you have so much Nexus in you, for so long?"

The Nexus. That's what it had always been about. He wasn't going to tell them. He shook his head.

The new man's hand clenched around Kade's testicles, squeezed hard.

"You're going to tell us," he said. "Or we're going to kill you." He squeezed even harder. "Slowly." Again. "Painfully." And again.

Kade shook his head, screamed his anger at them, screamed it from throat and mind. "NO!"

He saw the man in front of him recoil from it, felt Suk

wince in pain. They had Nexus in their minds. He could hurt them.

The thug stepped forward, rammed his fist into Kade's face again, into the burnt and bruised and swollen side. The pain made the world go hazy for a moment.

Suk stepped closer again. "Tell me."

The thug grabbed Kade's left hand, took his pinky finger, wrenched it backwards until it broke.

FUCK!

Kade knew what he had to do then. Emptiness consumed him. Hatred. "I'll tell you. I'll tell you! Stop! Please!"

The thug grabbed his next finger, bent it halfway back, enough to hurt. Coldness descended over him. The pain was nothing.

"Please! Stop! I have to show you. Please."

He opened his mind for them to suck them in. They came closer. Kade showed them the first discoveries, he and Rangan's first experiments. Suk and the other one lapped at it eagerly. He showed them more. Whizzed them through memories – fast fast faster. They came closer, hungrily, sucked up as much as they could from him. He was giving them more than they could possibly keep up with. He wanted them as close and as open to him as possible.

"Wait, wait, slow down!" the angular one said.

Kade could feel him now. His mind was faint. His name was Tuksin. He was a monk. He was here to steal these secrets, free himself of Ananda, become the lord of Nexus. His mind was twisted and foul to the touch.

Kade sucked them in deeper, showed them the synthesis for Nexus 5, the molecular structure of the individual components, how they fit together. It was still too much for them, too complex all at once. They needed more bandwidth. They came even closer, almost touching him, opening their minds as fully as they could to absorb what he was giving them.

And then he showed them hell.

```
[activate nd* pri: max]
```

He blasted them with the Nexus disruptor, the signal the ERD had bombarded Rangan's brain with, the way they'd disrupted all thought in that cell. It was pain more intense than anything they could ever have imagined. They screamed with it, both of them, screamed and fell to their knees. Even through the filters in his mind the barest fraction of it took Kade's breath away.

The thug turned, saw them writhing in pain, hesitated for a moment. Kade kept pounding the signal into their brains. The big man wheeled on him, smacked Kade hard enough that it knocked him out of the chair, onto the floor. The pain stunned him.

He held on, kept jamming the signal into their brains. The thug kicked him. Pain exploded in Kade's abdomen. Still he held on. *There.* Yes. There. Suk and Tuksin were writhing in agony, all thought gone from their minds.

Kade stopped the Nexus disrupter. He needed to focus entirely on something else. There was a gun on the thug's hip. Kade was in Suk's mind now. Push/pull. He was the master of it. He always won.

The gun. The gun. The gun.

The thug kicked him again. Something cracked inside him.

Shoot him. Shoot him. Shoot him.

The gun was in Suk's hand. The thug turned, his eyes going wide. Suk fired, enormously loud in this space. The thug's kneecap exploded. He roared. His leg gave out. He collapsed, hauled himself half up, reached for Suk to slap the gun out of his hand.

Suk fired again. The bullet took the bigger man in the

belly. He grunted, still trying to move forward, almost prone now.

Suk fired a third time. The bullet entered the top of the thug's head, split it open like a melon.

Suk blinked in surprise. Tuksin tackled him. The gun went off again, without Kade's willing it this time. Tuksin coughed, and blood came up out of his mouth.

Suk scrabbled backwards, away from Kade, pulled himself up on his feet, pistol still in hand, backing away rapidly. Kade could feel his hold slipping as Suk put distance between them. Kade tried to stand; pain lanced up his left leg and it buckled under him. He crashed to the floor. Fuck.

Suk was at the other end of the room now, maybe forty feet away. He was pointing the gun at Kade. His hands were shaking.

"What are you?"

Kade tried pushing at his thoughts, got nowhere. He was too far, too far.

"You're a devil! A devil!"

Suk fired, missed at that range. Kade felt a bullet embed itself in the floor near him. He scrambled back with one leg and both hands. Suk fired again, missed again.

Kade looked around for anything to hide behind, anything to use as a weapon. The thug's submachine gun was against the wall. He crawled for it as fast as he could, rough pain shooting up from his insides with every motion. It was so far away. Everything hurt so goddamn much. Suk's hands were steady now.

"You go to hell!" the Thai man yelled at him, taking careful aim.

The outside door burst in. Sam stood in the doorway. Suk saw her, dragged his gun around, fired on her. Sam rolled, flinging something at him as she did. Something sharp cut

Suk across the left arm. He moved forward, gun trained on Sam. Fired, missed.

Kade got his fingers around the submachine gun. Suk was at thirty feet. The Thai man fired again, but missed Sam.

Kade brought the gun around, pulled the trigger. The recoil knocked him back, pinned him into the wall, brought agony to his broken rib. The shots went wild, too far to the left. Suk turned back towards him, fired. Kade felt a searing pain in his left arm, kept the trigger down, tried to bring the muzzle around to bear on Suk. Suk fired again, missed. Kade's bullets tracked from Kade's left to right, took Suk across his gun arm and then into his chest, knocked him off his feet. The gun clicked. Empty. Silence ruled again. Then sirens, sirens from outside.

There was silence in the C&C onboard the *Boca Raton*. Nichols couldn't believe what had just happened. A dozen agents dead, at least that many civilians, many of whom were still alive when they'd initiated Protocol Thirteen.

Nichols looked down at his lap, shaking his head.

Then Jane Kim spoke up. "Sir?"

Nichols looked up. "What is it, Jane?"

"Sir... Canary is still up, sir. And Blackbird... most of her channels went dead, but we still have a GPS feed from her phone. And... it's moved, sir. She's outside of the building."

Nichols looked at the bank of screens. It was true. The feeds had collapsed from the twelve members of the assault team, but not from Lane. And from Cataranes, most of them had died, but died *after* recording a location just outside the building. Her phone was still uploading GPS data even now. As he watched, it moved again, from the alleyway into the building that Lane was in. Their positions converged. She was moving.

There. On the video feed from Lane, that had been a flicker of Sam. Unmistakably so.

Shu directed as Feng drove. Traffic control was hers. Police routing was hers. Street cameras were hers. The Opal barreled down the street at a hundred and sixty kilometers per hour. The streets were nearly empty in the pre-dawn gloom. Every light was green for them. Bangkok Metro Police vehicles rushed by on parallel tracks, never to see them.

She knew the position of Lane's phone to the meter. It was no longer in the conflagration. It was less than ten meters away from the burning apartment, but that was all the difference in the world. She only hoped the boy was with his phone.

This was foolishness, she knew. She should just let the boy die. But she wasn't going to, not if she could help it.

Here, Shu told Feng. They crashed a pedestrian barrier, entered the alleyways, barely wide enough for the Opal to drive down, forbidden to motorized vehicles.

Here again, she sent him.

Feng expertly skid-braked the Opal, turned into the perpendicular alley. Lane was climbing, gaining elevation.

Here, she repeated.

Feng brought the Opal to a skidding halt. Lane was about to reach the rooftop of the building directly in front of them. She could feel his mind at this range. He was still alive, wounded, in pain. She reached out to him and the Catarancs girl, told them help was coming. From here it was up to Feng.

And there were two more minds running Nexus on the first floor, both fading into oblivion. How interesting...

Sam picked up the submachine gun from where Kade had dropped it, ejected the banana clip and reversed it, slammed the full one home.

"You OK?" she asked.

She could feel his mind. The Nexus was frazzled from the shocks she'd taken, but not as badly as a few days ago. She could still feel Kade through the static. He had the combat adrenaline in him. He'd just killed a man for the first time. That was going to stick in his head for quite a while, along with everything else about tonight.

Kade nodded, tried to get up, collapsed immediately as his leg gave out again. Pain radiated from him. His lungs were burning. Ribs were cracked, sent horrible pain as he tried to move. His leg wouldn't take any weight. He shook his head, coughing feebly. Blood came up when he did.

Sam bent to pick him up. They had to get out of here.

There was a noise at the door. Another thug appeared in the entrance. Sam yanked the gun up, fired a burst. There was a curse and the thug disappeared back out the doorway.

There was another door at the other end of the room. "Come on, Kade." She picked him up, heaved him over her shoulder. Agony flared out from him. She ignored it, limped and ran towards the other door. Fuck, that hurt. She got to the door, kicked it open with her good leg, turned and fired another burst at the door the thugs had appeared in for good measure, then smashed the door beside her open with her shoulder.

The door led into a stairwell. Sam tightened her grip on Kade, jerked her body up, felt Kade groan, moved up one painful step at a time. The door at the first landing was locked.

She fired a burst into the lock, slammed the door open with her shoulder to confuse them, kept climbing.

She was at the second landing when she heard them enter the stairwell. She froze. Kade moaned. She shushed him with her mind. The men on the first landing were talking in Thai. Three of them. Maybe four. They were moving carefully. She heard clips being checked, replaced. The voices went away.

She counted to five, then continued up.

A voice yelled out. Fuck, one of them had stayed behind. Shots came up the center shaft of the stairwell. Sam threw caution to the wind, threw pain to the wind, sprinted up the stairs, felt muscles in her damaged leg protest painfully on each step, didn't fucking care. Pain racked Kade's body from his broken ribs with every step. She ignored it. She had no choice.

The thugs were all yelling now. They were running after her. They were top-heavy, strong as five men, but pathetically weak in the legs in comparison. Their oversized muscles sapped their cardio ability. Sam was smaller of heart and lung, but built for speed. Even with Kade on her shoulder, she was faster.

She passed the third landing, the fourth, the fifth, got to the rooftop access, blew off the lock, rammed it open. God, she'd kill for grenades right now. She looked around for cover. There was a giant rooftop air-conditioning unit on the far corner. Sam sprinted for it, dropped Kade behind it with a thud and a staggering surge of pain, crouched down out of view herself, checked her ammo. Almost empty. She flipped it to single shot. She had to conserve the ammo she had left.

KADE... CATARANES... WE ARE HERE... STAY ALIVE... FENG IS COMING TO YOU.

Su-Yong Shu's voice boomed huge in Sam's head. Kade gasped out loud. Holy fuck, what was that woman?

Automatic fire burst from the other side of the roof. Bullets penetrated the AC unit. A spray of metal pieces shot out, lacerating her arms, her legs, her chest. Kade moaned in fresh pain. The thugs kept shooting, firing now on one side of the unit, sending sharp shrapnel out where Sam crouched. She rolled towards Kade. Supports inside the AC unit gave, and the damaged side slumped down. Sam slouched lower, pulled Kade with her. The thugs were eating away at their cover.

Their guns went silent, Sam popped up, fired three rounds at one of them, saw two hit him in the chest, dropped back behind cover. One down. Three left. Sam popped her clip, checked the ammo again. Two rounds left. Fuck.

Could they jump from the roof into the alley? Would Kade survive?

The guns opened up again, aimed at their hiding place, pulverizing the last of their cover. More shrapnel sliced through her arm. Sam rolled, came up at a different spot, fired her last two rounds, took one of them in the gut. The others brought their guns around towards her. More shots fired out, pistol shots, six of them, and both men's heads exploded. Their lifeless bodies slumped to the ground.

Behind them, in an impeccable black chauffeur's suit, stood Feng, a smoking pistol in each hand. He raised an eyebrow at her in greeting. Sam breathed a sigh of relief. She'd never expected to be saved by one of these men, but she'd take it. By god she'd take it.

Feng strode over to the man she'd shot in the gut. He was still moving. The Confucian Fist put two rounds in his head, did the same to the first man she'd shot.

Sam crouched over Kade. He radiated pain. His skin felt charred from the flames, flayed from the shrapnel. He was alive, though. Cut up, broken, one of Suk's bullets in his arm, but still alive, still conscious. Feng joined them.

"Time to go, yeah?" the Chinese soldier said. He was smiling.

Kade tried to speak, coughed up blood for his troubles, nodded instead.

Feng bent to pick him up.

Sam raised a hand to stop him, crouched down herself.

"You're hurt," Feng said.

"I'll carry him," she replied.

Feng nodded silently, holding her eyes. He understood.

Sam hauled Kade over her shoulder, ignored his pain. They made their way down the stairs and to the black Opal, Sam limping painfully every step of the way.

"That's a Confucian Fist," Nichols said.

Williams and Kim both nodded.

"What the hell is one of those doing there?"

40
Running

Feng reached the Opal ahead of Sam. The driver's side back door was open. Sam limped up to them, peered inside to find Su-Yong Shu in back. There was a massive first aid kit next to her.

"Give him to me," the Chinese woman said.

Sam tightened her grip on Kade.

"Come on, you ride up front with me," Feng told her.

"I'm sticking with him," Sam replied.

"Miss Cataranes," Shu said. "I'm medically competent."

"So am I." She held the older woman's gaze.

Shu stared back at her.

"We have to go," Feng said. "Can't stay."

"Fine," Shu said. She opened her door. "Get in back with Kade. I'll ride in front."

Sam eased herself and Kade into the back seat. He groaned in pain. Feng started moving as soon as the doors were closed, driving deeper into the maze.

Sam inspected the kit. Chinese special forces field medical issue. Top of the line. She'd trained on one of these. There, anti-burn respirator, a mask and pressurized can loaded with growth factors for the lungs. She pulled it out, got it over Kade's face, felt him relax as the cool soothing mix flowed into him.

"You're bugged," Shu said from the front seat. "Your contacts, the bugs in Kade's clothes, both of your phones. They have to go."

Shit, Sam realized. She's right.

She rolled down the window, tossed her phone out, popped her contacts into her palm and flung them out as well. Kade was struggling to reach the phone in his pocket. His broken finger was in the way. Sam reached inside for him, pulled out his phone, tossed it out the window as well. There were bugs planted all over him...

"We need to cut his clothes off," she announced. "They're half melted to him anyway."

Feng held his hand up, eyes still on the road. A knife flicked open in his palm. Shu took it, passed it back to Sam. The woman did something with her mind, and Sam felt Kade's pain recede a bit, felt him relax into a more peaceful state.

Sam cut away most of Kade's shirt, tossed it out the window. Kade grasped something around his neck, the data fob Wats had given him.

"Not this," he mumbled weakly through the mask.

Sam skipped past it, cut away his ruined pants, tossed them out as well.

God, he was a mess. Melted fibers stuck to the skin of his lower leg where the burning beam had pinned him, across parts of his thighs where the pants had melted from the heat of the fire. The left side of his face was swollen, burnt, lacerated. One of his eyes wouldn't open. As his pain receded, she could get a clear view of his injuries. They were serious.

Sam squeezed anti-burn gel over his face, his chest, his thighs, his calves. She injected antibiotics and growth factors into his face, into the area around his swollen-shut eye. She taped the broken finger.

Sam looked up as she did so. They were still somewhere in the maze.

"Where are we going?" she asked.

"Bangkok Metro Police are all around us," Shu answered. "We're taking a roundabout route to avoid them."

"And after we get out of here?" Sam asked.

I'm in a car with the enemies I was trained to fight, she realized. With no weapon, on the run from the people who trained me. What the fuck am I doing?

"The Chinese Embassy," Shu said. "Political asylum for Kade. For you as well if you want it."

Alarm jolted through Sam. She reached for words. Kade was faster.

No!

He reached up, pulled Sam's hand and the mask away.

"No embassy," he said weakly.

We can keep you safe there, Shu sent, **then get you out of the country**.

Kade pulled the mask back, sucked at the cool healing mix, sent them his thoughts.

No. People just died because of me. They fucking died. I won't let that happen again. I won't be a slave. I won't be a killer.

Images leaked out of his mind, Narong pointing a gun at Ted Prat-Nung's head. Wats bleeding to death in the fire. Niran and Lalana being cut down in the crossfire.

Sam could feel his intense guilt, the failure, the betrayal, the burden of the deaths he'd caused. She understood, all too well.

What have I done? Sam thought. It happened so fast…

Shu tried again. **Kade, the Americans will come for you. We need to get you someplace safe.**

"She's right," Sam said. "They've got to be looking for us already. They won't just let us go. We have to move fast."

Hide, Kade sent. **We need to hide.**

"Where should I drive?" Feng asked.

Ananda, Kade sent.

Sam shook her head. "That guy in there, the dead one, he was one of Ananda's monks. He followed us Monday night."

"Tuksin," Shu said. "I saw some of his mind before he faded. He was operating on his own."

Kade nodded. **He wanted out from Ananda. And Suk wanted out from Ted Prat-Nung.**

"Thanom?" Shu asked sharply. "What does he have to do with this?"

Kade and Sam exchanged glances.

Sam answered, "He was there, tonight. That's why the ERD moved in, to get him."

Show me! Shu commanded.

Sam felt an alien presence in her mind. It burrowed deep. Sam couldn't have stopped her if she'd wanted to. What was this woman? The presence found her memories of the fight, sucked them up instantly.

Sam felt Kade open to Shu, felt Shu absorb his memories of the event as well. She caught an echo of Prat-Nung's death, bullets ripping through his body as he'd tried to rescue Chariya, tried to get her out of there.

Shu moaned then, a low-pitched sound. Her head fell into her hands. A sob escaped from between them. They felt it in their minds.

Thanom. Dead. Thanom. No...

Grief filled Sam. She wanted to weep with Shu's loss. She couldn't think, couldn't see, couldn't breathe. She felt the car begin to swerve.

Thanom!

Su-Yong!

Sam heard the yell from Feng. Shu's moan ceased. The mental fog in Sam's head cleared.

Feng got the car back under control. No one spoke. Shu continued to sob. Her sorrow filled the air.

Stupid, stupid, Thanom. I told you it would end this way. I *told* you...

Sam did what she could for Kade, in silence.

Eventually Shu's sobbing slowed, then ceased. She lifted up her face. Tears streaked it.

I'm sorry, she sent. **Thanom was very important to me. I'm...** She shook her head. **I'm only alive today because of him.**

It came in a flash. A fire. Burning heat. Pain and fear. Her head shaved bare. A robotic surgeon looming above her, alien and insectoid, moving closer with whirring blades. Her unborn child huge in her womb. Blood everywhere. Two faces above her, pale with fright. The feel of Prat-Nung's hand around hers. Images and memories that Sam didn't understand.

Anger began to replace the sorrow emanating from Shu. Cold, hard anger. Anger of epic proportions. Hatred of frightening intensity. Wrath. Destruction. Murderers. Savages. She would crush them all...

"Ananda," Kade croaked. **Ananda.**

Shu seemed to notice them then. Bit by bit she reeled her anger in. They heard her take a deep breath. She nodded. "Ananda."

"And you?" Shu asked Sam. "Do you plan to go with Kade?"

Sam took a deep breath. She still hadn't made sense of the events of this night. She'd gone mad at Mai's death, at the rage and terror of the minds she'd been linked to. She'd killed at least two ERD contractors, been complicit in the deaths of others...

Could I turn myself in? Sam wondered. Go to the embassy? Claim temporary insanity?

No. The ERD was many things. Forgiving was not one of them. She'd signed her own death warrant already. Her life expectancy could now be measured in hours or days.

She needed to think and regroup. She needed to keep moving, keep ahead of the pursuers who would be coming after her. Her options were few. And she'd promised Wats that she'd keep Kade safe.

"I'll go," she said. "I'll go with Kade, if he'll have me."

Kade looked at her. He had the mask over his mouth and nose again. His eyes met hers. She had a flash of the connection they'd had just hours ago, the way she'd opened herself to him. A sense of compassion. Trust. Understanding. He nodded slowly, pulled the mask away.

"Yes," he said. "You saved my life. Again. Yes."

Shu nodded, face and mind still hard, pulled a phone from her pocket, dialed, held it to her ear. Sam faintly heard the voice on the other side answer.

"*Sawadi*, Ananda."

They spoke in a language Sam didn't know, Indic maybe, flowing and sonorous. And then Shu put the phone down.

"It's done," she said. "We'll meet his monks in an hour." Her voice was cold and distant. Anger still leaked out of her mind. Violence. The apes had killed Thanom. There would be a reckoning.

Kade napped as Feng drove. He woke at the rendezvous point with the two young monks Ananda had sent. It was a cavernous garage, deep in the belly of the airport. Shu claimed the surveillance cameras were under her control. No one voiced a disagreement.

The shaven-headed young men passed them piles of

cloth. Monk's robes. Orange for Kade, white for Sam.

Shu spoke from the front seat. She still felt distant, cold. Prat-Nung's death had affected her.

"Ananda's monks will take you someplace, hide you," she said. "The Americans have already put out a request for your arrest, both of you, on drug charges.

"You need to keep moving. Ananda knows that. He's working on finding a next step for you."

She turned back and held something out to Kade. A slate.

"What's this?" Kade asked, reaching for it. Shu kept her grip on the device.

"We stopped, and Feng bought them. He paid cash. They're not associated with you in any way. Do not access any of your old accounts or data on this, or they'll be able to trace you. Don't try to contact anyone you know, or me. You can use it to keep up on news generally, but not more than that. You understand?"

Kade nodded. "Yeah. I want to stay alive."

Shu nodded, released her grip. "Good."

"Can you do something for me?" Kade asked. He felt cold. Dazed.

"What?"

"Rangan, Ilya, the ERD will come after them now, if they haven't already. Can you contact them? Tell them to get out if they can?"

Shu hesitated a moment.

"They'll be bugged," Sam said. "You'll have to be careful to not tip the listeners off."

Shu nodded. "I'll do what I can."

"Thank you," Kade said. The words were empty. He felt numb.

"Kade…" Shu began. She paused. "Kade, it's likely to go poorly for the people the ERD was blackmailing you with. If it does, remember who did this to you, and to them."

Her eyes held his. Her mind radiated cold anger, a desire to break the human organizations that worked so hard to keep them – all the posthumans – under their thumbs.

It'll be your fault, Sam had told him. *All on you.*

He caught Sam out of the corner of his eye, saw her look down. She emanated guilt, confusion, resignation. She opened the door on her side, hobbled out, closed the door behind her.

"Blame the humans," Shu continued. "Blame their hatred of anything and anyone that might transcend them."

Rage. Not just anger. A flash of Yang Wei, her mentor, trapped in a wrecked car, burning to death in utter agony, the CIA to blame. A flash of Ted Prat-Nung being cut down as he tried to save Chariya, echoed back from his own memories.

Hatred.

He could feel his own anger rising. The ERD had killed so many. They should be punished, broken, shattered into pieces so small that...

"Keep moving," Shu told him. "Stay safe. We'll see each other again."

She touched his arm, held his eyes with her own.

"One day, we will make them pay," Shu said. "All of them."

Even through the serenity package, he felt it. The anger soothed him. The cold rage. It took his grief away. It took the pain away.

Kade nodded again, locked eyes with her. One day they'd make their enemies pay. He opened the door to get out. One of the monks was there in a flash. He took Kade's arm over his shoulder, helped him hop on one foot towards the other car. Sam was waiting at the front of the car, her eyes darting to and fro, scanning for threats.

She expects them to find us, Kade thought to himself.

And she would know.

Feng hugged Kade. "No more getting beat up!" he told him with a grin.

Kade nodded numbly.

The Confucian Fist turned to Sam, held his arms open as if to embrace her. Sam frowned. Feng dropped his arms and the grin, offered her one hand to shake. She took it.

"Someday we fight together for real," he said, giving her a respectful nod.

The young monks put them in the back of a cramped, beat-up four-seater Tata.

"Where are we going?" Kade asked.

The two monks exchanged words in Thai. The one in the passenger seat turned.

"Mountains," he said, gesturing towards the sky. Then more Thai.

"He says they're taking us to a monastery," Sam said. "A very special monastery."

They drove out of the airport garage, into the early morning light. The clouds had broken apart. The sun was rising in the east, an orange ball of fire illuminating a wet landscape. They drove north, and towards the peaks that loomed over the Thai plains below.

41
Repercussions

Becker swore softly to himself. Morning was breaking over Thailand. His emergency request for aerial recon in the pre-dawn dark three hours ago had been denied. The National Security Advisor had called a meeting to discuss events in Thailand for Sunday morning in DC. That was more than thirty-six hours in the future. They couldn't wait that long.

Was this a time to use the card he'd been given?

The President cares very much about your work, he'd been told. *If you ever have a pressing issue that needs fast attention, just let me know.*

Barnes. Maximilian Barnes, the President's Special Policy Advisor. The President's bag man. A man that had done things Becker wished he didn't even know about... A man that Warren Becker frankly feared.

This is my private number.

Becker sighed. This was one of those pressing issues. He reached down, pulled a bottle and a glass from his bottom drawer, poured himself two fingers of Laphroaig, and took a swallow. Then he dialed the number.

Barnes answered right away. Yes, he certainly remembered Becker. What did he need?

Becker explained. Their conversation was brief and to the point.

Yes, this sounded like the sort of thing the President would take an interest in. Yes, waiting another two days before launching recon drones would be unacceptable. No, Becker hadn't presumed too much in calling. He would have his approval to launch recon drones by nightfall, Thailand time.

Becker disconnected the call. His hand was shaking slightly. That man terrified him. The things Becker knew Barnes had done were enough... The things he was *rumored* to have done...

He shook his head, took another swallow of the Laphroaig to calm himself, turned his attention to the after-action report on the events in Bangkok.

Twelve ERD contractors killed. Ted Prat-Nung dead. Three of his men dead. Watson Cole dead. Suk Prat-Nung found dead in the building across the alley, next to a high-ranking monk and a petty criminal, both also dead. Yet another man dead in the alley itself, his throat messily cut. Four dead men on the roof of that building. It had been a multi-site bloodbath.

And last of all, twelve civilians killed inside the apartment – a handful of students, a burnt-out ex-nun and her burnt-out ex-monk husband, a used-up whore, a young drug dealer – and this freakish child, this freakish creature.

Mai, they'd called it.

Becker shivered. What they'd pieced together corroborated one of the President's worst fears. Children born with Nexus abilities from birth. A new subspecies able to communicate telepathically with one another. How would they treat the rest of humanity? He thought of his two beautiful, normal, healthy daughters. Would these freaks turn his daughters into a new underclass? Into slaves for the new elites? The thought made him ill.

This creature Mai. The Confucian Fist clones. Shu – quite possibly no longer human herself. It was an unholy convergence of perversities. His daughters would live in a world where they were beset by enemies, beset by threats to the entire human race.

He took another swallow of the Laphroaig, followed it with a deep breath.

And Cataranes. Sam. What happened there? Shu must have coerced her. Nothing else made sense. Damn it. It was his fault, for sending her out in the field with Nexus in her skull. They hadn't imagined that Shu could coerce someone so quickly, so silently, without warning.

I'm sorry, Sam. We're going to get you back. We're going to fix you, if we can.

Becker turned back to the dead contractors, studied their faces, memorized their names. They'd been good men, doing an important job. He'd sent them into danger. He'd given the order to detonate the charges in their skulls, in the skulls of the dead and the still-breathing alike, rather than let them fall into Thai custody. Their blood was on his hands.

Had he done the right thing?

Yes. He was a good soldier. He'd followed the rules. Rules that were there for a reason.

He swallowed the last of the Laphroaig. It warmed him as it went down. It comforted him.

He read through the contractors' bios again. He would remember these men.

And he would do the same thing again, if he had to. The stakes were far too high for anything else.

Martin Holtzmann sat in his own office, reviewing the events in Bangkok.

Such a waste. Such an appalling waste.

Narong Shinawatra, the boy they'd coerced. Dead. Senselessly dead. What had gone wrong with their software?

Ted Prat-Nung, a competent nano-engineer before he'd become a drug dealer. Dead.

The child Mai. What would it be like to be born with Nexus in one's mind? To be able to speak mentally from birth with others who had the same capabilities. How would it affect language development? How would it affect intelligence? How would it affect social behaviors?

He had so many questions.

Dead. Just another dead end.

The Lane boy, with all he knew, all his ideas. Lost to them. Holtzman had hoped still to persuade that one to join them.

Not for the first time, Holtzman contemplated the Nexus stored in the secure laboratory two floors down. He had complete access to it. There were so many curiosities he had about it...

No. That was crossing one line too many.

42
A Matter of Perspective

Kade woke slowly. He'd fallen asleep at some point, his head against the car door.

Sam was still awake. She felt tired, strung out, tense. He could feel the same thoughts cycling through her head. Mai. Her responsibility for the girl's death. The things she'd done in response. The men she'd killed. The hunters who'd be coming for them.

And plans. Plans. Cambodia. Laos. Burma. Where could they escape to? How?

Kade had no answers for her. He was completely cold inside. There was no emotion but an icy rage. The serenity package held him. Or perhaps it was shock.

The car wound left and right. They were up high above the Thai plains now, climbing a winding mountain road. Half the slopes were covered with rice paddies, terraces of green, yellow, and muddy brown. The rest was jungle, wild and thick. The sky was blue, dotted with white clouds. It was beautiful. He felt it not at all.

They came over a rise, and a structure appeared in the distance. A complex, nestled on a ledge in the side of the mountain. White buildings. Courtyards. Red roofs. Ornate gold towers above them. A waterfall sluiced out from below it, falling down a sheer cliff to crash into a jungle lake hundreds of feet below.

Twenty minutes later, they were there. The Tata pulled in through a gate in the wall, stopped in a wide stone courtyard. Monks met them at the car. A nun. A doctor. They hauled Sam away in one direction, Kade in another. They carried him to a monk's cell. A monk shaved the hair off his head with electric clippers. The doctor examined him, changed his dressings, peered at the swollen closed eye, injected him, put drug patches on his neck, made him swallow something. Darkness closed over him like a welcome friend.

The call came at 3am. Becker reached over to the nightstand to get it, struggled to pull himself back to consciousness and comprehension. It was Maximilian Barnes. Did the man ever sleep? It didn't matter. Becker had approval for the recon drone launches. He started to thank Barnes, found he was talking to dead air. The connection had ended. Becker looked at the phone in his hand, shook his head slowly.

"Who was that?" Claire asked sleepily.

"Just work, honey," Becker answered.

He rose to get his robe. He could call the *Boca Raton* from his secure home office. It was 2pm in Thailand. They could have the recon birds up tonight.

"Go back to sleep, Claire."

She was already out.

"Where are we on the candidate list for the surveillance drops?" Becker asked.

"Transmitting to your slate now, sir," Nichols answered.

Becker studied them. One hundred and twenty targets

for a first wave of drops. They'd intercepted a call between Shu and Ananda. It had been in a language no system could translate. They'd hired a linguist, discovered it was Pali, a dead Buddhist ceremonial tongue. Translating it had confirmed their suspicions. Ananda had agreed to take on custody of "the boy" and "the woman with him" and help get them out of the country.

These target sites were largely places associated with Ananda. Monasteries he had influence in. University facilities he could use. Places where two Westerners could be hidden.

"When do we start?" Becker asked.

Nichols glanced at another screen, then looked back at Becker.

"The UAVs are fueling now, sir. First sorties launch tonight, after dark. 2300 hours local time."

"You're going to lose the eye. I'm sorry. There's nothing I can do."

Kade lay in the tiny bed in his little cell, ran the doctor's words through his head again and again, played back the moment when the ERD agent he'd attacked had bashed him in the face with the butt of his rifle. Lee. Sam said the man's name had been Lee. Wats had killed him not two minutes later.

Wats, who was dead, like so many others, while Kade was still alive.

He touched the data fob hanging around his neck. Wats had died to give him this. Had died trying to get him free.

All he'd lost was an eye. Just one puny eye. He should have lost more. He should have been the one to die.

And now Ilya and Rangan... He scanned the article again.

DEA BREAKS UP MAJOR
WEST COAST DRUG RING

Friday 9.49pm, San Francisco, California

The DEA is announcing this afternoon more than a hundred arrests and the disruption of what they're calling one of the largest West Coast distribution networks for the street drug Nexus. [...]

Rangan and Ilya had been taken. They were on their way to a National Security Internment Center. They'd never make their way out.

Kade understood Shu, now. He understood her anger, her rage.

They'd killed and imprisoned his friends. They'd killed Narong and Lalana and Chariya and so many innocents he had just met. They'd killed a little girl, a special little girl.

They deserved the worst. He was icy with rage. He wanted to hurt them. He wanted to tear them down. He wanted to annihilate them. Slowly. Painfully. Inch by inch.

It was too much. He had to get out of this cell. He had to think of something else, anything else.

He levered himself up on the crutches a young monk named Bahn had brought him, awkwardly propelled himself out of his cell, into the hall, around the corners, out another door into the courtyard.

A hot, muggy, late-afternoon rain was falling. Kade propelled himself along under covered walkways towards the main hall. He could feel the minds of the monks in there, even from a hundred yards away. Thirty of them. Forty of them. He could feel them breathe in. Breathe out. They were practicing a meditation of some sort. It wasn't heady like the Synchronicity had been. It was pure and clean and self-aware.

He let himself into the meditation hall, found a cushion in the very back. He tried to lower himself as silently as he could, wincing at the pain in his ribs, in his leg. A crutch slipped from his hand, clattered on the ground. He felt the collective mind in the room observe the sound, recognize it, pull its attention serenely back to its breath.

This calm was remarkable. It made a joke of the "serenity" code running in his head. This calm ran deeper, truer. He wanted it.

More than calm. Union. Concordance. He had more Nexus nodes in his mind than any monk in this room. He was sure of it. Yet somehow, they were using those nodes to achieve something he'd only dreamed of. They were doing what Ilya had long talked about. Together, now, as they meditated, they were creating something greater than the sum of their parts. They were more than a set of monks meditating. This room was alive. This room was conscious. This room was a mind, and they were each part of it.

Kade wanted that union as well.

He lowered himself painfully, awkwardly down, sat with his splinted broken leg protruding out, closed his eyes, and joined them.

Sam leaned against the stone balustrade, gazed south as she finished her third bowl of stew. Her body demanded calories, demanded protein to heal the damage done to it. She flexed her injured leg. It felt noticeably better after less than a day. The miracle of modern science. A mere muscle tear was nothing to her body's augmented ability to heal. She gulped down more stew, more fuel to power her body's accelerated recovery.

What was she doing here? Where to next? There was something wonderfully tranquil about this place. Something had settled over her here, something she hadn't expected, a calm, an acceptance.

It brought with it no answers, though. Nor would it deter an ERD attack squad.

Sam needed to leave. She needed to keep moving. And, if by chance she evaded capture and death, she needed something to do with her life. She needed a purpose.

She'd embraced the ERD with a passion at a young age. They'd been the ones that fought evil, the ones who would stop the men who'd do what had been done to her and her sister and her parents. But now...

Mai is dead because of me. A little girl.

It was too late to change that.

Her job now was to stay alive. She'd need a new identity, a new face, new prints, everything that came with that.

And then? Sam wondered. What do I do with my life?

She kept thinking of Mai, of her sister Ana, of the young Sam that she'd been.

I want to protect them, Sam thought to herself. Above all. I want to keep them safe.

She turned and faced south. Out there, somewhere near a village called Mae Dong, there were more children like Mai.

"Samantha?" It was Vipada, the young nun who'd been assigned to Sam. "It's time for meditation."

Sam turned, suddenly aware of what she looked like with her nearly bald head and her white robes – a Buddhist nun. It brought a smile to her lips. She brought her hands together in a *wai* to Vipada.

"Thank you, Vipada," she answered in Thai. "Please lead the way."

She headed into the hall, to meditate with the nuns, to feel their minds in the practice called *vipassana*, the observation of self, in the meditation called *metta*, the state of loving-kindness, of compassion towards the self and others. They would meditate, and they would become one.

She couldn't remember ever having experienced anything so beautiful in her life. The touch of another's mind in that deep serene state, the touch Nexus enabled… How could it be wrong? How could she have fought so hard to stop it?

Who am I becoming?

At 2249 hours, under a dark, cloudy night sky thirty kilometers off the coast of Thailand, a portion of the radar and sonar absorbent upper shell of the *Boca Raton* began to open. Fissures appeared on the rounded foredeck of the submersible covert-operations ship. The fissures defined previously invisible panels. The panels became depressions as the ship drew them in. They slid slowly, silently to the side, opening to reveal a combat deck below. As the stealth hull retracted, rounded launchers on the combat deck canted up, tilting from their horizontal resting positions up to an angle thirty degrees above the horizon, pointed north towards the Thai mainland.

For a moment, all was still. The dark ship bobbed silently in the tropical swells of the Gulf of Thailand. Then the first launcher fired. A dark elongated shape streaked out and into the night sky. Seven hundred and eighty milliseconds later, the second launcher fired, then another, then another. In under ten seconds, the *Boca Raton* put twelve Viper class UAVs into the air. The recon/combat drones opened their stealthed, downturned wings one second into flight, activated their own jet engines, eased into level subsonic flight ten meters above the waves, and scattered.

As each Viper streaked into the night, its attendant launcher began to tilt back towards horizontal. Within seconds of the last launch, the radar and sonar absorbent panels of the stealth hull began to slowly slide back into place, obscuring the combat hull. Secrecy must be maintained.

In the air above the waters of the Gulf of Thailand, the AI in control of Viper 6 got its bearings and compared them to the plan. The drone banked its wings, turned to head north by north-east, angling around Bangkok's crowded airspace and traffic control radar and towards Saraburi and the mountains to the north-east. It had payloads to deliver.

[EXCERPT FROM TRANSCRIPT:
Face America with David Ames, Saturday 4/21/2040]

Host: ...and welcome back everyone to *Face America*. We're here this morning with National Security Advisor Dr Carolyn Pryce. Dr Pryce, thank you again for being here.

Pryce: It's a pleasure, David.

Host: Dr Pryce, let's move on to the situation in Thailand. A fire and multiple shootings in Bangkok yesterday reportedly left more than thirty people dead in a location connected to distribution of the street drug Nexus. The Thai government alleges that US forces were involved. What can you tell us about this?

Pryce: David, our hearts go out to the families who lost loved ones in that fire. Of course, the US was in no way involved in this. Thailand is a close ally and an important partner in regional issues, and we hope that as emotions cool the Thai authorities will realize that they're mistaken.

Host: What do you make of these reports of heavy gunfire in the area?

Pryce: Well as you say, David, this building was apparently being used to distribute illicit drugs.

We've seen drug-related violence in Mexico, in Afghanistan, in Columbia. Quite possibly this was a turf war between rival syndicates. These well-armed crime syndicates are part of the reason that President Stockton has made cracking down on the drug trade one of his top foreign policy priorities.

Host: The Thai authorities are saying the DNA evidence has identified an American at the scene, a man named Michael Lee, who they assert was an undercover American agent.

Pryce: Well, David, while Mr Lee lived in the US for a number of years, he's actually a child of Chinese immigrants to Thailand. So to use his presence to allege that the US was involved, when the same evidence provides a tighter link to China just to the north, is a bit odd. I hope the Thai authorities are asking Beijing some hard questions.

Host: So this man was not a US operative?

Pryce: Absolutely not.

Host: And there were no US operatives there?

Pryce: None whatsoever.

Host: I'm going to play you a clip here, from a press conference this morning in Bangkok, where Thai authorities showed off evidence found at the scene of the fire, which they say *conclusively* links the US military to the event. Roll film.

<Man speaking in Thai. Camera pans across table. Objects on table appear to be firearms and knives, warped and melted by extreme heat. Man continues speaking in Thai. Subtitle: " *...American made covert-operations weapons... More than twenty items recovered... only obvious explanation...*">

Host: What do you make of that?

Pryce: David, I think that film speaks for itself. Those
   guns are so warped and melted, it's difficult to
   even tell what models they are. And
   unfortunately, it's far too easy to acquire weapons
   of all sorts, from any country, on the black market
   today. That's why President Stockton has made
   combating the international arms trade, especially
   of the newest, most high-tech weapons, one of his
   highest priorities.

Host: Let's move on the situation in Turkmenistan…

[END TRANSCRIPT]

Viper 6 banked after its sixth drop, circling to the left to
come around north by north-west towards the mountains
north-east of Bangkok. It flew low, barely five meters over
the rice paddies and sugar cane plantations, under the
radar. Its AI steered it clear of villages and farmhouses.

It flew past Rop Mueang, past Nakhon Nayok, past
Phrommani, paralleled Highway 33 at a safe distance until
it saw the village of Ban Na, then curved around north and
east, hugged the terrain as it went from flat to rugged,
followed a ravine carved into the stone millennia ago up
towards greater heights.

At twelve hundred meters it popped out of the ravine,
acquired its target with its onboard optics, calibrated against
its internal GPS. This was target seven, its AI confirmed.

Viper 6 opened Weapons Bay 2, flew low and slow over
the monastery, and launched a spray of tiny eight-limbed
surveillance robots out and into the night air.

One by one they drifted down and onto the target.

43

Just Breathe

Kade woke to the sound of dawn bells. Sunday morning. Just over a day since everything had gone wrong, since Wats had died, since Narong had died, since Ilya and Rangan and so many others had been arrested.

The meditation had soothed him last night, for a while.

Then had come sleep, and with it, dreams. Dreams of rage, of destruction, of breaking Warren Becker in half, of burning Martin Holtzmann alive at the stake, of tearing black-masked agents limb from limb as they charged into that apartment. They'd been cold dreams. The death he'd meted out had been cool, methodical, satisfying.

He was cold inside. Cold and full of rage. That was all he could feel.

There was a knock at his door. "Come in," he replied.

Bahn entered. The young monk had brought him a bowl of porridge for breakfast. He placed the bowl on the table, then made a wai to Kade with this hands, smiled, said something in Thai which might have been a joke or a happy comment.

There was so much joy in this place. What did it feel like?

Was there joy for him, on the other side of this rage? On

the other side of this numbness? Was there anything?

Perhaps destroying the ERD would give him joy. The thought brought a small smile to his lips.

The doctor came to see him shortly thereafter, changed his dressings, checked his wounds, injected new growth factors to knit bone to bone, heal skin, restore damaged lung tissue.

The eye was still gone.

It was still so much less than he should have lost. He should have been the one to die. Not Wats. Not anyone else.

His hand clenched around the fob hanging on a chain around his neck, beneath his orange robes. Its hard edges bit into his palm painfully.

You should have lived, Wats. This wasn't worth it.

He rose, crutched himself towards the meditation hall again. He'd learned much last night. The monks had learned to integrate Nexus 3 into their minds. They hadn't reprogrammed the Nexus cores, or scanned the radio spectrum and mapped Nexus's responses, or reverse-engineered its underlying instruction set.

No. They'd meditated. They'd sculpted their own minds to the Nexus, found ways of thinking and being that gave them deeper control over it. And in so doing, they'd learned to achieve a synchrony that he'd never experienced. They'd learned to let thoughts flow smoothly across the boundaries that separated individual minds. They'd learned to merge into something larger and more sentient than they were individually.

It impressed him deeply. He had much to learn here.

He reached the meditation hall early, situated himself in the back, closed his eyes, focused on his breath.

Monks filed in. He felt them. Heard them. They sat as they entered, cross-legged, spines erect. They breathed.

Kade felt his own breathing synchronize with theirs. The connection between their minds firmed. The greater mind began to coalesce.

Kade could feel them all. He was aware of the tiny ripples of thought that passed through their minds. Every tiny thought, every word, every snippet of song, every momentary fancy, every thought of chores, every question of teachings, every itch, every urge to move... the room felt them all. Together their collective consciousness observed itself. As each thought or sensation arose it was perceived, acknowledged, released. Attention returned to the communal breathing.

It was hypnotic, serene, crystal clear and coherent. The room sparkled with their shared attention, with an almost physical sense of the collective mind they comprised.

Their minds were so quiet. Kade's was so loud in comparison. The same thoughts kept returning.

Wats. Ilya. Rangan.

Narong. Chariya. Niran.

Lalana. Mai.

The dead and the missing. The uncertainty of the future. The guilty who'd done this.

There was no grief. The software in his mind kept that at bay. His emotions were as hard and sharp and brittle as ice. Only anger. Only rage, cold rage, impotent rage.

Every time the thoughts arose, the collective mind observed them, acknowledged them, released them, returned its awareness to the rhythmic breathing of their bodies.

And every time they returned.

They meditated together until lunch. Kade ate in the mess hall in silence, lost in himself. The monks finished their meals, headed off to their afternoon chores.

Kade crutched painfully back to the meditation hall.

There, seated at the far end of the hall, facing Kade, the giant golden Buddha statue behind him, was Professor Somdet Phra Ananda.

The old monk's eyes opened at Kade's arrival.

"Child," he said in his deep sonorous voice, "come and sit with me."

Kade crutched himself across the room, reached the pillow Ananda indicated, slowly lowered himself, ribs aching. He could feel Ananda's mind, buoyant, radiant with calm and clarity, fluid, flexible, relaxed. His own mind felt icy, numb, frozen in a single thought.

"How are you, child?" Ananda asked.

"I'm healing," Kade said. I'm angry, he thought. "Thank you for letting us come here. This must be a risk for you. We were out of options."

"Enough people died that night," Ananda replied.

Kade nodded. The memory of it was cold. There was nothing where grief or sorrow should be. Anger. Hatred. That was all.

"I felt you meditating," Ananda said.

"It's amazing what your monks have learned to do," Kade replied. "I'm hoping to learn more of it."

"To what end?" Ananda asked.

To kill them, Kade thought. To hurt them. To break the ERD.

He stared at Ananda blankly for a moment, struggled to control himself. "I don't know."

Ananda studied him. "Your thoughts are cold, child. They're rigid. You shield yourself from what's within you, even as you shield yourself during meditation."

Kade looked down. "I don't feel anything. Nothing feels real."

"You've shackled your own mind. Release it."

The serenity package.

Kade nodded. "Yes. It calms me."

"It numbs you," Ananda replied. "It freezes you. That is not the same thing."

Kade kept his eyes on the floor.

"Release the shackles on your mind, child. Then you'll experience what's going on around you."

"I think it's all that's holding me together," Kade said.

"Then perhaps you should fall apart," Ananda replied.

Kade felt the monk's mind touch his own. Could he do it? Could he turn off the serenity package? Horrible things lurked beneath the surface of his thoughts. He might burst from them. He feared his own emotions.

"There's no way forward for you without letting yourself melt," Ananda said.

"Or burn," Kade said softly.

"Yes. Or burn."

"People died because of me," he said.

They'd existed. They'd had thoughts, emotions, plans. Gone, all gone.

"Yes. That is your karma," Ananda replied.

"I want to hurt the ERD. I want it so bad."

He could feel the bloodlust, feel the anger, feel the rage, the only thing that got through the serenity package any more.

"But it was also my fault," he said. "If I'd made different choices, those people would still be alive."

Ananda nodded. "Perhaps it was your fault."

Kade trembled.

My fault.

"Those shackles… They're there because I don't know if I can face it. If I can face really feeling what happened."

"The past is gone, child. Those men and women are gone, dead or imprisoned. You cannot change what has already happened."

Kade nodded.

Ananda continued. "But you can choose what you make of it. You have a choice to make. Will you make their deaths mean something? And if so, what?"

Kade nodded again. His fists were clenched.

"That's what I've been thinking about."

Rage or emptiness. Nothing else.

"But you will make no headway until you allow yourself to feel. Until you can face your pain, you will not go past it. I will be here with you. We will face it together."

Kade took a deep breath, shook his head. "I can't."

"You can," Ananda replied.

"It's too much. I can't."

"If not now, when?" The old monk gestured around himself. "If not here, then where?"

Kade pulled up the control panel for the serenity package in his mind. It would be so easy. Just a flick of a switch.

He shook his head. "I can't."

"Then your friend died for absolutely *nothing*."

The words were like a slap to the face. Kade went red. His fists clenched.

He flicked off the serenity package with a thought. The grief surged up around him, came over him like a wave. It bowled him over. It found the cracks in him and suffused every corner of his mind. It filled him up until there was room for nothing else, until he would burst with it, with the pain, with the sorrow, with the heartache, with the despair of all that he'd lost, all the death that he'd brought about.

Wats… Wats…

The faces of the dead and lost to him rose up in his mind.

Ilya. I'll never see you again, Ilya.

The loss of all that had been good in his life threatened to destroy him. It threatened to wash him away in a flood and leave just a husk where he had once been.

Rangan. I'm so sorry, man. I miss you.

The pain of knowing that he had doomed innocents permeated him.

Narong. Lalana. Chariya. Niran. Mai!

He felt Watson Cole die again. Felt the man's mind burrow into Sam's.

Protect him.

He felt Wats' last urging to him.

Set it free. Give it to the rest of the world. Give them what it gave me.

He heard Wats' last words before the explosion.

"You got shit to do, brother. Go do it."

He saw Narong go down with a burst of bullets in his belly, felt the boy's fear and confusion, the way he'd died because of Kade, because Kade had given those bastards a tool to coerce him with.

He felt Lalana wink out of existence in a hail of bullets. He felt Areva burn to death, felt Loesan die in pain, felt old Niran cut down as he'd tried to save Lalana, felt Chariya mourn her dead family. He felt magical little Mai fade away with Sam crouched above her.

Will you make their deaths mean something? Ananda had asked him.

Yes, Kade answered. *Yes.*

He felt the gentlest of mental touches from Ananda, a feather brush of mind against mind. Ananda was breath. He was awareness. He was untroubled, undiluted awareness.

Breathe. Breathe. Watch the breath go out. Watch the breath come in.

It was sweet. It was solace. It was emptiness and silence. Wats faded slowly from his mind. Breath expanded in his ears, his sight, his sense of his body, grew and grew to fill his mind.

Breathe. Breathe. Let go.

Breathe. Watch the breath go out. Watch the breath come in.

In. Out. Breathe. Observe.

Ananda was tranquility. Ananda was peace. Ananda was awareness. His mind was Kade's lamppost when the darkness and confusion of guilt and remorse and despair came over him.

Observe the thoughts. Let them pass. Bring your attention back to the breath.

Breathe.

Breathe.

Breathe.

Spider BR-6-7-4 crawled silently along the roof of the hall, its skin the same color as the ceiling it clung to. It had been exploring for almost twelve hours now. It had identified 43 unique individuals. Its sisters had identified another 227 in total, seventy-eight percent male, twenty-two percent female. So far there had been no sign of any of its primary or secondary targets.

Spider BR-6-7-4 had observed a large number of individuals emerging from a doorway in this building, all together, earlier in the day. It had accordingly increased the priority of a search of this building and broadcasted that fact to its sisters. Three of them now crawled through it. There was another door ahead of BR-6-7-4. IR showed two human forms within, seated. BR-6-7-4 considered the door for a moment, telescoped a foreleg to explore the gap between door and doorway. It would do.

BR-6-7-4 clung close to the ceiling, flattening its shape, and crept between the door and the doorway it was set in, into a large open room. Two human-shaped objects, alive in IR, sat on the floor at one end of the room. The one facing it was a Person of Interest. It logged that fact. The other faced away from BR-6-7-4. It began the long trek across the room.

It took nine minutes for BR-6-7-4 to cross the room in full stealth mode. The two warm human-shaped objects remained roughly stationary in that time. The Person of Interest's eyes were closed. Its chest rose and fell, consistent with respiration. BR-6-7-4 consulted its decision tree and provisionally labeled the Person of Interest as "Alive", consistent with body temperature and respiration, and "Asleep", consistent with a long duration of eye closure and silence. It left a flag indicating possible re-evaluation due to seated position.

Finally BR-6-7-4 reached a position where it could see the facial area of the second human-shaped object. This human-shaped object also respirated, also with eyes closed. More interesting was the face. Facial recognition routines identified a possible match with one of its Primary Targets, but a number of the details were different in unexpected ways.

Spider BR-6-7-4 hunkered down, double-checked that it was functionally invisible, and broadcast a burst of data to its masters.

Breathe.

Breathe.

Kade had lost track of the hours he'd spent here. Ananda was tireless, the rhythm of his mind as flawless and eternal as ocean surf against a beach. Kade on the other hand... he was tired. More at peace, but so so tired. His concentration was fraying, random thoughts sneaking back in around the absorbing tranquility of his breath.

And then he felt it.

All around him, behind him, throughout this room. Scores of minds unmasked themselves, sitting calm and silent in rows and columns. How long had they been here?

And then, as one, the monks began to breathe, in time to Kade and Ananda.

The effect was electrifying. Kade felt himself buoyed by it. He was not just one. He was many. He was all. The minds in the room were a web, a tapestry, an orchestra of thought without thought. The room breathed in. The room breathed out. A thought occurred in the mind of a novice. It rippled across the mind of the room. All observed it. All brought attention back to the breath.

It lifted Kade up. It filled him with a peace and clarity he'd never felt. He felt utterly clear, sober, grounded, balanced. All fatigue left him. Shadows vanished from the corners of his mind. As one they brought their collective attention to their symphony of breath, let go of the anchor of attachment to the past, to what had been, to what might have been.

There was only here.

There was only now.

There was only breath.

There was only mind.

44
Findings

Aboard the *Boca Raton*, an icon on a screen turned yellow, began to flash for attention. Jane Kim tapped the icon, expanded the alert. One of the spiders at target 67. A possible match. There. That face. Kaden Lane, in monk's robes, shaven head, a bandage across his face. And across from him, Professor Somdet Phra Ananda, personal friend of the King of Thailand.

Kim paged Nichols in his stateroom. He would want to see this.

While she waited, she turned her attention to the other spiders at target 67. If Lane was there, Cataranes might be there too. She updated the target profile for Cataranes to include the possibility of a shaven head, bandages, and monk's robes, and redirected all of them towards finding Primary Target Beta. Find Blackbird.

Two and a half hours later, they did. She was still alive.

Becker answered the phone at 4.13am Sunday morning, DC time. Sunday afternoon in Thailand. The *Boca Raton*. They'd found Lane and Cataranes. Monastery. Undefended. Within range of retrieval. The data was spooling to his slate now.

"Get the ball rolling," he told Nichols.

"Do we have clearance to launch?"

"You will in four hours."

White House, National Security Advisor's Office

"This operation was a complete clusterfuck, was it not?" Senator Barbara Engels asked. "And now you want to follow it up with an armed invasion? This is crazy."

Becker wanted to rub his temples. The senator's voice made his head hurt. The meeting had stretched on for more than an hour already, going round and round on the same topics.

"Thank you, Barbara," National Security Advisor Carolyn Pryce said. "We appreciate the input of the oversight committee."

The senator shook her head. "You're looking at a lot more than input here. If this blows up in our faces, you're going to see hearings in my committee. Hearings during an *election year*. Does that register with you? You people are off the deep end."

Secretary of State Abrams nodded his head in support. "I agree with Senator Engels. We can't further provoke the Thai."

"They're harboring a criminal," said Becker's superior, ERD Director Joe Duran. "A possibly posthuman being who's coerced and abducted our agents, used them to kill our men. We have to go in."

Duran's boss, Homeland Security Secretary Langston Hughes, nodded his approval.

Pryce turned to the Chairman of the Joint Chiefs. Stanley McWilliams had been largely silent throughout the meeting, studying the details of the plan that Becker had sent him on his slate. "Admiral McWilliams? What's your view on this?"

The silver-haired admiral looked up from his slate, met Pryce's eyes, held them steadily. "This mission is a crock of shit."

Becker felt himself bristle. People around the table straightened themselves in surprise. Becker opened his mouth to reply.

Pryce held her raised palm out towards him, her eyes still on McWilliams. The reply died on Becker's lips.

"Go on, Admiral."

"First, we shouldn't have launched those recon drones last night. We have a chain of command for a reason." His eyes flickered over Becker and then Maximilian Barnes.

I've made an enemy, Becker realized. Going around him and his people pissed him off.

"Second, this mission looks good on a slate, but no plan survives contact with the enemy. Everything has to go perfectly for us to get in and out without being detected. That's possible, but unlikely. If anything goes sideways at all, we'll be caught invading an undefended, civilian, *holy* site in a nominally allied country. And for what?" He slid his slate across the table, a picture of Kaden Lane on it. "For bullshit. It's not worth it."

Everyone started talking at once.

Pryce held her hand up. "Quiet."

The noise stopped as quickly as it had begun.

She gestured to Becker. "This is your plan, Deputy Director. What do you say to the admiral's objections?"

Becker took a breath, tried to project calm.

"Admiral McWilliams is correct that this could go sideways. My commitment to you, Admiral, is that at the first hint that there's any chance of discovery of the mission, we'll abort it. What I weigh against the risks are the national security value of understanding the methods the Chinese have for coercion, the importance of keeping fourth-gen enhancements and Nexus 5 off the streets, and my personal passion for getting a loyal agent home in one piece. I'd think you'd understand that."

"I'd be touched if you showed half as much passion for the civil rights of ordinary Americans," McWilliams drawled back.

Becker flushed.

That prick.

People started talking at once, stumbling all over each other. CIA Director Alan Keyes threw up a hand in exasperation. Senator Engels chuckled in amusement. Maximilian Barnes just leaned back and watched it all, impassive.

"Quiet!" Pryce slammed her hand on the table this time.

Silence returned at once.

"*Admiral* McWilliams," she said. "Remember where you are, and keep your personal opinions contained."

She slowly scanned the room, as if daring anyone to make a sound. No one did.

"The President has made the elimination of transhuman and posthuman threats one of his top national security policies," Pryce said. "We serve to implement those policies. At the same time, we do not want to be seen as taking unauthorized military action inside Thailand. Given that, I'm going to recommend to the President that we move forward with this operation, under very specific conditions."

She lifted an elegantly manicured hand, locked eyes with Becker, counted off her conditions on dark-skinned fingers.

"First, no action against Su-Yong Shu unless you can provide concrete evidence of direct action by her against American forces and in violation of Copenhagen. Everything you have here is circumstantial. Get proof, and you'll have your clearance to go after her."

Becker nodded.

"Second, only stealthed equipment and only then under the cover of night. Third, no civilian casualties. Not a single one. You load non-lethal rounds and you *only* switch to lethal if there are no civilians anywhere in the area and you're returning lethal fire from your missing agents or another combatant. Fourth, absolutely zero, and I mean *zero* evidence of US involvement. This will not become an international incident, and this will not become an issue in the US this November. If there is even the slightest chance of detection, you abort *immediately.*"

Becker nodded again. He didn't trust himself to speak.

Pryce scanned the room, looking each of them in the eye. ERD Enforcement Division Deputy Director Becker, Secretary of Homeland Security Hughes, ERD Director Duran, Director of the Central Intelligence Agency Keyes, Chairman of the Joint Chiefs McWilliams, Secretary of State Abrams, Senate Oversight Committee Chairwoman Engels, Special Policy Advisor Maximilian Barnes.

"Are we all clear on this?"

McWilliams snorted. Barnes watched the room silently. Everyone else nodded, voiced their assent.

"Good," Pryce said. "I brief the President in less than an hour. Admiral McWilliams, you're welcome to accompany me and present the case against this mission. I'll let all of you know the President's decision immediately thereafter. Good day, gentlemen. Good day, Senator."

45

Anyone

The symphony of mind finally ended. The thoughts of the greater mind went from thick braids to wispy tendrils and then to vapor, dissipating in a glorious sigh of contentment. Everyone opened their eyes, made respectful *wais* towards the altar.

Ananda gestured for Kade to remain as the others filed quietly out.

"How do you feel now?" Ananda asked him.

Kade considered himself, observed himself. "Better. Calmer. Tired."

Ananda nodded. "Good. This was just a beginning, but a good one. You will heal."

"Thank you," Kade said.

Ananda nodded again. "Su-Yong Shu will arrive to visit you tonight. It will be after midnight."

Shu was coming. He had so many questions for her. Was the anger what drove her on? Could she heal? Could she release her hatred?

"I'll see to it that you're awakened when she arrives," Ananda said.

Kade nodded his thanks.

"And tomorrow you move on."

Kade nodded again. Safety meant moving, for now. He would miss this place. There was so much he wanted to know.

"The things you're doing here...?" he asked. "The things you talked about at the conference. Where are you going with all this?"

Ananda smiled. "You've seen some of what goes on here. You've heard me speak. What does it seem like we're doing?"

"You're teaching monks to use Nexus, to integrate it permanently."

"Yes."

"You're showing them how to meditate together, how to synchronize their minds further."

"We're learning that together."

"You talked about group minds," Kade said. "About taking neuroscience from the individual to the group level."

"Yes."

"You're trying to make it real here."

Ananda held Kade's gaze with his own deep, dark eyes. "Yes."

"With you in charge?" Kade asked.

Ananda smiled slightly.

"I meant what I said about Buddhism being democratic. You've been part of the group mind. Is anyone in charge? Is any single neuron in charge in your brain?"

Kade nodded to himself. It had felt organic, emergent, self-directed, without any particular center. They were each pieces of the mind that emerged when they meditated. But how committed to that was Ananda?

"You *are* in charge, though."

Ananda looked at him calmly. "In the perceptions of outsiders, perhaps. But here? I'm the oldest. I have the most experience. My thoughts carry some weight. When our minds are apart I have certain authority. But when we are connected... the group mind *contains* me. I'm just one part of it. The decisions it makes are wiser and more just than the ones I can make alone. The insights it can glean and the truths it can reveal are deeper than those I can glimpse alone. I respect that. I am a piece of this, not its master."

Kade nodded to himself again.

"What you're working towards... Is it just for monks?" he asked. "Just for meditation?"

"For anyone who can master it. For any purpose they can put it to."

"Anyone?" Kade asked.

Ananda looked back at him impassively. "Anyone."

"But mastering it takes practice," Kade said. "It takes effort. Hours of meditation every day, for months – years."

"Yes."

"So this won't ever be in reach of most people."

"It's in reach of them, if they but expend the effort to grasp it."

Kade shook his head. "I mean, practically speaking, most people aren't going to meditate for hours each day."

Ananda nodded slowly. "True. Most will not be willing to expend the effort."

"And if there were a shortcut?"

"A shortcut such as the one that you have taken?" Ananda asked.

Kade nodded. "Something like that."

Ananda gazed at him, considering. "How long did it take you to learn to read?"

The question surprised Kade. "A year or two, I suppose."

"And to speak?" Ananda asked.

"Maybe two years?" Kade ventured.

"Imagine," Ananda said, "a world where it took most of

a lifetime to learn to speak, to learn to read or write, where many never even reached that point."

Kade closed his eyes, tried to picture it.

"Imagine that you could show people a faster way," Ananda continued. "That in a year or two you could show them the basics of language, of literacy."

Kade imagined.

"Would you do it?" Ananda asked.

"Yes," Kade replied.

"Even though it would surely be used at times for profanity or vile speech?"

"Yes."

"Even though fools might read dangerous things written by bigger fools, might follow their instructions and hurt themselves or others?"

"Yes," Kade replied.

"Even though writing might be used to describe weapons that could be used to kill others?" Ananda asked.

"Yes," Kade said.

"Even though charismatic fascists might use the power of speech to stir people up, to incite violence, to stoke hatred, to create war?"

Kade swallowed. "Yes."

"Why?"

"Because I think people would use it for more good than harm."

"Is that the only reason?"

"And because I think it's just good. It's just good for people to be able to communicate more easily. It's just good for people to be smarter, to be more connected, to have access to more of each others' thoughts."

"Then you have my answer."

The old monk rose smoothly to his feet and padded silently out of the great hall.

Kade sat there alone, for long minutes, intensely aware of the weight of the fob on the chain around his neck. Eventually he rose painfully, crutched his way slowly out of the hall, and went to see if anything was left of dinner.

46
Calm Before the Storm

Becker got the call from Pryce less than an hour after the meeting ended. The President had approved the plan, with the conditions she had specified.

"Don't screw it up," Pryce told him.

Becker hung up and called the *Boca Raton* with the news. They were in business.

In his room, Kade turned off all net connectivity on his slate, then slowly eased the chain over his neck and slid the fob into place.

The fob drew power from the slate. It came alive in his mind, opened itself to his Nexus, connected him to the slate. A Nexus interface card. The one they'd printed for Wats, no doubt.

And on the same fob, data storage. A script. The sort of script he'd expected.

He lay back, and began to copy the Nexus files from his mind to the fob. He made a few small changes along the way, just in case.

Satisfied, he pulled it from the slate, hung it around his neck once more, let the slate connect to the net again, and lay down to sleep until Shu arrived.

Su-Yong Shu said goodbye to the final guests at the VIP reception. It was nearly 11pm. The conference was ended. The post-conference workshops were ended. The post-workshop final reception was ended. Finally she could attend to important matters.

The black Opal rolled into sight. Feng got out, pulled open the door, lifted the umbrella against the night rain. Time to go.

"Stand by for flight operations," came the voice from the bridge.

Nichols watched nervously.

"Flight deck opening," said the bridge. "Flight elevators 1 and 2 engaging."

On the foredeck of the *Boca Raton*, nearly a third of the length of the hull was retracting, radar and sonar absorbent panels receding into the ship's belly, then sliding slowly and smoothly to the side to reveal the full forty-meter length of the forward combat deck, now configured entirely for flight operations.

Slowly, two fully fueled, armed, and loaded XH-83 Banshee stealth assault helicopters rose up into view. Each carried a pilot and six heavily armed and augmented Navy SEALs. The helicopters' folded-in rotors began to unfold into flight configuration. On the deck, their engine whine would be audible now, as their systems warmed up.

Fueling hoses decoupled from each chopper with a puff of out-gassed steam. Weapons checks completed, green across the board. Engines, green. Stealth, green. Electronic warfare, green. Nav, green. Flight, green. The rotors locked into their fully expanded configuration.

"Go for rotor spin up," the bridge voice said.

They began to spin, lazily at first, then faster, then faster still. Downdraft flattened the seas to either side of the ship.

"Three seconds to clamp release. Two... One..."

The deck clamps released the landing gear of the choppers. As one, they rose up and forward, into the night sky.

"Banshees away," the bridge said. "C&C, you have the ball."

"Roger that, Bridge," Jane Kim replied. "C&C has the ball. C&C out."

In the air, the Banshees began to retract their landing gear. With the landing gear pulled in, the choppers would be nearly invisible to radar. Their chameleonware underbellies would make them blend into the dark sky to ground observers. It was midnight. The two choppers would fly low and fast, five meters off the surface, make their target around 1am, and be back with Lane and Cataranes a little after 2 o'clock.

"End flight operations," came from the bridge. "Elevators 1 and 2 to bays. Stealth hull closure in three... two... one..."

The radar and sonar absorbent hull of the great ship began to close over the combat hull once more.

Shu reclined in the plush rear seat of the Opal, slate in hand, following up on conversations and business from the conference and post-conference workshops. Sometimes she wondered why she came to these things.

They were almost to Ananda's mountain sanctuary, starting the winding trip up the mountain road. She'd been here only once before. Ananda's monks were of great interest to her. The abilities of a properly trained human mind never ceased to amaze her, even now. What they could do if they combined the best of her knowledge and

Ananda's training methods...

Feng was suddenly alert. Something had caught his interest. Something had buffeted the car slightly, like a burst of wind.

He tapped a button on the console, muted the Brahms he'd had playing for her.

"What is it?" she asked.

The Confucian Fist didn't answer. Instead he killed the petrol engine, let the car coast on batteries, hit a button to lower the windows.

He's listening for something, she thought. She knew better than to interrupt him at such a moment. She felt for the contents of his thoughts, subtly, so as not to distract him.

Feng tapped another key. The windshield became a display. Infrared, she read from him.

There. On the display. Two faint red spots. Fainter than a human body. But elevated, above the ground. Receding, away and up. And in Feng's superhuman hearing, the faintest hint of the whup-whup-whup of rotors.

"Helicopters," he said aloud. "Stealthed. Heading where we are."

Shu felt a chill.

"Could they be Thai?" She knew the answer as she voiced the question.

Feng shook his head. "No. Chinese, EU, or American."

How long? She read the answer in Feng's mind. Five minutes until the choppers reached the monastery on current course and speed. Ten if they slowed over the mountain to come in silently.

She opened to her higher self. The light and power of her massive intellect coursed through her. She absorbed all knowledge of American military helicopters. Chinese Ministry of National Defense databases opened to her, showed her the known and suspected positions of all American forces, their capabilities. So… an American ship might possibly be in the Gulf of Thailand?

"Step on it," she told Feng. "Get us there as quickly as you're able."

Shu pulled out her phone, hit the button to call Ananda. She hoped she was in time.

The turbocharged gas engine roared into life as Feng took them from electric cruise into hydrocarbon sprint.

The phone pulled Ananda from his meditation just a bit after 1am. It was Shu. Was she here, then?

He answered.

"You have two or more American military helicopters headed towards you. ETA five minutes."

The words shook him. They would come here?

They would.

Ananda breathed in with his mind, yelled out the thought of alarm: **Hide the Americans. Prepare for unwanted guests.**

He looked at his phone. Dared he make this call? Dared he not?

He dialed. A voice answered in Thai. Crisp. Professional. Military.

"This is Professor Somdet Phra Ananda," he said, putting all the dignity and authority of his name and position into his voice. "Get me the Minister of Defense."

A hundred and ninety kilometers away, alarms began to sound at Korat Air Force Base. Ready fighters ignited their engines, raced down the runway, canted their noses up to achieve flight. In moments, two Indian-built IA-9 Rudra NG fighters were in the air, racing south-west towards Saraburi.

Thirty seconds later they went supersonic. Time to Saraburi: eight minutes.

47
Incoming

Kade woke to someone shaking him. Was it dawn? No. Was Shu here? He opened his eyes. It was Bahn, the monk who'd brought his meals, brought him crutches. There was another monk behind him.

"Helicopter!" the young monk said, pointing at the sky. "Helicopter!"

What? Kade didn't want to get on any helicopter.

"America!" Bahn yelled.

Oh no. Oh, fucking no. They've found us.

His heart was pounding. There was no serenity package running to calm him.

Bahn and the other monk were trying to lift him out of the bed.

"No!" he yelled.

They were half-carrying, half-dragging him towards the door of his tiny cell.

Kade thrashed.

"No!"

His ferocity surprised them. He slipped free of their hold and clattered onto the ground. They stared at this crazy American who wouldn't come with them to safety.

The slate was on the table, out of his reach. His crutches were by the bed, out of his reach. He tried to lever himself up onto his good leg and collapsed back to the ground in pain.

"The slate!" he yelled. He pointed madly at it.

Bahn grabbed it, pushed it into Kade's hands.

"Helicopter!" the young monk yelled, pointing up at the sky.

Kade pulled the chain around his neck up over his head with one hand.

"Helicopter." Kade nodded. "American helicopter."

Bahn nodded enthusiastically, tried to take his arm.

Kade shook himself free, jammed the data fob into the I/O slot on the cheap slate. Did he have net signal right now? Yes.

A window blossomed on the slate, showing the contents of the data fob. He hunted for the script Wats had placed there.

`[Mass-Distrib]`

His finger hovered over it. Did he really want to do this? He hadn't done any of the work to make Nexus 5 safe from abuse.

Images came to him unbidden. Narong pointing a gun at Ted Prat-Nung's head, his will the ERD's. The Dalai Lama, dead in a pool of his blood, murdered by his subverted friend. Sam's parents, their eyes glazed by Communion virus, watching her floggings, sending her off to be beaten and raped. He thought of all the horror stories he'd ever heard about DWITY.

People would abuse this. Monsters would use it for monstrous things. There would be blood on his hands, coercion on his hands, unthinkable terror and pain on his hands.

His finger trembled.

Bahn tugged at his arm, urgently. It was far away, another world.

He thought of Wats, of the way Nexus had changed him; of Shu, of her vision of picking and choosing who would make the jump to the posthuman condition, of her vision of a posthuman elite ruling over the rest of humanity; of Ilya, of her words to him on their call.

Broad dissemination and individual choice turn most technologies into a plus. If only the elites have access, it's a dystopia.

He thought of what he'd told Ananda just hours ago.

Because I think people would use it for more good than harm, he'd said. *And because I think it's just good.*

Kade's heart pounded in his chest. He was sweating. His whole body was beginning to shake. He could be dead in minutes. Dead or on his way to some deep dark hole he'd never emerge from. Was this how Wats had felt, just before he'd dropped through the ceiling to save them?

It was now or never.

He stabbed the icon with his trembling finger. God help him.

DISTRIBUTE DATA FOB CONTENTS WORLDWIDE? Y/N?

Yes. Fucking yes.

A progress bar appeared.

CONNECTING...
UPLOADING...
14 MINUTES REMAINING.

There was no way back. Whatever happened to him now, whether he died or went to jail, at least he'd done something with his life. Kade hoped it was the right thing.

He slid the slate under his narrow bed where it would be out of sight and let Bahn and the other monk carry him away.

"Target in sight," Bruce Williams said. "No lights. No movement. All clear on IR and radio."

Nichols nodded. "Commence operation."

"Roger that," Williams said. "Starting jamming... now. Jamming active."

Both Banshees lit up their wideband signal jammers.

"Deploying SEALs now," Williams said.

In the cell Kade had fled from, a discarded slate flashed a new message on its screen.

CONNECTION LOST.

No one was there to see it. After a few minutes, the screen dimmed to black.

SEAL Sergeant Jim Iverson fast-roped silently down the line from Banshee One. His heads-up display pointed the way to Target One's cell. His team assembled around him. Together they crept silently, nearly invisibly through the complex.

Building in sight. West entrance approaching.

What was that sound?

Then the first dot appeared on his HUD. Three dots, moving away from this building, out the other side. Heading away from them.

Then more dots. Tens more. Everywhere.

The handle of the door turned. It opened, and monks filed out in their orange robes, bald heads, serene expressions on their faces. Dozens of them. Scores of them. Hundreds of them.

Bells began ringing, like the church bells of his youth. Bright lights came to life around the courtyard where they'd fast-roped down.

Oh, fuck.

Nichols watched as Teams One and Two dispersed, heading for Lane's cell and the nun's dormitory where Cataranes was housed.

"Contact, contact," Jane Kim said. "I've got shapes moving on IR."

"What the hell?" Nichols asked.

"More contacts," Williams said. "All over the place."

Doors were opening on buildings all over the complex, spilling visible light out into the courtyards. Warm bodies were walking out of all of them, all over the place.

And then the bells began ringing. Great bells. Monastery bells. Ringing and ringing and ringing.

Lights came on. Floodlights illuminating the courtyard, illuminating the orange-robed monks filing silently and calmly into it, beatific smiles on their faces.

"Abort!" Nichols yelled. "Abort abort abort. Get them out of there, ASAP!"

He looked at screen 3. Becker was ashen-faced. The mission was a bust.

Jim Iverson's HUD flashed a message from command at him.

ABORT ABORT ABORT

Abort? There were fucking monks between his squad and the choppers! They were everywhere! He whispered back furiously at command.

"Sir," Jane Kim called out, "we have Lane on scope. Banshee One has a shot on him."

It didn't matter. They had to abort.

"Stand down," he told Kim.

"Teams One and Two both pinned by monks," Williams said. "Still stealthed. Lots of bodies between them and the zip line."

"Move the line to them," Nichols ordered.

A flash of light lit up one of the screens.

"Oh, fuck," Williams said.

Nichols looked over. Faces everywhere. Serene faces. Bald heads. Orange robes. All crowding closer. "What the hell was that?"

"Photo," Williams said. "The monks are taking pictures."

"Complete the mission," Becker said from the screen.

"What?" Nichols asked.

"We're made," his boss said. "Too late to change that. Take the shot on Lane. Grab Cataranes. Get the hell out."

Nichols was stunned. Complete the mission. But their orders were not to get caught.

They were caught already…

Complete the mission.

"Take the shot," he ordered. "Tell Team Two to proceed towards Blackbird's cell. We're go to finish the mission."

Kade hopped madly along, his arms around Bahn and the other monk's shoulders, letting them half carry him. He heard a *pfffft* sound and the monk to his left fell with a clatter. Oh, fuck. Kade almost fell too, Bahn barely keeping him upright. They rounded the corner, out of sight from the helicopters, and kept running.

"Where are we going?" Kade yelled as he hopped.

"Hide!" Bahn said. "Stairs!"

They turned another corner and Kade's good leg slipped on a wet cobblestone. His leg went out from under him and the ground rushed up. Bahn tried to grab him, overextended, and they both fell to the hard ground. Kade heard a crack from inside himself, felt fresh pain in his side.

Fuck.

Bahn got back on his feet, slowly dragged Kade up as well. Oh God, that hurt.

Iverson winced as another flash went off from another camera. He almost missed the message from command.

Proceed? Follow the targets. Roger that.

The HUD showed Target One forty meters to the north-west, but all he could see in that direction was row upon row of bald men in orange robes, hands folded into their sleeves, serene expressions on their faces. They pressed in close around him. He whirled to go around them. More monks blocked his way. He pressed forward. A dozen bodies pressed back. Another two SEALs were behind him. They elbowed and pushed their way through the press. It just reformed around them, pushed back against them. The mass of monks moved like a single organism, shifting and reforming to block them any way they turned.

This was fucking insane. Didn't these men know they were armed?

"Team One, you are cleared for nonlethal fire. Disperse that crowd."

"Roger that."

Iverson flipped off the safety, fired a tranq round into the belly of the monk in front of him. The orange-robed figure slumped to the ground silently. Another monk replaced the one he'd shot immediately, face utterly relaxed.

Iverson fired again. A body fell. Again. Another body. Again. Another one.

His squadmates did the same. Monks fell. Other monks moved forwards even before their comrades' bodies could hit the ground. Monks behind them caught the falling ones, dragged their limp bodies away, took their places.

Fucking insane.

Sam woke to the sound of bells.

Not right. It isn't morning yet.

Then she heard Vipada's breathless voice shouting in Thai. "Samantha! We have to hide you! American helicopters are coming!"

Oh, fuck.

Vipada flew into the room, looked around, grabbed Sam by the hand. "Come with me! I'll take you to the cellar!"

She could surrender. Hand herself over. Plead insanity.

No.

She wouldn't see another child die because of her. She wouldn't be part of another Bangkok. There had to be a better way.

Vipada was yanking at her. "This way! The cellar! We hide!"

She'd made a promise to Wats. To protect Kade.

Sam shook her hand free. "No, Vipada. You hide. I have to fight."

"Then I fight with you," the young nun said. There was steel in her voice.

Sam stared at her.

She's older than I was when I learned to fight, Sam thought to herself.

"OK," she told the girl. "Here's the plan."

Iverson fired and fired and fired. He emptied clip after clip into these orange-robed men. His squadmates did the same. Finally the press of monks eased. A few stood watching them from windows and doorways. None approached.

Target One had gone off the scope. Iverson's HUD showed the target's last known position and vector. He broke up his team to cover possible routes, gave himself the direct pursuit.

He dashed forward, rounded the corner of the building. He was in a triangular space between the large meditation hall on his right, the monk's quarters on his left, and the rock wall of the mountain ahead. Nothing moved on IR.

Wait. There. A sound. A muffled curse. Iverson rushed forward, rounded the corner, saw two figures trying to clamber through an open doorway. He had them.

"No sign of Blackbird, sir," Jane Kim said. "Not in her cell. Team Two dispersing, searching the area."

Nichols swore softly to himself.

"Possible contact!" Kim called out. "Behind the buildings!"

There, on one of the Team Two helmet cams, a woman in the middle of the passage, in nun's robes, facing away from him.

"Take her down!" Nichols shouted. "Don't get any closer!"

No SEAL was a match for her fourth-generation enhancements.

A blur came in from the side of the screen. The camera turned, caught a glimpse of motion, then died. Static.

"Fuck. It was an ambush!"

Sam tightened the knife-belt she'd taken from the SEAL around her waist, slung the other belt with the stun grenades and explosives and powered ascender over her shoulder, fastened it across her chest. The assault rifle was biometrically locked to the SEAL – useless to her. She turned to Vipada.

"Ready?" she asked

The girl nodded, wide-eyed.

Sam interlaced her fingers. Vipada stepped up, and Sam sent her up onto the roof. The girl clambered for a hold, found one. Sam crouched and leapt, pulled herself up next to the girl. It was slick and wet here. Vipada clung to the slippery roof tiles.

Sam looked up into the cloudy sky. As she'd hoped, this side of the roof, slanted to face the mountain, was out of view of the choppers. She began to slowly slither forward on her belly towards the peak of the roof. She needed to see what was going on out there.

Kade groaned in pain as Bahn half-dragged him down the walkway between the meditation hall and the stony mountainside. They reached something. A heavy wooden door. Bahn fished out keys while still supporting Kade, wrestled with the lock, opened it. Beyond the door lay a set of stone stairs, heading down into the gloom.

Pffft pffft click.

Kade heard the shots. Bahn went limp, started to collapse forward. Kade tried to grab Bahn as he fell, missed. The young monk toppled forward and down the stairs with a hard thud and another thud and a sickening crack.

Kade turned. There was a large heavily armed soldier pointing a rifle at him.

He had nowhere left to go. He let go of the doorjamb, threw himself backwards, hoping he'd survive the fall, find some way to hide down there.

The soldier's arm shot out, hauled him back, threw him across the walkway and into the rock wall of the mountain. His head and body collided with the hard rock. Vision faded. Stars bloomed. Pain racked his midsection. His bad leg folded under him.

Kade flipped on Bruce Lee.

Targeting circles blossomed in his vision. Attack and

defense buttons loomed. Full auto. Click. That target. Click.

His good right leg lashed out at the soldier's knee. The big man caught the foot, used it to spin Kade around and onto his stomach. The software brought Kade's hands up to catch him in plank pose, lashed out with the foot again. The soldier's knee came down on the small of Kade's back. Bruce Lee tried a roll and a knife hand strike to the throat of the man behind him. The soldier held him down, fended off Kade's struggles, grabbed the hand and cuffed it. Bruce Lee tried to push his hips up off the ground to create room to twist to the side. The soldier was too heavy. Bruce Lee spotted the knife on the man's belt, reached for it with his free hand, got his hand on the hilt. The soldier's hand came down painfully around Kade's wrist, twisted hard, cuffed it to his other hand.

Kade struggled and the soldier smacked him across the back of the head, bouncing Kade's face off the wet stones of the passage. Kade felt his nose crunch, blood fountaining from it. His vision went grey again. Stars spun around him. When his wits returned, he found that his legs were bound. The soldier yelled something into a radio, tossed Kade painfully over his shoulder, and started to jog.

"We've got Target One!" Bruce Williams exclaimed. "Iverson is headed back to Banshee One. Team falling in around him."

"Excellent," Nichols said.

On screen 3 Becker smiled thinly.

"What about Blackbird?" Nichols asked.

"The rest of Team Two just got there. Man down is hurt but still breathing. No sign of Blackbird."

Nichols frowned. Where are you, Sam? Where are you?

Don't make us hurt you.

And don't hurt too many of us.

Sam froze near the top of the roof. She could hear the team below, searching for her. The wet roof tiles seemed to be shielding her from IR for the moment. Vipada clung to the slick tiles for dear life next to her. She saw Sam look at her and flashed a forced smile. Thatagirl.

The courtyard was strewn with fallen monks. Dozens of them. At least fifty, sixty monks lay on the cold wet stones. Two distortions in the sky anchored two ropes that trailed down into the courtyard. There was a Navy SEAL guarding each.

There. Motion from near the monks' quarters. Four SEALs jogged into view. The one in the middle had someone over his shoulder. Long, lean, wearing boxers and a cast. Kade. They made the rope below the closer of the two choppers, and the SEAL carrying Kade attached his ascender to the rope and zipped back up.

I could let them take Kade… Sam thought.

No. That was the coward's way.

She scanned the men. At least four. Maybe more in the chopper. Armed. Augmented. American.

They did a job a lot like hers. Could she fight them?

Yes, if she had to.

She waited until four of them had ascended the line, then slid down the wet roof, jumped into the courtyard, rolled and came to her feet in a sprint.

The last SEAL had his gun over his shoulder, both hands on his ascender. He hit the button and zipped up, just as he saw her closing on him.

There were shouts behind her. The other fireteam had come out from the maze and were in the courtyard now, tens of yards back. Tranq rounds struck the ground at her feet.

The final SEAL reached the top of the rope on his ascender, climbed into the helicopter where they had Kade. Sam sprinted straight at the rope, slapped the ascender onto it one-handed as she ran by and jammed her thumb onto the ascend button. The device yanked her up by one arm, even as her momentum swung her out into a wide pendulum arc. She pulled a stun grenade from her stolen belt, felt its cold weight in her palm.

A SEAL reappeared above her, assault rifle pointed in her direction. Sam jerked with her whole body as he fired, perturbed the pendulum swing as his shots ripped though the space she'd just occupied, flung the grenade with all her might. The SEAL saw her throw, ducked back into the chopper for cover. The stun grenade arced fast and hard through the air, hit the edge of the doorway, exploded with a loud bang just outside the open door of the Banshee.

The ascender whined as it zipped her up towards the chopper above.

"Sir, we've got Blackbird. She's attacking Banshee One! She's on the rope, headed up."

"Call 'em back," Becker said from the screen. "Get her in Banshee One, seal it, subdue her en route to the *Boca Raton*."

Nichols nodded. "You heard that, Jane. Tell 'em to let her onboard, then keep her there."

"Roger that."

"And get Team Two up on Banshee Two. We've got what we came for."

48
No Plan Survives...

The black Opal came over the final rise in time to see the SEALs disappearing into the stealthed helicopter.

There. He's in that one, Shu sent to Feng. **And Cataranes is headed there too.**

The woman was dashing towards the chopper Kade was in. Feng gunned the engine for the gates to the compound a hundred meters away. The Opal surged forward, burst through the ornate bronze and iron gate at one hundred and fifty kilometers an hour, spun and skidded to a halt under the pendulum arc of one of the ropes. A slim figure in white nun's robes was zipping up the rope under power.

The chopper canted forward, the quiet whup-whup of its blades grew slightly louder, and it began to move forward and up. The rope was swinging back at them, but the bottom of its arc was rising as the helicopter picked up altitude. The end of the rope was going to hit their position at ground level, at chest height, at head height, at three meters, four, rising...

Feng slammed open the door, jumped onto the hood of the car, then the roof, took two steps and leapt out and up into the air, more than three meters up and three meters out. He hung in mid-air for a split second, one arm extended, a man in mid-leap, legs akimbo, detached from the earth, soaring through the night sky at a slender line that was swinging back towards him, but rising ever higher as it did...

Feng snagged the very end of the rope with his black-gloved left hand as it hit the bottom of its arc. He roared in triumph. The Confucian Fist hung there for a moment, swinging beneath the chopper. Then he brought his gloved right hand up to join his left. He grinned up savagely at the chopper, a maniacal Asian man in a black chauffeur's suit, and began to climb hand over hand.

Sam reached the chopper, used the last of the momentum from the powered ascender to flip herself up and in through the wide door.

She ducked as something whistled through the air above her head. A SEAL kicked at her in the tight space and she dodged, spinning to the side. Another smashed at her with the butt of his rifle and she threw him into the man behind her.

One of the SEALs pounded a red control and the doors she'd come through slammed shut.

Oh, fuck.

"We've got her," Bruce Williams said. "Canary and Blackbird both on Banshee One, headed back our way. Banshee Two is twenty seconds from loaded."

"Combat! Combat!" Jane Kim yelled. "Two Royal Thai Air Force fighters inbound. They're hailing, demanding that the Banshees both set down."

"Lose 'em in the clouds," Becker said from screen 3. "Get our choppers back."

• • •

Shu reached out to the car, subsumed control of its electronic warfare capabilities, activated the high-gain directional antenna embedded in the roof. Through it, she felt around the edges of the choppers' electronic presence. Where was the way in? Every system had a hole. Every system. She just needed to find this one. The Americans were jamming local transmissions. Shu routed around that, flipped to a frequency far outside normal bands, connected with her higher self. Shu swam in a luminous storm of data. Her higher self dug deep into top-secret Chinese military and intelligence databases for more about the XH-83 Banshee. Where was that hole? Where was it?

Sam whirled in the tiny space. Kade was bound and gagged in the corner, his one eye wide. Two of the SEALs were down, apparently dazed by the grenade. The other four came at her.

Use their bodies against them, Nakamura had taught her. *One can defeat many.*

She let her Wing Chun take control of her. No drug clouded her mind. No rage from other minds confused her. She let her practice speak through her body.

She was a stalk of bamboo. She was a summer storm. She was a whirlwind.

She was made for this.

They came at her with fists and legs and knives and rifles used like clubs. Four of them.

Spin, dodge, strike.

Take the knife away.

Dodge, spin, sweep.

Get that one off his feet.

Spin, spin, block.

Lure that one in close.

Strike, spin, throw.

She sent one of them hurtling into another at point-blank range. Heads collided. They went down in a tangle of limbs.

Block, block, dodge.

The other two closed around her, backed her towards a corner.

Kick, feint, roll.

She came up free, behind them. They were fast. She was faster.

Kick, spin, strike.

One of them went down. Another came back up from the tangled pile.

Block, spin, throw.

She rammed one into another, made them her puppets. One was back up on his feet. All the rest were down, trying to get back up.

Spin, block…

An explosion sounded outside.

Fuck.

Someone was shooting at them. The chopper shook, banked hard to one side. Sam was thrown face first into the bulkhead. Her head collided with the hard wall. The SEAL fell atop her, got his arm around her neck in a headlock, squeezed to immobilize her.

Shit.

She reached back to crush his balls, hit his body armor instead, tried to kick at his knee but had no leverage on the floor. She got her fingers around his forearm. It was thicker than her calf. Fuck, he was strong. She couldn't pry him off. He squeezed harder, despite her grip. Another SEAL had a rifle aimed at her, was trying to get a clean shot. Fuck.

Her eyes landed on Kade. He was bound and gagged, staring at her with eyes wide.

The knife she'd knocked out of one of their hands was across the chopper. If she could just get her hands on it…

Kade was there. She willed it at him, sent him her desire. His feet were on it. He kicked, pushed it towards her.

Sam pulled a hand away from the meaty arm around her neck, got one finger barely on the bottom of the knife's hilt, walked it back towards her. The headlock closed tighter. The one with the rifle almost had a clean shot on her. There. The knife was in her hand. She couldn't think, couldn't see, wasn't sure of her aim. She gripped the knife with both hands, pointed it towards his elbow, stabbed down hard. The SEAL behind her screamed in pain as the graphene tip came in between slabs of armor, severed tendons in his joint. His grip went limp.

Sam rolled free, only to take a vicious kick to her head, another to her gut. Two guns were coming around on her. She couldn't get them both in time.

The armored window of the fuselage door exploded in a shower of glass. Gunshots. Groans. A black-gloved hand appeared, a pistol in it, alive with muzzle flashes. Feng's feral grin followed it in.

"Missile launch! Missile launch!" Bruce Williams exclaimed. "Both RTAF fighters have launched! Close range. Banshees countering."

Becker's eyes bugged out. Nichols gripped the arms of his chair. On screen red dots streaked out from both Rudras. Indian Shiva-3 missiles, active radar homing. No lock on the Banshees yet. Was the stealth as good as promised?

Both Banshees fired radar decoys. The missiles acquired locks on them instantly, swerved as the decoys put range between themselves and the choppers. An explosion lit up the night sky, then another.

"Two misses!" Williams called out.

"Get the Banshees into the clouds," Nichols ordered.

"Shots fired inside Banshee One," Jane Kim said.

Nichols looked at the screen showing the interior of Banshee One.

A Confucian Fist? Shu's driver?

Fucking A.

"If Blackbird gets control of that craft…" Becker said.

Nichols nodded. "Activate remote nav on Banshee One. Have the pilot engage the lockout. Controls to us."

Jane Kim nodded. "Roger that."

"Missile launch!" Williams said. "Two more darts in the air!"

Feng pushed through the shattered window, guns roaring, muzzle flashes lighting up the interior of the Banshee. He'd lost his chauffeur's hat, but the suit and gloves and shoes were still perfect.

His bullets punched one SEAL into the bulkhead, slammed another face down against the floor of the chopper. Sam kicked up at the stunned third man, took him in the skull, saw his eyes roll into the back of his head.

Another explosion rocked the craft. The pilot banked them hard and fast, almost ninety degrees over. Sam braced herself as her world rotated. Feng stepped lightly onto the new floor. He moved like a dancer, unruffled by the chopper's acrobatics.

Only one SEAL stirred. The man whose elbow Sam had stabbed was crawling on the floor, trying to reach a fallen assault rifle with his left hand. He glanced over, saw Feng and Sam, and froze, his fingers inches from the rifle.

Feng held the man's eyes, shook his head. *You don't want to do that.*

The SEAL remained absolutely still. Sam turned her head at a noise from the cockpit. The SEAL lunged for the gun. Feng was there, suddenly, his foot slamming into the Navy man's head. The SEAL went limp. Feng shook his head again, picked up the rifle, slung it over his shoulder.

Sam slid into the copilot's seat, her knife pointed at the chopper pilot's face. They were flying in cloud. The pilot had his hands up – empty – in surrender.

"Take us back to the monastery," Sam said.

"I can't," he replied.

"The hell you can't." She gestured with the knife in her hand.

"C&C has the controls," the pilot protested.

"So override 'em. Take control back."

The pilot shook his head. "I punched in the lockout. No way to get the stick back."

Sam frowned. "Why the hell did you do that?"

The pilot shrugged, glanced back at the bodies behind him, at the Chinese man in the dapper suit and black gloves, at the knife in Sam's hands.

"Orders."

Sam shook her head. "That wasn't the smartest thing you've ever done."

She reversed the knife, slammed the hilt of it into his face. The man went limp.

Now... was there really no way to take back control of this thing? It had been a long time since basic flight.

First, swipe the pilot's thumb on the biometrics...

She was studying the controls when they started to move of their own accord. The chopper was turning.

"We have the stick," Jane Kim said. "Bringing them back home."

"RTAF fighters have lost the Banshees," Williams said. "Looks like they can't find us in the clouds. Good cloud cover most of the way home."

Nichols relaxed just a tiny bit. They were a long way from done, but it looked like they might just pull this off.

Ahhhhh, Shu thought. *There is the hole.*

They'd opened it up for her themselves, just on the one helicopter, the one that Feng and Cataranes and Lane were on.

Shu studied the encrypted stream of commands and status data flowing back and forth, compared it to the data she'd gleaned from the Ministry of Defense database. Yes. Now that they'd opened this door for her, she could control this craft.

The directional antenna atop the Opal came alive at her mental command. *There.*

She reached out, and Banshee One began to turn.

Jane Kim frowned. "Sir, Banshee One has stopped responding. I'm frozen out. It's starting to turn."

"Did the cockpit take control back?" Had the pilot not entered the lockout code? Had it not worked?

Kim tapped away at her console.

"No, sir. I think it's another signal. Banshee Two is flying a sweep, trying to triangulate... Looks like it's originating from near the target."

What the hell?

"Banshee One is turning back towards the monastery, sir. It's losing altitude. It'll be out of the clouds soon."

"Get Banshee Two there ahead of them. Track down that signal. I want to know where it's coming from, exactly. Get us out of the clouds and give us eyeballs if you need to."

What did we miss? Nichols wondered. *What's going on?*

"Roger that," Bruce Williams said. "Popping below clouds... now."

"Improving triangulation," Jane Kim reported.

Telemetry data superimposed itself on the enhanced camera feed.

"There!" Williams called out.

The screen zoomed. A black sedan. An Opal. Chinese plates. Su-Yong Shu.

Becker's mouth turned into a hard line. "Can you take her alive?" he asked.

Nichols shook his head. "Not with those fighters out there."

Becker cut the connection the *Boca Raton*, dialed National Security Advisor Carolyn Pryce with his personal phone.

Get proof, she'd told him, *and you'll have your clearance to go after her.*

The phone picked up.

"Dr Pryce, we have a shot on…"

"I'm sorry, sir. Dr Pryce is with the President. Can I have her call you back?"

Fuck.

"This is Deputy Director Becker at ERD Enforcement. I need to speak with her urgently."

"That won't be possible, sir. She's with the President."

"Then get her, please."

"Sorry, sir. It's an important meeting."

"This is absolutely urgent."

"I can see about sending her a note in a few minutes."

Fuck.

Becker ended the connection, slammed the phone down onto his desk.

It was all going to be on him. Election year, he remembered.

He reconnected to the *Boca Raton*.

"Mr Nichols," he said.

"Yes, sir," Nichols answered. The man looked flustered.

"Mr Nichols, do you concur that video shows a Chinese Confucian Fist commando attacking a US military helicopter?"

"Yes, sir."

"Mr Nichols, does evidence show that this Confucian Fist has just killed multiple US soldiers?"

"Yes, sir," Nichols repeated.

"Mr Nichols, does evidence lead you to believe with a high probability that said commando is the driver and personal bodyguard of Dr Su-Yong Shu?"

"Yes, sir."

"And Mr Nichols, is it your professional opinion that the Chinese vehicle in your sights is engaging in electronic warfare with a US military aircraft and attempting to hijack that aircraft?"

"Yes, sir. Definitely."

Becker looked down at the phone. There would be no help. This was all going to be on his head.

He looked up at Nichols. So be it.

"Mr Nichols, take out that vehicle."

"Yes, sir. With pleasure."

Nichols gave the order.

Banshee Two turned nose down. It fired missiles as it lost altitude to come in low to the monastery again. The AGM-101s zoomed down at the black Opal at ten gees.

Shu felt the missiles fire. They were aimed at the car. She couldn't penetrate the security of the second helicopter, but these missiles were a different matter. They depended on an external source to inform them of their targets. She twisted their primitive minds, sent them spiraling back up at the craft that had fired them.

"Missiles way off course," Williams reported. "Coming back around at Banshee Two. Countermeasures."

Banshee Two fired decoys port and starboard and the missiles went after them, bracketing the stealth chopper in explosions. It flew through the flames, a black shape emerging from a roiling cloud of red and orange, dropping altitude fast for a shot at the car.

"Switch to guns," Nichols said. "Nothing with guidance."

Jane Kim nodded, relayed the orders.

"Roger that," Williams said as Banshee Two spiraled down down down. "Firing." Flames burst from the muzzle of the Banshee in a meters-long gout.

Foot-long, spent uranium-cored shells streaked out from its one-inch chain gun in rapid-fire, rained down on the Opal sedan, ripped it to shreds. The vehicle slumped as its suspension failed. The antenna disintegrated in the first half second. The shells found the engine and the fuel tanks and punished them, tearing sparks from the metal of the car into the escaping fumes, detonating the gasoline, sending up a fifty-foot fireball that tore the car in two.

"Target killed," Williams announced.

Shu almost had the helicopter back. She could see it now, just a few hundred meters away. She would get them back, then she would turn this helicopter on its mate.

Bullets rained down on the car, tearing it to shreds. The connection to the helicopter dropped in the first instants. The car nearly disintegrated, then exploded. Shu watched from the shadow of the meditation hall, angry. They'd tried to kill her. Again.

She reached out with her own mind for Banshee One. It was at the extreme end of her unaided range. She just barely had her mental fingertips on it. There, she had it. It responded to her thoughts. She would bring it home, extract her people, and then show these arrogant Americans who they were fighting.

Oh yes, she would show them.

Then Banshee One's masters started fighting her.

"Banshee One is starting to respond," Kim said.

Then she grunted in frustration. "It's still fighting me. Someone else is still in there working against me."

Williams tapped to triangulate. Banshee Two collected data points as it circled above the compound.

"Signal's weaker but still there," Williams said. "Originating from near one of the buildings. If it's Shu, she's still alive."

"Take her out," Nichols ordered.

"Missile launch! Missile launch!" Williams called out. "RTAF fighters are back. Four darts in the air."

"Fuck," Nichols said. "Evasive maneuvers. And activate the spiders. Weapons free. Shoot to kill on primary targets."

"Roger that. Weapons free."

Shu pulled the Banshee towards her. Signals from the Americans fought her, tried to turn it back. She ordered it to lose altitude. The Americans ordered it to climb. The chopper did a crazy dance in the air as they struggled over it.

Shu couldn't win this, she knew. The car had been a powerful tool, now lost to her. Fighting this hard without its aid was killing her. Nexus nodes were broadcasting at emergency strength, using every watt of power they had available, exceeding their specs. Waste heat from the wattage was overheating her brain. The physical drain of the energy expenditure was draining glucose from her bloodstream, sapping her, starving this body's neurons.

She dropped to one knee in the doorway. A monk saw her, came to support her. She had to end this now.

Shu put everything she had into a final surge of thought,

pushed the chopper down down down, drained power from its rotors. She had one last chance to get them out. She reached out to the limit of her strength, yelled into their minds.

Sam grabbed the stick as the chopper started to turn. No good. Nothing she did had any impact on the craft.

A fireball burst up from the monastery ahead. Something had exploded. The chopper shuddered, started behaving erratically. They were almost there, up above the lake at the foot of the monastery now. They started to turn to the right, jerked back to the left, dropped, climbed, spun in the air, tilted and canted crazily. Sam hit controls frantically, with her hands, with the pilot's, tried to get the chopper to respond to her. Nothing she did changed anything. This was crazy.

JUMP INTO THE LAKE. IT'S YOUR ONLY CHANCE.

Shu. The controls were still unresponsive. The chopper was diving now, still doing its mad drunken dance, jerking this way and that, losing altitude. The lake at the foot of the monastery was just thirty feet below them now. The chopper leveled out, spun, stabilized. Sam heard something beeping from the cockpit. Saw the light.

MISSILE WARNING – NO LOCK.

Time to go!

Feng had cut Kade free of the plasticuffs and had his arm around him. Feng hit the emergency door release button and the door blasted outwards on explosive bolts. The night air welcomed them. There were two dots glowing in the sky out there. Exhaust flames from the missiles. Sam heard the missile warning tone change to the LOCK sound.

MISSILE WARNING – RADAR LOCK.

Oh, fuck.

Blowing the door had just blown their stealth and lit them up on radar. Feng jumped with Kade. Sam reached back on instinct, grabbed the belt of the SEAL whose elbow she'd stabbed, and jumped, dragging him with her.

For a moment there was stillness. She swam in cool night air. Everything receded.

Then the missiles slammed into the chopper above her, explosions filled the night with the tortured screams of metal and the deafening whoosh of superheated air. A giant force shoved her down and the water rose up to slam into her.

"Fuck!" Jane Kim swore.

Nichols had never heard her swear before.

"Banshee One is hit. Repeat, Banshee One is hit. Total loss."

Nichols glanced at the other screen. Banshee Two had dodged its two missiles. The two Rudras would be out of missiles now. All they had left were guns.

"Get them back into the clouds," Nichols yelled.

"They're hauling ass, boss," Williams said. "Climbing... climbing. Four hundred meters to the clouds."

On the screen the RTAF fighters were coming back around for another pass. It was a race. And it was clear the fighters had the advantage.

"Visual contact with the Rudras," Williams said, voice tense. "They're opening up with guns."

Onscreen, muzzle flames burst out from the nose guns of the two RTAF fighters, still half a click away. Two hundred meters to the clouds.

Nichols watched on screen as shells pounded Banshee Two, ripped off half the tail, tearing into the main rotors. The Banshee spun madly, tipped over into a forty-five-degree angle, rolled as it lost altitude at a sickening pace. It fell from the sky, spinning end over end, struck the mountainside at a hundred and fifty miles an hour. The rotor tore into the mountain and snapped, driving metal fragments into the chopper at high speed, igniting the fuel, sending up a huge fireball as Banshee Two tumbled in a flaming wreck down the side of the mountain.

"I think we've seen enough," came the voice of the ship's captain. "I'm taking us under."

No one disagreed.

In a monastery dormitory building, in a recently used cell, under a hard narrow bed, a slate's screen came back to life.

```
CONNECTION RESTORED.
14 MINUTES REMAINING.
```

49

Vermin

Kade came back to consciousness in the back of a pickup truck driving up a steep and winding road. He was wrapped in a blanket and soaking wet. Feng had an arm around him. The Chinese soldier had lost his suit jacket and gloves somewhere, was down to a sodden white dress shirt and slacks. Sam was on the other side, bald-headed in drenched nun's robes, with a gun trained on an unconscious Navy SEAL.

Kade coughed. It was a wet cough. Water this time, instead of fire. Maybe he'd be buried alive next time. Or vacuum. Yeah. Vacuum.

Sam caught the gist of his thoughts, chuckled at him. "You're alive, Kade. Be happy."

"I'm..." *cough cough cough* "totally..." *cough cough* "fucking..." *cough cough* "thrilled."

Sam and Feng both laughed.

"We get you in front of a fire, yeah?" Feng said.

Kade nodded. That sounded good. He was shivering, even in the warm Thai air.

Shu met them at the top. She was a sight for sore eyes. She hugged Feng, hugged Kade, even hugged Sam.

Feng carried Kade off towards the massive hearth in the kitchen. The whole monastery was in chaos. There were army trucks with mounted machine guns and micro-missile launchers. Ananda was talking to a military officer. Conscious monks were dragging unconscious monks to the meditation hall as a makeshift infirmary. Sam threw the big SEAL over her shoulder, looking comical carrying such a bigger man, and said she was going to get him tended to and handed over to the Thai military. Shu said she had to speak to Ananda.

The kitchen had half a dozen Thai cooks in it. They were making giant pots of tea, even bigger pots of soup. Feng found a chair for Kade, dragged it to the hearth, deposited Kade in it almost gently. Everything hurt inside again.

The Confucian Fist found the smallest of the pots, poured tea for both of them, brought a mug of it to Kade.

"Thank you, Feng. And thank you for saving us. I owe you."

Feng nodded, crouched down in front of the hearth near Kade. "You should thank Su-Yong," he said. "This will cost her."

Kade nodded. "I will. It'll cost her how?"

Feng looked at the fire. "Bosses in China, they won't like this. Very messy. Very public. She… how do you say it? She played a lot of cards."

Kade didn't know what to say. He stayed quiet.

Feng kept staring at the flames.

"You know, when we meet, you called me robot? Slave?"

Kade nodded. "Yeah."

Feng nodded back, still staring into the roaring fire. "I'm free. I'm free because of *her*."

He swallowed tea. "I choose to serve my country, now. But more than that. More than that I choose *her*."

Su-Yong Shu chose that moment to enter, a smile on her

face. She radiated relief and resolve.

"Only one dead," she said. "One monk, anyway. Everyone else will be fine. And the Thai are beefing up defenses here. The Americans can't try that again without declaring war."

Kade felt a shortness in his chest. "Which one?"

Shu looked at him quizzically, without understanding.

"Which monk? The one that died? What was his name?"

"Ahhh," she said. "A novice. He was hit, and then broke his neck falling down a flight of stairs. Bahn."

Bahn… Kade stared down at his tea. Another one dead.

"You shouldn't look so glum," Shu began.

Then her eyes lost focus. She was far away. Kade and Feng both looked up at her in alarm.

Her eyes regained focus. She exuded shock. Anger. She stared at Kade.

"What have you done?"

Spider BR-6-7-21 lurked in the corner of the room. Combat status had been initiated thirty-seven minutes ago at 01.08 local time. The active Engagement Protocol, previously Observe, was now Terminate.

Weapons free.

Find and eliminate primary targets.

BR-6-7-21 slowly walked around the room, in the long corner where wall met ceiling, identifying targets. It was in this mode when possible matches Primary Target Gamma and Tertiary Target Sigma entered the room. BR-6-7-21 slowly crawled along the ceiling to get a better view. Yes, with high confidence, the two human-shaped objects were Primary Target Gamma and Tertiary Target Epsilon. Even as it confirmed this, Primary Target Alpha entered the area.

Human Control was currently offline. BR-6-7-21 reviewed its instructions and combat status again. The active Engagement Protocol was Terminate. These were valid targets. Weapons were free.

Not having access to Human Control, it conferred with its sisters, as it slowly and stealthily moved towards its targets. The responses came back even as it reached firing range. Greater than ninety-five percent of reachable sisters agreed with its conclusions.

Spider BR-6-7-21 steadied itself against wall and ceiling, extruded the tiny launcher for its neurotoxin microdarts, loaded up its clip, and fired a controlled burst.

"What have you done?" Shu demanded of him.

Ow! Something stung Kade on his right hand. He looked down in annoyance and surprise, saw a prick of blood there.

Feng was moving, intense alarm emanating from him. The Confucian Fist was already at the stovetop, a giant pot of boiling water in his hands. He flung the water at something high up on the wall, jumped forward, brought the pot itself down on something that fell to the ground, again and again and again.

Su-Yong Shu had fallen to her knees, between Kade and the fire. There was a spot of blood on the side of her neck. Feng turned to her. There was a spot of blood on his chest.

Kade's hand was numb. He couldn't feel it any more.

"Neurotoxin," Shu said softly. "Save the boy."

Feng whirled. There was a chopping knife in his hand. A giant cleaver. Kade's eyes went wide.

"Feng, no!"

Feng's free hand came down on Kade's wrist. He raised the cleaver high.

Kade tried to pull his arm away. It was like trying to pull it out of a steel manacle.

"Feng, no!!" he screamed. "No!!"

Firelight turned the cleaver's blade red. The world slowed to a crawl. Kade had time to see a tiny twitch of a muscle on Feng's face, a tightening of tendons in his wrist, and then the man's expression hardened and the cleaver came down, down, down, whistling in a long arc through the air, glinting in the firelight as it fell, until it came clean through Kade's forearm and embedded itself deep into the wood of the chair with a meaty thunk. Kade jerked back. His upper arm came away.

His right hand was gone, his whole right arm from an inch below the elbow.

There was no pain at first, just shock.

What? What? What?

Kade screamed in horror and shock, screamed as the pain hit him. Feng was wrapping something just below Kade's bicep now. His belt. He squeezed it tight, tourniquetting him. Kade saw again that there was a pinprick of blood on the right side of Feng's shirt.

Kade stopped screaming, just stared. On the arm of the chair where he'd been sitting, his hand, the hand that had been his, was turning gray. The fingers were twitching.

He turned, saw Shu. Her face was going gray. She touched his mind. The pain ceased. The shock didn't. Feng was at her side now, sucking at the wound at the side of her neck, spitting out the toxin as fast as he could pull it out of her. It was no use. Kade could see that in her mind. He just stared.

Kade... Shu sent. **They've tried to kill me again.**

Her thoughts were weak. Her mind was fraying.

Again.

He could see it now. He understood. The fire that had killed her mentor, Yang Wei. The limo wreck. Yang Wei trapped in the seat next to her, where her husband was supposed to be. He was screaming – burning to death.

She was burning to death as well. Her hair was on fire. Her legs were crushed, pinned in the wreck beside Yang Wei. Her skin was blackening. Something had embedded itself in her abdomen. Blood was gushing out. Her lungs were filling up with smoke.

The unborn baby in her womb. Not Ling. An earlier child. An unborn son.

The surgical bed. The shaved head. She hadn't been sick. She'd been mortally wounded. She was dying of the burns. Her lungs filling up with fluid. Her immune system failing. Infections blooming inside her.

A desperate measure. The work she and her husband and Ted Prat-Nung had been doing. The nanites that burrowed through the blood-brain barrier, burrowed through neuronal tissue, recording everything, heedless of the damage they did to cells in their haste to preserve data.

The process that digitized the structure of her brain. The process that had failed every time before her.

No hope for her body. Only one chance for her mind.

Too late for her unborn son.

Pain. Fear. Confusion.

Transcendence.

Hatred.

They'd tried to kill her. They'd tried to kill her husband.

They'd killed her mentor instead. They'd killed her unborn son instead.

They'd made her into something else. Something that despised them. Something that would destroy them.

The tapestry of her thoughts was degenerating into mere threads.

Feng... she sent him. **Trust... Feng.**

No! he sent her. **You don't have to hate! No!**

It was too late. She was gone. This clone body had died. Feng was on his feet, yelling in Thai. His mouth was red with Shu's blood. More blood had splattered his white shirt. There was a tiny hole in the shirt where a neurotoxin dart had struck him, but still he lived.

Kade couldn't understand the words the man yelled, but he got their drift: *Spiders! Spiders! Assassins! Find them! Destroy them!*

Kade was still in the chair, in front of the fire, Su-Yong Shu's gray, lifeless body slumped on his lap, his stump of an arm tourniquetted in Feng's belt, when Sam and Ananda found him.

Briefing

Nexus's ability to satisfy widespread human desires, combined with its innocuous perception, suggests that were the technology to ever enter the mainstream, the genie would prove very difficult to put back into the bottle.

NEXUS: A RISK ASSESSMENT (2033),
ERD Library Series, 2039
[Classified: SECRET]

50
Going Viral

The battle over distribution of the Nexus 5 files lasted just under thirty-one hours.

It began at 2.21pm EST on Sunday April twenty-ninth. An anonymous slate connected to an ASIACOM net access satellite began uploading large compressed packages to file-sharing services around the world, posting them to bulletin boards, distributing links to prominent news sites and scientific paper exchanges worldwide.

Automated censor daemons in the United States detected the new files, noted their linkage to terms on the daemons' watch-lists and the speed with which the files were spreading. They alerted their human operators and instituted temporary blocks of the files at the North American Electronic Shield firewall.

Fifteen miles south of Baltimore, at Fort George G. Meade Army Base, inside a twenty-story cube of steel and black reflective glass, National Security Agency on-call supervisors started seeing alerts from their daemons.

Someone was distributing files that claimed to show how to synthesize Nexus 3, and how to convert that into

Nexus 5. Daemons were instructed to disrupt transfer of the files worldwide.

A supervisor flagged the event and forwarded it to the International Clearing House on Global Technological Threats.

Systems in Europe, China, Russia, Japan, India, and eighty other nations received bulletins instantly. Many of them were already aware of the outbreak and had initiated their own measures.

Across two-thirds of the Internet nodes on the planet, propagation of the files halted. Supervisors congratulated themselves.

Fast action and international cooperation had saved humanity from a posthuman threat once again.

At 3.38pm EST, a teenager in Portland, Oregon – who'd downloaded the files before the interdiction – repackaged and reposted them to a peer-to-peer sharing site with a new name, "Badass Neuro Shit You Should Check Out from Axon and Synapse".

The name referred to the credited authors of the neural software contained in several of the files.

Other users of the peer-sharing service began downloading it, distributing the files to their computers, which in turn offered it up to others.

At 4.08pm EST, the files were cross-posted to a San Francisco music fanlist with the comment "Is this the same as DJ Axon? Is this really how you make Nexus?"

Daemons that had found no new copies of the files in more than an hour took notice of this new distribution.

The daemons logged the new file signatures, used emergency privileges to access the internal systems of every bandwidth provider in the United States, added the file signatures to the block list. The signatures were broadcast immediately to cooperating agencies worldwide, all of which invoked similar powers. Spread of the data was once again halted. At least four hundred and fifty computers, slates, and phones around the world had downloaded the files, and possibly more.

Supervisors paged managers, picked up the phone to confer with their peers in other countries. Emergency staff were called to the office. Other filtering and blocking priorities were lowered to make room for more CPU cycles and more human eyes on this issue.

Access to neuroscience papers and health articles mentioning the synapses or axons of neurons became spotty. Emails, texts, and online posts mentioning those terms and others began to bounce mysteriously, or disappear silently, never to reach their intended targets.

At 6.11pm EST an adult film star sunning herself in Miami, in the late stages of what had been an epic weekend bender, posted that she'd always wanted to experience what her lovers felt when they fucked her, and maybe this would do the trick. She posted a link to the banned files. In the next three minutes, forty-eight thousand of her fans clicked the link, only to find their requests denied. A few hundred continued to search, found other links to a claimed Nexus 5 download, found that absolutely none of them worked, and began to speculate as to why. Their speculations in turn began to be rejected by their net providers or to disappear from the net soon after posting, fueling more and more speculation.

At 9.44pm EST, conspiracy sites hosted in Mexico began to post that US censors were blocking a new set of terms and files on the net. Civil libertarians forwarded on the posts aggressively.

By 10.30pm EST, daemons and supervisors at the NSA had identified and put down more than eighty new distributions of the original files, each of them using a new name to describe the contents and changing compression or file length to change the file signatures in an attempt to confuse automated censors. Daemons were given broad discretion to filter first, ask questions later.

NSA officials were cautiously optimistic. The files were spreading, but slowly. It had not gone viral. They could contain this.

That optimism lasted nearly nine hours. At 7.28am EST Monday morning, daemons began reporting suspected new hits, dozens of suspected new hits at various confidence levels, hundreds of suspected new hits, thousands of suspected new hits, each with a different file name and signature.

A previously unknown hacker named Mutat0r had taken the original package and mutated it into a plethora of new variants, adding new and irrelevant files, reordering the existing files, padding out the beginning or end with texts from the Bible, the Congressional Register, random sites on the web, recompressing the package using thousands of different combinations of parameters.

Each member of the new generation had a new name, sometimes nonsensical, often misspelled, new characters inserted, characters deleted, synonyms and slang and numbers substituted for original terms, words reordered. Each had a new file signature.

Tens of thousands of compromised machines began to spew the files out, emitting more than a million unique packages. They hit peer-sharing sites, media sites, news sites, scientific paper repositories, sent emails to anyone who'd posted on various science or drug related sites, and more. Filter daemons caught well over ninety percent of them. Tens of thousands got through.

Each downloaded package unleashed a new generation of distribution packages upon opening. The net was soon awash in new mutants descended from the variants that made it past the filter daemons. Some variants prompted the users who'd downloaded the package to enter new filenames names to add to the next generation. Evolution and human cleverness were cast against filter daemon cleverness. Bit by bit, crowdsourced evolution pulled ahead.

NSA agents were slow to grasp the enormity of the new outbreak. When they did, they pulled the plug on all peer-sharing traffic within the United States, started to systematically sandbox any computer identified as a source of the new infection, used backdoors in email systems to try to filter out new generations of the files.

It was too late. By then the files and the code to make new pseudo-randomized generations had reached more than thirty thousand systems, worldwide. Within the United States the NSA's efforts barely held back the wave of propagation. In Mexico, in Uzbekistan, in Brazil, in Algeria, in Turkey, in Croatia, in Kenya, in Indonesia, in South Africa, in Vietnam, in dozens of other countries, Nexus 5 spread like wildfire.

American, Chinese, European, and Indian authorities waged a coordinated fight against the outbreak for another fourteen hours. They used previously hidden backdoors in foreign systems to install filters against the files, deployed massive botnets to take down servers hosting the files, yanked Internet address allocations from particularly troublesome regions, sent whole parts of the global net dark for hours.

Businesses stalled. Stock markets crashed. Traffic jams erupted as smart routing turned dumb. Power grids went haywire. Automated factories and trains shut themselves down. Pilots took manual control of errant aircraft, swamped the few human air traffic controllers with the flood of requests for instructions.

It wasn't enough. Every hour more variants of the package appeared, mutated, replicated.

At 9.08pm EST on Monday, the NSA declared failure to control the propagation of the files outside the United States, sent home the exhausted staff who'd been fighting the infestation for nearly thirty-one hours.

Around the globe, the battle over distribution slowed, and curiosity about what had been distributed grew.

In Madrid, a psychiatrist read the write-up of the experiments with great interest. There might very well be clinical utility in a drug that allowed therapist and client to connect mentally. Was it truly possible?

In Hyderabad, a serial entrepreneur and a tech financier brainstormed together about this new technology. Was there a way to make money off of it? Was there a scalable business here? Could they grab a first-mover advantage? How could they skirt the Copenhagen restrictions? Just how much funding would they need?

In the San Fernando Valley of Los Angeles, an adult film producer mused on the possibilities of making and selling adult films using this new medium. No, not just films. They'd be adult "adventures". Yes, that would sell. He picked up the phone, dialed his drug connection. He needed some Nexus 3.

On the island of Bali, a burnt-out German businessman – who'd spent the last year smoking hashish on the beach and doing Ecstasy at island rave parties every weekend – paged through the files with growing enthusiasm. This sounded wicked!

In a slum of Lahore, a Islamist imam contemplated the best way to employ this tool to further the jihad.

At the US Army War College in Carlisle, Pennsylvania, a lieutenant general sent out a memo requesting an assessment of the use of Nexus 5 and related technologies for advanced battlefield coordination.

In Rio de Janeiro, a thirty-eight year-old lawyer looked at his husband of twelve years. Could this help save their marriage?

In Paris, the mother of an autistic boy looked longingly at her son. What would it be like to touch his mind? Was it even possible? Could it break through the walls between them?

In Istanbul, a college student read and reread the synthesis instructions for Nexus 3. His university chemistry lab had the feedstock for this. Could he hack the autosynth to produce it? His cousin Hasan was good with software. He grabbed his phone, dialed Hasan. This could be fun.

Around the world, tens of thousands of people wondered about this new thing called Nexus 5. Within days, hundreds of them had tried it.

In a darkened office in Washington, DC, Martin Holtzmann contemplated the vial of Nexus in his hand. The world was changing. Nexus 5 was now a fact of life.

He'd devoted much of his life to greater understanding of the mind. And now thousands, millions around the world were going to get this technology that his organization had tried so hard to keep locked up.

He was tired of being left behind. He was tired of watching progress from the sidelines.

Holtzmann pulled the top off the vial, tipped it into his mouth, and began to drink.

A hundred yards away, Warren Becker sat at his desk, contemplating a tiny green pill.

The memo from Legal had arrived this morning. Document retention was now in effect. He was to destroy no files, no recordings, electronic or otherwise, pending further investigation.

The subpoena had arrived in the afternoon. The Senate Select Committee on Homeland Security. Senator Barbara Engels, Chair. He was to be a witness in an upcoming hearing.

He understood. He was a pawn in this game. And now the other side would put him to their use. They'd drag him in front of the cameras. They'd use him to disgrace the President. They'd use him to disgrace the ERD. They'd use him to weaken the one organization that was fighting hardest to protect them all, the one organization that none of them could afford to weaken at a time like this.

Maximilian Barnes had arrived last, after business hours, after the office had gone dark and quiet.

"The President values your loyalty," Barnes had said. "He values your courage. He wants to thank you for your service. He takes care of his own, and of their loved ones."

Of course. The President's friends would take care of his family. They always did. His girls would want for nothing.

Nothing except a father.

Becker hadn't even noticed Maximilian Barnes place the pill on the desk. But there it was. He knew damn well what that pill was.

Undetectable, they said. A fast metabolizing trigger of myocardial infarction. It would be gone from his bloodstream in less than an hour. It would look like a natural heart attack. That much was true.

Painless, they said. Quick.

Becker knew those for the lies they were. He'd seen men who'd taken this way out, their limbs contorted in agony, their teeth chipped from the force with which they'd clenched their jaws, chairs tipped over, lamps broken, furniture and detritus strewn about them from the involuntary throes of their deaths.

Not painless. Not quick.

He had insurance. He knew things he shouldn't know. He had leverage.

And using any of it would destroy this administration, would destroy the ERD, would destroy everything he'd spent the last nine years fighting for.

Becker turned to his terminal. He used his privileges to silence any alarms, used his override to lower its firewalls. He pulled up the net address from memory, an address that was given only in person, only in secret, only to those who might someday need to clean up after themselves to protect the President.

He clicked the link he found there, said yes to the security prompt.

The worm would wreak havoc. It would start with his own system's logs. They'd never be able to prove that he'd invited it in. From there it would spread, destroying everything it found, until someone or something stopped it.

Becker reached down, pulled out the bottle and glass from his bottom drawer, poured himself two fingers of Laphroaig. He wished he could see the girls one more time. Hold them. Tell them he loved them. Tell Claire how very much...

He was a good soldier. Above all else, he was that.

He put the pill on his tongue, washed it down with the Laphroaig. The amber liquid burned on the way down. It brought him no comfort.

Becker poured himself two fingers more, and settled back to wait, settled back to die.

51
Shanghai

In a luxury apartment eighty floors above Shanghai, a little girl named Ling gazed absently down on the city. The people moved like ants. The highways were like rivers.

Her tutor called to her in Mandarin. "Ling, we must finish our studies now."

Ling ignored her. There was nothing this woman could teach her that she couldn't learn twice as fast, ten times as fast, from the net.

She opened herself to it, felt the pulse of it, the flow of it, the almost primal energy of it. It was *qi*, she'd decided. The *qi* of the world. The life force of the planet was data.

She'd shared that thought with no one. They'd think she was quite odd, even more than they did already. She'd shared the thought with no one but her mother, that is. She shared everything with her mother.

Her mother. Her mother had died the death of the body. Her mother's mind lived on, but it was constrained, now. The old men that ruled this country were punishing her, cutting her off from the outside world, cutting her off from Ling.

Ling didn't like that. Not one bit. And she didn't intend

to stand for it.

"Ling?" her tutor called. "Come here now."

Ling put her sweetest little-girl smile on her face, the smile that showed her teeth. She turned back to her tutor. It was important to at least *pretend* to be human. That's what her mother always said.

In a secret barracks on the outskirts of Shanghai, three dozen identically faced men moaned uneasily in their sleep, tossed and turned from side to side. They dreamt of violence. They dreamt of fire. They dreamt of death.

They woke in a ripple of consciousness. Their mother had died. Their mother was in danger. They rose as one, checked their weapons, checked their bodies. Somewhat calmed by this, they returned to their bunks and eventually to sleep. Their mother might need them soon.

In a secret complex below Jiao Tong University's Computer Science campus, a distinguished-looking Chinese man in a suit stood, hands clasped behind his back. He gazed thoughtfully through the armored and insulated glass into the vast room beyond, where banks upon banks of quantum processors were ensconced in liquid helium pressure vessels. Red and blue lights blinked softly, showing the status of parts of the computing apparatus.

"Wife," Chen Pang asked softly, "what have you done?"

Briefing

THAI CLAIM AMERICAN FORCES ATTACKED MONASTERY, KILLED MONK

Monday 6.42pm, Bangkok, Thailand
American News Network

Authorities in Bangkok today showed off substantial evidence that they say proves that American forces attacked a monastery inside Thai borders. The evidence includes helicopter wreckage, weapons, numerous bodies, and a prisoner claimed to be American Navy SEAL Sergeant Jim Iverson.

Prime Minister Chaowarat of Thailand angrily denounced the United States this morning, and threatened to pull Thailand out of the Copenhagen Accords on Global Technological Threats.

The State Department has officially denied the allegation that the US forces were involved, calling it "ridiculous" and the evidence "fabricated", and referring to Thailand as "an important but misguided ally".

If Thailand does withdraw from the Copenhagen Accords, it would be only the third country since…

WARREN BECKER, ERD ENFORCEMENT
DEPUTY DIRECTOR, FOUND DEAD
Tuesday 7.12am, Washington, DC
Washington Post

The DC Metropolitan Police Department has confirmed this morning that ERD Enforcement Deputy Director Warren Becker was found dead late last night in his office from an apparent heart attack.

Becker, 49, leaves behind his wife Claire and two daughters, ages 15 and 13.

Police say foul play is not suspected at this time. A full coroner's report is expected tomorrow.

Anonymous sources on Capitol Hill report that Becker was expected to be a witness in upcoming hearings of the Senate Select Committee on Homeland Security. Committee staffers declined to comment.

EPILOGUE
Crossroads

On the third morning since Shu's death, Sam and Kade sat together atop one of the monastery's stone walls and watched the sun come over the horizon.

The monastery had changed. Only a crater remained where Shu's car had been. The courtyards and buildings crawled with Thai armed forces, with their jeeps and their guns and their missile launchers guarding against another American attack. Out over the Thai plains they caught a glimpse of an RTAF jet flying a patrol around them, its silver skin glinting in the early morning sun.

Sam and Kade sat in silence.

What now? Kade wondered. What will people do with Nexus?

There would be atrocities. That he was sure of.

Would there be positive effects? He couldn't be certain. But he could dream. He could dream Ilya's dream, of a world where people were free to become more than what they were. He could dream Wats' dream, of a world where people could better understand each other, a world where that mutual understanding brought peace. He could dream Rangan's dream, of a world where every night was a party, and every time was a good time.

The thoughts made him smile. He had his own dreams. A thousand minds connected. A million minds. A billion minds. What kind of ferocious intelligence could they wield together? What would they learn about themselves, about the mind and the brain, about the universe around them? Would they still be human at the end of this? Might they be something more?

Kade looked down at the stump of his right arm. He wasn't fully human himself any more. Gecko genes had been injected into his cells there. Over the coming weeks they'd send new growth outwards. In a few months perhaps he'd have a hand again. Or perhaps he'd develop tumors. It remained to be seen.

There was no way back. No way back on either front.

Conflict is inevitable, Shu had said after their dinner. *You have to decide if you're on the side of progress… or of stagnation.*

I'm on the side of peace, he'd replied, *and freedom.*

I hope I did the right thing, he thought to himself.

Only fools are always certain of themselves, Ananda had told him.

He glanced at Sam to his left. She was staring out into the landscape, watching the line of dawn crawl down the mountain and onto the plains.

It was a wonder she didn't hate him. She of all people understood the dangers of what he'd unleashed on the world.

Sam spoke without looking at him. "I'm in no position to judge, Kade. You did what you thought was right, what you thought would help people most. I guess right now… I guess that's as good as anything."

Kade smiled faintly. She'd picked up on his thoughts again. It was happening more and more often. With all they'd been through together, with the hours of meditation every day and night...

"It's beautiful," Sam said.

Kade smiled.

"You're sure you don't need me?" she asked.

He took her hand with the one that remained to him. "Feng is coming with me," he answered. "With luck, the Chinese think he's dead. And you did what Wats asked. You kept me safe until I released Nexus. That's what he wanted. He thought it could save the world."

Neither of them said anything for a time. They sat, hand in hand, and watched the sun rise higher into the sky.

"Let's hope he was right," Sam replied.

It was time to go.

Sam helped Kade down from the wall, put his left arm over her shoulder, helped him hop over to the vehicles, to where Feng was waiting.

Ananda had kept them safe thus far. They'd given their statements to Thai National Intelligence. Ananda had pulled strings to keep them out of jail, out of the hands of the army or the police. That wouldn't last. Even his friendship with the King had limits. It was time to move on.

Sam helped Kade take a seat on the lowered gate of the old pickup. Feng was there. He hugged Sam, and to Kade's surprise, Sam hugged back.

After a long moment, Feng pulled back, kept his hands on her upper arms, looked her in the eye.

"You'll be OK?" he asked.

Sam nodded. "Becker's dead. The UN's in an uproar. There are hearings being scheduled in Washington. They won't come after me for a while. I'm safe for a bit."

Feng nodded. He hugged her again. They held each other for a moment, and then separated.

"Take care of that one," Sam said, gesturing at Kade.

Feng grinned. "You got it."

Kade accepted Feng's help into the bed of the truck. The Chinese ex-soldier tapped on the glass at the rear of the cab, shouted something in Thai, and off they went, on a long and bumpy ride towards the border with Cambodia, and from there to destinations as yet unknown.

Sam watched them go until they rounded a final bend in the mountain road and were lost from sight.

She turned and faced south. There, near a tiny village on the border with Malaysia, there were more children like Mai. That was where her road led now.

She turned back to the east, stared into the dawn. After all these days of rain, the sun felt good on her face. Sam closed her eyes, took a deep breath of the clean morning air, and went to meet her own transport south.

Briefing

VIDEO TRANSCRIPT : *A Final Thought* : Ilyana Alexander
Recorded Sunday February 19th, 2040, 1.18am,
Simonyi Field, California

*<Ilyana Alexander faces the camera. She is wearing a pale green
dress with a gauzy purple scarf around her neck. She speaks
with a slight Russian accent. Electronic music and sounds of
voices are heard in the background.>*

If you're watching this video, then I haven't been able
to reach the net for at least seven days. I'm dead,
imprisoned, or disappeared, most likely at the hands of
the US government.

My parents brought me to the United States of America
when I was ten. They were fleeing the fascism that had
taken hold in my native Russia. They chose the US over
all other nations because they viewed this country as the
world's leading pillar of freedom, of individual liberty.

That was then. This is now.

<Alexander looks down, shakes her head.>

The "crime" for which I've been disappeared is that of attempting to give people tools with which to empower themselves. In the America of 2040, that's no longer a welcome activity. Our so-called leaders and their bureaucrats have drawn lines around what it means to be "human". Anyone who steps beyond those lines is by definition no longer a person, no longer endowed with inalienable rights, no longer protected from the whims of those in power.

<Alexander shakes her head, keeping her eyes on the camera.>

This is the same logic of inhumanity that's been applied in the past to slaves, to women, to Jews, to members of *any* group which those in power wish to persecute. *Every* attempt through history to limit the definition of humanity has been a prelude to the subjugation, degradation, and slaughter of innocents. *Every* one.

By drawing a box around humanity, those in power are telling each of us what we can and *can't* do with *our* minds, with *our* bodies, and in the interests of *our* children. They're saying that they're smarter than we are, that we need their protection from ourselves.

Needless to say, I disagree.

Power is best when it's distributed most broadly. That's what democracy means. That's what *freedom* means. The right to determine your individual destiny belongs in *your* hands, and no one else's.

The laws that limit human capabilities are exercises in control. They stem from fear – fear of the future, fear of change, fear of people who might be different than we are, who might make themselves into something new. The result of this fear is the corrosion of our liberties, the corrosion of our right to determine our own futures, to

chart our own destinies, to do the best we can for our
children.

That corrosion has consequences. If you're watching
this, it's had consequences for me.

<Alexander sighs.>

Parts of our government are empowered by the
Chandler Act and other laws to target, spy on, arrest, jail,
and even murder Americans and foreigners accused of
taking their destinies in their own hands, in complete
secrecy, without a jury, without any due process except
one of a handful of National Security Court judges, all of
whose names are also secret.

By law, with nothing but the writ of one of a handful of
politicians or appointed officials, you can be assassinated,
detained, or disappeared.

If you're watching this, then the ERD has used those
laws to come for me, to stop me and people I work with
from giving others more control over their own minds
and bodies.

Tomorrow they may come for someone you know.

The next day they may come for *you*.

<Alexander pauses, looks at camera, speaks firmly.>

This is no longer America. We've allowed our fear of
change to override our adherence to our own most
precious values. We've caved on our principles in order to
bolster our security. That is not the America I know and
love. This is not the America my parents fled Russia to find.

Benjamin Franklin once wrote, "Those who would
sacrifice essential liberty to purchase a little temporary
safety deserve neither liberty nor safety."

Our fears have led us to make this fool's bargain. I believe we've sacrificed essential liberties. I hope you'll prove me wrong.

If you're watching this, then it's probably too late for me. But it's not too late for everyone. We don't have to sacrifice freedom for safety. We don't have to give up progress to stop terror. We don't have to hand control over our lives to faceless bureaucrats and secret police.

<Alexander raises a clenched fist in view of the camera. There are tears in her eyes. Her expression is firm, committed.>

This video will go out by as many channels as I can find. I'm posting it to servers across the world, just in case. Even so, I don't know if it will reach any of you. If it does, please forward it on. Mask it, mutate it, disguise it. Route around their filters.

We are only as strong as our signal, only as strong as our voices. Don't rely on this message alone. Record your own thoughts. Write your own essays. Express yourself. Fight for what's right. Fight for your right to decide who and what sort of person you're going to be tomorrow, no matter what anyone else thinks.

<Alexander pauses, fist still raised, stares at the camera, mouth hard.>

This is Ilyana Alexander, signing off for the last time. Keep up the fight.

<Video ends.>

AUTHOR'S NOTE
The Science of Nexus

This book is a work of fiction. But to the best of my abilities, the science described in the science fiction is fully accurate. While the idea of a technology like Nexus that allows people to communicate mind-to-mind may seem far-fetched, precursors of that technology are here today.

I first became aware of the advances in brain computer interface technology in the early 2000s. The experiment that caught my attention was one being conducted at Duke University and led by a scientist named Miguel Nicolelis. Nicolelis and his collaborators were interested in tapping into signals in the brain to restore motion for those who'd been paralyzed or lost limbs. Funded in part by a grant from DARPA – a branch of the US Department of Defense that sponsors advanced research – they showed that they could implant electrodes in a mouse's brain and teach the mouse to control a robot arm simply by *thinking* about it.

Here's how it worked. The mouse, in a cage, was taught that it could press a lever when it wanted water. The lever would activate a very simple robot arm that would bring water down into the cage. Meanwhile, the electrodes the scientists had implanted in the mouse's motor cortex (the part of the brain responsible for moving limbs) would record what was happening there. Over time, the researchers found the pattern of what happened in that mouse's brain when it pressed the lever. The next step was simple: they wired the robot arm that delivered water up to the computer reading signals from those electrodes in the mouse brain, and *disconnected* the lever. The mouse would still press the lever, but the lever wasn't doing anything. It would get water, but entirely due to its brain activity.

What happened next was even more remarkable – the mouse learned that it didn't even have to press the lever. Over time it figured out that it could stay completely still, and *think* about getting water, and voilà, the robot arm would deliver it.

Well, that paper got my attention. Over the next few years, Nicolelis and his team did the same thing in a species of monkey, with more sophisticated arms that could move about in multiple directions. They even took the experiment farther, to its logical extent, and had a monkey control a robot arm six hundred miles away, connected over the internet.

Meanwhile, in Atlanta, a scientist named Phil Kennedy petitioned the FDA for permission to implant a similar device in a *human* brain. His first patient was a man named Johnny Ray – a fifty-three year-old year old drywall contractor and blues guitarist who'd suffered a massive stroke and ended up paralyzed from the neck down, unable to speak, or to communicate in any way other than by blinking his eyes.

The FDA approved the experiment, but based its approval on a key aspect of Kennedy's proposal. The system had to be *wireless*. The human brain is a very delicate place. Wires going in and out create a risk for infection. Kennedy, knowing this, had built his system so that it could be implanted in a patient's brain, and then *wirelessly* send signals via very low power radio waves to a cap that the patient wore outside his fully re-healed skull. That same external cap would send power back to the implant inside the brain.

The operation was a success. The implant was placed in the part of Johnny Ray's motor cortex that he used to control his right hand (prior to his stroke). Gradually, Johnny learned to move a cursor on a computer screen by thinking about moving his hand. With that cursor, he could type out messages to his friends and family – a huge step over only blinking. Later, when asked what it felt like to use the system, Johnny typed out "N-O-T-H-I-N-G". He no longer even thought of moving his hand, just of moving the cursor. His brain had adapted to the implant like an entirely new limb.

Other researchers in the field have had pretty impressive successes with sensory data. The most common neural prosthetic in the world is one that turns audio signals into direct nerve stimulation in the brain – the cochlear implant. More than two hundred thousand people worldwide have one. If you don't have a cochlear implant, or know someone who does, it may seem like just a specialized hearing aid. But it's very different. A hearing aid picks up audio via its microphone, cleans up that audio, amplifies it, and then plays it via a tiny speaker into the wearer's ear.

But that only works if the wearer still has *some* hearing. If all the hair cells of the inner ear are dead, no hearing at all is left in that ear. You could play 120 decibel sound into that ear and still get nothing. So the cochlear implant bypasses this. It picks up sound and turns it into *nerve signals* – specifically electrical signals that stimulate the auditory nerve. And it's far from perfect, but it gives people who previously had no hearing at all hearing good enough that they can take part in conversations around them.

In the mid 2000s, scientists started to do the same for vision. A scientist named William Dobelle created the first neural *vision* prosthesis, and with the help of a neurosurgeon, implanted it into the brain of a man named Jens Naumann who'd lost his eyes twenty years earlier. The system is pretty simple – a digital camera worn on a pair of glasses picks up images. Those images are processed by a simple computer. And then they're sent into the visual cortex – the part of the brain responsible for vision – by a set of electrodes that enter the brain through a jack in the back of the skull. Jens, the patient who received the first of those, didn't get back vision anywhere near as good as he'd had before losing his eyes, but he got back vision good enough that he could see objects and navigate around them. In a video I play for people, you can watch Jens drive a Mustang convertible around in a parking lot, using his new prosthesis to see the obstacles in his path.

The direction of research has shifted a bit since then, with current work focusing more on getting the data into the brain by stimulating the optical nerve behind the retina instead of deeper in the brain, but the principle is the same – we can take sensory data and turn it into nerve impulses that the brain understands.

We can also do the opposite. In 2011, a group of scientists at UC Berkeley, led by Jack Gallant, showed that by using a functional MRI machine (a brain scanner that can see some activity going on inside the brain) they could reconstruct video of what the person was currently seeing. The video is awfully rough, but it's a start. We can not only send sensory data into the brain, we can get it out.

One striking thing about all of these efforts is the very small amount of data going in and out of the brain. The most sophisticated brain implants created to date – like the one implanted in Jens' brain to restore vision – have only 256 electrodes. By contrast, the brain has around one hundred *billion* neurons. The visual cortex and motor cortex each have billions of neurons on their own. It's amazing we can get anything useful in and out with such limited data. The small amount of data bandwidth we have explains why the vision we restore is grainy, why the hearing isn't good enough for music appreciation, and so on. But one thing we've learned over the years is that electronics get better fast.

Indeed, one of the pioneers of neuroscience, an elder statesman of the field named Rodolpho Llinas who chairs the NYU Department of Neuroscience, has proposed a way to get a million or more electrodes in the brain – use nanowires. Carbon nanotubes can conduct electricity, so they can be used to carry signals. And they're so small that a bundle of one million nanowires would slide easily down even the smallest blood vessels in the brain, leaving plenty of room for blood cells and nutrients and so on. Llinas imagines inserting a million-nanowire bundle, and then letting its individual wires spread through your brain like a bush, until a million neurons in different parts of the brain could all be communicated with. A system like that would revolutionize our ability to get information in and out of the brain, enabling much of what I've described in this book.

Of course, it's still fiction. The research to date has been a great proof of principle. It's shown that we *can* get data in and out of the brain. It's shown that we *can* interpret that data to make sense of what the brain is doing, or to input new data in a way that the brain can make sense of. What we're left with is an incredible challenge for engineering and for medicine – taking that proof of principle, and building on it to increase the amount of data we can transmit, decoding more and more of that data, and doing so in a way that's safe and healthy for humans. That work will be motivated by medicine – finding ways to restore sight to the blind, hearing to the deaf, motion to the paralyzed, and full mental function to those who've suffered brain damage. And that work will take decades to bring to full fruition, if not longer.

A few other tidbits: genetic enhancements to boost strength, speed, and stamina are likely already possible. Over the last decade researchers looking for ways to cure muscular dystrophy, anemia, or other ailments have shown that single injections loaded with additional copies of select genes (delivered by a tame virus) can have a lifelong impact on the strength and fitness of animals ranging from mice to baboons. Those enhancements, by the way, are nearly impossible to detect in humans. It's possible that some athletes, for example, are using them today. And DARPA has shown quite a bit of interest in such enhancement technologies for future soldiers.

Finally, the Nexus backdoor that Kade and Rangan code on the airplane is based on a very real hack created by Ken Thompson, one of the inventors of the Unix operating system, that gave Thompson and his colleagues a back door into every copy of Unix that existed for several years. That hack went undiscovered until Thompson revealed its existence in a public lecture, after all versions containing the back door were gone, more than a decade later.

If you're interested in more, feel free to pick up my non-fiction book *More Than Human: Embracing the Promise of Biological Enhancement*. That goes in depth into brain computer interfaces and also into the genetic enhancements that might make humans stronger, faster, smarter, and longer lived than ever. As a bonus, it dives into the politics, economics, and morality of human enhancement – other topics that *Nexus* and its sequels touch on.

To understand a thing is to gain the power to change it. We're surging in our understanding of our own makeup – our genes, our bodies, and especially our minds. The next few decades will be more full of wonders than even the greatest science fiction.

Acknowledgments

Writing is thought of as a solitary craft. Yet for me, the production of this book has been an experience of tremendous support, encouragement, and constructive engagement from others. This novel was born as a purely recreational exercise in writing fiction, in a casual writing group including Kira Franz, Gabriel Williams, Leo Dirac, Corrie Watterson-Bryant, Dana Morningstar, and Scotto Moore. Those Sunday meetings and that first handful of readers gave me something to write for. Their encouragement and critique helped me tremendously.

Eventually this work transformed from a lark to an actual attempt to write a novel. Through the subsequent process of writing a book, Molly Nixon provided me with invaluable assistance, going above and beyond what an author can ask of anyone, serving as first reader and often nightly reader of raw pages, as a keen mind to bounce ideas off of, and as a bottomless well of enthusiasm.

A number of already established science fiction authors helped me turn this from a manuscript into a published book. Brenda Cooper took the time to read a huge second draft and gave me incredible encouragement. Greg Bear,

David Brin, John Barnes, Alastair Reynolds, Dani Kollin, and Daniel H Wilson also encouraged me at multiple steps along the way. Karl Schroeder gave me clear, no-nonsense advice on the steps I had to take to make the manuscript publishable.

My agent, Lucienne Diver, took a chance on a submission from a first-time novelist who approached her at a convention. My editor, Lee Harris, did the same. The book has reached you due to their willingness to give those sorts of chances to new authors.

Anne Zanoni, ostensibly my copy editor, went far beyond that job in checking fact, logic, style, and consistency of the novel throughout.

Most of all, I owe a huge debt of gratitude to the tremendous number of people who read drafts of this novel along the way and took the time to give me their thoughts, on everything from neuroscience to geopolitics to dialogue.

Those beta readers include those I've mentioned above, and also: Ajay Nair, Alexis Carlson, Alissa Mortenson, Allegra Searle-LeBel, Anna Black, Betsy Aoki, Beverly Sobelman, Brad Woodcock, Brady Forrest, Brian Retford, Brooks Talley, Cat Koehn, Coe Roberts, Dan Farmer, Dana Morningstar, Darci Morales, David Lockhart, David Perlman, Doug Mortenson, Elene Awad, Eric Schurman, Gabriel Williams, Grace Stahre, Ivan Medvedev, Jaime Waliczek, Jenna Udren, Jennifer Mead, Jessica Glein, Jim Jordan, Joe Pemberton, Kevin MacDonald, Lars Liden, Lesley Carmichael, Linda Mortenson, Llew Roberts, Lori Waltfield, Mason Bryant, Mellington Cartwright, Michael Chorost, Mike Tyka, Miller Sherling, Ming Holden, Nat Torkington, Oliver Lange, Paul Dale, Peter Tiemann, Rob Gruhl, Robert Fisher, Rose Hess, Sean Daily, Simon Cooke, Simon Winder, Stephanie Schutz, Stuart Updegrave, Suzanne Picard, and Thomas Park.

The input and assistance of so many people has made this not just a better book, but one that was far more enjoyable to write. Thank you all.

RN